Safe Home

W.A. PATTERSON

CHAPTER 1

Liam Flynn was waiting for his eldest son to arrive for their afternoon's labour. Robbie had gone across to his cottage, 'for a bit of dinner' he'd said. He was probably chasing that new wife of his around. Liam propped open the door of their carpentry shop to let out the stale air and welcome in some fresh. July had been unseasonably hot and sunny so far, delighting farmers the length and breadth of Ireland and bringing a welcome uplift in spirits to the tiny Tipperary village of Gortalocca. The mild, wet spring had given way to a glorious long summer of hot, sunny days and that meant a bountiful crop was assured. The 1720s had been a decade of crisis in Ireland and it was taking time to recover from the early famine years, when two seasons of failed crops had devastated a country already on its knees.

There was still no sign of Robbie and his father's mood began to sour. They were mid-way through an important job, fabricating an armoire for the wealthy Butler family in nearby Nenagh, and he wanted Robbie to help him move a pile of wooden planks. The wood he needed for the doors was near the bottom. He decided to start shifting them on his own and found the top ones to be surprisingly light but, as he got towards the middle, they became heavier. He felt a sharp pain in his left thumb. At almost forty-seven, he was no longer a young man and, if nothing else, Robbie was useful for the lifting and carrying. The job had to be done and so he pressed on.

The sweat on his leine made the shirt stick to his body and he stopped to straighten himself up for a moment, wiping the sweat away from his eyes with the back of his hand. A pain shot up the inside of his left arm to the elbow but he ignored it and attacked the woodpile again. He had barely begun when an overwhelming sense of nausea came over him. He sat down on the wooden stool in the workshop to rest for a minute or two. A searing pain shot through his chest and it was a pain like no other he'd experienced. Where's Michael? No, not Michael, he thought, he left long ago. Where's Robbie? An iron fist seemed to crush his chest in its grasp and he fell from the stool as the pain gripped him. He tried to get to his knees, using what little life was left in his body and, as he sank back down to his face on the hard packed floor, he wished he'd been able to see Rosin one last time.

*

Roisin sat alone in the gloom of her tiny cottage, the only light cast by the glowing embers of a turf fire. Her blue-grey eyes were a relentless basin of tears and she dabbed at them for the hundredth time that day, her liquid gaze resting on the lifeless body laid out in front of her … her husband of twenty-four years.

As she looked down at Liam's now ashen countenance, she thought of how she'd kissed his face that morning as he left for work. She closed her eyes to imprint the memory on her brain. The early sun had warmed them when they'd stepped outside their thatched cottage. She had watched her husband walk away, down the only street in the village of Gortalocca, and he had raised his hand, knowing that she would still be standing at the cottage door, watching him until she could see him no more. Roisin wished she could open her eyes and discover this was just a dream but this was Ireland, and death was a silent and constant companion.

Thoughts fluttered around her mind, like a butterfly going from one blossom to the next, each thought leading to another. As she raised her face to pray, her gaze came to rest on the huge gilt mirror which hung over the fireplace, prayer could wait. She thought back to when Liam had carved it, soon after they were married, and she remembered how she'd chided him for wasting time making such a foolish extravagance for such a simple cottage. Her eyes welled with tears again as she recalled the hurt on his face.

'But it's for your birthday,' he had said.

She had relented then, her heart full of pride for the man she had married, the endearingly simple and frustratingly complicated young carpenter. The gold leaf was beginning to peel from the mirror frame now, revealing the red sizing beneath. If you had peeled off the thin, stoic, veneer of her husband's Presbyterian heritage, Liam Flynn had been a romantic underneath.

Roisin picked up the crocheting she had begun just the night before. If she busied her hands, perhaps the pain of her broken heart would ease, if only briefly. She thought about how she'd watched Liam immerse himself in his work when they had lost their infant, their only daughter, eighteen years before. He had focused all his efforts on a job he'd been commissioned to do by the Otways, in an attempt to relieve his grief.

A wave of anger washed over her now and she put the wool down. She got up from her chair and addressed her husband's dead body, as if an argument might rouse him from his slumber.

'How am I supposed to live without you, Liam Flynn? Damn you for leaving me! I should have told you how much I loved you, but…' Her eyes filled again. She noticed a smudge on the mirror and went to it, using a corner of her apron to clean off the mark. She looked at herself and smoothed down her hair. Strands of platinum now mingled with the golden ones, and there was no denying that she was thicker around the waist than she'd been on that day when she first met her 'raggedy man'.

Her thoughts now darted back to the days when Liam had first arrived in Gortalocca. That had been 1704 and almost everyone from those days was gone now. She looked down at his face again and had to swallow her bile. His once ruddy complexion was pallid and his lips were grey. She felt a sudden need to see his crystal clear blue eyes one last time, those eyes which didn't just look at something but saw everything. Roisin knelt next to her husband and touched his face, his skin was cool. She recoiled at first but pressed on, opening an eyelid. The pupil was dilated now but it was unmistakable, the blue that she had lost herself in so many times. But it was different now. Everything was different now. The eyes that had once been so full of life and enthusiasm, no matter how bad a situation got, were distant, as if gazing at something far, far away. She kissed his cold face, not for the last time.

Roisin returned to her chair to resume her vigil over the deceased. She pulled a shawl onto her lap and let her mind wander again, back to that afternoon when she had met the raggedy fellow, covered in mud. Their first encounter had been anything but auspicious. She hadn't thought much of his looks. He was ordinary, she was bored, and had delighted in an opportunity to tease the poor fellow for her own amusement. Looking back, she reflected on how churlish she had been, but that was long ago, when she had been a spoiled and self-centered young woman of nineteen. She knew now that, if anyone ever treated either of her sons that way, they would incur a mother's wrath that they wouldn't forget in a hurry. She wished Michael was with her. Mikey was their younger son. Robbie had spent the afternoon with her but now he had gone home to his wife. They lived in Paddy's old house across the road.

She thought about Paddy, the pig farmer. She missed him almost as much as she missed her own father. Paddy Shevlin always had a joke to tell, or a story to relate, and he never knew how funny he was. Whatever came out of that gob of his was always a surprise, even to him. Fat little Paddy wasn't just a friend and a neighbour to Roisin, he was like a favourite uncle. He had shared many a meal at their table with them, here in the cottage, and many a beer across the road in the bar, both when her da ran the place and after his death too. She made a mental note to put a sign up on the door of Hogan's to notify people that it would be closed until further notice. Hogan's hadn't closed since her father died, almost twelve years before, but she didn't have the heart to open it now. There would be too many questions to answer and she needed to feel stronger before she faced people again.

She thought about the little spirit grocery which she had helped her da run since she was eleven. She hadn't changed the name of Hogan's after he died, she hadn't had the heart to do that either. It would always be Michael Hogan's place in her mind and she knew everyone would still call it Hogan's, no matter what they changed it to, and so she'd left the sign up outside. Liam and Roisin had called their younger son after her father. She wondered where Mikey was now.

He had been well on his way to becoming a blacksmith, as Liam's own da had been, when he had astonished everyone by announcing, out of the blue, that he was going to become a priest. Liam had been disconsolate at his son's decision and had tried his best to talk him out of it, but Mikey was like his father. Once he had an idea in his head, he turned it into a plan, and once the plan was made, neither God nor man could deter him from it. Mikey would be almost twenty-two now and his mother hadn't seen him for four years. If he had become a priest, she knew that he would be a wanted man now. Catholic priests had been incarcerated, some had even been executed, for spreading sedition against the English crown by defying the edict which banned them from practicing their faith. Despite the threatening possibility, Roisin's instincts told her that her son was still alive. As his Mother, she would surely sense if any ill had befallen him. Right now, she just wanted to see him again, and look into his eyes. He had his father's eyes and Liam's disposition too, quiet, modest and unassuming, but with a will of iron. If anyone could survive these wicked and treacherous times, it was her boy, Mikey Flynn.

Roisin thought back to the summer her father had died. It had been a wet one and the winter was even wetter. Crops failed and times were lean for almost everyone. Liam had commissions from the wealthy English families to build furniture, so he was able to support his wife and children, but most Irish families suffered terribly. Late that autumn, an epidemic had spread through all the townland communities around Lough Derg. It started with a fever and aching joints, but in just a matter of days, it suffocated many of those who contracted the disease, especially the old and the very young. In spite of old Moira's best ministrations, Roisin's father had died just a week after he became ill, his last short breath just a bubbling gasp. Roisin's eyes moistened again, she hadn't thought about her father's last few moments for a long time. The babies died that year too. Jamie Clancy, the orphaned neighbour who Liam had taken in, lost his wife and two children that murderous autumn. Jamie was young and had eventually recovered from his terrible loss. He was married to a girl from Ballina now and Roisin smiled through her tears as she thought about their newborn. Life goes on.

Roisin's thoughts landed on Paddy Shevlin and she smiled. A person couldn't help but smile when they thought of Paddy Shevlin. Paddy had suffered the same fate as her father a few years later, but with one difference … Paddy had welcomed death. He had been lonely and no one knew it until those last few days, because he was always the life of any gathering. When he knew he was dying, Paddy had said he wanted an Irish wake and that Liam could pay for it. He told Liam and Roisin that he had talked to his dead wife every night since she'd died, before he went to sleep. He told them he wanted to be buried next to her in the old churchyard at St. Patrick's, and that he wanted a pig engraved on his gravestone. Liam had tried to talk him into something more dignified and funereal but Paddy had insisted.

Paddy Shevlin had a wake that no one ever forgot and he was buried under the only tombstone in Ireland with a swine on it.

Paddy had been a witness at Liam and Roisin's wedding, along with old Moira. Father Patrick Grogan had presided over the ceremony. It was performed deep in the woods, at Lodge, and Liam had dressed in his 'gentleman suit' for it, even putting on the shoes he hated so much. Roisin had been dressed in a muslin shift, dyed blue with woad in the traditional fashion. She was barefoot with a wreath of wild yellow flowers in her hair. She thought back to Liam's tenuous relationship with the priest. If he'd had his way, he would have had another priest marry them, but Father Grogan was the only one left. They'd had an official ceremony at nearby Johnstown's Church of Ireland too, a few days later. Roisin had been reluctant but she knew it was the only way their plan could succeed. Father Grogan gave her absolution but Liam had declined.

Father Grogan had always been a mountain of a man but he began to lose weight, in spite of eating and drinking as he always had. He seemed to be always thirsty, drinking cup after cup of whatever fluids he could get his hands on, and he smelled of urine. His sight failed him and old Moira, whose own sight was dim, had to lead him around. Finally, he became too weak to walk at all, and his feet broke out in foul-smelling ulcers. His breath smelled like sickly-sweet spirits and Moira said he was dying from what she called 'sugar poisoning'. He had collapsed and died shortly after he presided over the funeral of Sinead, Liam and Roisin's baby girl. They'd had to carry the priest, on a litter, to the field at the back of their cottage to conduct the service when they buried the three year old near the faerie ring. Roisin's eyes filled again. Her daughter, her little girl with hair the colour of ripened wheat and blue eyes … planted in the ground, like a potato. When she fell asleep in the chair, the tears were still wet on her cheeks.

CHAPTER 2

Roisin opened her eyes to her new world. There would be visitors today, they would be coming to pay their respects. She decided she would put on her Sunday best finery. She tried to focus her thoughts but, again, they were like leaves in the wind. Her eyes wandered to the little door next to the fireplace, which led into the small bedroom. She had been pregnant with Michael, and Robert just a toddler, when she'd asked Liam if he could put in a little window next to the fireplace, to let in more light. She shook her head now and managed a faint smile as she remembered. Whenever she had asked Liam for something, it was sure to be SOMETHING. He had promptly begun to build an extension onto their little cottage. A window would have been sufficient but, of course, it had turned into a project. For almost a month, the cottage had been in total disarray … and so had her temper. When the job was completed, Roisin had to admit that having the extra space, and a modicum of privacy, was welcome, but she'd had a hard time saying so. It didn't matter. Liam knew she appreciated it and that's all that mattered to him.

Before she headed to the bedroom to get herself changed, Roisin looked down at Liam's lifeless body and the now familiar sting threatened tears again.

'I'm going to miss you so much, my darling,' she said out loud to him. She and Liam had never been apart for more than a matter of hours since the day they were wed. In the bedroom, she took off her worn linen dress and put on her Sunday clothes. She thought about her husband, the yeoman carpenter, who had shed his labourer's skin so many times to become the country squire, and how uncomfortable he had been with the hypocrisy of it all.

'Clothes make the man, they tell me,' he had said and shrugged his shoulders. She had always known that clothes didn't make Liam Flynn. No, Liam Flynn was an exceptional man, no matter what garments he wore.

She returned to the parlour now. She lit an oil lamp and stood in front of the big mirror, frowning as she tugged at her dress, it was tight in a few places. Her figure was no longer the girlish one she imagined it still was in her mind, but was undeniably taking on the fuller form of a matron. Again, she addressed Liam out loud.

'Why didn't you tell me I was gettin' fat, ya sod?' She knew it hadn't mattered to him. To him, she was always his 'beautiful Irish girl'. He had said it often, whenever they'd shared rare moments alone together. Another of Liam's expressions came to her mind now too.

'It's all in the perception, Roisin,' he had told her repeatedly. 'Reality has nothing to do with it. We see what we want to see.'

'Alright, Liam, it's my turn to be brave,' she said, sitting herself back in the rocking chair which he'd built for her when she was expecting Robert, their first child. She caressed the chair's well-worn arms and her mind drifted back to Hogan's bar, one night many years before. Paddy Shevlin had been leaning a bar-stool back on its hind legs.

'You'll break the legs off that thing, ya old toad!' she'd scolded him. Paddy had ignored her until, as predicted, one leg snapped, sending him sprawling onto the floor. Paddy had glared indignantly at the stool as if it had done something wrong. Even though Roisin was heavy with child, she had helped Paddy up by grabbing his ear.

'Easy woman! Yu'll pull me ear off o' me head!'

'I'll pull the head off yer shoulders, ya old sausage,' she snapped back. Liam had been watching the goings-on through squinted eyes.

'I think I have an idea,' he said, quietly. Those words always made Roisin's blood run cold and she raised her eyes to the heavens. Paddy held his hand against his still smarting ear and saw an opportunity to change the subject quickly.

'Whaddya got in mind, boyo?' he asked, keeping one eye on Roisin.

'I just built a cradle for the baby…' Before Liam could finish voicing his thought, Roisin interrupted.

'If you're gonna build a cradle big enough for Paddy, you'll have to rock it yourself.'

'No, no,' Liam explained, smiling at his wife. 'I'm going to put a chair on top of it.'

Liam had Paddy's attention now but Roisin was still in a sour mood. She looked at the destroyed chair and then at her husband.

'Get away outta that,' she said. 'Just fix the chair, Flynn, and no more of your daft ideas. You stole the stays outta me corset when you built that ridiculous portable roof!'

Paddy laughed out loud, but clapped his hand over his

mouth when Roisin gave him a withering glare.

'Ah, she's right, man,' he agreed, in an attempt to soft-soap her. 'Ya did look like a harse's arse wit' dat t'ing over yer head.'

Liam's face flushed. 'Maybe so,' he said, 'but at least I was a dry horse's arse.'

Liam built his 'rocker' chair. The first one was a disaster. He brought it into the cottage to demonstrate it and, as soon as he had seated himself, it dumped him over backwards. Roisin had tried to stifle a snigger and said that it wasn't much of an improvement on the barstool Paddy had 'modified' for them. Liam got up and stood with his hands in his pockets, regarding the offending piece of furniture.

'It needs a little more work, alright, but the idea's sound.'

Roisin had shaken her head. 'Like the sound when your head just hit the floor, you mean?'

Liam built another rocker chair and it was better. The third one was perfect, so perfect in fact that, when Squire Johnson saw it, he asked for six just like it for his porch. When the Otways and the Tolers saw Johnson's rocker chairs, they wanted some too and Liam had ended up building dozens of them for the English gentry.

A wan smile played around Roisin's lips as she rocked in her chair, conjouring up visions of them all rocking back and forth in theirs. She was roused from her thoughts by the sound of a horse's hooves outside. She was expecting a visit from Liam's brother, the High Sherriff of the Tipperary barony of Ormond Lower. She stood and straightened her clothing as she went to the front door. It wasn't the sherriff, it was Mick Sheridan, the master of hunt and horse. Mick worked for Squire Johnson and had been a close friend of Liam's, especially since the death of Paddy Shevlin. Mick was in his fifties now but he was still a striking figure of a man. He stood well over six feet tall and the uniform he wore bulged with his muscular frame.

Mick had already dismounted when Roisin opened the door of her cottage and she saw that he was holding a note of some sort in his hand. He cleared his throat and said, in a formal tone,

'Dis is from Squire Johnson. Himself sends 'is condolences, an' if it were permissible, he'd like t' call by dis afternoon in person.' Mick lowered his voice now, 'but if ya please, he'd radder dat no 'bog Irish' be present when 'e calls.' Roisin bristled at the phraseology, even though she knew that certain proprieties had to be met.

'Bog Irish, is it? Does that mean I have to leave me own house?' she asked rhetorically. Mick thought she was asking a question and, even though he was a man of few words and even fewer sentiments, he said,

'I don't t'ink so. I t'nk maybe d' auld fella carries a wee torch fer ya.' Roisin looked at him aghast. Harold Johnson was now well into his eighties and, admittedly, she had noticed that whenever she and Liam were in the old fellow's presence and he was addressing Liam, more often than not, he would be looking at her. She had just assumed that he held her in polite regard. She gathered herself.

'Well,' she said, 'you can say to him, "You're welcome to visit, ya auld buzzard, but Mrs. Flynn can't guarantee your beer won't be tainted by the lingering smell of the bog!" '

'Now, I'm not sure I should be callin' 'is Lordship an auld buzzard,' replied Mick innocently, 'ev'n dough it is what we call 'im behind 'is back.' Roisin rolled her eyes and ushered the big man into the house. Mick stood in the tiny room, making it look even smaller, and gazed at Liam. After a few minutes, he addressed him directly, as if he could hear. Roisin stood back and listened.

'Ah sure, we had some mighty adventures, didn't we, boyo. Hey, d'ya r'member when we borried Harry Johnson's prize ram to service your ewes?'

'The pair of you didn't borrow that sheep,' interrupted Roisin, 'you stole it!'

'Agh, woman, we only borried d' ram. Stealin's a sin. We jus' borried d' Protestant, English purebred, an' den we brought 'im back again. Anyways, sheep stealin' is fer folks from Roscommon. Here in Tipp, we jus' borry 'em.'

'As I recall, that ram was the worse for wear when you brought him back.'

'He wuz, but he wuz a happy sheep.'

'How did you two pull that one off, anyway? Liam wouldn't talk about it.'

'I tol' auld Harry dat I saw a wolf up around Coolbawn. He gathered some farm hands, an' 'is men-at-arms, an' den I led 'em all away. Liam had built a pair o' short stilts wit' wolf feet carved on 'em, an' 'e made tracks in d' dirt by Ballycolliton. When dey wuz all busy chasin' wolves, Liam snuck in an' stuck a rope aroun' d' sheep's neck, an' led 'im back t' my place.'

Roisin shook her head in amazement, but not even she could deny the results of their shenanigans. In a single generation, the weight of the sheep they produced had doubled. Mick interrupted her thoughts.

'It jus' goes t' show,' he said, nodding earnestly at her, 'mixed marriages can work. Protestant rams, Catholic ewes, an' d' lambs is all brought up Catholic!'

Mick appeared satisfied with the results of his and Liam's grand idea and he thought he had finished the story, but Roisin hadn't quite heard enough. She couldn't help but smile as she looked down at Liam's dead body, and she turned to Mick.

'So, how did you manage to return the ram that you 'borried'?'

'Wellll', he drew out the word as he tried to think of how he could say it to a lady, 'we put 'is arse in a pasture wit' a few dozen ewes dat wuz … let's say ripe, an' 'e bred an' bred. Da bugger went from one to anudder an' never ate a bite o' grass fer two days, an' when 'e wuz finished 'e tried t' start all over again! Liam asked me if I knew anyt'ing about sheep an' I tol' 'im dat all I knew was dat dey tasted grand. He wasn't sure whedder a ram could breed 'imself t' death, so we finally got 'im away from d' ewes. D' poor bastard, beggin yer pardon missus, couldn't hardly stand up on 'is own, he w's so exhausted. So I carried 'im back t' my place t' get 'imself rested, cuz 'e w's too big fer Liam t' carry. Dat night I returned 'im t' d' place where 'e got lost an' Liam put down more wolf tracks wit' 'is stilts.'

'And did you two geniuses ever consider that a wolf was unlikely to return a sheep that he'd stolen?'

Mick rolled his eyes up into his head as if the answer was written there, even though he wouldn't have been able to read it if it was. 'No missus, we never t'ought o' dat. I have t' git goin' now, 'r Johnson'll be wonderin' where I've gone to.'

With that, Mick gave Roisin a slight bow and a deeper one to his dead friend, and left the woman alone again. She wouldn't be alone for long.

CHAPTER 3

The weather changed as fast as an eye could blink and the wind began to blow. Roisin's mood changed too. A few moments earlier, she had been smiling as Mick told the story of how he and Liam had 'borried' the sheep, but now she settled back in her chair, letting clouds fill her mind as they filled the sky. There was a quiet knock on the door and her eldest son, Robbie, came in with his wife, May. Robbie walked over to his mother and kissed her cheek and the scene was repeated by his sixteen year old wife. The young couple looked down at the lifeless body lying on the floor and Robbie was the first to speak.

'I have some work t' do, Mammy.'

Roisin dabbed her eyes. 'You do what has to be done, lad. May can stay here with me. Dig the grave next to Sinead, near the faerie ring. That's what your da would have wanted.'

Robbie nodded. Any words he spoke now would have caught in his throat. He hesitated for a moment and it gave young May a chance to speak.

'Tell me about your courtship, Mam.'

'Ah, go way,' Roisin smiled, 'sure haven't you heard it a hundred times, m'cuishla.'

'But I love t' hear it. And dis time tell it all at once, not a little at a time like ya usually do. Ah please, Mam.'

Roisin slumped wearily into her rocker and grasped the arms of the chair. May sat herself on the floor at her feet, like a child waiting to hear a story. Robbie decided that the work could wait, he wanted to hear this too. Jamie Clancy came in with his wife and tried to whisper something in the other man's ear, but Robbie held up his hand to silence him. Kathleen, Jamie's young bride, sat herself next to May, the baby cradled in her arms. The room was starting to fill up. Roisin sighed and closed her eyes, letting the memories find tongue.

'It was April of 1705,' she began. 'A cold, clear night it was when Sean Reilly and his henchmen set fire to this cottage, but not before they'd beaten Liam to within an inch of his life.'

Robert interrupted, 'That divil, Reilly, got his comeuppance from Sherriff D'Arcy, though, didn't he Mammy.'

Roisin cast a look at Robert that would wither a barrel of apples. 'Do you want to tell this story or will you let me tell it, ya magpie?'

Robert snapped his mouth shut like a mousetrap. 'Sorry Mam,' he said, 'you tell it better.'

Roisin rolled her eyes. 'I should think so, ya natterjack, I was there. You weren't even a gleam in your da's eyes … well, maybe just a fleck.' Roisin gave a weak smile and looked at Jamie, now a tall, lean man of thirty-six years. 'That was some night, wasn't it, boyo?' Jamie nodded. He was a man of few words, like his own poor dead father.

'I r'member it well,' he said. 'I r'member aul' man

McCormack kicked me down d' road like a ball.' Roisin waited to see if Jamie had anything more to add, he hadn't, she continued.

'Where was I?'

'We was talkin' about foot-ball,' said Robbie.

'You are thick as shite, Robert Flynn,' said his mother, and took up the story again.

'After a few days, Liam was able to get out of bed, but he was so badly busted up inside that he wasn't much use, so Jamie and Paddy busied themselves rebuilding this cottage. Mick Sheridan and Matt O'Brien helped when they could, and in a month, it was all done except for the furnishings. I'd had a…,' Roisin cleared her throat, 'let's say a heart-to-heart talk with me da about Liam during that time and I'd told Liam there was something important he needed to talk to me da about. Liam was scared shiteless, of course. He hobbled over to Hogan's on that auld walking stick over there in the corner,' Roisin motioned with her head to the polished holly cane that still stood by the door, 'and I went with him. Da was sitting at a table in the bar in his best church clothes, with a sheaf of papers in front of him. "Did you want to see me about something, sir?" says Liam. Me da had a bewildered look on his face. "I thought it was you who wanted to see me, sure," says he.

'Both of them looked at me so I kicked Liam in the shin to egg him on and he stammered, "I … I would like to ask your permission to see your daughter sir." Well o'course this wasn't going at all how I wanted, so I had to take matters into my own hands. "Shut up, Liam," says I, "I'll do the talking from now on. Now, Da, this gentleman, Liam Flynn, is requesting the honour of courting me, in pursuit of eventual marriage. Alright, Da, it's your turn to speak now."

'Da followed my lead. "May I assume, sir, that your intentions are honorable?" says he. "Sweet Jayzus," says I, "this is Liam! He couldn't do anything dishonorable if he tried, except maybe lie to Protestants. You shut up too and I'll talk for the both of ye. Alright so, Liam says his intentions are honourable. Now we have to discuss the dowry." Me da shuffled the papers and coughed, then he looked at me for permission to speak. When I nodded, he says, "My daughter comes with a sizable fortune. By my calculations," says he, "it comes to almost nine pounds sterling."

' "Well," says I, "you'd better re-sharpen yer quill! I keep the books around here and I know that there's almost thirty pounds in the till and I want my half!" Me da looked at me like a bedbug caught in the light. "The rest will go to you when I die," says he. Can you believe it? I told him that if he didn't want to get patted on the face with a shovel before the sun went down, he'd better come up with a more realistic number. He did, and the fortune amounted to close on fourteen pounds.

'Anyway, the courtship went smoothly. Liam and I hardly ever had any arguments. I had my own opinions about things and, by the time I'd finished with him, he thought they were his own. Ah sure he'd get his own way on occasion. He had this way about him of being infuriating and endearing all at the same time, and he knew it. There was one incident though that almost mucked up everything.

'Not long before the wedding, old Father Grogan was in the bar and he was in his cups again. He let it slip that me da would need to give the bride away at the Protestant church of St. Mary's, as well as at St. Patrick's in the village. Well! Me da exploded like a barrel of beer on a bonfire. He swore he'd rather be dead in a pigpen then ever go into a Protestant church. Father Grogan tried to explain that it was necessary, but Da was determined and he wouldn't budge. Even I couldn't convince him, I couldn't even browbeat him into it. He said that's what he got for letting a black Protestant close to the family. That was a fierce bad week and he and I barely spoke to one another. Everyone knew Michael Hogan was my da and, if he didn't attend the service at St. Mary's, there was going to be a lot of questions asked.

'Finally, two days before the event was to take place, old Moira came and spoke to Da alone. After that, he agreed to give away the bride and he even told us he'd look happy when he did it, if you please! Well, a week after the wedding, I asked Moira how she'd done it. "It was easy, my dear," says she. "You know how vain yer da is about being bald? Well, I told him I could make him up a potion that would put the hair right back on his head." I asked her if she could and she shook her head. "That noggin of yer da's is as barren as the burren," says she. "Only God can grow roses on a stone." '

Roisin laughed as she recalled it. 'It didn't matter, sure, Da rubbed that bloody stuff on his head every night and morning for a month. He kept asking if I could see all the new hair sprouting. I told him I could and that soon I'd need to cut his locks with sheep shears.'

'That story gets better every time you tell it, Mam,' declared Robbie.

'Ah well, that's the way Irish stories are,' she said quietly. The joy of relating the tale had evaporated and the melancholy had returned. 'Jamie,' she said, 'you spent as much time with Liam as anyone. Tell us a story about him.'

'Well, emmm, I r'member when auld Moira disappeared,' he said, uncomfortable at having everyone's eyes on him. 'Me an' Liam spent days searchin' d' forest lookin' fer 'er. We never saw a sign nor a track … but we kep' lookin'. After a coupla weeks, Liam jus' said, "She's gone". He was sad … said d' aul' lady took all her wisdom wit' 'er.' Jamie looked down at Liam and everyone could see how painful it was for him to relate the tale. 'Dat auld woman saved me life … an' me dog's too. Ya know I used t' go back t' dat ol' mud house she lived in. I alw'ys hoped dat, one day, she'd come back. Sometimes Liam'd come wit' me … said 'e could feel Moira's spirit dere. I couldn't 'cuz I w's young, but I bet if I wen' back dere now, I could.'

Roisin had been reflecting back on Moira as Jamie spoke. The old crone had been as much a part of the landscape as the forest she lived in. Part Druid and part Catholic, she'd dispensed her wisdom as casually as she dispensed her remedies. One day, she simply wasn't there anymore. Liam and Jamie had searched every inch of the forest, but she'd vanished without a trace, and with her went the knowledge of the old ones. Moira had believed in the spirits of the natural world as fervently as she believed in the Holy Trinity.

Roisin felt a wave of profound sadness and nostalgia wash over her. So many years had passed and so many of the people she knew and loved had gone. 'Have you got another story for us, Jamie,' she said, 'maybe something to make us laugh?'

Poor Jamie thought for a moment. 'I don' feel very funny right now, Roisin, but I'll give it a try.' He thought for a moment. 'Did ye ever hear d' story about me t'ree legged table?'

Roisin forced a smile. 'It's still over there in pride of place by the window, Jamie. Liam was as proud of you as any da could have been.' Jamie blushed and looked at his feet, just as Liam had done a thousand times, whenever she embarrassed him. 'C'mon, tell us about it,' she encouraged him.

Jamie didn't look up, he just began the story quietly. 'Liam was still laid up an' I wanted to surprise 'im wit' d' table. I worked at night at d' ol' rectory so's I could keep it secret. I wanted it t' have dem oak leaves carved on d' legs, so's he could see dat I was payin' attention when 'e made dat big desk fer Johnson. Well, t'ree o' d' legs looked just grand but d' fourth had a mistake, an' d' more I worked on it, d' worse it got. In d' end, I had wood chips all over d' place an' d' leg looked like it'd been chewed by a dog, so I took d' t'ree good ones and built d' table on top of 'em. When I brought it back, Liam looked at it an' he scratched 'is head an' he put 'is hand on 'is chin and he says to me, "Dat's an' interestin' concept, Jamie. I wonder why nobody ever t'ought of dat before." I'll tell yous now dat I was so proud o' meself, I wanted t' cry, but Liam tol' me dat men don't cry. I wanna cry now cuz I miss 'im, but I won't.'

At Jamie's words, Roisin's tears began to flow and she put her arms around his neck and patted his back. She felt his warm tears on her shoulder and knew he had lost the battle with his emotions. He pulled away from her and tried to gather himself. His throat was thick with the words as he said, 'What'll we do widdout 'im?'

Roisin had been wondering the exact same thing as Jamie spoke the words. She swallowed hard, and in a voice barely above a whisper, she said, 'We'll carry on as usual, Jamie, my son from a different mother. It's what Liam would want.'

May and Kate left the cottage to get some food to bring back and Roisin sent Robbie and Jamie across to the shop, to collect a keg of cider and a firkin of beer.

She was neither hungry nor thirsty but, if this was to be a proper Irish wake, then things must be done right. She was alone again now with her thoughts and her mind wandered back, once more, to her youngest son, Michael. Mikey was Liam's legacy. He looked so much like him and even sounded so much like him that, often times, she wondered if they were one and the same person, just a quarter of a century apart. She would give anything to have him back here with her right now.

CHAPTER 4

The day wore on endlessly for Roisin. As the widow of the deceased, she had to listen to all the stories about Liam, most of which she'd heard a hundred times before, and many of which bore little semblance to the true facts. A grave had been dug near the faerie ring and Jamie had needed something to busy himself with so he was out building a coffin. Robbie had offered to help but Jamie told him his time would be better spent keeping his mother company.

Mr. Johnson, now well into his eighties, had dropped by and in contrast to the message he'd sent earlier, he did enjoy a drop of poteen with the locals. He even told a story about Liam that had happened years before. He told the assembled gathering about the time he'd invited Liam on a hunt and told them that Liam didn't have the proper attire and so he'd got out an old set of riding clothes for him. Although they were two sizes too small, Liam had managed to squeeze himself into them.

'He looked like an English sausage, but with an Irish flavour,' he joked, and continued the tale.

It seems that, when the hunt was over, Liam was nowhere to be seen so Johnson had sent Mick Sheridan out to find him. First, Mick had found Liam's horse grazing placidly and, when he backtracked, all the while shouting 'Hellooo!', he finally got a response. But it wasn't from ground level, it came from a tree. Liam's horse had run under an overhanging branch and, with a bit of help from sod's law, the end of the branch had gone up inside the cuff of his right sleeve and out at the collar. The horse had run on and Liam was left dangling from the tree. The riding jacket had pulled so tight that he couldn't unbutton it and so he was left helplessly hanging there, amongst the squirrels and birds. Johnson told them that Mick who, he acknowledged, was often not the brightest flame on the candelabra, had asked Liam what was he doing in the tree and Liam had answered, 'I'm waiting for you, ya pickle, cut me down.'

Mick took out a knife he wore at his belt, looked at it, then at Liam. 'Ah no,' he said. 'I'd best not cut d' squire's clothes. I'll go get d' man 'imself instead.' Liam was left yelling obscenities at Mick as he wandered off to get Johnson and the rest of the party.

Johnson laughed heartily as he retold the story and Mick looked slightly indigant.

'It was a good tale alright, Squire, but I promised Liam dat I'd never repeat it.'

'So did I,' laughed Harry Johnson, 'but now seemed like as good a time as any to break my vow.'

Roisin poured a big slug of the good stuff into Harold Johnson's cup and he downed it in a single gulp. He leaned over and whispered in her ear.

'I always knew about the conspiracy.' He smiled and kissed the back of her hand.

Roisin's eyes widened. 'How?'

He went on in a low voice. 'It was on the night of your wedding, when my late wife and I hosted the reception party. Your da, Michael, got in his cups and let it slip that you'd already been married by the old Franciscan. I told the old bugger to shut his mouth or everyone would get into trouble.'

Roisin's mouth fell open and she felt her blood rise. 'If that old soak was here now, I'd fetch him a clout around his ear,' she said.

Johnson gave a nod. 'I'm sure you would, my dear,' he said, patting her hand, 'but there's no harm done.' He bade everyone farewell and said that, since he had no family in Ireland, perhaps they'd give him an Irish wake one day, and then everyone could tell Harry Johnson stories.

He looked at Liam's body before he left. 'I'll be seeing you again one day soon, my old friend,' he said and then left, leaving those assembled with a slightly better opinion of the old goat, even if he was English.

Sooner or later, the story of Sean Reilly's hanging was bound to come up and Roisin had dreaded it. Every story needs a villain, however, and Sean Reilly was the perfect scoundrel. Time had served to dim the memory of his misdeeds in many people's minds, but Roisin still loathed him for what he had done to Liam. It was Matt O'Brien, the blacksmith, who told the tale.

It had been a beautiful day in late April. It was a Saturday and the market in Nenagh town was crowded. All commerce had ceased for the day because a hanging was a cause for diversion. Hucksters moved amongst the crowd, selling drink and food. There was entertainment in the form of Punch and Judy shows and dog fights. Sean Reilly and Conor McCormack had a trial that lasted all of fifteen minutes, before being found guilty of treason and sedition, with violence. The sherriff had gone in to interview each of them in their prison cells at Nenagh castle. He offered a reprieve to McCormack but told him he would have to suffer some kind of punishment. He had his nose and ears cropped and he was banished to Connaught. If he was ever seen in Tipperary again, he would forfeit his life. The same offer wasn't made to Sean Reilly because Sherriff Robert D'Arcy had no mercy for assassins. Reilly was escorted, or rather dragged, to the gallows by two deputies and, when asked if he had any last words, he began to rant and rave, saying it was all Liam Flynn's doing. Sherriff D'Arcy had planted a foot in the small of the man's back and the only sound he made after that was as his neck cracked. The crowd cheered and D'Arcy shot a pistol into the air, quietening the mob.

'A man just died here,' he told the hushed crowd, 'and I will suffer no celebration, even if it was his just deserts.'

They left the body hanging from the gibbet until it was almost dark, then it was removed and buried in an undisclosed location. It was widely reported that the High Sheriff had a smile on his face when he booted the man from the gallows, but Liam had told Roisin it was a grimace, that Robert had no love of hangings.

Roisin thought about Robert Flynn D'Arcy, Liam's half-brother and High Sheriff of Ormond Lower. After having been parted for many years, the two brothers had stumbled upon each other purely by chance. Liam had thought he was about to be arrested when the warrant came for him to report to the High Sherriff in Nenagh, but instead it had turned out to be a reunion. Robert was feared by most, with a reputation for being a ruthless lawman of the King but, in his own way, he was an Irish Nationalist. He was subtle in the way he enforced the laws, and he never allowed his deputies to get involved in evictions. Robert was getting on in years now, he was already in his early sixties, but Roisin considered him timeless, like Mick Sheridan. Robert made frequent visits to Gortalocca but never in his uniform, and he always rode into the village on a modest horse, rather than the charger he rode in his official capacity. He said there was no need to scare the shite out of the villagers, which it surely would have done. In some ways, the two brothers were very alike, in other ways very different. Both men were single-minded when there was a task to be done, but, whereas Liam wore his heart on his sleeve, Robert, with those dark green-brown eyes of his, suppressed emotions as best he could and never revealed what thoughts lay behind them. One thing that could be said about Robert D'Arcy was that he was a man of his word. He had made a promise to Liam that he would watch over the village of Gortalocca and he intended to keep his promise. Robert was to come and pay his respects to his dead brother, and Roisin was to ask him one last favour.

It was growing late and the weather had cleared. The dying sun warmed the land and it would be a rare hot and sultry night. Only Robbie, Jamie and Mick Sheridan were left in the cottage with Roisin when they heard the sound of a heavy horse galloping down the village street. Robbie got up and went to the door. They had been expecting a visit from the High Sheriff and, after he tied his horse, he motioned for his nephew to come to him and the two men spoke in hushed tones.

'What happened, Robbie?' asked the sheriff, straightening out his uniform.

'Da died,' said Robbie, deadly serious.

The sheriff shook his head in disbelief at how dim-witted Robbie could be sometimes. 'I know that already, boy. I'm asking you how it happened.'

'Ah right. Well, I'd just gone home for a bit to eat at

dinnertime and when I came back, he was dead on the floor.'

'Had he been ill?'

'No, not ill, but for the last couple o' weeks he'd sometimes get the sweats, even when he wasn't working.'

'It sounds like he had a heart seizure.' Robert D'Arcy nodded grimly. 'I want to see your mother.'

Robbie ushered his uncle inside the cottage. Both Mick Sheridan and Jamie Clancy knew the sheriff from his visits to the Flynn cottage and they nodded a sombre greeting to him. The dark man ignored them and went straight over to Roisin, who was sitting in the rocker. He knelt down next to her.

'I'm sorry for your loss,' he said, 'and I'm sorry for my own too. Liam was the best of us all.'

Roisin's eyes teared up and she grasped Robert's hand. 'You were Liam's hero. Did you know that?'

His eyes glazed over too and he swallowed hard before he spoke. 'He was the hero. I always envied the life he led and so many times I thought that, if I'd listened to my own Da and taken a different path forty years ago, I could have had a blacksmith shop and a family, and maybe even a piece of land.' Robert D'Arcy checked himself. He stood up straight and changed his demeanor, he'd said too much. 'But the past is dead,' he said with a flat expression, 'and the last of my family is dead too.'

Roisin didn't let go of his hand. 'You still have family, Robert,' she said, 'and you always will.'

Robert's shoulders slumped perceptibly 'Thank you,' he said quietly and softened his countenance once again.

'I have a request to make of you,' whispered Roisin, 'and you don't have to give me an answer, now. I'll wait until the men have gone before I ask you.'

Mick overheard Roisin, and the big man put his hands on Jamie and Robbie's shoulders and led them out of the cottage, leaving the sheriff and Roisin to talk in private.

CHAPTER 5

As soon as they were alone, Robert spoke bluntly. 'Tell me what your request is,' he said, 'and if it's within my power as sheriff, I will do my upmost to grant it.'

'I'm not asking you as a lawman,' she said, 'but as Liam's brother.' She hesitated for a moment. 'I want to see Mikey.'

Robert closed his eyes. 'My nephew made his decision to pursue a dangerous profession, Roisin. Being a priest makes him wanted by the law, and it puts him in the same category as any bandit.' He paused for a moment. 'I've earned my reputation as a man-hunter, because I do my thinking and my preparation first and only then do I set out to track down my target.' He sighed. 'Tell me what you know about his last known whereabouts.'

'I haven't heard from Michael in more than a year,' Roisin told him, 'and that was only a cursory note, saying he was well and living on the Cork and Kerry border.'

Robert gave a low whistle. 'That's wild country, a fierce big area, full of rebels and other nefarious types.

It's also out of my jurisdiction, Roisin, I'll have to do some research and study the situation first.'

'I know it's an awful lot to ask of you, Robert, and I wouldn't blame you if you decided that it's too difficult or too risky'.

Before she could speak again, Robert interrupted. 'I've already made my mind up. I can't help Liam any more, the least I can do is to help his widow. You try and get some sleep, I'll be back tomorrow for the burial.'

Roisin buried her face in her hands and wept, the word *burial* was so final. Robert turned and knelt beside Liam's corpse. He smelt the familiar odour of death as he whispered in his brother's ear, so low that the woman couldn't hear.

'I know what you meant now, brother. When she looks into your eyes and asks you to do something for her, it's impossible to say no.'

Roisin's curiosity was piqued. 'What did you say to him?'

Robert smiled sadly at her. 'I told him I would take care of everything' he replied.

*

It was long after dark when Robert and his lathered horse galloped through the gates of Nenagh Castle. The guards stepped aside and saluted him, but he didn't bother to return the salute. He dismounted and gave the winded horse a pat on the neck, before handing the reins to a groom.

'Cool him down,' he said, 'and give him an extra measure of grain after you've done it.' The groom made a half-hearted bow and the sheriff scowled. The boy made a deeper bow. Robert strode to his office and, when he got there, he immediately pulled out some ordinance maps of West Cork and South Kerry. He wanted to evaluate just how difficult a task he was about to embark upon. He rubbed his right shoulder, it was stiff. He was beginning to feel his years, even if they didn't show yet. He was going to have to make arrangements for his absence very soon. As it is with all plans in their beginning stages, Robert's mind was flooded with arrangements and preparatory measures.

*

The night had been hot and humid and the day had begun the same. Almost from the time it rose above the horizon, the sun was hot, and the smell of death grew stronger. Liam's body was placed in the plain, pine coffin which Jamie had made. Before the lid was nailed shut, Roisin kissed his cold lips and tried to control herself. Every fibre of her being wanted to cry out in anguish because this was to be their last ever mortal kiss.

Robbie and Mick stood on either side of her and helped to support her. Roisin had never fainted in her life, but now she could feel her knees try to buckle under her own weight. Her mind was in a fog and there was little thought there, just unadulterated grief. She felt as if her heart had been torn from her chest and laid inside the simple coffin next to her dead husband. The sound of the hammer resounded as it drove nails into the coffin lid and the only other sound was the coo of wood pigeons from somewhere inside the faerie ring. Even they sounded sombre.

Robert Flynn D'Arcy had come to bid a final farewell to his only sibling. He wasn't dressed in the crisp uniform of High Sheriff, but in the simple clothes of an Irishman.

Sweat trickled down his brow and the yellow leine stuck to his skin. For a brief moment, he wished it was he who was going into that hole in the cool earth, but he snapped himself away from those thoughts. He had a job to do and, even if this was the last thing he ever did, he would reunite his dead brother's wife with their boy. The task came first now, death was just a momentary interruption.

There was no crowd there when they buried Liam Flynn, master carpenter. All the well-wishers from the day before had to get back to work and all the stories about Liam were already forgotten. He would have preferred it that way. He would have been mortified to hear all the talk about him and his adventures. Jamie and Mick Sheridan began to fill in the grave and the sound of earth and gravel hitting the top of the casket had a hollow ring, like a muffled drum. Those assembled were silent. There was no priest here to say any final words. Liam was laid to rest as quietly as he had lived his life, a shorter life than some, but a fuller one than most.

As they walked the short distance back to the cottage, Jamie spoke quietly.

'I have t' put a stone over Liam,' he said, 'somet'in' t' mark where he is, f'rever like.'

Roisin squeezed Jamie's hand gently. 'No, Jamie, make it out of wood.'

'But wood'll rot,' he protested meekly.

'Wood was what Liam loved and it's what he'd have wanted,'

'It'll be wood, so,' Jamie pronounced, 'the very best I can carve.'

Roisin shook her head, 'No, lad, something modest, Liam was a simple man.' As soon as she said the words, she realised it wasn't quite that way. Liam had indeed lived simply, without any great needs, but he was as complicated as anyone could be. Her husband had been a complete paradox, sophisticated and crude, a believer and a blasphemer, and, most of all, a dreamer and a practical man. Her tears began to flow silently again and she wondered if she would ever be able to think about her poor dear Liam without crying.

Before they reached the cottage, Robert called Mick Sheridan aside.

'I need to speak to you,' he told him. A look of fear crossed Mick's face. 'Don't worry, you're not in any trouble, Mick. I have need of your expertise in a matter concerning horses.'

Mick was relieved. 'I'm at yer service, sir,' he said.

'I need to buy a pair of horses for a specific purpose.'

Mick was intrigued. Whenever he was talking about horses, he was entirely comfortable. 'What'll ya be needin', so, sir?'

'I need two mountain horses, about fifteen hands tall. I need animals with endurance, horses that can put on a burst of speed with a rider on board. They have be able to live for a couple of weeks on a sparse diet and still keep up their strength.'

'Ah, yeah.' Mick smiled now. 'Yu'll be needin' a horse with some arse t' get uphill, an' a pair o' shoulders on 'im fer getting' down. It sounds t' me like ya need Hobbies but dere ain't any Hobbies around here anymore.' Mick scratched his chin and thought for a moment. 'Dere's an' auld feller up in Folly dat's got a couple wit' d' bloodline. I don't know if he wants t' sell 'em, dough.'

'Money's no object, Mick. If those horses fit the bill, I want them.'

Mick looked quizzically at the sheriff. No one had ever asked him to buy a horse without first setting a budget on it and he felt the responsibility weigh heavy on him.

'I'll go check d'horses first t'ing in d' mornin', sir.'

'They'll need to be dead broke, and fit to ride as soon as you can get them ready, Mick.'

Mick scratched his head now. 'A week,' he said, 'maybe two. Would dat be soon enough fer ya?'

'As soon as you can is as soon as I want those animals,' said Robert slipping a pound into the big man's hand.

Mick looked down at the coin. 'Beggin yer pardon, sir, but dat ain't gonna be anywhere near enough t' buy dem creatures.'

'That's for you, Mick, for your trouble. I'll be back tomorrow afternoon, then you can tell me what the price is and we'll make the deal.'

Mick held Robert's gaze for a moment. 'Yer goin' after Mikey, ain't ya, sir?'

'I am, Mick, and I'd appreciate it if you'd keep it under your hat, at least until a couple of days after I've left.'

They had reached the cottage now and the two men went inside to eat dinner with the others. When the meal was finished, Robert announced that he had some business back in Nenagh and that he would return the next afternoon. Roisin was surprised. It wasn't usual to see the sheriff more than once or twice a month, and then only briefly. He was a busy man. But then, nothing was usual anymore, so much had happened in such a short time.

True to his word, Robert arrived the following afternoon, dressed in his uniform and riding the big chestnut charger. He stopped by the cottage briefly. He had a satchel with him and he placed the leather sack on the table.

'I'm leaving this with you for safekeeping, woman,' he said.

Roisin heard the metallic sound of coins as Robert put the sack down. 'How much is in the bag?' she asked.

He smiled. 'Enough to live on for two lifetimes,' he said. 'I've made a lot of money as High Sheriff, and as a soldier of fortune before that. You're to keep it for me and, if I need any of it, I will send for it.' With that, Robert strode out of the tiny cottage, mounted his charger, and headed at a gallop down the road, toward Micks house. Roisin was alone with the satchel and she eyed it suspiciously, as if it might bite her. She tentatively lifted the flap and gasped as she peered inside the leather pouch. She had never seen so many gold coins in one place in all her life. She lifted up her goose feather mattress and stuffed the pouch deep underneath.

CHAPTER 6

Robert rode to Mick's cottage, his mood strangely upbeat. Trees lined the side of the road, their branches meeting overhead to form a green, leafy tunnel, and the hoofbeats of his big chestnut horse resounded as they pounded the road with the rhythm of a bodhran. He felt more alive than he'd felt in a long time.

Robert Flynn D'Arcy had lived through a hundred, maybe a thousand, adventures in his life and he had thought those days were gone. Now, here he was, about to embark on another, perhaps the best one of all. He felt the long-forgotten tingle of excitement, like a charge of electricity, as the adrenaline coursed through his veins. He felt young again.

Robert had already decided to leave the office of High Sheriff when he returned from his quest. He had grown weary of sitting behind a desk and, although his hair was still dark, his beard had become grizzled with age and the wrinkles on his face deepened with each passing day. He had forgotten the thrill of the chase, until now. He had eliminated any local banditry long ago, and considered that he'd probably already hung every interesting person there was in North Tipperary. His job had become little more than that of a desk clerk, writing reports and shuffling papers and, for a man like Robert Flynn D'Arcy, the mind-numbing occupation of an administrator was fatal.

He reined the chestnut to a trot, then to a walk, as he approached Mick's paddock. Mick's horses whinnied a greeting at the approach of the big steed and Robert's horse nickered in reply. Sheridan was waiting for him.

'Howaya!' he called.

The horse had barely come to a halt when Robert swung himself out of the saddle. 'Well?'

'Well, I got some good news, an' I got some bad news.'

'Give me the bad news first.'

'The bad news is dat 'e wants eight pounds each fer d' two geldings.'

Robert gave a slight smile through gritted teeth. 'He can take ten for the both of them.'

Mick looked sceptical, 'Ah, I don' know, now. Callahan's a slick aul' horse trader.'

'I'm telling you, he'll take ten for the both. C'mon, Mick, saddle up, we're going for a ride.' Robert watched impatiently as the big man saddled a nicely-built paint cob.

'Dis is Aoife,' he informed Robert, stroking the horse's neck. 'I named 'er after a mare I had donkey's years ago.' Robert nodded. He was anxious to get started so they could negotiate the deal for the horses.

The ride to Folly didn't take much more than fifteen minutes at a relaxed canter but, even so, the horses were breathing heavily when they arrived at a whitewashed, mud cottage. An old fellow stood outside waiting for them. He was thin with a pot belly, and it occurred to Robert that he looked like a length of rope, with a knot tied in the middle of it. The man's jaw dropped when he saw the sheriff.

'Let's go and inspect the stock', said Robert and, as he was led to the pasture where the two geldings were grazing, he heard Callahan whisper to Mick,

'Jayzus Christ, man! Ya never tol' me dat d' buyer was d' sheriff!'

As they got closer to the horses, Robert could see that the two bays were put together well, straight-legged and short-backed, deep-chested and well-muscled about the hind quarters and shoulders. The three men approached and Mick examined the feet and teeth of each, running his ham-sized hand along each of their backs and legs. Robert thought he was almost tender in the way he handled the animals.

'Alright, let's see 'em move,' said Mick decisively, giving a piercing whistle and throwing his arms in the air.

Callahan was startled and jumped at the sound, 'Jayzus, man! I almost shit meself,' he yelled.

'Almos' don't count,' said Mick. 'Ya eider shit yerself, or ya don't.' Robert stifled a grin.

As the horses galloped around the small pasture, Robert scrutinised their gait. They appeared sound, and they could certainly put on a burst of speed to match even his own heavy horse, but they looked able to sustain it for much longer.

'They'll do,' said Robert finally. 'Give me a price.'

Callahan looked the sheriff up and down, then looked at the two horses, then back at Robert, scratching his head as if pondering on the price which he'd already decided on.

'I want eight pounds apiece,' he said, 'but I'm willin'

to sell 'em both t' ya fer fifteen.'

'It's illegal for an Irishman to own a horse worth more than five pounds,' said Robert, 'and you don't look like a thief to me, so I'll give you ten for the both of them.' Now Mick understood why the sheriff had worn his uniform to come and buy horses.

Callahan looked startled. He realised he could be in a serious predicament and he hummed and hawed a little.

'Could ya ever see yer way to making it just a wee bit more?' he whined.

'I could,' replied Robert, 'but then I'd be a criminal too and, as well as arresting you, I'd have to turn myself in. Here's what I'll do. I'll give you the ten pounds for the horses and another pound as a gift, so you can buy yourself a jug of poteen to salve your wounds.'

'Will ya make it two pounds?' the skinny man bellyached. 'Dem wounds is fierce deep?'

'Mick, confiscate the horses. They're evidence in this crook's trial.'

'Noooo, no, no!' interrupted the horse trader. 'Let's not be hasty, now. I t'ink me wounds is healin' already. Ten pounds an' a jug'll do just grand.'

The two men shook hands and the money was exchanged. As they led the horses away, Robert heard the old fellow say, 'I hope d' horse t'rows him on 'is arse.'

The sheriff stopped and turned slowly around. 'Did you say something, Callahan?'

Callahan gave a little bow. 'Ah, I was just sayin' dat if you need anudder horse anytime, just ask.'

Mick took the saddle off his own horse and placed it on one of the bay geldings to give it a trial, and they led the animals down the road towards Gortalocca. The animal was spirited and tried a side pass as they cantered down the lane. Mick gathered the horse and smiled.

'Dis one's grand and frisky,' he said. 'He has some vinegar in 'im.'

'You'll need to sweeten him up, Mick. I might have to depend on him for my life.'

Mick nodded. 'I understand, sir. I'll get d' edges polished off in a few days, no bother.' As they rode, Robert led the other two animals while Mick began schooling his own mount. By the time they reached Mick's place, the horse had settled down.

'I have some work to attend to in Nenagh,' said the sheriff, 'but, God willing, I'll be back in a few days,'

'Yer doin' God's work, sir,' replied Mick, 'so I'm sure He'll be willin'.' As he turned and began rubbing the horses down, Robert wheeled own horse around and headed west, towards the market town. God's work, he thought. It was a long time since anyone had accused him of doing God's work, in fact he'd been damned by many men with their dying breath. He closed his eyes now and let the sun shine on his face. His horse knew the way, but it slowed instinctively as they neared Liam and Roisin's cottage.

'Not this time, old fella. We have some work to do before we get home.'

He crossed the bridge over Nenagh River at Ballyartella's mill and the horse wanted to keep going towards town. Robert pricked the animal's side with his left spur and pressed his thigh against the creature's flank. The horse turned abruptly right at the cue. He reigned it to a halt, dismounted, and tied the reins to a ring which had been set in the wall of a small, stone building. He drew his sabre from a scabbard which hung from the saddle, and he ducked through the low door of Matt O'Brien's forge. The smell of charcoal brought back memories of being with Liam, back in his own da's smithery. Neither Matt nor Jamie looked up. They were busy building wheel rims, and the constant hammering at the anvil had partially deafened them, so they didn't hear his approach. When Matt looked up at the man with an unsheathed blade in his hand, he put his hand out to stop Jamie working and they both took a step backwards. Robert realised that he'd unwittingly unnerved them and he placed the sword down on a work table near the door.

To diffuse the tension, Robert spoke first. 'Good day to you, gentlemen. I have a task that I would like you to perform'. The two smiths opened their eyes wide with surprise. Robert turned, picked up the sabre and held it towards them, handle first. 'Here, I'll describe my requirements. I want the blade shortened to sixteen inches. It will no longer be a slashing weapon, so I want the tip to be sharp. You have to lighten the hand guard too, so that it balances right in front of the hilt. I don't want it to be shiny so you're to take the polish off it, and brown the blade and basket like a musket.'

Matt spoke now. 'Beggin' yer pardon sir, but dat blade's the finest I've seen. It'll look like shite if we do what ya ask. Anyway, why don'cha take it t' d' armourer in d' castle?' Jamie had taken the blade and hefted it slightly. It was so beautiful that he forgot, momentarily, how deadly it could be in the wrong hands.

'Can you do it, or not?'

Matt hesitated for a moment but Jamie leapt in. 'We can, sir, o'course!' The smith looked at Jamie dubiously, but the young man continued. 'It should be straight and pointy, so's it won't hang up when ya stick somebody. An' it must have a blood groove, t' lighten d' blade wit'out givin' up d' strength. Da guard should be t'ick at d' front, in case ya have t' fight a man wit' a sword, or break somebody's jaw.'

Robert smiled. 'You could be an armourer yourself, lad,' he said. 'You just described precisely what I want.'

Jamie's face flushed and Matt scowled at him, he didn't appreciate being upstaged by his student. 'As ya know so much about swords,' he told Jamie, 'you c'n do d' job yerself, an' den, if dere's any complaints, d' sheriff can cut off yer ear!'

'There won't be any ears cut off, Mr. O'Brien,' said Robert. 'In fact, here's ten shillings for the job, and I don't care what you do with the steel from the half blade you cut off.'

Matt was elated at receiving this unexpected payment and some quality spare steel, but Jamie blurted out,

'I'll make anudder knife for ya, sir, a long skeane, so's ya c'n keep it hidden mostly.' Another cloud crossed Matt O'Brien's face. He'd already decided he would make a knife for himself out of the extra metal.

'Yu'll do dat job too, so,' he groused, and went back to furiously pounding the wheel rim. Jamie shrugged and grinned at Robert, who remembered how infectious his brother, Liam's enthusiasm had been too.

'I'll be back in a few days to check on the progress of the labour, and I hope I can trust you two gentlemen to keep this in confidence.' Matt looked up from his work and grumbled. Jamie nodded enthusiastically.

Not long after Robert had ridden away, Matt's foul mood had been replaced by one of curiosity,

'What d'ya suppose yer man is up to?' he said, watching the doorway where Robert had exited just minutes before. It had been a rhetorical question but Jamie offered a reply.

'I t'ink he's goin' t' find Mikey.'

'Sure Mikey is probably as dead as his auld man by now.'

Now it was Jamie's turn to curdle. 'Roisin said he's not dead, an' Liam always said dat Robert got every man he hunted down.'

'Agh! You an' yer Liam dis an' yer Roisin dat. Dat feller's got as much chance of finding d' stupid boy as he has of findin' a snowball in dat fire d'ere.'

Jamie ignored him and began work on the blade.

CHAPTER 7

Less than a hundred miles away, as the crow flies, another young smith was beating a piece of iron on an anvil. At the same time, he was wrestling with his own internal demons. It was a crisis of faith and a contest he couldn't win.

His name was Michael Hogan and his smithy was in the village of Ballyshee, in the west of County Cork. It was the perfect place for a body to re-invent himself, nestled as it was in a little valley amongst fierce and almost uninhabitable mountains. There was only one road to it, and that lay mostly ignored by the authorities. There was hardly ever a stranger to be seen in Ballyshee and, if one did make a wrong turn on the way to Macroom or Bantry and wander in, they left as soon as they'd obtained directions back out.

Mikey had arrived here two years before, a skinny, sandy-haired boy of twenty, carrying with him a sack containing the grey frock of a Franciscan. He was the son of a carpenter and, in his previous life, his name had been Michael Francis Flynn. He had assumed his grandfather's surname of Hogan in his efforts to protect the family he'd left behind in Tipperary.

Ballyshee's village smith had died of consumption four years before, and the village had gone without, until Michael came. They had also been without a priest for almost as long, since he'd been caught saying Mass in Gougane Barra. There were spies everywhere, and priests were hunted as if they were wolves. It was a new witch hunt but this time, Catholic priests were the quarry.

Michael wasn't an ordained priest. After the two years he'd spent in the seminary, it had been closed by the authorities and the teachers arrested. Only a few students had managed to escape, and they dispersed themselves throughout the country. He wasn't even a proper blacksmith, having left Matt O'Brien's forge before he'd completed his apprenticeship. Nevertheless, he was the best the little village of Ballyshee could get until someone more qualified came along. None of those things were a problem for Mikey, he could live with them. Michael Francis Hogan's problem was that he had fallen in love.

They had been warned in the seminary about 'occasions when sin would present itself' and had been told that, above all things, they must not abuse their power. To be a priest in Ireland meant that your status was only just beneath that of an angel. To be ordained meant that you were Christ's representative on earth and, as such, you transformed from a mere human being into something supernatural, with the ability to change water and wine into the blood of Christ and bread into His body. But Mikey had never been ordained. He hammered the iron on the forge harder now, as if it might help to exorcise the demons which threatened to invade his body.

Morna O'Malley was sixteen years old, the only daughter of farmer Jack O'Malley. Mikey thought that Morna had been an ill-suited name for the girl he loved.

It meant lively and energetic and his Morna was far from that. She was a quiet and timid girl unlike his mother, both in appearance and demeanor. She was small and petite. Her auburn hair was the colour of burnt honey and hung in loose curls down her back, her emerald green eyes flickered like there were flecks of light in them. If someone was to paint a picture of the quintessential Irish lass, he thought, then Morna would surely make a perfect subject. Of course he would think that, he was in love with her. His thoughts flew wildly again, like a flock of grouse. If only he was just the village blacksmith.

It was Friday today and this coming Sunday would be the third one in July. When Mikey thought it safe, he tried to hold Mass once a month, on an island in the bog, near Macroom. It was at least a day's walk and was better made after dark. He would start out tonight. He would rather travel after dark and risk bandits, rather than by day and face the possibity of encountering British cavalry. If he was caught, however, his calloused hands would work in his favour. He'd had a couple of close calls so far, but one look at his hands had convinced those who apprehended him that he was only a yeoman and not a man of the cloth. He would leave his Franciscan robes behind and take with him only the linen stole which he wore during Mass, hidden at the bottom of his sack in the secret pocket he'd sewn there. He placed a lump of rancid pork on top of it, to deter anyone from searching further, and then a loaf of bread and piece of cheese for his victuals. He tied the ends of some rope to the top corners and slung the bag over his shoulder. It wasn't the professional highwaymen who concerned him, after all he'd heard most of their confessions, it was the roving bands of half-starving orphans who posed the greatest danger. These were boys of between eleven and seventeen years of age and they were ruthless. Life had no meaning for them and they would do anything to get the money they needed for ale and cheap poteen. He would rather run into a company of English grenadiers any day than have an encounter with those murderous young thugs.

The first part of his journey was safe. No one except the residents of Ballyshee trod the road he used but, when he got to the main road, he had to be more careful. He draped his dark grey, felt brat over his shoulders, obscuring his faded yellow leine. His trews, or trousers, were dyed with woad and weld, to give them their olive green colour. Dressed like this, on a moonless night like tonight, it would be relatively easy for him to become invisible to prying eyes. Silence and darkness were his allies and stealth was his companion.

The first few miles out of the valley were all uphill and the rope cut into his shoulder, so he kept shifting his sack from one side to another. It was an hour and a half before he reached the summit but he knew then that the rest of the journey would be rolling hills and easier for him to negotiate. He stopped for a moment to let the fresh night air cool him. The past few days had been hot and humid and perhaps this new breeze meant that more seasonal temperatures were on their way. He hadn't eaten any supper, so he tore a lump off the loaf and took a bite of cheese. He uncorked his water bottle and washed down the mouthful, wishing he had a drop of beer to help it on its way.

The first few hours after dark would be the most dangerous. After that, even if the youths positioned a lookout, whoever it was would most likely fall asleep. Michael began his long walk, one foot in front of another, each step taking him closer. The sound of his rhythmic footsteps on the path was hypnotic and lulled him into a reverie. He thought about the story his father had often told him, about the long trek he'd made many years before from Thurles to Nenagh, pulling a wagon behind him. Well, he thought, at least I only have a sack to carry. I don't have to drag a few hundred pounds of wagon and a box of heavy tools. He walked for another hour, lost in a hundred thoughts, mostly about a young girl with emerald green eyes and copper hair. He was wrenched from his fantasy by the high pitched voice of a boy.

'Hey! I t'ink I heard someone!'

'You better be right, ya stinkhole!' The voice from the dark was a little deeper.

Michael slipped the bag off his shoulder, slowly and quietly, and gradually slid into the shadows beside a hedgerow. Now, silhouetted against the dark sky, he could see two figures looking in his direction, one taller than the other. Soon there were four of them. They were only thirty yards or so away from where he lay crouched and he controlled his breathing. It seemed hours, but was probably only minutes, when finally, the tallest of the four, and the one with the deepest voice spoke.

'I don't see anyt'ing but if yu're sure, you g'wan an' take a look.' With that, he gave the smallest one a mighty shove that sent him sprawling. The boy got up and dusted himself off.

'Feck you,' he said over his shoulder. He ventured a few steps in Michael's direction, then stopped, turned, and spoke to the shadows behind him. 'What if it's a feckin' wolf?' There was some laughter amongst the bigger boys.

'Den he'll eatcha,' one of them called, 'an' d' rest of

uz'll be safe. Now g'wan!' The small lad retreated backwards, retracing his steps and, when he reached the bigger boys, one of them gave him a smart slap on the back of his head.

'Hey you!' said another. 'Dat's me brudder! If anyone's gonna wack d' little fecker, it'll be me.' With that, one of the other older boys gave him a second slap.

'I'm d' leader o' dis outfit,' roared the third, 'an' I'll do d' whackin', if yous don't mind!' He took a shot too and a brawl broke out, with the bigger boys throwing punches at each other and the little one trying to join in. This was going to be a long night and Mike was getting a cramp in his leg. When he straightened it, the small boy yelled out.

'Hold yer whisht! I heard it again!' The rest of them stopped fighting each other and set about the boy.

Michael didn't dare to close his eyes for the rest of the night and, just before dawn, he slipped past the now sleeping sentry and headed down the road towards Macroom. He got to the safehouse around midday and he knocked on the door in code, as was his custom, one loud and three soft. A stout old woman opened the door, grabbed him by the shirt and yanked him in, then poked her head outside, looking in both directions to see if he'd been followed.

She was agitated and wrung her hands. 'Dis is d' las' time ya c'n stay here, Farder,' she said quietly. 'I'm sorry, 'tis gettin' too dangerous fer an auld woman like meself.'

Something had changed. 'What's happened?'

'Da English, dey've got a man-hunter, Farder,' she told him. 'He's lookin' fer priests. Dey've given 'im a whole company o' soldiers t' help 'im.'

This was news to Michael. Generally, the authorities used local spy networks to uncover clandestine church services.

'What do you know about him?'

'I heard tell he was in Kerry, an' dat he tracked down a couple o' priests an' hung 'em. He even killed one wit' a sword near Glenbeigh. He got mad 'cuz nobody had turned 'im in, so when he found 'im travellin' at night, he stuck 'im t'rough d' middle wit 'is saber!'

Michael gave it some thought. That was astute for an Englishman, anyone out on the road late was probably up to no good. That meant he'd be better off travelling by day and taking his chances with the local sheriffs. Agh! Redcoats chasing priests, he thought, cynically. What the English need is a good old-fashioned war with France to keep their army occupied. Michael thanked the old woman and retired to a little room off the kitchen to get some well-needed sleep.

CHAPTER 8

One of the things Robert needed to do before he left on his mission was to appoint an interim sheriff. He already had someone in mind, a young man who had been his adjutant for the last six years. Bernard Higgins was capable, although perhaps a little stuffy for Robert's taste. He was the third son of a lower level English nobleman, and young at just twenty eight, but he had an advantage which many in his position did not. He had been raised in Ireland since he was an infant.

Bernard Higgins had never been particularly ambitious, which had turned out to be an asset, but he did understand Ireland. He was even-tempered and uninclined to temper tantrums, as many pampered sons were. The office of sheriff no longer called for a man of action, the duties having become more administrative than anything. Robert sat back in his chair and put his feet on the desk, his gaze wandering up to the ceiling. He thought about the days when he had chased bandits through the countryside, and the dangers it had presented, and he longed for them. The job of a bureaucrat did not suit him at all well. He did what was necessary but he did it grudgingly.

He carried on with his plans for the task ahead of him. Although he knew could make it alone, he also knew that an extra set of eyes would be useful and to have an extra man-at-arms wouldn't go amiss. He already had someone in mind for this job too, Ned Flood. Ned was a young man of action but, unlike most, he was able to think on his feet. He had acquired his current position as deputy by mere chance, several years before, when he'd worked as a stable-boy here in the castle. His duties had been barely more than that of a janitor back then, shovelling horse dung and providing clean bedding for the animals. One afternoon, two of the senior deputies had got themselves into a dispute, Robert couldn't remember what it was, a gambling debt, or a woman, or some such nonsense. The argument had escalated into a fistfight, down in the courtyard below, and Robert had watched the proceedings from his window. He left them to it for a while, aware that sometimes it was better to let men get their frustrations out of their systems, but soon the altercation had begun to grow out of hand. Just as he was about to go down and separate the two burly fellows, a young stable hand had come out and intervened, and what an intervention it was.

Initially, Ned had tried to sandwich himself between the combatants, in an effort to split them up but, when they turned on him, he had made quick work of them both. There had been consternation and amusement at the time amongst the other men because the two big men-at-arms had been soundly whipped by a lanky boy. Robert was already considering introducing some fresh blood into the corps, and Ned's fearlessness impressed him. The boy had casually returned to his work mucking out the stables, and Robert made his way down, to find him shovelling another pile of dung onto a wheelbarrow.

'Do you have a name, boy?' he asked, sternly.

Ned was afraid that he was about to be punished or, even worse, that he would be dismissed from his job. 'Me name is Ned, sar,' he stated.

'Ned Sir, is it? That's an unusual surname you have there, Mr. Sir,' Robert joked, attempting humour in an effort to allay the boy's fears.

'No, sar,' corrected the young man, 'it's Ned Flood, sar'. He didn't understand the joke.

'Can you read, Ned Flood Sir?'

'No, sar, nary a word.'

'Are you an idiot?'

'I'm no eejit, sar.'

Robert saw the colour rise in the boy's face. 'Do you think you could learn?'

'If I got d'chance, I could larn.'

Robert interrupted his own line of interrogation. 'You don't have a Tipp accent, boy. Where do you hail from?'

'Oy'm fr'm Cark, sar. Fr'm West Cark.'

'Interesting,' mused Robert. He turned and went back to his office, and the boy went back to shovelling manure.

Robert hadn't forgotten his conversation with the sandy-haired lad who had smelled of horse urine and dung. The very next day, he sent his adjutant to the stable with a thin, dog-eared book. Higgins had handed the book to Ned, and walked off without a word. When he returned to the sheriff's office, Robert stood with his hands on his hips.

'That was fast, Higgie,' he said.

Higgins bristled at the familiarity and straightened his back with indignation. 'I did as you instructed, sir.'

'Go back down there and teach that boy to read, if that's not an offense to your sensitivities.'

Bernard Higgins was totally taken aback by this commoner's effrontery and sneer of resentment wasn't wasted on the sheriff.

Robert sighed deeply. 'Let me put it to you this way, Higgie. Do you like your job?'

Higgins winced at the thinly-veiled threat. 'As you wish, sir,' he said. He knuckled his forehead in salute and sulkily went down to the stable.

Higgins followed his orders and finally got over his snit. A week went by and, one morning, he went into Robert's office.

'Permission to speak sir.'

Robert looked up from the papers he had been shuffling, fully expecting to hear some complaint from his adjutant.

'It's about that stable-boy from Cork sir.'

'Continue,' replied Robert.

'That filthy bog-Irishman must be some sort of genius or other.'

Robert held up his hand to warn the young officer. 'Watch your tongue, Higgie.'

Higgins ignored the familiar term and continued. 'He has devoured that primer already and now he's asking me to teach him his numbers, if you please. He even had the gall to ask me would I get him another book. Said he was getting tired of reading the same one over and over!'

Robert smiled, it seems he had completely underestimated his new discovery.

'And another thing,' said Higgins. The sheriff was sure this would be some complaint or other.

'When I told him I should flog him for his impertinence, he looked at me like a wolf and said that if

I did, it would be the last time I flogged anyone!'

Robert shook his head, the lad had gone too far now.

'I'll speak to him. Perhaps I can scrape some of the Cork off. In the meantime, Higgins, if you'd like your features to stay as they are, I recommend you don't threaten the young sod again.'

Robert left the papers scattered on his desk and immediately left for the stables. Higgins smirked, satisfied that his complaint had been taken seriously for a change. He hoped there would be a flogging, at least it would provide entertainment after the evening meal. That hope couldn't have been further from the truth.

Ned was busy mucking out stalls when Robert arrived, so he stood in the doorway and watched him quietly until the boy finally became aware of his presence and put the pitchfork against the wall.

'Sorry, sar, I didn' see ya standin' dere.'

'Listen to me, Ned.' It was the first time he'd used the young fellow's name.

The boy held himself erect and looked directly at the sheriff, 'Ef it's about me t'reat'nin' d' depuddy, I'm sorry, sar. It won' happ'n again. He joost made me mad when 'e said he'd beat me.'

Robert returned the boy's direct gaze and his face was stern. Finally, the young man looked away and hung his head. He was genuinely sorry for speaking on impulse.

'I have t' larn t' control me temper,' he said quietly.

'You do,' replied Robert with an edge in his voice. 'How can I make a deputy out of you if you can't control your own emotions?'

The boy's head snapped up now. 'Ya can't make a lawman outta me, no matter how haird ya troy.'

Robert wasn't used to being told he couldn't do something and it reflected in his voice, 'So you'd rather piss your life away shovelling shit, would you?'

The boy shook his head agitatedly. 'No, sar. It ain't dat. Dere's anooder reason.'

Robert raised his eyebrows. He realised he knew nothing about this bright boy, except for their brief conversation a week before.

'Well tell me, so.'

'When I tell it t' ya', you won't want me fer a depuddy.' The boy had Robert's complete attention now. 'Me da an' me ooncle … dey w's both hanged, down in Glengarriff, about ten years ago. They was bandits, 'r at least me ooncle was. I t'ink me da jus' wen' along fer d' craic. Dey tried t' waylay a gennelman on d' rawd t' Bantry. It tarned out he w's bait fer a troop o' cavalry some smairt young Anglish officer was leadin'. Annyway, dey got run down by d' harses, an' d next marnin' dey hung 'em both from Cromwell's bridge.'

'That wasn't any wrongdoing of yours, boy. How did your family survive?'

'I didn' have any fam'ly, sar. Joost me da. When he w's gone, I stairved fer a few days in me house an' den I hit d' rawd t' make out 's best I could.'

Robert considered Ned's words for a moment. This was a story which repeated itself all too often throughout Ireland. Most orphans starved, but a few of the more resilient ones managed to survive, at least for a while. Ned's story gave testament to the resourcefulness of the young man standing here in the stable.

'Tell me about your da.'

The boy looked down. He was loath to speak of his father, but this man had shown him mercy where another would have flogged him, so he deserved a response.

'He beat me all d' time,' he said quietly. 'He'd get drunk on whiskey an' he'd smack me 'til 'is hands got sore. Den he'd beat me wit' a willow switch until he couldn' swing it anymore. Boot, he w's me da, sure, an' I loved 'im joost d' same.'

Robert had never been married and he had no children, none that he knew of anyway, but he never understood how a child could be subjected to such abuse by a parent, yet still love their abuser. Robert had heard enough. He told Ned that what they'd talked about was just between the two of them and that the young man should, under no circumstances, repeat it again. Ned understood. He had never told the story to anyone else, out of shame and embarrassment.

'Clean those rags you have on you, boyo,' ordered the sheriff. 'You might as well start learning to take care of yourself.' As soon as he'd uttered the words, Robert thought how redundant his statement was. If there was anyone in this whole green island who knew how to take care of himself, it was the young fellow who stood before him now.

CHAPTER 9

Roisin was kept busy in Gortalocca and she often thought about Michael, wishing he was there to help. Robbie did his best, but the unvarnished truth was that he was about as much use as her own dear father had been. They still owned and ran Hogan's, the village store, but business had been poor since so many had been evicted from the area.

Roisin would open the store for a few hours in the morning, for women coming to buy their supplies, then again in the evening in the hopes there would be a gathering of the locals for a bit of gossip and a pint or two. Her best customer was Robbie, who would share a drop with anyone who stopped by. He suffered from the publican's curse, sampling too much of his own product, so she had to keep an eye on him. Roisin doubted that Hogan's would last another generation. Her fears were not based solely on the poor business, and her dear Liam's death, but the thought of what legacy might be left behind when her time came. She loved her son Robbie dearly, but she seriously doubted his capabilities. It wasn't that he was stupid or ignorant, he just didn't care enough. Robbie's only concern was his next meal and flagon of beer. If Mikey were here, things would be different. Mikey truly was his father's son.

Liam's experiment in socialism had failed dismally. He had thought, by having community-owned land, although for legal purposes it was his name on the deed, the farmers would be more productive. Liam's plan was that a quarter of the profits would be set aside, to cover the tithe which had to be paid annually to the Church of Ireland, and the rest would go towards buying seed and livestock for the coming year. That way, if the crops failed, the community wouldn't starve as they had done in other parts of Ireland during famine years. There were so many homeless families that Liam had no problem finding people. The problem was that, when it came time to divide the profits, they regarded Liam with the same animosity they would any tax collector, even though they were living better and more securely than they had ever lived in their lives.

There had been a few exceptions. When the Reilly family left their farm and moved to Clare, Liam had bought it and settled a young family from south Tipp there. The Kellys had understood. They raised sheep, the likes of which had never been owned by an Irishman before. Roisin smiled to herself as she remembered that those sheep were the progeny of the 'borrowed' Protestant ram.

Managing fifteen farms … Roisin put her face in her hands, she felt like crying. She didn't know how in God's name Liam had done it. She had the now familiar thick feeling in her throat but the tears wouldn't come this time, she had cried herself dry. She knew it was time to pull herself out of her misery and to get on with things. She made her way from her cottage, across the little village street, and opened Hogan's for the first time since they buried Liam.

*

Michael Flynn Hogan had just finished saying Mass in the bog outside Macroom. On any other occasion, he would have been invited to eat a meal with a local family, but today was different. After Mass, everyone had dispersed into the swamp. They were afraid and wanted nothing to do with the priest. There was nothing to do but start the journey home. He would travel by day, hoping to avoid not only the bandits, but also the redcoats. He packed his stole under the piece of rotten pork, got a small loaf of bread from one of the old women parishioners, and headed off back to safety.

He had covered almost half the route back to Ballyshee but the sun was getting low now and Mikey knew he must find somewhere to spend the night, far away from the more travelled road from Macroom to Bantry. His thoughts were with his empty stomach instead of in his head when he came to a small road crossing.

'Halt!' yelled a red-coated man who had stepped out from behind a stone wall with another. The first man was shaped like a barrel and he held his musket at port arms. The other younger man had his weapon pointed at Michael and he heard the unmistakeable double click of a 'Brown Bess' being cocked. Mikey froze in mid-stride, wishing that he'd been paying more attention. At this range, there would be little chance of a miss, and a seventy five caliber lead ball left no apologies.

'State yer business, you Irish pig!'

Michael heard the undeniable Irish in the man's own

accent. Sometimes, the Irish in the King's employ were even more English than the English, he thought.

'Putcher hands over yer head, Paddy.' Mikey did as he was instructed. 'Are ya deaf? I said state yer business! What are ya doin' on d' road?'

'I'm a blacksmith,' replied Michael.

'O'course ya are,' sneered the barrel-shaped corporal, 'an' I'm d' King o' England.' He turned and addressed the trooper. 'Go and check 'is bag. An' put dat gun on half cock, so's ya don't blow yer own head off.'

The second man lowered the hammer on the flint lock and went over to Liam's bag. He opened it up and, when he smelled the contents, he turned and gagged.

'Jayzus have you got a dead pig in there?' he spluttered, clouting Michael on the side of the head with a gloved hand.

By now the smell had reached the thick corporal. 'Jus' see if 'e has somethin' t' eat in dere, den kick 'im in d' arse fer offendin' me nose.'

The trooper pulled out the loaf and then, as instructed, kicked Michael's arse.

'Show me yer hands,' barked the corporal. 'I c'n smell a priest a mile away, an' y' got dat stink about ya.' Michael held his hands out for inspection. The corporal turned them over, then threw them down roughly. 'Get yer sorry self outta here an' get off me road before I spend a bit o' lead an' powder on ya.' Michael wasted no time in heading down the road and didn't slow his pace until he was sure he was out of musket range.

Even when he knew he was out of view, the young man's heart continued to pound in his chest. That was two close calls on one trip. Mikey didn't mind a little excitement in his life, but this was too much for his temperament to withstand. He thought about Gortalocca and his mam and da. The land up in Tipperary was a lot more hospitable and his uncle, the sheriff, had cleaned out most of the bandits long ago. Except for a few roving bands of youths, it was safe to travel day or night. There were only a few red-coats stationed at Nenagh Castle, and even they were mostly brought out for ceremonial purposes. Mikey had begun to get homesick for the rolling Tipperary fields which gave up their fruits so willingly. The mountains around him now were majestic, to be sure, but a man can't eat beauty and what bounty they did give up, they gave up grudgingly.

He found a place to rest for the evening, behind a thicket of gorse. He had nothing to eat now, the troopers had seen to that. He counted his blessings, however, that the rotten pork had done its job and that the English hadn't probed any deeper into his sack than they had. He slept fitfully, woken several times by the sound of hoof beats on the road just below where he rested. The night was no longer his friend.

The next day, the sun was directly overhead when he walked into Ballyshee Valley. The sky was cloudless and the sun had grown hot. He had forgotten about his empty belly. Empty stomachs were something the Irish had grown used to. He looked forward to washing the road grime off himself with the clear water which ran in the little stream at the back of the forge. He would sit in the sun and let himself dry. He thought about sitting there with Morna, as the sun descended beyond the mountains, and the shadows creeped across the land. He was startled from his daydream by a voice he always half-hoped for, and had even begun to expect, each Monday when he returned from Macroom.

'Yer late. Oy bin worried aboutcha.' Michael smiled for the first time since he'd seen her a few days before.

He couldn't help himself. Whenever he looked into those beautiful green eyes, he got lost. Her red hair was tied tightly back, exposing the nape of her neck and Mikey felt a stirring that wasn't at all priestly. Morna walked over to where he stood and took his bag out of his hands. She was so close now that he could see down the collar of her dress, but he didn't let his eyes linger there long. Morna O'Malley was blossoming into a woman and she had the same feelings for the young smith as he had for her, but he wasn't aware of them. They walked together to the wooden bench which stood next to the cold forge and he sat heavily on it, slumping his shoulders with exhaustion. Morna sat down too and slid across the bench so that their hips just touched. He didn't care whether they spoke or not, as long as the girl was sitting beside him, but she said,

'It's long past toime dat we put t'ings on d' table.' Mikey was torn between inching away and wrapping his arms around her, pulling the delicate young woman to him. 'Ya know, Mikey, all d' eligible men here in Ballyshee aire joost overgrown boys.'

Mikey gave her a perplexed smile, 'They're Irish lads sure,' he said. 'It's hard for them to let go of the boys they once were.'

'Oy have sumpthin' t' say, Mikey Hogan.' Her pretty frow furrowed. 'An' if ya get me confused, Oy won't r'member d' speech Oy been goin' over in me head!' Michael lowered his head in mock penitence but she had his complete attention.

'It's like dis, Michael. Oy bin talkin' t' a couple o' d' udder garls, Kathleen Finnegan an' Mary Galvin, an' dey've taken a shine t'ya too.'

'What about the priest thing?'

'Shut yer trap, Mikey, yer makin' me ferget me speech.

Anyway, yer d' only one aroun' here dat t'inks yer a priest. Ya a'ready tol' evryb'dy dat you ain't took yer final vows, so ya ain't a real priest yet, an' if Oy get my way, d' only vows you'll take is weddin' ones. Now see what ya did, ya sod, ya made me ferget me speech! Oy'll jus' say dat ya have somethin' t' talk to me Da about an' Oy expec' ya t' say it really soon, befar dem udder garls talk t' ya.'

With that, Morna hurried away for a few steps, then slowed, tossed him a skittish smile over her shoulder and sauntered off in the direction of her family's cottage. Michael was flummoxed, completely taken by surprise at the young woman's boldness. She might not look like me mam, he thought, but it was like herself talking to me.

CHAPTER 10

Robert D'Arcy was as meticulous in his plans for this mission as he was in planning strategy for a battle. He strode towards his office and spoke to his adjutant on the way.

'Come with me Higgins. I have something to discuss with you.' Higgins was completely caught off guard and, from the tone of the sheriff's voice, thought he was surely in trouble for something. He snapped to attention.

'I can explain, sir,' he began.

Robert stopped and turned to his subordinate. 'Shut up, Higgie,' he said, 'you're not in any hot water. In fact you're getting a promotion.' Higgins' jaw slacked and, mutely, he followed Robert into the office. 'Shut the door, Higgins, this isn't a barn.' The adjutant meekly did as he was told. 'Now, take a seat.' Robert pointed to the chair behind his desk and sat himself at the one in front of it. Higgins lowered himself gingerly into the big chair and fidgeted for a moment before settling in.

'Gives you a different perspective, doesn't it?' asked Robert rhetorically.

'Yes, sir… but do you think I'm ready?'

'You're a gobshite, Higgins. You know as well as I do that you've lusted after my position from the time you arrived here.'

'Well, yes sir, but…'

'False modesty doesn't suit you, Higgins. The job is temporary. You'll only be keeping my seat warm and if you do it well, I might recommend you for the post. But first, I have a request to ask of you and a piece of advice to give you. The request is that you keep an eye on the little village of Gortalocca. I have a special interest in some of the people there. The advice, Higgie, is stop being such a snob. This is not Staffordshire, it's Tipperary and it's not Lichfield, this is Nenagh.'

Higgins was astonished that the High Sheriff even knew where his family came from, and he chose to ignore the 'snob' comment. The adjutant nodded and said he would do as requested.

'Now go back to your desk. You'll be sitting in my chair soon enough.' Higgins rose reluctantly and returned to the outside office. Robert followed him out and went straight to the armoury.

Rows of muskets were lined up in racks against the wall, along with every kind of bladed instrument of mayhem, which were rapidly becoming obsolete. The old man who tended the arsenal stood up as Robert entered.

'C'n I helpya, sir?' he inquired, from the dimness. There was only a single small window providing the light. Any open flame, like that from a candle or an oil lamp, could ignite the gunpowder stored here.

'Have you got any caltrops?' asked Robert.

'We have o'course,' said the old fellow. 'We've sacks of 'em,' With that, he disappeared into the dark and returned with a vicious, mediaeval-looking device made of iron, with four three-inch spikes sticking out from it in a manner such that, if thrown on the ground, one of the spikes would always point straight upwards. The old man handed one to Robert and the sheriff turned it over in his hands. He shook his head.

'It's too big and heavy. I want two dozen of them, made with one inch spikes. How long will it take?' The armourer took the caltrop back now he turned it over in his hands.

'Vicious t'ings, dese,' he mused. 'Dey could lame a man 'r a harse wit' one step. I could get d' smith t' make a bunch in a day 'r so.'

'Make it so', ordered the sheriff, 'and one more thing. I want a pistol which can be hidden in a pocket.'

The old fellow beamed a toothless grin, 'I made t'ree o' dem fer Sir Howard some years back,' he said, 'fer 'is own personal protection like, but he tol' me dat I was a toymaker. I ev'n have 'd bullet mould fer dem. I'll get dem fer ya.' The armourer again disappeared into the darkness and Robert could hear him rummaging around. The old man reappeared with a box and, when he opened the lid, there were two complete pistols with barrels about four inches long, and a third one without a lock mechanism. Robert picked up one of the two finished guns and put it in his pocket. When he tried to withdraw it, the dog ear of the hammer caught in his clothes.

'Can you take most of the ear off the hammer?' he asked.

The old armourer looked a little doubtful. 'I can, o'course, sir, but it'll make it harder to cock d' piece.' The sheriff shrugged and the armourer added, 'Dese t'ings won't be much good after 'bout ten feet, sir.'

Robert smiled openly, 'As long as they can outreach a sabre, that will be sufficient.'

The old man nodded in affirmation, 'Ah, dey'll do dat sir, unless d' man swings a mighty long blade.'

Robert stepped outside the darkness of the armoury

and squinted his eyes against the harsh, bright sunlight. If he'd had more time, he would have stayed and talked to the armourer for a while longer. The old fellow was interesting, in a murder and mayhem sort of way. He headed back towards his office and noticed that his adjutant wasn't at his desk. I hope the fecker isn't getting drunk, he thought, as he opened the heavy door to his inner office. There sat the adjutant, behind the desk, with his feet up. A decanter of whiskey and a smoking pipe sat on the desk in front of him.

'I bet you wouldn't jump in my grave that quick, you shitwad!'

Higgins jumped up and stood to attention. 'Begging your pardon, sir. I was just trying the chair out for size, sir.'

'Well try your legs out for size and run yourself back out to your own desk.' Higgins did nothing better than follow instructions, there wasn't a creative bone in his body, so he made his way to the door. 'And send for Ned Flood, if you can manage to find him. Tell him I want to see him.'

When he was alone in his office, Robert slouched down in his chair and closed his eyes. He was tired and could easily have dozed off right there and then. He was sixty-one years old and, although he didn't look it, there were times when his years felt like a hundred and sixty-one. His right shoulder ached when he used it too much, or when the weather was cold and damp, and there were times when, if he sat for too long, his knees felt like they had rusted tight. It was time to give it up and perhaps find a little place to spend his dotage, maybe even Gortalocca. It was just the right size and everyone there knew him. His reverie was interrupted by a loud knock on the door.

*

Mikey made his way along the floor of the valley and started up the slope which lead to the O'Malley cottage. It wasn't far, less than half a mile. He was surprised at how calm he was and he thought about the story his mother had told him about how nervous his father had been when he had asked permission to court her. Michael, by contrast, was as calm as a man could be under the circumstances. He had dressed in his best clothes. It was an easy choice since they were the only clothes he had, except for the grey Franciscan robe. Thankfully, the day had been sunny and warm and so he'd had the opportunity to scrub his leine and trews. They hadn't quite dried but they were dry enough. This was going to be one of those moments that he needed to remember, although he wasn't sure what he was supposed to say. He had decided he would simply react to whatever was said to him and take it from there.

As he approached the cottage, Michael could see that the upper half of the door was open, and he could hear the soft murmuring of voices from within. He didn't have to announce himself, it seemed that he was expected.

'Come in, boyo, an' have a drink wit me', said Jimmy O'Malley. Mikey noticed that O'Malley's face, which was normally split in two by a huge smile, was unusually sober. Jimmy was a short, stocky fellow with white hair and a ruddy complexion. Mikey estimated him to be in his mid-fifties. When his eyes got used to the dark, Michael saw the faces of Caroline O'Malley and Morna, equally as grim, and he could tell they'd been crying.

'Maybe this isn't a good time' he said.

'Nonsense, boyo, dis is d' parfec' toime. C'mon, we'll

have a drink an' den we'll take a walk, an' leave d' women t' talk.'

There were only two little stools and a table in the house and they constituted the entire furnishings, so the men stood and the older woman and the girl sat mutely. Jimmy downed the cup of poteen in a single gulp, it wasn't the first drink he'd had that afternoon,

'Drink oop, lad, an' we'll stretch our legs.' The homemade whiskey was strong and when Mikey drained the cup, it burned his throat and took his breath away. Jimmy ushered the young fellow out and they walked together for a while in the warm afternoon sun. When they reached a stone wall, the old fellow rested his forearms on it and Mikey mimicked him.

'It's beautiful isn't it, boyo,' he said. They both looked out over the valley floor, dotted with cottages, some made of stone and some of mud. The afternoon sun glazed the valley with a golden hue and it was indeed beautiful.

'Boot it's a terrible beauty, boyo,' Jimmy continued. 'It c'n killa man as sure as pyson.' Mikey wrinkled his brow in confusion.

'How auld d' ya t'ink Oy am, Michael?' Mikey shrugged, he knew this kind of guessing game was one you couldn't win.

'Oy'm t'arty eight years auld, an' me woife is t'arty six. Dis land has sooked d' loife outta us, an' Oy don' wannit t' kill my Morna too.' Mikey exhaled deeply as Jimmy continued.

'When me granda came t' dis valley, sixty years ago, dere was only a few families here. Dey grazed sheep on d' slopes, and dey raised mostly oats an' wheat. Da soil was deep enoof on d' floor o' d' valley t' grow a crop o' veg'tables too. Dey had a good life here. Den dey brought in d' spuds an' a man could feed a fam'ly on an acre 'r two o' land an' more people came. Da spuds was both a blessin' an' a curse fer Ireland. Have ya noticed dat dere ain't no auld people here, or kids between d' ages o' five an' ten?' Mikey raised his eyebrows in realisation. 'Well, dat's because dey all stairved t' death, a few years before ya came here. We had a cold, wet winter an' a wet summer, followed by anudderer wet winter, an' two crops o' p'tatoes failed. We lost Morna's younger brudder an' sister. We ate grass soup an' we all stairved. D' lambs doid from d' cold, an' a lot o' da ewes doid fr'm d' hoof rot, so dere was nutt'n t' eat but d' grass from d' hills. Liddle childr'n have always made mud pies, boot Oy betcha nev'r saw dem eat dem as well.' Michael shook his head. 'Well, dey did it here t' keep d' hoonger pains outta dere shtoomicks. Sure it broke me hairt, an' it broke ev'ryone's hairt, boot dats d' way it was.'

Mikey's eyes were glassy now and he saw that Jimmy had tears running down his face. He remembered back to 1722 and 1723 but the horrors of those periodic famines were something he had only vaguely heard about. He had never witnessed, firsthand, the desperation of the victims of one of these holocausts. Things did get lean in Gortalocca at the time, but his father had made sure everyone ate at least once a day. Michael realised that, even though he'd known Morna for two years now, he had never heard her talk of those times. He had oft times spoken about his own life in Gortalocca, and she had always listened attentively, but now he knew there was much more to this sweet young girl than he had ever imagined.

CHAPTER 11

In a mansion overlooking the bay in Glengarriff, a middle-aged English officer stood at the window of his office and stared down at the anchorage, feeling very sorry for himself. How could such a promising career have come to this? He'd been posted to Ireland more than ten years before and he despised the country and every living thing in it. He'd had the best education available and had excelled in the study of tactics and military history. Now, he'd been a Captain for nine years with no prospect of promotion. A rat-catcher, that's all he'd become.

Percival Grey, the eighth child born to the Duke of Suffolk, turned away from the window and stood in front of the full-length mirror he kept in his office. His eyes saw a military hero and he turned sideways to admire himself. He thought that, given the opportunity, he could rival Hannibal, or even Alexander, with his military acumen. His own eyes didn't see what the mirror saw. He was almost six feet tall and weighed not much more than a hundred and thirty pounds. His eyes were too close together, making his face foxlike in appearance, and he had a long prominent nose and less-than-prominent chin. His shoulders were too narrow and his hips too wide but, in his own eyes, he was Hercules reborn.

He had thought that by now, at the age of thirty-three, his military career would be over and he would be married to a plump girl, perhaps the only daughter of a rich English nobleman, and have an estate to rival his father's. He would regale people at parties with tales of gallantry and heroics on the battlefield, yet here he was hunting Papist priests.

A fine crystal decanter of French brandy sat on his desk and the captain stared at it for a long moment. Bloody French, he thought, all they know how to do is make liquor and lose wars. Why can't they start one up now? Then, when we defeat them, I can go back to England and write my memoirs. He rang for his butler, Joshua. The poor, unfortunate man had worked for the Grey family for many years and knew that, when Percival was in foul temperament, it was best to say nothing and await orders. He sometimes wished he was back in the cane fields of Jamaica, where Percy's father had bought him, on a trip he'd made there twenty years before. He had brought back his pet 'darkie' to show off to the other gentry and, when he'd grown tired of his new 'toy', he had assigned him to serve Percival. Joshua had become oblivious of the younger man's insults and derision and he'd also become accustomed to being flailed with whatever the Captain might lay his hands on. Joshua poured his master a snifter-full of brandy and waited to be dismissed. Percy waved him away.

Percival Grey hated his life and firmly believed that his circumstances were no fault of his own, that it was the stupid narrow-minded pigs in London who kept him here. An older brother of his had been posted to the

Virginia colony and now he was married to a planter's daughter, standing to inherit a very profitable tobacco plantation. His oldest sibling would become heir to his father's title and estates and there would be nothing left for poor Percy. He hated his name too, and his mother for burdening him with it … Percy. His peers at boarding schools had bullied him and called him 'Pussy'. He wished he could run them through with a sabre and watch them squirm, as they had made him squirm all those years before. Percival Grey saw himself as one of life's victims and he had always blamed the world for making him feel that way. Now it was his chance to even up the score, and the entire country of Ireland would be the object of his animosity.

*

Robert Flynn D'Arcy was sitting behind his desk when Higgins ushered Ned Flood into the room. The young man stood to attention and the door was closed behind him.

'At ease,' ordered the sheriff, and Ned separated his feet, placing his hands behind his back. 'Take a seat Ned. I have a request to make of you.' The young deputy was used to taking orders from his superiors and this last statement made him curious. He seated himself facing the older man and stared at the horse pistol on the desk, pointing directly at the chair he was sitting in.

'Sorry,' Robert smiled, 'that's just for show.'

Ned smiled back. 'Well, I wish yu'd show it t' d' wall. It makes me narvous having dat t'ing pinted at me.'

Robert turned the pistol butt towards the young Irishman. 'I'm going on a mission to west Cork,' he told him.

The deputy's grin became wider, 'Dat's my aul' stompin' ground.'

'I know. I was wondering if you might be interested in joining me on an adventure, Ned.' The boy's face lit up and Robert knew he had the fish hooked. 'There may be some danger involved,' he warned. 'That's lawless territory down there.'

'It won' be lawless when we get down dere. When are we goin'?'

'Whoa! Hold your horses, boyo. You don't even know what we're going there for.'

'It don' matter. I been gettin' homesick fer d' mount'ns.'

'We have to go as civilians, Ned. We have no official jurisdiction down there.'

'Aire we chasin' villains?'

'No.'

'Boot it's 'n advent're, right?'

'Yes.'

'An' it could be dangerous, right?'

'Yes.'

'What more could a Carkman want, so. When'r we leavin?'

'I have a little more work to do here, but it will be soon, probably by the end of the week.'

'Oy'm game. You jus' let me know an' Oy'll be saddled oop ready.'

Robert stood up and walked around the desk. He shook the young fellow's hand, 'Thank you, Ned,' he said. 'When we get back, you'll be promoted to corporal.' Ned Flood nodded and waited to be dismissed. Robert hesitated. 'First we'll have a drink to the success of our adventure,' he said, and poured a healthy measure of good whiskey for them both. When Ned left the room,

Robert heard him give a loud hoot and Higgins shouting at him to shut up. He went back behind his desk and poured himself another drink. As he sipped it, he smiled and thought back to the long-forgotten days in his father's forge when he, too, had thirsted for adventure.

*

Roisin was beginning to formulate an idea of how to keep the village of Gortalocca sustainable, now that Liam was dead. She knew that if anything was to happen to her, then everything would be lost in short order. Liam had been the heart and soul of the town and the father of it too and, like all good fathers, he'd had his rules. To keep order, and to stay below the scrutiny of higher authorities, he'd had to impose a few. He had made sure that the debacle they'd had with Sean Reilly wouldn't happen again. Sean had been spoiled as a child and had become a petulant adult, subject to rages, believing that everything related to him. Although he'd been generally tolerable when sober, he was dangerous in his cups and, when Liam tended the bar at Hogan's, there had been times when Liam had cut off the supply of alcohol, even to the extent of shutting down the bar, if he thought there was a threat of violence.

His other rule was that the taxes and tithes must be paid at harvest time. To wait any longer would invite wild spending sprees, followed by destitution. It was the only way the community could survive through the bad years as well as the good. Their eldest son Robbie was a good hearted man, generous to a fault. He lived to be liked and, because of his good nature, he was an easy mark. Roisin knew only too well that the most difficult time of year was when the bills became due, and she also knew that Robbie was too easy-going to press anyone for payment. She wondered how she could approach Jamie Clancy to do the job, without evoking any jealousy or resentment from her oldest son. Liam had looked after Jamie from the time he was eleven years old, and Roisin knew him well enough to know there wasn't a dishonest bone in his body. It was only July now, but she knew she had to start making plans for what must happen by the end of September. If only Liam was here to give her counsel, she thought. But Liam had lived his life as if he'd live forever … but he hadn't. Roisin dabbed her eye with the corner of her apron. 'Damn you, Liam Flynn, you're going to make me cry again', she said aloud.

Roisin was well aware that delicacy and diplomacy were not her forte. She was as blunt as a shillelagh. She thought perhaps she'd speak to Jamie first. He had spent so much time at Liam's side that, sometimes, he even sounded like him. Some people, for whatever reason, were born wise and didn't need a pile of decades under their belt to be prudent. Jamie Clancy was one of those, just as Liam had been and her youngest, Michael, was. Mikey, I wish you could hear me, she thought, I wish you'd come home and help me. She put her hands under her apron, pulled it up and buried her face in it. Her heart ached.

CHAPTER 12

The one-roomed cottage in Ballyshee was dark, except for the glow which ebbed and flowed from the turf burning in the fireplace. The temperature outside had plummeted as soon as the sun descended behind the mountains. Twilight lasted forever here in the valley. The four people inside talked intermittently, the women occasionally shedding tears. Michael and Morna sat on the floor, while the two chairs were occupied by the girl's parents. Jimmy O'Malley and his wife approved of the match but there were certain formalities to be discussed. It would be unseemly for the young couple to court openly, at least until the rumour mill had announced their intentions. There would be some who would not accept the fact that Michael wasn't a 'real' priest, since they had confessed to him, and he had dispensed penance, and had transformed the water and wine into Christ's body and blood at Mass on Sundays. Jimmy chose to disregard those arguments. He wanted to get his daughter out of this beautiful, terrible valley.

The valley was remote enough to be untouched by the stranglehold which the British yoke held over most of the country but, sometimes, it was the land itself that could grind a man's soul into grist … Ireland's endless, unpredictable cycle of boom and bust. Depending on the vagaries of the weather, one out of every four years, it seemed, a crop would fail. If two bad seasons followed one another, the result was catastrophic and there would be a famine. Sometimes the season of privation was local but, once every twenty years or so, it was countrywide. The condition was exacerbated by the explosion in the population of Irish peasants. The lowly potato was a blessing and a curse, as the Irish people became more reliant on a single crop for their very survival.

Jimmy O'Malley almost always had a smile on his face. He was good-natured and cheerful but, underneath it all, lay a sense of dread or foreboding. He was happy enough with his lot, but a fear of the future haunted him. Like the land itself, he was pleasant and engaging at first glance but, underneath, lay a fierce unpredictability. The Irish and their mentality were largely shaped by the ground beneath their bare feet.

Jimmy tried to persuade his daughter to leave with Michael but Morna resisted, partly because she was afraid of the unknown. She had rarely left the confines of Ballyshee, and the outside world, with all its uncertainties, terrified her as much as the future frightened her father. She would miss her parents desperately too, if she was to strike out with Mikey. She worried that perhaps she didn't know the young man, sitting beside her on the floor, well enough to make such a momentous decision. Michael had the advantage, he had heard her confessions.

He provided them with a possible solution. Since it was customary for parents in their dotage to live with one of their children, he and Morna would go to Gortalocca and, once they were settled, would send for Jimmy and his wife. O'Malley was dubious about this plan.

'Wit' t'ings bein' d' way dey aire, boyo, d' roads'll be too dangerous t' travel wit' a woman, 'specially one as young an' pretty as me dotter. Yu'd have t' travel overland, an' dat'd be some haird goin' 'til ye get outta dese mountains. Ye'll have t'carry yer provisions, an' I got no money t' give ye.'

Mikey gave a passing thought to how effective the rotten pork had been in dissuading the troopers from searching his belongings. Perhaps he could secrete the foul-smelling stuff about Morna's person, under her clothing. He thought about the many times, as a boy, when he'd come up with some hair-brained scheme, only for his father to ask, 'What kind of feckin' nut are you, Mikey?' Having seemingly already branded his son a nut, he was just curious to know which particular variety of 'feckin' nut' he actually was. The memory of how he and his da used to interact made him smile involuntarily. They were two peas in a pod.

Jimmy O'Malley interrupted his train of thought. 'Ain't nuthin' funny here, boyo, dis could be life an' death … 'r even worse!'

Mikey snapped back from his reverie and apologised to the farmer. 'I'm sorry, sir, I just was thinking about me da.'

Jimmy was perturbed. 'Well stop t'inkin' 'bout yer da, take a look at dat garl settin' nex' t' ya dere, an' stairt t'inkin' 'bout a safe way t' get 'er outta here.' Michael looked at the delicate young girl by his side and his heart pounded. O'Malley was right, of course. The thought of any harm coming to her was enough to focus his attention.

'I will, sir, you mustn't worry. I have to give it some thought but I'll come up with a plan that will work, I promise.' The older fellow was satisfied. After all, Michael was a learned man who had attended the seminary.

'You make yer plans, boyo, an' when ya tell dem t' me, Oy'll try an' poke holes in 'em. Between d' two of us, we'll work somethin' out. Now kiss d' garl on d' cheek an' stairt yer planning.'

*

Just over a hundred miles away, in the market town of Nenagh, another plan had almost reached completion. Robert went down to the armoury and was greeted enthusiastically by the old armourer. It wasn't often that dignitaries visited him and, when they did, it was usually to tender some complaint or other. Here, he'd had two visits from the sheriff in almost as many days. Robert extended his hand in greeting and this was another new experience for the armourer. Those in authority never proffered their hands to those who worked in the dark recesses of the castle. He was more accustomed to the back of someone's glove across his cheek.

'Oy have sumthin for ya, sir.' The old fellow held out a closed wooden box for inspection and the sheriff opened the lid. Inside were the two small pistols which the armourer had modified. Robert took one out and turned it over in his hand. The dog ear of the hammer had been shortened to a nub. Robert slipped it into his pocket and withdrew it and, as he did, he cocked the hammer. He smiled at the craftsman.

'This will do nicely,' he said. He repeated the action and the gun slid in and out of the pocket of his greatcoat easily.

'I had d' flintnapper make some fresh flints fer dem,

an' I cast some extra lead balls too. I'll make a powder horn wit a plug t' measure d' right amount fer d' load, t'day.' Robert nodded and shook the man's hand again.

'I have sumthin' else for ya, sir,' said the armourer, delighted that his work was approved of. He picked up a leather bag from his table and handed it to Robert. The sheriff hefted it on his open palm and noted that it only weighed little over a pound. He untied the string at the top and reached inside, it was the caltrops. He fingered one of them and, again, a hint of a smile crossed his lips. Yes, this was more like it.

'Dey'll lame a horse 'r a man if dey step on one o' dose t'ings.' Robert emptied a few of them out onto the table and they did, indeed, all lie with a deadly point sticking straight upwards. The spikes were about an inch long, placed at a hundred and twenty degrees from each other and tapered into a razor tip. 'I had t' use a ledder bag 'cause d' tips poked t'rough a cloth one.'

The armourer had surprised Robert by exceeding his expectations. He had thought of everything. Destruction and mayhem were his life's work and he clearly excelled at both. Robert had a surprise for the old fellow too. Before he left the armoury, he handed the old man a gold coin. The fellow looked at it and, involuntarily, bit into it to see if it was real. Robert was amused by the action and grinned to himself as he snatched up his packages and left.

The sheriff handed a note to a courier who was due to head along the same route Robert proposed to take down to Kerry and west Cork. The note was for the new sheriff in Kenmare, informing him that he could expect a personal visit within the week. He also penned a letter addressed to the Lord High Mayor of Nenagh, informing him of his absence, without indicating the reason, and a final note to Roisin. He sealed each of them with red wax, onto which he impressed his mark. He would leave the last note with Roisin when he got to Gortalocca. He would have to go out that way anyway, to check on the two horses he'd left with Mick Sheridan and also to see if Jamie had finished work on the blade. He told an orderly to get his horse saddled.

July was coming to an end and it was a glorious morning, the oppressive heat wave having been broken the night before by a fierce thunderstorm, and the stagnant air having been replaced with a fresh new breeze. Robert passed a few groups of people on foot, as they trudged into Nenagh on the still wet road. As soon as he left the confines of the town, he spurred his horse into a gallop. After the last week's hot sultry days, it felt good to have the cool air wash over him. The horse's hooves slashed through the puddles which still lingered from the previous evening's tempest. Robert felt like the young man he had once been. An adventure was imminent and he was becoming as enthusiastic about it as his young travelling companion had been a few days before. 'When are we leaving' were the last words Ned Flood had spoken to him in his thick Cork accent. If all went well, it would be within a day or so.

Robert slowed the horse to a long trot as he approached the bridge at Ballyartella. He was loath to slow the horse because the exuberance of youth had overtaken him, and he had to remind himself that he was getting long in the tooth. He had forgotten the aches which plagued him each morning. He had a mission to accomplish and it could quite possibly be the most important one of his life.

Jamie was expecting the sheriff and, when he heard the horse approach, he appeared at the door of Matt

O'Brien's forge with a sheathed sword in his outstretched hands. By the very manner in which the young man handled the sabre, Robert could see it had been made much lighter. He dismounted his charger and, without a word, slid the blade out of its scabbard. The balance was superb and, by shortening the edge, the yeoman had created something brand new. The removal of the added length had made it handier. Robert tried it out, stabbing and slashing at the air. The basket was still substantial enough to parry a thrust but light enough to keep it in balance. He was pleased.

'You've proved your worth, boyo. For a man not schooled in the use of such an instrument, you've created an excellent piece of work. Jamie looked down and kicked the dirt at his feet. It embarrassed him to receive praise.

'Ah sure, I jus' did as ya told me sir.' Then he remembered something. 'Dere's somethin' else here for you,' he exclaimed, and went it inside to retrieve the dagger which he'd fashioned from the leftover metal. The blade was nine inches long and double-edged, and the wooden handgrip had been riveted in place, full tanged, then bound with rawhide, rough side outwards. 'It won't slip in yer hand if it gets sweaty,' beamed Jamie, proud of his innovation. Sweaty, thought Robert, or bloody?

'It's too long to be a skean, Jamie,' he said, 'so it's neither sword nor skean. Since it's your invention, you shall name it. What's it to be?'

The young man was not as adept with words as he was working with iron, so he pondered for a moment. 'It looks like ol' Paddy Shevlin's pig sticker, so I'll call it a paddy.' Robert had to laugh at the total absence of complication about the man in front of him.

'Well, let's hope that 'paddy' never has to do any

work, other than sticking a pig.' Robert held his finger up to his lips as indication for Jamie to be quiet, then handed him six shillings for his work. 'This is for your labours, Jamie,' and, before the younger man could object, he tied the short sword, in its sheath, to his saddle and slipped the 'paddy' into his boot.

CHAPTER 13

Michael counted the money he had, it was two shillings and four pennies. That was almost enough for the coach fare to Limerick, but only for a single person. He needed to work out how he could get both himself and Morna to Nenagh. Judging by the behavior he'd experienced from the parishioners in Macroom, he had to assume that there were spies or informants there. They could stay in the wild mountain country all the way to Mallow, but it was a long and arduous journey and Mallow was at a crossroads, so it was certain there'd be troops garrisoned there. It wasn't just the bandits and roaming youth gangs who troubled him, but the troops too.

Half the British army comprised of the dregs of England's society. There were recruiting officers at every courthouse in the land and, oft times, petty criminals would be offered a choice between prison or service in his majesty's forces. Life for English peasants was almost as brutal as it was for the Irish. Poverty and injustice, with all the callousness they brought, had created a segment of society who believed that cruelty was simply a part of life. The other half of the military was foreign, the majority of them Hessian and Prussian professional soldiers, bred to fight battles for the highest bidder. There was also a smattering of French Huguenots who had been persecuted by the Church for their beliefs and had fled to England for asylum. Like most refugees, they were particularly bitter.

*

Percival Grey sat at his desk, dressed in a blue silk dressing gown. He was growing impatient.

'When will my bath be ready, you tar-faced imbecile?'

Jacob was lugging bucket after bucket of hot water up the stairs to fill a copper tub, so the officer could take his bi-weekly bath. The black man didn't reply. With Percy becoming impatient, anything he said could easily result in another flogging. There came a tentative rap on the office door.

'If this isn't important, I'll see you skinned!' snapped the captain.

The door opened just a crack, and a timid young adjutant poked his head in. The lieutenant had recently graduated from a new military college at Sandhurst in England. He had realised, soon after his posting, that Percival Grey was jealous of him and bitter about the fact that new graduates were on the fast-track. This young fellow would probably be Grey's superior in a few years and, one day, would likely lead an entire army.

The young man saluted but the captain didn't return it. 'Well? Have you been struck dumb? Make it quick, my bathwater is getting cold.'

'We've arrested the tinker, sir.'

Percival allowed a mirthless smile to crease his

chinless face. The young officer thought he resembled one of those long German sausage dogs, and he smiled, not with him, but at the buffoon.

'Wipe that stupid grin off your face. It bothers me,' snarled Percy.

'What shall I do with him, sir?'

'Throw him in the gaol, you fool. What did they teach you at that military academy, idiot?'

'I need to file charges, sir.'

Percy was becoming petulant, the water in his bath was cooling. 'Sedition,' he sighed, 'it's always sedition.' He shook his head in disbelief.

'But we have no proof, sir.'

'He's from Cork, that's proof enough for me! Everyone in this damned county is a rebel and the sooner you realise that, the better.'

'He's old and frail, sir. The cold and damp of the gaol will likely kill him.'

'Good! That'll be one less feckin' Irishman. If it bothers you so much, why don't you give him your own bed?'

The lieutenant could see that this debate was hopeless. 'As you wish, sir.' He knuckled his forehead in salute and, when none was returned, he did an abrupt about-face and left the room. He made his way to where two troopers stood, holding the arms of a small, thin old man, with a nest of white whiskers down to his chest, his clothes hanging off him in rags. He ordered the men-at-arms to throw the old sod into a cell, but to give him something to eat first. He knew he wouldn't last much longer than a couple of weeks down there in that stinking hole.

Percival Grey strolled into the room where his bath stood waiting, and allowed his robe to drop to the floor.

He was feeling satisfied with himself. The water in the big copper tub was just the right temperature and Jacob had remembered to scent it. He stepped in, one boney leg at a time, then slowly lowered himself into the hot water until it came up to where his chin should be. He tipped his head back and thought about the network of spies and informants he'd placed in the bars and inns. They hadn't managed to ferret out the Papist, so he must send a spy out amongst the people. He wanted the priest caught unharmed so that he could personally hang him from Cromwell's Bridge or, better yet, sever the man's head with a stroke of his sabre. For Percival Grey, this was personal.

*

Roisin opened the store every morning. Reality had finally started to sink in and she had begun to act like a widow. Robbie was just being Robbie, always saying what he would do, but never actually doing anything. He would check in regularly, along with his wife, May. She was a pretty girl, vivacious when you got to know her, but she was a girl and not yet a woman. Roisin hoped that soon she would be with child. She thought that a child might make a difference, the new responsibility making a woman of May and, perhaps, forcing Robbie to grow up too.

She thought back to the times when Liam had a project and Jamie Clancy was busy at the O'Brien forge. He and Robbie would do the work alone and, sometimes, Liam would come home for supper and say that if brains were gunpowder, that boy wouldn't be able to blow his own nose. Robbie was better at talking about work than actually doing it and, most likely, that would never change. She thought about Mikey now, he was different. When you gave Mikey a task, you didn't worry that he would waste his time looking up at the clouds to watch them change shape. He was a true Flynn, as Liam had been, and as Liam's brother Robert was. When those men began an undertaking, it was as if they had taken an oath on their almighty souls. Robert had promised to find Michael. To most people, promises were like flowers … lovely at first but, after a while, would wither and soon be forgotten. To the Flynn boys, a promise was a vow, inviolate and inescapable, until it was fulfilled.

Roisin's thoughts were interrupted by the sound of a horse galloping down the road at a rapid clip. She looked out the window and saw the sheriff on his big chestnut. He saw her too and gave her a simple wave of acknowledgement before passing by. Roisin felt just a little disappointed when he didn't stop, but thought he must have something important to do because he always made time to stop, if only to have a chat with Liam. Perhaps the fact that Liam was no longer here made a difference. The thought made her sad, everything was changing.

When Roisin had first met Robert Flynn D'Arcy she hadn't liked him, in fact she had despised him. His dark green/brown eyes narrowed when he looked at you, as if he was trying to see into your soul. He had first appeared in Gortalocca, those many years ago, as a sinister stranger, sitting at Hogan's bar and conversing with the farmers who were, at that time, in fear of being dispossessed. He hadn't revealed then that he was Liam's brother but, when Liam had been badly beaten by Sean Reilly and his gang of thugs, Robert had visited him and Roisin had realised then just how unscrupulous he could be. He had used his own flesh and blood as bait for his trap and had almost got Liam killed in the process. Roisin shook her head at the thought. But over the years, she had come to have a grudging respect for the man. He had promised them he would watch over the village of Gortalocca and he had been true to his word. When other towns fell into decline, Gortalocca, in its own way, managed to survive with the help of his protection.

The sheriff had the note for Roisin in his pocket, he would stop on his way back to Nenagh and drop it off. First, he was anxious to see how the horses were coming along at Mick Sheridan's farm. When he arrived, Mick was in the big round pen, schooling one of the geldings. Mick gave a wave of acknowledgement and carried on with what he was doing. He was finished after a few minutes and he rode the animal up to the fence where Robert stood with his forearms on the top rail, resting his chin on his hands.

'Dese 'r some harses,' said Mick, with childlike enthusiasm. 'I fergot how good Hobbies c'n be. Look at dis!' He dropped the reins and got the horse to go round in circles, first in one direction, then the other. He grinned. 'Ya c'n ride 'em off o' leg. Ya don' even need t' use yer hands.' He stopped the horse in front of the sheriff. 'Give'm a try! I t'ink he's goin' t' be a fine mount fer ya.'

Before he put his foot in the stirrup, Robert asked, 'How's the other one?'

Mick could barely contain himself. 'I t'ink he's just 's good, maybe even bedder!' Robert took the horse out of the round pen and Mick held the gate open for him. 'Take'm out on d' road an see what he's got!'

Robert did just that. He spurred the horse into a gallop and then gave him a bit more leg. The animal increased velocity so quickly that it felt like he'd been shoved by an unseen hand. Robert wheeled the horse at speed and fought to keep himself straight in the saddle. He streaked back to the paddock.

'Jayzus!' he cried. Even he found it hard to contain himself. 'Are they ready, Mick?'

'Dey're 's ready 's I c'n make'm. I been feedin' dem oats so's dey'll be fit fer d' trip. Dat auld horse trader knew what he had.'

Robert felt a twinge of guilt for virtually stealing the geldings and using the law to do it, but before the thought had manifested itself into words, Mick laughed.

'Dat ol' sod's bin skinnin' people fer years. It's 'bout time 'e felt d' knife 'imself.' Robert felt relieved that at least he hadn't stolen from an honest man. 'I wish dat I could own a horse like dese ones,' Mick said, longingly, but without envy.

'Well, Mick,' replied Robert, 'I'll make a deal with you. When I get back, I'll give you the horses, but on one condition.' Mick waited excitedly, there was no condition that he wouldn't consent to. 'One day you and I are going to take these horses out and go have an adventure, like when we were kids.'

Mick looked puzzled. 'I ain't never had an adventure,' he lied.

Robert laughed. 'Borrying the squire's ram sounds like an adventure to me.'

Mick looked down at the ground and wondered where the lawman could have heard that. He quickly changed the subject back to horses.

'Da Hobbies c'n go faster an' further dan d' big chargers c'n.' He shot a glance at the sheriff's warmblood and addressed the horse, 'Beggin' yer pardon, sir.' Robert tried to keep a straight face. He too had been known to carry on conversations with the dumb beasts, and had even apologised when one had been shot out from under him, or he'd had to put one down. Such was the way of a horseman.

Mick placed the rope halters and lead lines on each of the horses, and Robert could tell that he would be sad to see them go.

'Mick,' he said, 'I'm getting too old to be sheriff. Perhaps, when I get back, the two of us will buy a big farm and become horse traders together.'

The big man smiled. 'Ah sure, I'd like dat altogether, sir,' he replied.

Robert gave him a wink. 'I'll see you in a month or so and I'll bring you your horses,' he said. He turned and set off down the road towards Gortalocca at a walk, with the geldings in tow behind the big chestnut.

'Safe home!' he heard the big man yell as he rode away and, without turning, he gave him a wave of his gloved hand.

Roisin was tending the flower garden which Liam had planted in front of the cottage. He had wasted so much time on those silly flowers, she thought, but he had loved them. She was so lost in her thoughts that she was startled when she heard Robert shout, 'Halloo!' from behind her. Her first inclination was to scold him for scaring the shite out of her but, for once, she held her tongue. He took a leather gauntlet off and reached into his pocket for the note, holding it down to her from his saddle. She took it and looked up at him quizzically. His face was stoical and devoid of expression.

'If I'm not back in five weeks,' he said, 'open the letter.' A wave of anxiety washed over her. She had known that the task she'd asked of him bore its risks but, if Robert Flynn D'Arcy was in doubt, then it must be far more dangerous than she had ever imagined. Here was a man with iced water in his veins, fearless, without reservations. His doubts meant that he was more like Liam than she had imagined.

Flatly, and without betraying himself he asked, 'Do you have any of Liam's old clothes? I'd like two sets, but if you can't manage that, can you get some from Robbie?'

She went inside the house and returned immediately with a couple of leines and two pairs of trews.

'Why do you want two sets?' she asked. She knew he wouldn't have asked unless there was a good reason, that was another characteristic of the Flynn siblings.

'I'll have a travelling companion with me,' he said tersely.

Roisin handed him the clothing and he balanced it on the saddle in front of him. He turned the horses wordlessly and headed up the road, out of the village.

'Godspeed, Robert Flynn!' Roisin shouted after him.

He turned and said, in a voice she could barely hear, 'Goodbye, Roisin.'

There was something about the way he said it that brought a lump to her throat and tears to her eyes and, as Robert rode away, her vision of him became blurred. She wondered if she would ever see Robert Flynn again.

CHAPTER 14

It was almost dark and the sky over Clare still had an orange tinge to it, when Robert arrived back at the fortress in Nenagh with the three horses. He dismounted the big brown and handed the reins to a waiting groom, telling him to have the big one saddled and ready for him at dawn the next day. He ordered that an extra measure of oats be fed to each horse, then went straight to the mess hall. The deputies were all seated on benches at both sides of a long table. The food had just been served, some kind of stew with a little meat and a great deal of potatoes in it. At his appearance, the men began to stand, but he motioned for them to sit down. Ned Flood sat attentively, watching the sheriff, and Robert gave a slight motion of his head towards the door. The young man stuffed as much food into his mouth as he could in one go, then leapt out from between two burly lawmen, accidentally kicking one of them in the process.

'Watch it, arsehole,' the man growled. Ned ignored him and and headed straight for the door, accompanied by Robert. When they were out of anyone's earshot, Robert said,

'You ready for an odyssey, boyo.'

'Oy dunno what dat is, boot Oy can't swim, so if it's got anyt'ing t' do wit' d' sea, Oy'll havta larn, sar.'

Robert stifled a grin. 'It's a story by a Greek man called Homer, it's about the greatest adventure that ever was.'

'No boats, right sar?'

'The story's full of boats, but we're going to use horses.'

The young deputy looked relieved. 'Well, if a harse goes lame, I c'n alw'ys walk. If a boat springs a leak, Oy'll havta say 'n Act o' Contrition.'

Robert knew that if he didn't get back to the subject at hand, Ned would go off on another unrelated tangent so he asked him, 'Did you draw a horse pistol from the armoury?'

'Oy did, sar, an' I tried it out too, boot the ol' man down dere said I cootn't hit a bull in d' arse wit' a han'full o' oats, so 'e loaded it wit' goose shot.'

'Good man yerself, Ned,' said Robert. He found himself imitating the man's west Cork accent and shook his head. 'Get your gear together and we'll leave at first light.'

'T'ankya, sar. Oy won' let ya down.' Ned forgot about his food and went straight to his quarters. Robert returned to his own room and, even though he'd packed and repacked a dozen times, he felt compelled to do it once more.

The old man slept fitfully and finally he gave up trying, long before the first rays of sun had shown themselves in the east. He dressed himself in his best uniform and sword, and carried his belongings out to the stables. He wanted to be gone before most of the men in the castle roused themselves so he didn't call for an aide.

When he got to the livery, Ned was already there, waiting for him.

'Oy cootn't sleep a wink las' night 'cuz o' d' noise me shtoomach wuz makin'. It sounded loike Oy swallied a dog.'

Robert knew it wasn't hunger that had kept the boy awake. He remembered when, a hundred times before he'd gone into battle, his nerves had pulled as tight as a harp string.

'Let's saddle up our mounts, Ned. No reason to wait for the lazy louts to get here.' The two men saddled their horses and stowed their gear. Both hung their horse pistols where they could be drawn at a moment's notice and Ned carried a Brown Bess musket, slug across his back. It was still an hour or so before dawn when they walked their steeds across the courtyard and out the gate, past the sleeping guards. Both had one of the Hobbies in tow. When they got about twenty yards from the gate, they mounted up and started the ride towards Limerick, the first stage of their journey.

'How'r we gettin' down t' Cark, sar?'

Robert thought he'd have a little fun with Ned, it was good to build a degree of camaraderie for an expedition like this.

'I thought we'd go by horse, Ned.' He could see Ned was confused but he kept it going. 'I had planned for us to go by boat, but you told me you can't swim, so I decided we've use horses instead.'

Ned ruminated on the sheriff's words for fully two minutes before a look of realisation crossed his face and he got the joke. 'Ah, sure ya can't take a boat t' Cark fr'm here.' Robert rolled his eyes. If Tipp fellows can be as thick as shit, what did that make a Cork man?

'So, what rawd aire we takin', sar?' asked Ned.

'We going by way of Kenmare.'

'We could get dere a day quicker if we head t'ward Mallow, sar.'

'We're going in by way of Kenmare because that's the back door.'

Ned rode in silence for a while and wondered if he was riding alongside a madman. He'd been all over that part of Cork and had never seen either a front door, or a back one. They travelled on and, by mid-day, they had crossed the Clare River into County Limerick. There was an inn there where they could get something to eat, but first they watered the horses.

'When we get past Limerick city, we'll find another an inn,' said Robert, 'and, maybe tonight, we'll get some sleep.' Ned told him he'd been sleeping in the saddle for the last two hours and Robert realised that was the reason his companion had been so quiet.

'Well, it's a good thing you didn't fall out of the saddle, so.'

Ned grinned sheepishly. 'I'm starvin' hungry now, sar.'

Robert snorted. 'Yes, well that's what a nap does to you old fellas,' he mocked.

By late afternoon, they had passed the city of Limerick. Ten hours in the saddle was enough, they had covered just over thirty miles and the horses needed a break, so did Robert. His bones ached and he wanted a flagon of ale and a hot meal but, mostly, some shut-eye.

'Mind that the horses are fed and rubbed down, will you Ned, I'll arrange the accommodations.' The inn was almost full and he was only able to get the one room for them both. Revitalised by his snooze, Ned had his talking head on and, finally, Robert had to order the Cork man to shut his gob and let him sleep.

The next morning, they were up long before dawn.

Robert's bones ached. He hadn't spent that long in a saddle in many years and it was going to take a while to get his arse back. Today's destination would be Newcastle and, after that, he expected the going to be slower, as the hills began to become higher.

The day was uneventful and it was growing late in the afternoon when they approached the town. The density of the woodland had increased now and, occasionally, they heard rustling in the undergrowth, where people had recognised their uniforms and had ducked for cover.

When they arrived at an inn in the town, they found it to be a hive of activity. There were parties of gentry there to hunt the wild boars which were prolific in the forest, where they rooted for acorns and hazel nuts. Most of the gentlemen were in their cups and one of them, on seeing the uniformed men, came over and sat himself at the table with Robert and Ned.

'Would you two gentlemen be interested in accompanying us on a hunt tomorrow?' The young deputy shot Robert a glance and gave a slight nod of his head, his eyes wide. The sheriff was annoyed that his meal had been interrupted and, without a word shook his head, no. Ned looked plaintive but Robert asserted himself.

'I said no, Ned. We have no time for frivolity.'

The gentleman was offended, 'Frivolity, is it? I'll have you know that it can be very dangerous. Why, I saw a man get his middle finger bitten off by one of the beasts, I saw it with my own eyes.'

By now, Robert had lost patience with the man, 'Well that's too bad for his feckin' wife. Tell me, have you ever cut off a man's head with a sword?' The man got up so fast that he upset the chair.

'Well, I never…'

Robert stood up and addressed the crowd. 'No, you never. And that's because people like you get people like me to do your dirty work, so you can spend your time hunting little piggies in the woods.'

The room had fallen silent and Robert looked around, suddenly ashamed of his outburst. He usually had better self-control and didn't allow himself to lose his temper like that but his bones ached, and his arse was sore, and he just wanted to finish his meal and be left alone. He and Ned slept in separate rooms that night and Robert got the decent night's sleep he needed, and not a moment too soon.

The next morning his mood had lightened and he even joked about the previous evening's scene at the inn. He told Ned he doubted if they would make it to the town of Castleisland that night because they'd have to cross a pass in the Glanaruddery Mountains. The mountains weren't much, as mountains went, at least not like those that would come later, but they would make for slower going with the horses. He didn't want to use the beasts up before the more arduous trip ahead. They left an hour before dawn and were well on their way before the gentry had roused themselves for their hunt.

The sides of the road were much more densely forested now and they passed only the odd remote cottage here and there. Eventually, as the road climbed, even they disappeared and the woods became primeval. It was getting late and the sun was beginning to set when they came to the crest of a pass in the hills. If they were to push on, it would be several more hours before they reached Castleisland, but Robert didn't like the look of things here. It would make a grand place to be ambushed. The thought was still fresh in his mind when, out of the shadows, stepped a man with a gun in his hand, and pointed it directly at the lead rider. Ned reined his horse to a halt as two more men, with pikes, stepped out five yards further on and pointed them at the animals. Robert noticed that the gun pointed at Ned was an old match lock and that the slow match was glowing. Many men had lost their lives to a primitive hand canon such as this, loaded with stones and nails and whatever else could be rammed down the bore.

Before the man could pull the trigger Robert said, 'Wait, I have a purse here in my pocket.' He reached his right hand into his pocket and cocked the little pistol. The man fired before Robert could get his gun cleared from his greatcoat, but the powder just fizzled. The condensation from the night air had dampened the priming powder in the flash pan of the old matchlock. Robert whipped the gun out of his pocket and, at the range of only around two feet, he put a hole through the outlaw's head. The other two highwaymen were caught by surprise at first, but then they charged at the horses with their pikes. Ned had drawn his horse pistol and now he let fly. The black powder shot a cloud of smoke into the air, which obscured their vision, and both lawmen reached for their sabres. There was no need because, at a range of around ten feet, Ned's goose shot had downed both the pikemen. One of them moved, the other having taken the brunt of the blast. Ned was transfixed by the bodies in the road and Robert snapped him out of it.

'Come on, let's get out of here, there might be more of them.'

They galloped the horses downhill until about a mile had passed and only then did Robert slow down and stop.

'We have to reload, in case we meet more of the Kerry bastards.' Ned was visibly shaken. He had never killed a man before and now he'd just slain two. Robert looked for something to say to calm him.

'Now you have something to tell your grandchildren,' he said, 'how you killed two desperadoes with a single shot.' It didn't help to quieten Ned's nerves.

They arrived in Castleisland before midnight.

CHAPTER 15

'How can we be married, Michael?' Morna had been tormented by the question for the last few days and had finally worked up the courage to put it into words. 'Dere are no priests.' She gazed plaintively at this young man of hers who, if he could read the words printed in a book, must surely have the answer written somewhere.

It was a question Mikey had been asking himself, and he thought he had finally come up with the answer. His own parents had been married twice … once, secretively, by an old Franciscan, in a place hidden deep in the forest … and again in the Church of Ireland, for appearances' sake.

'Don't worry,' he consoled her. 'We'll be married in the eyes of God.' Morna wasn't satisfied. She and the other girls had often talked of how wonderful their weddings would be and how grand the occasion, but the reality of how impossible it all was had taken its toll on her and, although tears hadn't yet fallen yet, Mikey knew they weren't far away. He knew he'd have to resolve the problem and, as he was his father's son, he set out to make the impossible happen.

He retrieved his little copy of the church rituals which he still had from his days in the seminary, and he thumbed through the book until he came to the part concerning the nuptial ceremony. He had looked for a passage which might possibly alleviate the girl's distress and had found it. Now, he held the book open at the page in front of her.

'It says here,' he read aloud. 'What God has put together, let no man put asunder.'

She looked bewildered. 'Oy unnerstand d' God pairt, Michael, boot what does d' udder pairt mean?'

'It means that if we go to a holy place, and I put a ring on your finger there, then we are married in the Eyes of God.'

'Widdout a priest? Wouldn' dat be a Martal sin sure?'

'It doesn't say anything here about a priest.' Michael stretched the truth; the book plainly assumed that a priest would be reading it.

'It still sounds like a sin t' me,' she said doubtfully.

'What is a sin, Morna?'

'Accardin' t' d' aul' priest who use t' live here, he said dat anyt'ing dat causes happiness 'r pleasure is prob'y a sin an' ev'n t'inkin about dose t'ings is a sin.'

'Well he was wrong, Morna. Which commandment says, Thou shall not be happy?'

'Den what is a sin, Farder?' Morna caught herself, 'I mean, Michael.'

Mikey pretended not to notice her accidental lapse and went on, 'If you do harm, or even if you intend to do harm to another person on purpose, that's a sin. All the other stuff's just pishogue.'

Morna smiled. She still wasn't wholly convinced that the Church would approve of what Michael was suggesting but she so badly wanted to marry him.

'When will you make the ring?' she asked. 'I want to be your wife.'

'I promised to have this chain repaired this morning so I'll make the ring this afternoon, then tomorrow we can go to Gougane Barra. It's a rough walk across the mountains, but it's only five miles.'

'After tomorro' den, we'll be husban' an' wife,' she said, looking up at him. When she tilted her head back and kissed Michael's lips tenderly, impure thoughts raced through his mind and coursed through his body.

When he'd finished the chain which he'd been constructing links for, he put it aside and set to work making the ring which he would place on his bride's finger tomorrow. He would cast it from the same tin he used to mend pots. He had a few silver coins, but he didn't dare use those because they would need them when they made their escape from the valley of Ballyshee. While he worked, he reflected upon Morna's concept of sin, which was the same one most Irish people had. The concept of happiness had been distorted by dried-up old priests who had never truly experienced it, and whose vision of it pertained only to spiritual matters. What good was spiritual happiness when each day was a drudge to the common people? Where was the good in dangling a faint hope of eternal bliss in front of an oppressed people, at the same time destroying any chance of joy for them? In Michael's mind, the most grievous sin was to use guilt to manipulate an ignorant populace, and he was sure that Jesus must be as appalled as he was. He felt himself becoming angry and tried to shake off the train of thought. There was work to be done, and this work was something he would put his whole heart into, the ring which would bind he and Moira together for eternity.

He gouged a circular ring into a piece of old wood, about a quarter of an inch deep, and a quarter of an inch wide. He left the inside diameter at what he estimated would be a little smaller than her finger. He dampened the board, then set about melting an ounce of tin in a small iron crucible on the forge. As soon as it was molten, he poured the metal into his mould and the wood sizzled and scorched. Within a few minutes, it had cooled enough to remove the rough blank, and he started to shape it. He placed the ring onto a ream, a tapered piece of iron which he used to enlarge holes. He tapped it with a hammer until the ring was perfectly round, then thinned it out until it was, at most, an eighth of an inch thick and three eighths of an inch wide. Mikey ground it to as fine a polish as he could on a sharpening stone and, in less than an hour, he had made the ring which Morna was never to remove from her finger.

*

Robert and Ned didn't get the early start they'd planned. The horses had needed the extra rest and so had the men. The incident from the night before had clearly shaken the young man; the sheriff tried to block it from his mind. Even for someone like him, who had grown accustomed to violence, blowing a man's brains out from just two feet away had a sobering effect. For the deputy, it was worse. He had killed one man in an instant, and left another mortally wounded, leaking his life's blood out onto a lonely dirt road.

'Oy can't help t'inkin' we shoulda helped dat poor sod in d' rawd.'

'He wouldn't have given you the same consideration, Ned, and we couldn't wait to see if there was a nest of vipers in earshot. We announced our presence and our mission comes first.'

'Agh, I know sure, but it still bothers me.'

'Good, I'm glad it bothers you, and I hope that every time you have to use a weapon on a man, you react in the same way. It isn't a trivial thing to end a man's life, but it's better for you to have your regrets than to be feeding jackdaws and wild pigs with your own arse.'

Ned shuddered at the thought of the man's body, or indeed his own, being eaten by wild creatures.

'Oy don' wanna t'ink aboot dat,' he said.

'He's beyond feeling any pain now, Ned, except for the hellfire that he deserves,' said Robert, thinking about the close call he'd had. If they had arrived at the scene an hour earlier, the gunman's powder would likely have been dry enough to fire the weapon, and he himself might be lying there on the road, feeding wild boar. Life is full of near misses, he thought, and he'd had more than his fair share of them already. He shook himself from his dark thoughts and began to get the horses ready for the ride into Killarney.

Ned was silent for much of the journey but finally, in an attempt to assuage the boy's conscience, Robert spoke.

'I do know how you feel, Ned. I still remember the face of the first man I sent to perdition, years before you were born.' He had Ned's attention now. 'It was my first combat. The battle was lost and most of our own officers had ridden off to save their own skins. A retreat wasn't drummed so it was disorganised … just small clusters of men fighting for their lives. I had no powder or lead, so I threw the musket away. A young English lad with curly blonde hair and blue eyes confronted me with a bayonetted musket, and he lunged it out to stick me in the middle. His teeth were gritted and he had blood splattered all over him. The ground was slippery and he fell on his face, so I sat on his back and held his head down in the mud until he stopped moving. I grabbed his weapon and ran off. I found out afterwards that he'd still had powder and ball in the gun and that, if he'd pulled the trigger, I would have been lying there instead of him. He was probably as shit-scared as I was.'

'Oy can't imagine you ever bein' scared, sar.'

'I'm always afraid, man. I might be old, but I'm not ready to die yet. I've learnt, over the years, to wear a brave face … but shit, even last night, after we escaped, my heart was pounding so hard I thought you'd hear it over the hoof beats. My hands were shaking so hard that I had to wait until we were down the road from those bandits before I could reload my pistol.'

'T'anks, sar, Oy'm feelin' a liddle bedder now.'

'Good man, now shutcher gob and let's go and see Killarney. They say it's the most beautiful place in Ireland.'

It was mid-afternoon when the two men rode into Killarney. Although Robert hadn't know exactly what to expect, he couldn't help being a little disappointed. There were only a few streets and even those were narrow and muddy. Vendors, with their carts, lined the road and a few people hurried about. Robert and Ned's uniforms were conspicuous because everyone else was grubby and dressed in rags. As they advanced though the town, the two men attracted attention, far more than Robert was comfortable with. He spotted a livery directly across the street from an inn and he turned in, Ned followed. They dismounted and a filthy young fellow took the horses and began to lead them back to stalls.

'I want them fed and watered,' instructed Robert, 'and

I'll pay extra for some oats.'

The ragamuffin laughed derisively. 'Oooh, his majesty wants oots fer d' animals,' he snorted. 'Ain't we fancy.'

Robert glanced at Ned. 'Well, Ned, what do we think of this Kerryman?' That's all it took. Ned took off one of his leather gloves and began to give the insolent youth a shellacking with it. After seven or eight swipes with the glove, he drew back his fist and Robert intervened.

'That's enough, boyo. I think he's learned to curb his tongue, with us at least.'

Ned glared at the youth. 'Oy'll be back later t' check on me harses… an' dey bedder be smiling, ya gobshite.'

The men took their weapons and made their way across the street to the inn to secure two rooms for the night. 'I hope d' Kerry bedbugs don' have a taste fer Carkmen,' said Ned.

'Just don't start anything here, Ned, we want to leave early tomorrow morning.' A rough-looking, one-eyed fellow had been sitting at the bar, and now he turned towards them.

'Whar will ye be headin'?' he asked.

'Macroom,' said Robert immediately.

'Agh, dat's 'n Cairk,' and he spat on the floor. Ned took a step forwards but Robert grabbed his arm.

'Easy, boyo.'

The rough codger at the bar looked Ned over, as if sizing him up, then grinned, showing a row of brown teeth. 'Dat boy ye lathered in d' liv'ry's got t'ree brudders, so Oy'd hold me hand on me arse if Oy wuz you, Carkman.' Robert kept the restraint on Ned, whose face was flushing crimson. The old fellow was satisfied that he'd had his fun but thought he'd said enough, so he left and hurried down the street.

Word travels fast in a town as small as Killarney and,

shortly afterwards, a smartly-dressed young deputy came into the bar and saluted the two men.

'Sheriff Higgins is expecting you in Kenmare,' he said. 'He sent me here to escort you.'

'You from Kerry?' growled Ned.

'No, sir, I'm from Kilkenny,' replied the deputy.

Ned rolled his eyes towards heaven. 'Agh, dat's almost 's bad,' he said, and went to get himself a beer.

CHAPTER 16

The three uniformed men sat together in the bar having supper and a beer. The sheriff and the young deputy from Kilkenny discussed the route they would take in the morning and Ned listened in silence. When their business was done, Robert turned to him, the beer having loosened his tongue and put him in a jovial mood.

'So Ned, is it true that Cork people hate folk from Kerry?

The hint of a smile played around Flood's face as he thought up an answer. 'Nah. Carkmen an' Kerrymen are like brudders ...' There was a long pause as Ned took another swallow of ale, '…ef ya can't stand yer brudder.' They all shared a laugh.

'What about Kilkenny?' enquired the deputy.

'Yer d' farst man fr'm Kilkenny Oy aver met, so Oy'll resarve me opinion 'til Oy got one.'

'I thought you had an opinion about everything, Ned,' said the sheriff.

'Oy do,' said Ned, 'an' sometimes, Oy might ev'n be right.'

The three lawmen shared a few stories and a few laughs, until the subject came around to the incident with the highwaymen on the road. Robert told his side of the story dispassionately and, when he had finished, the young deputy looked enquiringly at Ned for his version. Ned's expression was serious now.

'Oy'd like t' tell ya a good story, boot d' truth is, all Oy saw wuz dat big gun pintin' at me noggin an' Oy almos' shit me britches. Oy sart'o heard the sheriff's gun go off an' Oy only r'member pintin' me own gun at d' udder villains, an' closin' me oyes, an' poolin' d' trigger. When d' smoke cleared, dey wuz on d' ground.'

The mood had become sober, even if the men had not. Just then, three hefty young men, dressed in ragged clothing, strode into the bar and one thing was clear. They were spoiling for a fight.

The largest of the three spoke. 'We haird dat a feckin' Cairkm'n plast'red 'r baby brudder 'cross d' street,' he said. 'an' we're here t' square t'ings up.' Ned stood up and assessed the three of them. He calculated that he could easily take care of the two smaller ones, but the big one who did the talking was a different matter.

Robert was trying to avoid any trouble so, before Ned could open his fat mouth and start a donnybrook, he said, 'I apologise for the incident and, to show my sincerity, I'd like to buy you gentleman a bucket of beer for you to take over to your wounded brother and share between you.'

The three brutes formed a small circle and held a conference. They quickly decided that, even though a fight would be great craic, a bucket of ale would be even better. When they broke the scrum, the biggest one spoke again.

'We accep' yer offerin', and we t'ank ya, … an' if ya

t'row in a few spuds, we'll go back an' finish d' job ye stairted across d' street.'

Robert held up his hand. 'There's no need for any further mischief,' he said, 'just take your brew over the road and enjoy it.' He ordered up the beer and the three brothers took their spoils back across the street to their brother. In no time at all, they could be heard brawling amongst themselves.

'Oy coulda tak'n dem,' said Ned sullenly.

'I have no doubt that you could, Ned,' replied Robert. He was anxious for them to get an early start in the morning and, no matter how early they set off, he doubted they would reach Kenmare in a single day. The highest mountains in Ireland stood in their path, Macgillycuddy's Reeks.

'One t'ing Oy wanna ask, sar,' said Ned. 'Whoy did ya tell dat oogly bastard we was headin' t' Macroom?' Robert put down his empty tankard, stood up and smiled.

'Good night, Ned,' he said. 'When you've slept on it, you'll work it out.'

*

Mikey had slept fitfully and was up long before dawn. He had to admit to himself that he was more than a little nervous. Up until now he'd had two options. He could relinquish his status as a novice priest and take his final vows, that's if he could find a bishop to perform them, or he could continue his career as a blacksmith. In just a few hours he would choose the path that he would take for the rest of his life. He closed his eyes and imagined how it would feel to lie next to the girl he loved, and he knew he was taking the only course that was right for him.

He packed a morsel or two of food, along with a small iron pot, inside a thin blanket and he stuffed it into the sack he always carried to Macroom. The iron pot was heavy and he decided he would buy a small copper one from the tinker, who was due to visit Ballyshee in a week or so. That way, when he and Morna travelled up to Tipperary, with less weight, they'd be able to carry more supplies. Now that he knew it was imminent, he was looking forward to seeing his mam and da, and showing off his new bride to everyone in Gortalocca. He had left there as a boy, to become a priest, and now he'd be returning as a family man. He liked the sound of that and he was certain it would please his parents.

When the time came, Jimmy and Caroline O'Malley accompanied their daughter to the forge. Morna was their only surviving child and, since this was to be her wedding day, they would travel along with her to Gougane Barra. They, too, carried bedrolls. Even though the round-trip was little more than ten miles, there were three steep mountain ridges to cross, with precipitous valleys between each, so they had prepared themselves to spend the night there. Michael had no doubt about his own ability, nor that of Morna and her father, but he harboured reservations as to whether Morna's mother, Caroline, was capable of the journey. He did know of a flatter but longer route, a little path which had been made by pilgrims over the centuries and connected the Bantry to Macroom road to the holy site of St. Finbarr, but that would mean them travelling on the busy thoroughfare. If they took that route, the round-trip would be over thirty miles, most of it on well-patrolled road, and that would be far too dangerous for a pretty young thing like Morna. Michael thought that the trip they were about to take would be good practice for the longer odyssey which he and his new bride were soon to make through the high country.

He had made this hike numerous times, to say Mass at the site of St. Finbarr. Morna and her family had travelled it too, when the old curate who lived like a hermit there, had said Mass. He had been captured by priest-hunters long ago, and turned over to the authorities for a bounty. He had never been seen or heard from again. As far as Mikey knew, he himself had been the only priest to practice the ritual in the area for several years. Now, he would be making the journey as a simple blacksmith.

The wedding party of four set out, crossing the little stream at the back of the forge, then beginning the climb out of the valley of Ballyshee. From afar, the hills didn't look much. They didn't seem overly high or too steep but, once the hike was underway and the mountains grew closer, the reality of their menacing elevations loomed only too clearly. Morna's mother had already begun to limp and, although she did her best to keep up with the small party, the rugged terrain was proving too much for her.

'Lean on me, woman, take me hand an' Oy'll help ya along,' said Jimmy, but it was no use. The path they had to negotiate was too strenuous for her.

'You go, Jimmy,' she said, 'Oy can't make it. I have a fierce pain in me hip an' it's gettin' warse.'

The young couple had walked on ahead and now they stood and turned, waiting for the girl's parents to catch up. They could see that Jimmy's face was sombre.

'Caroline can't make 't,' he shouted ruefully, 'an' Oy won' leave 'er, so you two g'wan an' Oy'll take the woman back t' d' house.' Michael and Morna climbed down to where her parents stood with pained looks on their faces. Jimmy kissed his daughter on the cheek.

'We loove ya garl,' he said. Then, to Mikey's surprise, Jimmy moved over to him and kissed his forehead. 'An' you too, son.'

Tears of sorrow and nostalgia rolled down Caroline O'Malley's cheeks as she watched her daughter leave. Her little girl would return a woman tomorrow but, from now on, she belonged to someone else.

Mikey and Morna came to the first ridge in no time and, as they walked downhill into a wooded valley, the coarse grass, heather and gorse soon gave way to a forest, so dense, that they could barely see the sky. When they forded a small stream at the bottom and began to walk back uphill, the sky opened up to them again. They could feel the muscles in their thighs start to bite now but they kept going. They would stop as soon as they crested the next peak for a bite to eat, then, without lingering, they would forge onwards.

The last ridge wasn't as high as the others and, from it, they could see the same beautiful lake St. Finbarr had seen centuries before, when he'd made this the site of his hermitage. The sun sparkled on the pristine water and, the closer they got, the more they sensed the sanctity of this isolated place. Mikey wished there was a priest here. Then he could confess his sin of deceiving the girl and they could have the wedding she deserved. The burden of guilt lay heavily upon him, but he was first to break the silence.

'I've seen a cathedral, Morna, but this place is even more beautiful and seems even more sacred.' He took Morna's hand and squeezed it.

'Do ya t'ink heav'n 's like dis, Michael?' she whispered.

Mikey whispered back, as if they were in a sanctuary, 'I think heaven is even better.'

She smiled up at him and it was the most beautiful smile he had ever seen. 'Even if it ain't,' she said, 'Oy'd still be happy.'

They walked down to the shores of the lake, to the place where the Mass Rock stood. Without hesitation, Mikey reached into the little pouch he wore on his woven belt and produced the tin ring he had made. He took Morna's left hand in his and slipped the ring on her fourth finger, it fit perfectly.

'I will be your husband forever and ever,' he said quietly.

'And Oy'll be yer woife ferever an' ever.'

Mikey closed his eyes and kissed her soft mouth, his lips lingering on hers for a long time. When he pulled gently away, they gazed into each other's eyes. Her look made him feel like the most handsome man who had ever lived and she felt like the most adored woman in the world. And so the wedding ceremony was over … no priest and no witnesses, other than God Himself and the souls of all who had visited this holy place.

The two newlyweds sat hand-in-hand in comfortable silence on the shores of the Lough, and they watched as the shadows fell over the mountains which loomed over them. There was no need for words, they just basked in each other's company and dreamed of how their lives would be. Each was lost in their own thoughts, never imagining for a moment that they shared the same dream.

Morna was the first to speak. She turned and looked directly at Mikey, her limpid green eyes full of love, and lust, for her husband.

'Michael … have ya any … ya know, experience?'

Mikey did know, his thoughts had been along the same vein. He cleared his throat. 'I … I was almost a feckin' priest sure. What experience could I have?'

'Well, ditn'cha see yer parents do anyt'ing?'

'My da had built a bedroom on the house before I was born, so I never got to see … anything.'

Morna beamed, 'Well Oy did,' she said triumphantly. 'Oy grew up in a one-roomed cottage, an' Oy peeked when me mam an' da … ya know.'

Mikie exhaled deeply. 'Oh?'

'Don'cha know anyt'ing, Michael?'

'I do, o'course. Haven't I watched sheep … do it … and geese?'

'Well, Michael Flynn, p'raps ya didn't notice, but Oy aint a sheep an' Oy ain' a goose,' she said with a hint of exasperation, like a schoolteacher with a slow child. 'Oy'll show ya what Oy know an' let's hope d' rest'll come nat'rally.'

Michael and Morna Flynn made perfect love for the first time, under a beautiful starlit Irish sky, in the Valley of Saint Finbarr, and the angels blessed them.

CHAPTER 17

There was a storm brewing in Gortalocca. Roisin had already determined that Robbie had absolutely no head for business, so they were going to need some help from Jamie Clancy. There was already a rivalry between the two men, at least on Robbie's part. Liam had taken Jamie Clancy as an apprentice when Jamie was just eleven and, when the lad's parents died, he had raised the boy as his own. The Clancy boy idolised Liam and had emulated him in every way. People always said Jamie was the carpenter's shadow, they were as close as father and son.

Roisin had been carrying out an inventory of the stock when Robbie came into the store. He went straight behind the bar and poured himself a beer. He was his usual cheery, ebullient self and, as he sipped his beer, he asked his mother if she'd heard any new gossip. Roisin turned away from the shelves she'd been inspecting to face him, and tried to form the words as delicately as she could.

'You know, Robbie, it will be time to collect the taxes in another month or so.'

Robbie shrugged his shoulders. 'Yeah? So?'

'Well, I was thinking, maybe Jamie could help you this time.'

Robbie's good mood evaporated instantly. 'Do you think I can't handle it?' he snapped.

'No, I was just thinking that it's such hard work and that maybe …'

'Do you think I can't handle hard work?'

'No, that's not it at all,' she lied. 'It's just that last year, when your father sent you to collect the taxes from Joe Finnegan, the pig farmer, you came back empty-handed, except for the sob story Joe had given you. Your da already knew that Joe had sold twenty or more pigs at the auction in Nenagh, and had made a good profit on them. He and Mick Sheridan had to go back and collect the money because Finnegan had already given you his bullshit story and didn't want to pay.'

'Alright, so I make one mistake and now you think I'm completely incompetent? Whenever Da had anything important to do, he always took that Clancy with him. He always liked that sod better than me, and now you do too?'

Roisin felt her ears burning, she was becoming angry with her son. 'You know very well that, when you came of age, your father sent Jamie off to Matt O'Brien's to learn smithing so he could take you on as an apprentice.'

'Oh yeah but, whenever he had something important t' do, he'd bring dat shite-fer-brains back t' help him.'

Roisin's face flushed now as she tried to hold her temper. 'Sure you'd be busy picking the lint out of your bellybutton while your father was working. He knew Jamie would have his mind where it mattered, instead of floating off in the clouds somewhere.'

She flinched as Robbie threw the clay cup against the wall, smashing it.

'Well, feck you, and feck everyone else for that matter, especially that sneakin' earthworm Clancy. He ain't even family! Michael's dead and I'm all you got!' Robert stormed out. It was a characteristic of his to appear even-tempered and likeable to the rest of the world, but to throw temper tantrums with members of his own family.

Roisin breathed heavily. That hadn't gone at all how she'd planned. She took consolation in the fact that Robbie would be back as soon as he was thirsty, and that he would be as endearing as ever, and repentant for his outburst. She realised that it was impossible to repair what was between Robbie and Jamie. Jamie would never understand Robbie Flynn and Robbie Flynn would always harbour resentment for Jamie … but her son's remark about Michael being dead had cut deeply. Roisin felt her eyes sting with tears. Michael is alive, she told herself, for the hundredth time, and Robert D'Arcy will bring him home.

*

Robert Flynn D'Arcy was on the road out of Killarney early, and he and his two young companions had begun the arduous trek up Magillicuddy's Reeks. His head throbbed and he hoped it was no more than the effect of the previous evening's drink and that it would soon wear off. Each fall of the horse's hooves pounded inside his head and the pain made him particularly irascible.

'Tell me what you know about Sheriff Wentworth,' he snapped at the young guide.

The deputy looked at him with a bewildered expression, he had been perfectly amiable the night before. 'Well, what do you want to know?' he asked. 'He's a decent enough sort.' Robert was becoming impatient and could see that he would have to ask his questions in the form of an interrogation.

'How old is he?'

'In his early thirties, I think, sir.'

'Is he Irish?'

'No, sir, he's from somewhere called Conventry, in England.'

'Do you mean Coventry?'

'Yes sir, sorry sir, that's the place.'

'Is he noble born?'

'No sir, I believe his father is a merchant.'

The High Sheriff had enough information to satisfy him for the moment. At least he wouldn't be dealing with a dandy, like his own adjutant. His head still throbbed. He had packed a powder for relieving pain in his kit. He knew that it was made from an extract of poppies and he decided that a pinch of the remedy might give him some relief. He didn't particularly like the way it made him feel, but it was better than this relentless headache. He called the party to a halt and rummaged through his bag until he found it. He took a pinch of the bitter concoction and, within minutes, he was feeling better. He resumed the game of questions with the young lawman.

'So what does this sheriff of yours do in his spare time?'

'He always has 'is nose in a book. The wall in 'is office is full o' books. He reads 'bout the animals an' the flowers, an' he even reads 'bout the rocks. An' he thinks a lot. He's the cleverest man I ever knew. Before he does anyt'ing at all, he t'inks about it for a long time and, when he makes a decision, it's always the right one. When he first came, a few years ago, the men weren't so sure about him but after they saw how he works, we all came t' respec' the man. He got the bandits an' the gangs cleared out, an' he hardly had t' kill anyone. An', if I might say so, sir, he always talks about how you did the same in Ormond.'

'Does he have family?'

'Well, sir, 'is folks is in England but he's courtin' an Irish girl, she lives out Lissyclearig way.'

Robert's mood was much less testy now that the medicaments had started to work and he was able to think more clearly. It seemed his host was an intellectual commoner and, if he was seeing an Irish girl, then he undoubtedly intended to put down roots here and not head back to England. Robert was amused that this man of letters should hold him in such high esteem. To most people, his reputation was that of a man of action, not the thinking man that he actually was.

The scenery around them was breathtaking and the sheriff allowed himself the luxury of taking in his surroundings. The forest spread out for miles around and reflected itself in a large lake near Killarney town. The mountains created an ever-changing backdrop with the light from the sun. He toyed with the hope that perhaps one day he could come back here and, instead of passing through, he could sit by the shores of the lough and maybe even paint a picture. He shook his head to clear his mind, aware that his thoughts were not his own, but merely the spell cast over him by the headache remedy.

The three men continued their climb until, early in the afternoon, the guide stopped at a wide place in the road, high above the loughs.

'Sheriff Wentworth wannid me to stop here and show ye this place,' said the deputy.

Robert and Ned looked down and, stretched out before them, was the most magnificent panorama either of them had ever seen. Three lakes were in full view in the valley below and the verdant emerald hills around them were punctuated by craggy outcrops of granite and limestone. The lakes shimmered a sapphire blue, with glistening golden spangles cast by the afternoon sun.

'The sheriff calls it The View,' he added. Even the world-weary Robert D'Arcy was overwhelmed by the carpet of beauty that was spread out before him.

'This must be what God sees,' he said quietly. He tried to memorise the spectacular vista … to burn it into his memory so he would never forget it. Even Ned Flood had to admit he had never seen its like, not even in his beloved Cork.

The horses had rested for long enough and the party climbed onwards towards Moll's Gap. They had decided they would stay at the stagecoach layover for the night and continue on to Kenmare the next day.

'A lot of the gentry stay here cuz it's quieter, an' it smells better'n the town does,' volunteered the deputy from Kilkenny. 'If a coach is pulled by four horses, it c'n make the trip fr'm Kenmare to Killarney easy in a day, that's if there ain't no rock slides to block the An Mhor Chuaird. That's what dey call dis road.'

The five horses were taken to be fed and watered and the men retired to the inn for a meal and a night's sleep. Robert decided against drinking this evening, he didn't want another headache like this morning so, when he'd finished eating, he left the two young deputies at the table and wandered outside. The air was crisp and the stars shone in their thousands. The moon was so bright in the crystalline air that Robert thought a man could easily read a book by its light. High up, on the slopes above him, he could see a herd of red deer grazing. This was a sight seldom seen in Ireland, most of the larger wildlife had been harried and hunted to extinction. He watched them for a while and imagined that this was how the whole island must have looked to the first settlers. He wondered what life must have been like for them here, what hopes and dreams they had. He shook his head again but realised that the medicine he'd taken had long since worn off and the only intoxication he felt was the spell cast upon him by the Kerry mountains.

The herd of deer must have numbered over thirty creatures, he tried to count them but lost track. A single animal stood perfectly still, watching him warily. Ah, you've posted a sentry, he thought, that's wise. Robert became mesmerised and he knew he wouldn't leave until the deer did. Without uttering a sound, he raised both hands above his head. The sentinel flinched, then coiled itself and bound away, flashing its white rump in alarm. The others took flight and followed their leader, over a little rise and down into a depression in the mountain, out of sight. Robert looked around him and wondered if it would always be as perfect here. Agh, if I know humans … and I do, he thought bitterly … this won't last forever. He took one last lingering look and went back inside.

CHAPTER 18

Mikey had slept soundly on the shores of the lough at Gougane Barra and had woken in the light which came just before dawn. The orange-coloured moon was just setting and the sun hadn't yet risen over the peaks which surrounded this peaceful valley. He thought how different this place was to the world outside it. He studied the features of the lovely young girl who lay slumbering beside him. Her green eyes were closed now but her aquiline nose and her full lips were arousing his passions. He touched her gleaming copper hair gently, hoping it might wake her, but she slept on. He slipped out from beneath the woollen blanket they'd slept under and went to the edge of the water, where he washed himself. He wished he could wash away the sin as easily as he could the dirt. As soon as they found a priest, he would seek contrition and put things right.

He remembered the promise he had made to Morna's father. He had given him his word that he'd get her out of the valley of Ballyshee and, now, he wondered if it was possible to forego the oath. Perhaps if he remained the village blacksmith, in time the residents would forget he'd ever been a priest. He knew in his heart that wasn't a possibility, that Ireland was a country built on memories and the fact that he had been the village priest was one memory which would never be forgotten. He thought about the journey back to his home in Gortalocca, it would be fraught with perils. He was well able to make the trip by himself but now, with his beautiful young wife accompanying him, he had the added responsibility of keeping her safe from harm. The thought of her being violated was abhorrent to him. He would stall their departure for a couple of weeks and they would leave only when they had to.

It was getting lighter now and the sun had risen enough for him to see the young woman stirring. She beckoned him to come back to her. He slid back under the blanket and she put her arms around him.

'Tell me about Tipperary,' she asked softly. Michael began to describe the green rolling hills and the gentle farmland, while the girl listened dreamily. Abruptly, she interrupted.

'What about yer fam'ly, do ya t'ink dey'll like me?' Mikey smiled and told her the tale of his father's arrival in Gortalocca, all those years before, and the way he had duped the authorities, and how his mother and father now owned and ran the village spirit grocery. He told her about Jamie Clancy, the orphan who his father had taken on as an apprentice, and how Jamie had been more of a brother to him than his own. He spoke about how Jamie had helped his father build the family home when he was just a boy and how the raiders had burned it down, and how his father had taught Jamie to read.

Morna interrupted again. 'But Oy can't read 'r write,' she groaned. 'What'll dey t'ink of an ignerint farm girl fr'm Cark?'

Michael pulled her tightly to him. 'They will love you because I love you and, as far as reading and writing are concerned … well, do you want to learn?'

Morna squeezed Michael so tightly that he could barely inhale. 'Oy'll make ya so proud o' me, Michael Hogan, yu'll see.'

Michael smiled and corrected her. 'Michael Flynn,' he said. 'The name I was given at my Baptism was Michael Patrick Flynn. I took Mam's maiden name to protect my family from persecution when I went to the seminary.'

Morna released her grip. 'Who air we, so? Flynns 'r Hogans?'

Michael gently pulled her head to his chest. 'We're Hogans,' he said, 'and when we can find a priest, we'll have a proper ceremony, after we've confessed our sin.'

The girl understood Mikey's guilt but, with the dearth of priests in Ireland now, she was certain that ceremonies such as the one they'd had yesterday must be commonplace throughout the land.

*

The passage to Kenmare was uneventful for the three lawmen. The road twisted and turned through the mountainous terrain, sometimes even doubling back on itself. They walked the horses uphill and trotted them down and the miles passed. The two deputies engaged themselves in lively banter for most of the way and Robert dropped a distance behind them, lost in his thoughts. The pain in his head had come back with a vengeance and, at times, it was so bad that it was all he could think about. Whenever it abated, he let his mind drift around in random thought. He had chosen to take so many paths throughout his life and he wondered, if he'd chosen different ones, what things would have been like for him now. If he had remained in his father's forge, he would undoubtedly have a shop of his own now. What would life be like if he hadn't got some hair-brained notion about Irish independence, and gone off on a fool's errand to fight for the Jacobite cause? What would have become of him if he hadn't assumed the guise of his dead officer D'Arcy? He would probably have been left in Ireland to become a highwayman instead of a lawman. If he hadn't gone to France to be a mercenary soldier, there would be at least forty dead men who would probably still be alive now. He thought about the Commandments. 'Thou shalt not kill'. If one mortal sin would send your soul to perdition for eternity, he mused, how many times would God condemn him? 'Thou shalt not covet thy neighbour's wife.' It's a good thing there wasn't one which said 'Thou shalt not covet thy brother's life.' He had visited Liam hundreds of times in Gortalocca and he had often felt envious of his brother. Poor dead Liam had the life he wanted for himself, but it was too late for that now. He wallowed in his own self-pity and damned the headache that plagued him. I'll do what I promised, he thought, I'll bring Mikey home to his mother.

Ned Flood slowed his horses and allowed the sheriff to catch up.

'Beggin yer paird'n, sar, butcha ain't tol' me much about 'r assignm'nt.' Robert realised that Ned had followed him this far on blind faith alone and that he deserved to know what was expected of him.

'We're going to find a priest.'

Ned recoiled at the thought. 'Oy ain't no priest-hunter,' he said, sharply

'Don't worry, Ned, we're not doing the devil's work.

We're bringing this one home to his mother.' Ned looked less agitated now and curiosity had taken over.

'Why, sar?'

'Because he's my nephew, and I made a promise to my brother's wife that I'd deliver him home safely to her.'

'Tell me whatcha know about 'im sar. Dat way, if sumthin' happens t' ya, I c'n keep goin' 'till I find 'im.'

'He's about your age, Ned, and about your height and build when I last saw him.'

'Dat ain't much t' go on. Dat d'scribes most o' d' blokes in Wes' Cark.'

'He was a blacksmith's apprentice when he got the daft notion about being a priest and he speaks with a Tipp accent.'

'Beggin' yer pairdon, sar, boot dat ain't a daft notion. Dats what dey call a 'callin', sar. He mus' be a brave fella t' become a priest in times like dis.'

'He's a fool, Ned, and that's something I know about.'

Ned smiled and reassured Robert that a man with a Tipp accent shouldn't be too hard to locate but that, since the mountain people have no trust in strangers, it would be better if he did the talking and Robert just did the listening. Robert thought for a moment and agreed. Ned was wiser than he had imagined and he began to soften his opinion of this feisty lad from Cork. As the young fellow made to ride off, Robert said to him,

'You know, Flood, I'm getting tired of being sheriff.' Ned turned as if he'd been poked with a pointed stick. 'And I have an idea about what I want to do next.'

'Ah sure yu'll alw'ys be d' sheriff, sar. It's whatcha do,' Ned dismissed the statement as if it wasn't even an option. Robert's head throbbed. He closed his eyes to the glaring sun and drifted off to sleep in the saddle.

The three men rode through Carhoomeengar, stopping for a quick meal of bread and cheese and, just as it was getting dark, they entered the township of Lissyclearig. It wouldn't be long now before they reached their destination, Kenmare. It had been a long hard day in the saddle and Robert finally relented and took another pinch of the headache remedy. He reminded himself that he needed to stay alert because he was soon to meet the young sheriff in town.

Kenmare was a new town, by Irish standards. In days past, it had been a monastic site, but the town itself was only around forty years old. It owed it existence to the beautiful anchorage and the fishing that it provided. The sheriff's office had been built for the purpose, unlike Robert's office in the old Norman castle and this new construction, although practical, lacked the character and gravitas of his own.

Robert handed Ned a shilling and told him to see to the horses, while he went to meet the sheriff. He warned the young deputy not to get into any altercations with the Kerrymen and not to get too drunk. They would be leaving first thing in the morning.

Nigel Wentworth was an enthusiastic young sheriff. To Robert, he looked to be little more than a boy, but Robert was under no delusions. He knew that he was getting to the age, now, when all young men seemed like children to him. The young fellow greeted Robert enthusiastically, shook his hand firmly and bade him to sit, then poured them both a glass of sherry.

'I'm honoured to meet you, sir, you are somewhat of a legend around here,' he said, raising his glass. Robert was embarrassed and ignored the remark. He took a sip of the sherry and looked around him at the vast library of books and framed paintings the young man had on his wall. He noticed a section of books on natural history and science.

'Have you read all of these?' he asked, hoping to change the subject.

'I have, o'course, sir.' It amused Robert to note that the young fellow from Coventry had allowed Irish colloquialisms to creep into his speech. His attempt to change the subject hadn't deterred the new sheriff from pursuing his original line of conversation. 'I've heard stories of how you swept the bandits from the Wicklow mountains,' he said excitedly, 'and then went and did the very same thing up in North Tipperary.'

'Agh, the time for men like me is past, Sheriff Wentworth.'

'Please call me Nigel, sir.'

'Very well, Nigel. Those days are all but over. Now, it's time for young men like yourself, who use your intelligence, not for brutes like me.'

'You are too modest, sir. You have a reputation for always being fair and never killing anyone who didn't deserve it. Whenever the situation called for action, you were the man, and when it called for intellect, you were equally able to perform those duties too.'

'I'm too old and too tired to argue with you, Nigel. You'll just have to take my word for it that men like you are the future of our country.' Robert had chosen his words carefully, with the intention of testing the young man.

'If you mean that our country has seen too much violence, sir, then of course I concur.' The young fellow had passed Robert's test with flying colours, referring to Ireland as 'our country.' Ireland had swallowed another immigrant whole.

'So tell me, sir, what brings you so far from home?'

'I'm looking for someone, Nigel.'

'He must have done something seriously wrong to bring you all the way to Kerry.'

'It's serious, indeed, he's a priest.'

Nigel stood up from his chair now and held himself erect. 'I'll have no business with priest-hunters here,' he stated bluntly. 'It's a detestable duty you're performing, sir.'

Robert smiled. 'The priest I'm looking for is my brother's son. My brother died and I promised his widow that I would bring her son home.'

The young man relaxed and sat back down. 'In that case, you had better find him quickly. There's a notorious priest-catcher in Glengarriff and, if he finds him before you do, he will most certainly hang him.' This was news to Robert and it added a note of urgency to his task. He wished he had followed the advice of his subordinate and come into the mountains by way of Macroom.

'What do you know about this priest-hunter?'

'His name is Percival Grey, sir, Captain Percival Grey. He's a mean spirited, ugly pig, so full of himself that I don't even care to be in the same room with him. He's a sneaky, conniving bastard, who even his own mother couldn't trust. The worst part is that he's as smart as a fox. He has everyone intimidated and, in his conceit, he believes that it's respect. He hates all things Irish, especially the people themselves, and he's not afraid to use cruelty and terror to accomplish his goals.'

Robert exhaled audibly. 'I'll be needing a letter of introduction from you. I hope we don't have to use it, because I'd rather not cross paths with the man.'

Sheriff Wentworth opened the drawer of his desk and, as he was writing, he said, 'Did you know I'm Catholic?'

Robert was astounded. 'I didn't,' he blurted. 'I

thought there were no Catholics at all left in England.'

Now it was the young man's turn to smile. 'Oh, there are,' he said. 'Not many, of course, but trying to get rid of us is like trying to get rid of nits. They'll always be a few of us left. If you're surprised by that, then you'll be even more surprised to hear that my father's mother was a Jew. That's where he got the money and the expertise to start the textile business. My father was a cobbler.

Robert shook his head in astonishment. 'It seems we both have secrets to share then, boyo.'

Nigel poured them each another glass of sherry.

CHAPTER 19

Michael and Morna decided to take a more direct route back to Ballyshee. The ridges would be just as steep but the valleys were more densely wooded. As they crested a hill, they saw some people coming out from a copse of trees. This was Sunday and Michael told Morna he thought they must have been to a Mass, that there was no other reason for them to be out here in such a remote place. The young couple changed course and headed towards the woodland where the people had come from.

There, amongst the trees, they saw a large granite outcrop with a flat surface. Michael went over to the rock and noticed traces of candlewax, confirming what he had suspected. This was a Mass Rock and secret church services were undoubtedly held here. He looked around him, hoping to find the priest, but there was nobody to be seen so he and Morna sat on the stone and opened the sack which contained their food. Michael had been disappointed not to find someone who could marry them properly and he reiterated his promise to Morna that, as soon as it was possible to do so, he would make his confession and then they could be married in the eyes of the Church. He had only just finished expressing himself when a rasping voice came out of the shadows.

'Da oyes u d' Charch air on ye now!' it croaked.

Michael almost jumped out of his skin as an old mendicant moved out from the shadows.

'Oy haird ya, boyo,' he said, 'an' Oy'll give ye yer penance widdout hearin' a c'nfession. But Oy'll have a bit o' dat bread an' cheese first.' The old fellow grinned at the young couple, who were staring at him in astonishment, looking as he did like a spectre, with his grey robe draped over skin and bones. Still dumbfounded, Michael held out the lump of bread he'd been about to eat and the old man grabbed it and ate hungrily.

'An' ef ye got any beer in dat water boddle, Oy'll give ye a plenary indulgence too.'

Mikey proffered the leather sack to the old priest and found his voice. 'It's only water,' he said.

The wizened man waved his hand in dismissal. 'Ah sure, Oy'll give ye d' indulgence anyways.'

He drank a good few slugs of the water, gave a loud belch and handed the water bottle back to Michael, who, he could see, was surveying him from top to toe.

'Agh! Oy wuz a fat fella once, back when toimes w's good. Now Oy'm just a bagga bones, b't Oy thanks ye fer sharin' yer repast wit me. Now tell me, what is it Oy'm fergivin' ye fer?'

Michael liked the cut of this old fellow and explained to him how he'd been less than candid with Morna concerning the mechanics of the marriage ceremony they'd had. Morna watched Michael's face as he told the priest their circumstances and, when he'd finished, she spoke.

'Mikey, Oy might be ignerint, boot Oy ain't no eejit. Oy knew you was jus' tryin' t' foind a way t' get me t' say yes, and Oy said yes befar ya hadda chance t' change yer moind.'

The old priest jumped in before Michael could reply. 'Da marriage jus' needs d' blessin' o' d Church, so kneel yerselves down.' The two young people knelt down in front of the old cleric, who spoke to Morna first. 'Take off d' ring, garl, so's he c'n poot it back on yer finger.'

'No,' said Morna firmly. Michael looked at her in surprise but the old man just shrugged and began.

'In nomine Patris, et Filii, et Spiritus Sancti … dere, you're married with d' blessin o' d' Church.'

Michael looked doubtful. 'Are you sure you're a priest?' he asked.

Mikey's question irked the old man. 'D'ya t'ink Oy'd be stairvin' t' death if Oy w's d' King o' England? Oy use t'be a fire an' brimshtawn sart o' priest, wit ev'ryt'ing coot an' droid, boot me years in exile taught me dat dere ain't nuthin black 'n white. Moses wen' oop Mount Sinai an' come back down wit' a cupla shtones dat had all d' sins written on 'em. If d' Pope went oop t'day, sure he'd need a harse an' cart t' carry all d' shtones!'

Michael felt a little ashamed at his lack of faith regarding the old priest and he spoke to Morna in whispers for a few moments. They decided they could easily return to Ballyshee without eating any more food so they left the remainder of their victuals with the old mendicant. They thanked him and bade him good day and, as they walked away, they heard him bless them for their generosity.

A few minutes into their hike, Morna suggested that they bring the starving man home with them. Michael didn't have to think long before he gave her his decision.

'No,' he replied. Morna was surprised at her husband. She had thought it would be the Christian thing to do.

'The old man is simple in the head so he's dangerous,' Mikey told her. 'If we bring him back with us, sooner or later he'll attract attention to the village and that will bring the troops. They'll burn the houses and drive off the livestock and do God-knows-what other mischief if they think the village is harbouring a priest.'

Morna wasn't satisfied and harped on with her argument but Michael was accustomed to women. His mother had always got her own way, even when she'd been wrong, but the prospect of the village being burned down was no trivial matter, especially going into harvest season.

'It's not like bringing home a stray collie dog, Morna,' he told her. 'This is a priest, and a mad priest, at that.'

Ireland was full of the starving dispossessed. From late autumn until April, the roads were littered with the dead. Often, the skeletal bodies were just shoved into the ditches to be left as carrion for the foxes and crows. After a while, even the most sensitive of people became hardened to sights which would previously have sickened them. Death, whether sudden or by starvation, was a part of life. It had to be accepted and accept it the people did, believing that all things, good and bad, were God's will and that He must let them happen for a reason.

Morna knew she wasn't going to change Michael's mind and so the young couple continued their journey with no further mention of the old priest. It did bother Michael that they hadn't asked the priest his name. It troubled Morna too that they had been married in an unnamed valley, among a grove of trees, by a priest whose name they would never know … but the marriage was sanctified now and that was all that mattered.

*

Percival Grey sat in his office planning his latest scheme, which was to ferret out the younger of the two priests who, he'd been told, had encroached on his jurisdiction. Percy disregarded, but had not forgotten about, the old priest … that old Papist would probably not last through to the autumn. No, he was particularly interested in the younger one and he had received a valuable piece of information that would help to trap him. An informer from Macroom had reported that the man's hands were hard from manual labour and that meant he was, most likely, disguising himself as a farmer. Grey's usual practice of offering a bounty for information in towns like Glengarriff, Bantry or Macroom had brought results in the past, but the Irish pigs who lived and worked in the more remote and rural communities were tight-lipped. The only way to glean information from them was to put a rat amongst them. He rang for his adjutant to come to his office.

'Have we got a bloody Irishman to put on the tinker's wagon yet?' he barked to the young lieutenant, who stood with his hand raised to his forehead, waiting for a return salute. When none was forthcoming, he eventually lowered his hand.

'We have, sir, several,' the young man replied. 'They're from Derry.'

'That's no good, you idiot,' snapped Percy. 'They sound more like Scots than Irish. Didn't we get one from Cork City last year?'

'We did, sir, but you hanged him for striking a corporal.'

'Damn it! Anyway, if I remember rightly, you executed him,' contradicted Percival.

'Under your orders, sir,' protested the lieutenant.

'No matter. Put one of the Derrymen on the wagon and send him out to the lice-infested hovels. I'll smoke that bloody Papist out before the leaves fall.'

*

Robert D'Arcy's plan to find his nephew was reaching its final phase now and he told Sheriff Wentworth they would leave their uniforms and chargers under his care until they returned from Cork. From this time onwards, he and Ned would become common Irishmen, albeit on uncommon horses. They dressed in the clothes Roisin had given Robert, in order to pass more easily into the territory which he knew to be patrolled by Percival Grey's company of redcoats. With Ned Flood as his guide and mouthpiece, they would find Michael and return him to his mother.

Robert checked his bag one last time, laying his supplies out on a blanket he'd spread on the stable floor. There was a small brass spyglass, a compass, the two small pistols, the blades and the sack containing the caltrops. He checked his purse. He had almost two pounds, much of it in shillings and pennies. When he found Michael, he would take him out of reach of the priest-hunter, then put him on a stagecoach and send him back to Nenagh. He and Ned would follow.

The two men began their journey to Glengariff. Ned wasn't at all comfortable about being unarmed but Robert explained that two armed men might be mistaken for highwaymen.

'Sure, dat's no problem where we're goin',' protested Ned. 'Highwaymen is held 'n high regard boy d' locals. Ya see, bandits air look'd on as a sart o' rebel against d' English, an' d' people here 'n Wes' Cark love deir rebels. Ya jus' gotta be careful, cuz some o' dem moight wanna tarn ya in fer a reward. Me cousin, who was d' son o' me ooncle dat got hung in d' Glen wit' me da, prob'ly still lives dere, near where we're goin', so we c'n stash our goods an' harses dere an' walk intuh town loike a coople o' beggars.'

Robert was glad that Ned had already filled in the details of the plan because truthfully, up until now, he really hadn't a clue as to how they would find Mikey. It seemed that his young compatriot, on the other hand, had given it considerable thought and Robert vowed he wouldn't underestimate his inexperienced deputy in the future. He appreciated and respected guile in a man, whether he be a partner or an adversary, and the success of any plan relied heavily on one's companions.

The two Hobby horses covered the ground quickly and easily at a long trot, the low coastal hills proving effortless to them. They had been bred in Ireland since the Normans arrived, replacing the big cumbersome heavy horse with the more durable and agile Hobby. The English had never appreciated the breed, even after they'd had to ban the exportation of them to Scotland, during the time of Robert the Bruce. The Scots had used the Irish horses to harry English garrisons in a guerilla war which lasted for many years.

When they got to within five miles of Glengariff, Ned reined his horse to a halt.

'Da English'll be puttin' out pickets to guard d' road,' he told Robert. 'Dey know dat dey only own d' land in d' towns hereabouts, an' dat d' countryside belongs t' us when we're outside o'musket range. We'll tarn off d' main rawd here an' go t' me cousin's house.'

The path climbed steeply up into the hills and sparse trees gave way to gorse and heather, rocks protruding from the ground as if they were the very bones of the land. The afternoon sun was fading now and night was approaching. Ned knew the way and led on. In places, the path folded back on itself and they could see the bay stretching out into the ocean. The moon had passed full and was rising now, the colour of a pumpkin, but it was all the light Ned needed to negotiate the tortured path.

Robert had just begun to wonder if they'd ever arrive at the cousin's house, when it was as if his companion had read his mind.

'We'll be dere in anudder hour 'r so,' Ned assured him. 'R'member now, let me do d' talkin' an' no madder what Oy say, you jus' keep yer trap shut … sar.'

The two riders arrived at the mud cabin in the time Ned had predicted. 'Keep yer hand on yer pistol,' Ned told Robert. 'Me cousin ain't d mos' trustin' fella, an' Oy'd trust im more if ya kept 'im covered.'

Robert took out the little pistol, put the hammer at half cock, blew the powder from the pan and re-primed the piece. Ned approached the door and announced himself.

'Who's dere?' growled a decidedly hostile voice from behind the locked door.

'It's me, yer cousin Ned, let me in.'

'Ned's dead.'

'Feck you, Jawsef, I ain't dead, it's me … an' Oy got some money fer ya.'

The door opened a crack and a hearty laugh came from inside. 'Sure Oy knew 'twas yerself when ya called me Jawsef, ev'rybuddy round here calls me Joe. Who's dat on d' harse out dere? Show yerself!' he shouted. Robert walked his horse a few paces forward. 'Poot dat gun away man, an' c'mon in, yer both welcome here.'

CHAPTER 20

It was as Roisin had predicted. A few days without beer was enough to smooth Robbie's ruffled feathers, and although he didn't come back repentant, he came back having forgotten the entire altercation.

'I haven't seen ya fer a couple o' days, Mam.' He grinned at his mother, who just grunted and carried on with cleaning the bar. 'I had this thought, Mammy.' Roisin knew only too well that, when he called her Mammy, he was trying to get past her defenses.

'And what thought did you have, Robbie?' she asked. She still hadn't looked at him.

'I was thinkin' that all this work is too much for a woman of your age.' Robbie had lit a fuse and it was burning rapidly.

'Really? Well, I'm not sure a woman of my advanced years is capable of understanding the workings of a man's mind but tell me, I'm curious, was is it that you propose?'

'I was thinking that I could take over managing this place for you and you and Jamie could watch over the farms.' This was vaguely similar to Roisin's own plan but putting Robbie in charge of the store, where the beer was kept, was a little like putting a fox to guard a henhouse.

'Well now, Robbie, if ... and I said if ... I was agreeable to your plan, when I come back in a month's time to check the books, will I find the inventory tallies with the income?'

Robbie put his arms around his mother and hugged her. 'You will, Mammy. I swear I'll be able to account for every drop.' Roisin had no doubt that her son could account for the beer, as most of it would be running through his own bladder, but she wasn't in the mood to argue, even if he had implied she was getting old. She agreed to give his 'amazing and original' idea a try. It wouldn't work, of course, but it would buy her another month by which time, hopefully, Michael would be back.

*

'Jayzus, Merry an' Jawsef, Ned, when Oy saw youse comin' t' d' door, sure I t'ought ya was a ghost! I ain't seen ya since dat night when we was all in our cups fr'm d' poteen we stole fr'm d' travllin' man. Ya jus' stood oop an' said, 'Oy've had enoof', an' Oy t'ought ya meant ya had enoof whiskey, an' Oy was glad cuz dat meant dere was more fer us, boot ya never came back. I figgered d' law got ya, or ya stairved, now here ya aire wit' yer own band o' scalawags.'

'What happ'ned t' d' rest o' d' orphans, Joe?'

'Agh! Sure after ya lef' we got careless. You was alw'ys d' brains o' d' crew. 'About a month later, we went an' mobbed a travellin' salesm'n's wagon, an' sure 's shite, it had four redcoat troopers inside. We all scattered an' Oy was old'st an' had d' longes' legs, so Oy got away. Dem troopers caught d' kids an' dat miserable fecker Pussy

Grey hanged ‘em all, includin’ Gallagher, an’ he wasn’ ev’n twelve years old yet.’

‘How did ya get by, Jawsef.’

‘Oy jined oop wit’ a crew fr’m down east. We had a leader, an’ aul’ fella fr’m Cark City, an’ we plied ‘r trade on d’ roads fer a coupla months ‘til d’ ol’ boy said it was gettin’ too hot here an’ he took d’ crew down t’ d’ Beara. Oy made me livin’ borryin’ d’ odd sheep dat gets lost in d’ hills an’ here I am. What’ve you been about Ned?’

‘Me partner here an’ Oy been ridin’ d’ rawds in Narth Tipp, boot we decided dere might be bedder huntin’ down here.’

‘Narth Tipp, is it? Oy haird dere’s a sheriff oop dere dat’s ev’n more bloodtharsty den Pussy. I haird dat he killed a hun’red men in Wicklow, an’ more ‘n Tipp. Ya must be as smairt as ever t’ be avoidin’ dat bastard.’

‘Yeah, he’s is a rough coostomer, a’right.’ Ned gave an almost imperceptible wink towards Robert, who rolled his eyes.

‘It’s getting haird fer a man t’ make ‘n honest livin’ deese days,’ lamented Joe. ‘Let’s have a swalley. Ya got any?’ Ned pulled a small flask from a pocket of his trews and Joe looked disconsolate. ‘Sure dat ain’t enoof t’ wet d’ back o’me t’roat. Ya ain’t taken d’ pledge have ye?’

‘Not on yer nelly, Joe. We jus’ don’ drink when we’re warkin’.’

Joe laughed, ‘Dat’s where we differ cousin. Da mar I wark, d’ mar mooney Oy have, an’ d’ mar mooney Oy have, d’ mar Oy drink.’ He tipped the little flask up and sucked it dry in one swallow. He looked at Robert, who promptly produced his own flask, opened it and took a sip. ‘Waw! Don’t be drinkin’ it all, ya pig, save some fer d’ landlord.’ Robert passed the flask and, as before, Joe turned it on its head and drained it.

The horses needed to be seen to and Robert whispered something to Ned, who conveyed the message to Joe.

'We need a bucket fer d' harses, Joe.'

'Oy got two buckets,' replied Joe. 'One's fer me water, an' one's fer me t' take a piss in. Oy don' want harses slobberin' in me water bucket, so yu'll have t' em'ty d' piss bucket, 'cause Oy ain't done it 'n a coupla days.'

Robert conferred with Ned again, who passed the message on. 'Me friend'll give ya a penny fer d' water bucket.'

Joe looked at both pails, then at the penny Robert was holding out to him.

'Ah sure take d' water bucket. A liddle harse spit ain't gonna do me no hairm.' Robert picked up the wooden tub and left.

'Yer friend don' say mooch, does he?'

Ned chuckled and touched his head. 'Don't mind him, he's an eejit.'

Joe laughed back. 'Well, dat explains what he's doin' wit' you den, don' it?'

The two men talked, as young men do, remembering stories about their misspent youth and all the close calls they'd had, and Joe became nostalgic for a time when adrenalin and alcohol had fueled their escapades.

'If yer t'inkin' 'bout puttin' t'gedder a crew,' said Joe, 'count me in. Dis runnin' down t' Beara fer a sheep 'r two ain't very profitable, an' Oy might be a bit more useful den dat auld man yer travellin' wit'.'

Ned Flood felt his hackles rise. 'Oy seen dat auld man kill a fella d' udder day,' he said, 'an' not ev'n blink. Besoides, we're partners, we travell'd a long way togedder.'

Joe understood. Men who engaged in a dangerous

occupation such as banditry formed bonds like brothers. 'Well, yous two give 't a t'ink, an' r'member, Oy'm available.'

Robert had been out with the horses too long for Ned's liking and he told his cousin he'd have to check on his 'eejit' companion. As he walked outside the dark cabin, the light of the moon illuminated Robert, who had been studying a hand-drawn map. Ned walked over to where the old man was seated on the upturned bucket.

Robert looked up. 'Can we trust him?'

Ned shrugged his shoulders. 'If dere's some easy money t' be made, we c'n trust 'im.' That was good enough for Robert. He folded the map and, when he and Ned returned to the unlit cabin, Robert spoke to Joe for the first time.

'We need you to watch after our belongings for a day or so.'

'What koind o' feckin' accent is dat?' said Joe, wrinkling his nose as if someone had passed wind under it.

'It's a Tipp accent.'

'Jayzus, someb'dy oughtta teach youse lads t' talk oop dere.'

Robert held out two shillings and Joe's eyes lit up. 'Ah now, dat's a language Oy unnershtand.'

'Tell us what we're up against.'

'Pussy Grey is an aul' fox,' Joe explained. 'E's got troops on d' road, mos'ly at night. Dey're tryin' t' catch some priest 'r udder somewhere b'tween here an' Macroom. 'E t'inks d' priest'll have t' go out t' say Mass on Sundays so, on Frid'ys, he sets men out at all d' crossroads.'

'What about the troops?' asked Robert.

'Dey's mos'ly English, Germans, an' a few Frenchies,

boot d' mos' dangerous ones is d' Prussians. He got a half dozen o' dose fellers dat 'r hunters. Dey don' carry muskits, dey carry a diff'rint kind o' gun an' dey c'n hunt a man an' shoot 'im almos' as far as dey c'n see 'im.'

Jaegers, thought Robert, professional Prussian hunters, he had seen them in action in Europe. They were excellent trackers and marksmen, raised in the forests and mountains in Bavaria. They used rifled muskets and instead of relying on massed fire, like the common troops, they could pick a man off at two hundred paces. It was considered ungentlemanly to target officers in times of battle, but the unwritten code of conduct was oft times ignored.

'Dey're like Pussy's pack o' hounds,' continued Joe, 'an' dey sit in d' Boar's Head bar in town, an' dey wait 'til Pussy calls dem out. Oy wouldn' wan' dose lads huntin' me.'

The Boar's Head, thought Robert. If that's where the captain's troops loitered, then that would be an excellent place to gather intelligence. He and Ned would go and have a couple of beers there tomorrow, and listen.

The next afternoon, having walked around the town of Glengarrif, the two beggarly-looking men wandered into the Boar's Head tavern. There was a scattering of red-coated men in there along with a few civilians. As his eyes grew accustomed to the dim light, Robert scanned the place. All eyes were on the two Irishmen and the conversation inside ceased for a moment, until they sat themselves down at a table and ordered a beer. The table next to them was occupied by four smartly-dressed young men conversing in low German.

'What d' feck aire we doin' in dis place?' Ned whispered.

'Whisht, Ned, I can't hear what's going on.' Robert

spoke fluent French from his years in exile as a mercenary, but his German was poor. He relaxed nonchalantly in his chair and casually tipped it backwards, onto its back legs, to get closer to the conversation behind him. He sipped his beer and concentrated. Ned just sipped his beer. As best the sheriff could make out, they were talking about a tinker. It seemed Percival Gray had bribed a tinker to locate a priest. Grey was indeed a crafty fox, thought Robert. If brute force and fear didn't produce results, then guile was called for, and a tinker would have free access to the communities without arousing suspicion. Very clever … Robert thought he'd garnered enough information for now and he drained his beer tankard, signalling to Ned to do the same. Robert was just about to stand when his chair was kicked out from beneath him and he fell backwards onto the floor. Ned stood to defend his companion and was immediately shoved to the table on his chest and his arms were pinned down. Robert lay motionless on the floor with the tip of an English trooper's bayonette just inches from his throat.

'Don't fight, Ned, they've got us.'

CHAPTER 21

Michael and his new bride arrived back in the village of Ballyshee just after dark. They went directly to the cottage which Morna had shared with her parents all her life, in order to retrieve her meagre belongings. From now on, they would share the little room which adjoined the forge where Mikey worked. While the girl told her mother about their encounter with the priest, Jimmy called Michael outside.

'Have ya given any t'ought t' how ye are goin' t' get all d' way t' yer home?'

Mikey nodded. 'We'll stay in the mountains.'

Jimmy shook his head. 'Yu'll get yerself lost, an' dat ain't no account t' me, but we're talkin' about me dotter here.'

'Don't worry,' Mikey replied. 'I've worked out a way that we can head in the right direction, even in the dark, or if it's raining.'

'If it's got anyt'ing t' do wit' witchcraft, Oy'll have nutt'n t' do wit it.'

'Not witchcraft, Jimmy, I'll show you how when I make the thing.'

O'Malley still looked doubtful. 'Dem mountains is barren an' yu'll have t' carry provisions. I don' t'ink yous c'n carry more 'n a week's warth.'

'I worked out we'll be three weeks in the mountains, Jimmy. I have a little money to restock ourselves when we start to run low.'

'What way aire ye takin, boyo?'

'We'll go straight north to the Derrynasaggart Mountains, then northeast through the Boggeragh. When they wither, we'll go north, cross the Galtees, then on to the Silvermines after that and we're nearly home.'

'Ya make it soun' easy, boyo, but cher takin' d' toughest way dere is.'

'If you have a better way, Jimmy, I'll be glad to hear it.'

'Agh, Oy don' know sure… When are ye t'inkin' o' leavin?'

'I'll wait until I can buy a small copper pot from the tinker. Probably within the week.'

Jimmy wasn't at all satisfied with the plan but, since he had never travelled further than Macroom or Bantry in his whole life, he wasn't able to offer an alternative.

'Alroight, boyo, Oy'm trustin' ya wit' me mos' valu'ble possession, so Oy'll say a prayer an' hope ye change yer moind.'

The two men went back inside the cottage just in time to catch the remains of a heated discussion between Morna and her mother, Caroline.

'C'mon Michael,' said Morna, sulkily. 'We have t' be goin' home … t' OUR house!'

Mikey complied as directed, bidding the O'Malleys good night and following Morna out. He knew from the set of her chin and the pace she was walking, that something had gone on while he and Jimmy were outside. Discretion dictated that he wait awhile before he spoke, lest he be the target of the girl's wrath. Mikey had learned, from watching his da's dealings with his mam, that Irish women are like a bear trap. Sometimes, you can jump up and down on the trigger and nothing happens. Other times, the draught from a butterfly's wings can set it off and there's the divil to pay. He didn't have to wait long to find out the reason for her indignation.

'Da brass o' dat woman! Suggestin' you go t' Tipp an' leave me behoind an' send fer me later. Would ya believe it?'

Mikey ventured a response. 'She's just worried about your welfare.' The trap was sprung! The delicate girl grew two sizes larger and, even in the moonlight, Michael could see her face flushing red as she faced him, her green eyes blazing. She put her hands on her hips and he braced himself for a broadside. For what we are about to receive Lord, he said to himself, we thank You. She began with a phrase he would hear many times in the years to come.

'Michael Hogan!' That's my name, he thought, so whatever comes next is mine forever.

'Michael Hogan! Oy'll be thankin' ya, not t' be takin' soides wit' me mudder 'r anyone else dat Oy'm havin' a discooshun wit in d' future. Ever! D'ya hear me?' There are many hundreds of words in the Irish language, and thousands in the English, but the only word that might possibly save a tongue-lashing is 'sorry' and, even then, it can be taken in one of two ways. It can mean 'I'm sorry for being stupid and opening my big fat mouth', which might possibly get you off the hook, or it can mean 'I'm sorry I took sides against you', which throws another log onto the fire. There's another potentially more dangerous alternative, you can grab the woman and kiss her on the mouth. If she kisses you back, all is forgiven. If she kicks you in the groin, then you can be sure you won't be sleeping in her bed tonight. Morna kissed Michael back … it was a newlywed's advantage.

When the young couple were back in the small room on the side of the forge, which served as living quarters, and now as the honeymoon suite, Michael tentatively broached the subject of the discussion he'd had with Morna's father. Morna sensed a conspiracy and began to fume again.

'Dem auld sods musta bin talkin' about me future, an' me not able to get a ward in.'

Michael spoke to her as if he was trying to soothe a spirited horse. 'Easy woman. I told him I had everything worked out and that he had no choice but to accept it. We're married now and that means we're together forever. From now on, wherever I go, you come with me.' It seemed he'd got it right this time because Morna smiled up at her new husband, put her arms around his neck, then shoved him backwards onto the straw-filled mattress.

*

Robert and Ned were dragged, pushed, pulled and prodded at the tip of bayonettes to a small room in a cellar, which was occupied only by a frail old man huddled in a corner, trying to keep out the damp and cold. The only light came from a tiny barred window above their heads and the stench of bodily waste hung heavy in the air, mingling with the smell of death which permeated the cell.

'Oy never t'ought Oy'd end me days loike dis,' lamented Ned, as the heavy door was slammed shut behind them. 'Oy alw'ys t'ought Oy'd be dead on some road, like dem highwaymen we run intuh. Ya shoulda let me put oop a fight. At least Oy'da tak'n one o' d' blaggarts wit' me.'

'Were not dead yet, boyo,' said Robert.

The old man in the corner cackled like a half-dead rooster. 'Tis dead y'aire alright, lads. When Grey puts ya in a cell, ya eider leave feet farst 'r at d' end of a rope.' Ned shuddered at the thought of having a noose put around his neck and being dropped from Cromwell's bridge, as his father had, ten years before at the hands of Percival Grey. Robert scanned the cell and looked up at the tiny window. The old fellow watched him with amusement.

'Ain't no escapin' yer fate, fella. Yer a dead man,' he croaked in a weak voice.

'What did he charge you with, old timer?' Robert asked the feeble creature, interrupting his exploration of the tiny chamber for a moment.

The man looked up at him with rheumy eyes. 'Sedition, boyo, it's alw'ys sedition. Dat way, dey c'n hang ya, dat's if ya don't die in dis cesspool, farst.'

'And what did you do to get the captain's attention, old man?'

'Ya c'n stop callin' me auld man, me name is Fergusson, ev'rybuddy calls me Fergus. Oy was a tinker befar Oy doid, an' dead Oy am. Oy plied me trade in d' townlands here in d' mount'ins fer farty odd years, paid me taxes t' d' crown, an' ev'n paid d' toll aul' Pussy Grey charges t' do me business hereabouts. Ya got any food? Only Oy ain't been fed 'n two days.'

'We haven't got anything to eat, Fergus, I'm sorry.'

'Agh, it's a'roight, Oy wasn't expectin' ye did. In a few mar days Oy'll be dead anyway, so if ye did, Oy wootn't blame yuz if ya kep' it. Whaddid dey get you lads far?'

'Fer drankin' a feckin' beer!' chimed in Ned. 'We wen' in t' d' Boar's Head fer a swalley an' nex' t'ing ya know, here we are.'

'Ah, dat's whar d' king's men hang out. Dey'll charge ye wit sedition too. Pussy says all Carkmen are rebels an' trait'rs an', if 'e had 'is way, he'd hang 'em all.' The feeble old man eyed Robert. 'Yer no Carkman. Oy c'n tell boy d' way ya talk.'

'No,' replied Robert. 'I'm from Tipperary.'

Fergus turned his attention to Ned now. 'An whar do ya hail from, boyo?'

Ned pulled himself up to his full height. 'Oy'm a son o' Cownty Cairk,' he said, drawing out the accent to make it more pronounced.

Fergus cackled. 'Dat ya aire, boyo, Oy c'n tell boy d' proide in yer vice.' He turned back to Robert. 'Oy've haird yer accent befar, not s' long back, boot me moind is foozy an' Oy can't r'member whar it was.'

Robert did his best not to appear too interested. 'There can't be too many men from Tipp around here.'

'No, joost d' one, boot Oy can't r'member whar. It'll come t'me after awhoile.'

Escape had became a priority for Robert now. At first he had been willing to allow time for Percy Grey to read the letter of introduction he'd brought from the sheriff in Kenmare and send for the prisoners, but now there was a sense of urgency. If the old man recognised the foreign accent from Tipp, then so would Percy's spies, and anything that drew attention to Michael would be his downfall.

The massive door to the cell had heavy iron hinges and, when Robert pushed on it, it barely moved. He peered through the door's tiny opening, about six inches wide and less than a foot long and, when he pressed his head hard against the iron bars, he saw there was a huge padlock holding it shut. He reached out tentatively, expecting at any second to be rewarded for his efforts by the butt stroke of a musket. None was forthcoming but, try as he might, he couldn't reach the lock. He decided to try the window.

The bottom sill was about seven feet off the ground and Robert guaged the opening to be a foot wide and a little less than a foot and a half tall. There were two rusted iron bars blocking the aperture which faced out towards the bay and Robert reached, grabbing hold of the edge of the sill to haul himself up, so he could clutch one of the bars. The sill cut into his forearm and he couldn't hang on for more than a few seconds before the pain caused him to release his grip. He motioned for Ned to come closer and told him to get down on all fours. He stepped up onto Ned's back so he could get a better look at the metal staves. The salt air had caused the iron to corrode and expand, cracking the mortar that held them in place but, when Robert put both hands around one of them and shook it with all his might, it didn't budge. He tried it with the second bar and that didn't move either. Ned suggested he should give it a try.

'Oy might be a liddle stronger den you aire,' he whispered. Robert got down on his hands and knees and the young deputy stepped up but, try as he might, the metal didn't budge. The men took turns all night long, shaking the bars and trying to turn them, to break the rust free. Finally, just before dawn, one of the pickets moved a little and the two men, flushed with success at loosening at least one of their restraints, doubled their efforts.

'We need a plan,' whispered Robert. The old tinker snored so loudly that he woke himself.

'Oy see youse lads have fin'lly giv'n oop. Joost as well. Aband'n hope all ye who enter here.' Robert recognised the quote from something he'd once read, and he quoted something back at the codger

'Where there's life, there's hope.'

The tinker grinned a melancholy smile. 'Tell me dat when d' noose tight'ns aroun' yer neck, boyo.' The sheriff and his deputy huddled in the corner to get warm. They were exhausted after a frenetic night's work and both fell asleep, each dreaming their own terrible dreams.

CHAPTER 22

Michael needed to prepare for the journey ahead. His first job was to build a compass of sorts, so that he and Morna would know which direction they were travelling in, day or night. When he'd been a child, Mikey had been fascinated by a compass his Uncle Robert always carried, and his uncle had explained to him it had something to do with a magnetised needle which always pointed north. Michael knew from his experience in the forge that when you forged steel, it attracted filings and shavings of iron particles. He didn't know how it worked, he just knew that it did, and that was enough practical knowledge for him.

While Morna heated porridge on the turf fire, he heated iron in the forge. He took a small billet of iron and flattened it, so that it was an inch wide and three inches long. He balanced it on the edge of the anvil and punched a hole at that point, so that it would hang freely from a bit of string. Michael knew where north was from the position of the North Star he'd seen on so many nights but, when he tested his makeshift compass, it lied, pointing northeast. He thought perhaps there was some miscalculation on his part so, while he ate his gruel, he gave it a bit more thought. Maybe it was something to do with how the metal was positioned while he beat on it with a hammer. He left his bowl of half-eaten oatmeal and stoked the forge again. This time, he oriented the long axis of the iron in a north, south direction and hammered the red hot metal on the anvil. When it turned a bluish colour, he quenched it in water and the steam sizzled. Again, he hung the pointer from the string and, this time, it pointed north. He turned, and the steel still pointed in the same direction. They had their compass.

The cloth sack which had served Michael on his forays up to Macroom wouldn't be adequate if he and Morna were to carry provisions, as well as their few possessions, on their journey through the mountains. Morna had been watching as Mikey prepared for the long hike and, when he sat to think about how they would carry their supplies, she asked him why he was wasting his time sitting around. He looked at her in surprise.

'Whoy didn'cha joost ask me?' she said. 'We c'n use willow baskets, like we use t' carry turf from d' bogs. Oy c'n make dose in a few hours. Oy'll weave d' baskets an' poot fleece on 'em so dey don' rub against yer back.'

Michael smiled, their problem was solved. His wife not only had the answer but the expertise too. He stood and held her to him, kissing her tenderly. She kissed him back, then pulled herself away.

'Oi, Mister!' she laughed. 'We got wark t' do!'

*

Fergus poked Robert with a bony finger as he slept, waking him up with a start.

'What is it?' he hissed.

'D' man…'

'Which man?' Robert was still groggy.

'D' man wit d' foreign accent.'

Robert was wide awake now, Ned too. 'You mean the Tipperary accent?'

'Yeah.'

'Well? What about him?'

'Oy r'membered. Oy r'membered whare Oy met 'im.'

'Where, ya auld bugger?'

'In one o' dem towns, near Gougane.'

Ned looked at Robert. 'Dere's only a few,' he told him. 'Ballingeary is on d' main rawd t' Macroom, so 'e won' be dere. Dat leaves jus' Cappaboy Beg, Lackabaun, Turnispidogy an' Ballyshee.'

The tinker was listening. 'Well, it ain't Cappab'y,' he said. 'Oy ain' been dere 'n months an' Oy haird 'is voice jus' d' udder week. It was eider Lackabaun 'r Ballyshee, and dey both oonly got d' one road inta town.'

'Dere oonly 'bout a mile apairt, sar,' said the deputy, with a hint of excitement. 'One on eider soide o' d' ridge dat's b'tween dem. It'll be easy t' foind 'im.'

'That's good news, Ned, but first there's the small matter of us getting out of this shit-hole. I've got an idea. Do you think you can squeeze through that window up there with one bar missing?'

'Can Oy?' Ned smiled, rubbing his hands together. 'Oy'm like a feckin' rat, sar. If Oy c'n squeeze me head t'rough, Oy c'n wiggle out.'

Robert took a look at the boy and was glad he still had the leanness of youth. 'Here's the plan, Ned. Tonight, at about midnight, I want you to slither out and go to your cousin's house. Get him to help us, even if you have to threaten him. We'll need a diversion for when we escape, tomorrow night.'

Ned interrupted, 'Don'cha mean t'night?'

'No, Ned, you'll break out tonight, but you'll come

back here before dawn and we both break out tomorrow night.'

'Feck, sar, ya mean Oy havta break out twice?'

'Yes, Ned. Don't worry, it'll be grand. Do you think you can do it, boyo?'

'Oy c'n do it, sar. It seems a bit half-arsed t' me, boot you're d' boss.'

'Good man, now here's the rest of the plan. Give Joe one of the small pistols and tell him to go to the west side of town, fire the gun, then get the hell out of there. That ought to attract the attention of the guards and the rest of the troopers. Have him bring the horses and the rest of the supplies to a place near here, so we can find them quickly in the dark. While the redcoats are out looking to see where the gunfire came from, we'll be heading north into the Sheehy Mountains on horseback. We'll make our gaol-break tomorrow at midnight. Do you have any questions?'

'Oy gots one prob'em wit' yer plan, sar. Whoy don' we bawth escape t'noight?'

'Because I can't fit through that opening in the little window, and I can't move as fast as you. I'm sixty-one years old.'

Old Fergus overheard. 'Oy'm awnly four years aulder den ya,' he cackled. Robert looked at wizened old man. Jayzus, he thought, he looks older than dirt … and I'm right behind him.

Ned whistled, he'd never thought about his boss's age until now. 'Chroist, sar, yer t'ree toimes aulder den meself!' Robert shot him a look and he coughed. 'Whaddaboot d' guard out front, sar?' he asked, getting the subject back to the plan.

'If he doesn't take the bait when Joe fires the shot, you'll have to get rid of him.'

'D'ya mean kill 'im?'

'Whatever it takes, Ned. If it's too dangerous, then you have to carry on the mission by yourself. Don't go back to Nenagh without Michael, no matter what happens to me, do you understand?'

Ned pondered for a moment. A lot of things could go wrong. The plan did seem half-arsed, but surprise was on their side. He extended his hand to the sheriff.

'Ya got me ward on it, sar,' he replied, shaking Roberts hand. 'T'morry noight, we'll be free men an' gallopin' off inta d' mountains.'

The day passed excruciatingly slowly for Robert and he thought about all the things that could go wrong with his plan. Ned slept peacefully in the corner with his back against the wall. Sometimes Robert sat, and sometimes he paced around the tiny cell, lost in his thoughts. He had been in many dangerous situations in his life but none seemed as compelling as this one. If anything happened to the young deputy, the entire scheme would unravel like yesterday's knitting. He knew his age was not his ally. Physically, all the injuries he had suffered in his life had begun to lay heavily upon him of late, wracking his body with aches and pains. He glanced over at Fergus and saw that the old man was studying him in the dim light of the cell. Robert went over and sat himself beside the skeletal old tinker.

'Dat lad takes arders froom ya, like ya w's a gen'ral,' Fergus said, his voice low.

Robert looked at Ned sleeping. 'Yes, he's a good man,' he replied.

'Yer no farmers. Oy been dealin' wit' farmers me whole loife an' yer no farmers. I was t'inkin dat maybe yer hoywaymen, boot dere's sumpt'in aboot ya dat says youse ain't dat eider.'

Robert realised, for the first time, that the old man had seen and heard too much and that he could be dangerous, so he told a small truth wrapped in a small lie.

'I was a Jacobite officer in the war,' he told him, 'with the Parliamentarians. Then, when the war was over, I went to France.'

'Ah, den yer one o' d' Woilde Geese!' The tinker had raised his voice now and Ned stirred in his slumber.

'Whisht, man, let the boy sleep. He'll need his rest for tonight.'

Fergus lowered his voice again. 'So was Oy,' he said with a touch of pride. 'Oy was at d' siege in Limerick, boot d' Gen'ral made a deal wit' d' English t' get all d' soldiers out an' sent t' France.'

'You had a good man so. Most of the general officers just saved their own skins and left their men behind.'

'Aye, sar, he was d' foinest altogedder,' said Fergus, with a touch of sadness and nostalgia.

'How long did you stay in France?'

'Ah, Oy got hoomesick fer county Cark, sar, an' as soon as Oy could, Oy got on a boat an' came home.'

'I wish I'd been as smart, Fergus. I stayed for ten years, fighting for whoever paid the highest price.'

The two old soldiers grew silent and remembered the glory of their youth. The truth was, of course, that there was no glory, only youth. Robert thought how easy it was to forget the tribulations and to remember only the good times. Fergus did the same.

The tinker broke the silence first. 'Tell me d' troot. What aire ya' really doin' down here.'

Robert's opinion had softened towards this wreck of a man who had once, many years ago, been a comrade-at-arms.

'I've come here to rescue… ,' he corrected himself.

'I've come here to find my nephew and take him home to his mother.'

Fergus smiled his toothless smile. 'Dat's a noble cause, loike d' ones we once fought fer. All men die, boot if yer goin' t' be dead, it moight 's well be doin' God's wark.'

'I can't pretend to know what God's work is, Fergus. I just want to do something that feels right for a change.'

'Den youse go an' foind d' priest 'r blacksmith 'r whatev'r he is an' ya bring 'im home t' 'is mam.' Robert's heart skipped a beat and his mouth fell open. The starving tinker had listened to every word the two men had spoken, even when they'd thought him asleep, and he had put it all together. He chuckled now.

'When ye spoke aboot d' Tipperary man, Oy knowed who ye meant froom d' farst, boot Oy wudn't sure if ye was spies Pussy'd sent t' get d' information from me. Yer boy's in Ballyshee.'

'Thank you,' said Robert, sincerely.

'Don't t'ank me,' said the old man, 'when ye leaves dat door open, Oy'm goin' straight t' Pussy's house an' t'row a rock t'rough d' window. Dat way, he'll get mad an' shoot me. It's bedder fer a soldier t' doy wit' a lead ball 'n 'is hairt, den t' rot here in a hole 'n d' groun'. Now, Oy'm gettin' toired an' Oy wanna sleep, boot Oy'm glad we talked. It'll gimme sumptin t' dream aboot.'

CHAPTER 23

By early afternoon, Morna had finished weaving the willow baskets which the young couple would carry into the mountains. Michael went about getting the foodstuffs they'd need for their journey, ground oats and bacon. He cut the meat into thin strips and strung them up, high over the forge. He didn't want them to cook, just to dry a little more to prevent them from spoiling quickly, also the smoke would give the bacon a little flavour. Morna watched as her husband worked.

'Moy clever man,' she said lovingly. 'Show me dat t'ing ya made so's we don' get lost.' Michael reached into the collar of his leine and pulled out the home-made compass he had hanging around his neck on a length of string. The metal swung and turned about and eventually pointed north. Morna smiled. 'It points t' home,' she said. Michael was happy that she was proud of her husband's resourcefulness.

'There's only one more thing we need now, sweetheart,' Michael told her. 'When the tinker gets here, we'll buy a little copper pot to cook on and then we'll be ready to leave.'

Michael wondered where the old tinker had got to, he'd been due to visit the village days ago. If he didn't show up soon, they'd just have to leave something else behind so they could carry the heavy iron pot across the mountains. One way or another, Michael was determined that they would begin their long journey within the week.

'Go and visit your mam and da, Morna. You haven't seen them since the quarrel and, after all, it'll be a while before you see them again, before we can bring them to Gortalocca.

Morna wrinkled her brow. 'Alright, Oy will,' she said, 'but if dey troy an' talk me out of it again, Oy'm comin' roight back.' Morna kissed Mikey's cheek and looked into his eyes. 'Oy love you, Michael Hogan,' she said, 'an' Oy'm only happy when Oy'm nex' t' ya.'

'Go way outta that,' laughed Mikey and watched her leave. Even when she was only at her parent's house, his world grew a little smaller. 'Tell them I'll be over in a little while,' he shouted after her. She flashed him a smile, picked up her skirts, and ran the rest of the way.

*

The afternoon wore on endlessly in the cramped cell and Robert went over the plan with Ned, and over it and over it again. He must be stealthy, Robert stressed, and, under no circumstances must he be seen by anyone other than his cousin, Joe. They could trust no one, Percy had eyes everywhere.

The dry weather had ended abruptly and a weather system had moved in from the southeast, bringing a cold front with it. Although the old tinker suffered badly because of it, the change was an advantage for Robert's plan. Even if the sentries did see Ned, the powder in their muskets would be useless and the big guns, with their bayonets, would be no more effective than pikes. Nevertheless, if he was seen, he would have to abandon the plan and search for Michael without the sheriff.

Ned had grown tired of rehearsing the plan. He knew, as well as Robert did, that a plan as vague as this one would need some degree of flexibility.

'Let's talk about sumthin' else, sar. We still got hours t' wait.'

'Let's talk aboot food,' chimed in Fergus. The poor creature hadn't eaten but a single bowl of thin porridge in five days now. 'Oy'm so weak, Oy don' think Oy c'n stand oop anymore,' he said. 'Oy'd give ev'ryt'in' Oy own fer a spud.'

'Oy'll bring ya back some spuds,' said Ned. He felt bad for the pathetic old man but he too had gone several days now without eating and the thought of food made his mouth water.

'If ya bring back a nip o' d' good shtuff, Oy'll tell ye a secret,' said the tinker, weakly, his voice just a rasp now. He was dying and he knew it. He had something to say and he wanted to say it before he met his maker.

'Oy'll do me best,' said Ned.

'C'mere, lads' said Fergus, motioning for the two men to come closer. They formed a huddle around him. 'Oy bin plyin' da backroads an' villages roun' here fer a lotta years,' he whispered. 'Oy buried me poke in one of dem caves d' monks use in Gougane. Dere's two grottos nex' t' d ' lough. Ain't no monks dere now. Dey was easy t' foind an' d' English rounded 'em oop years ago. In d' cave on d' left, I buried me purse oonder a flat shtone, in d' back. Loike Oy said, if ya bring me a spud, Oy'll give ya all me earthly posseshuns. Oy'm a man o' me ward an' Oy won't be needin' mooney whar Oy'm goin'.'

Ned looked at Robert, his eyes wide with excitement, but the sheriff brought him back down to earth. 'We don't have time for a treasure hunt, boyo.'

'It ain't no hoont,' interrupted Fergus. 'I tol' yous where d' purse is. Oy'd radder dat you fellers foind it den a tot'l stranger … an' anyway, ye have to go t'rough dere t' take d' shartcoot t' Ballyshee.'

'How much is dere?' asked Ned, still excited at the prospect of getting something for nothing.

'Joost shart o' foive pounds,' whispered the dying old man, 'a fartune dat Oy was savin' fer me auld age.'

Ned sat back against the wall and, as if he already had the money, he thought about what he could do with it. He asked Robert what he'd do.

'Agh, I'm too old for any more adventures after this one, Ned, but if I were your age, I'd go to the colonies in America. There's fertile land there. No one owns it and there are no authorities to answer to. I heard of a place called Mary Land where a man could make his fortune. If I was your age, I'd find a nice Irish lass and take her to the new world, and raise fat babies who'll be free to decide their own future.'

'Dat's it so!' Ned had forgotten his current circumstances, his head now full of a bright future. 'Oy'll take d' mooney an' Oy'll go t' d' colonies, wit' an' Orish garl an' we'll raise some animals an' have arselves a fairm.'

Robert felt a twinge of envy, he had dreamed that dream for himself. 'Get yourself some sleep, boyo,' he told the young man. 'You have more of an incentive to get out of here now and you'll need to be well-rested for your escape in a few hours.'

The three men huddled together in the corner for warmth. The pouring rain had blown through the little window and had turned the putrid floor of the cell into a quagmire.

The time came and the rain hadn't let up. Fergus slept on, his breaths coming in ragged gasps, Robert wondering if each would be his last. He turned his attention to his young deputy.

'Alright so. I'll get down on all fours, you climb on my back and shake the bar loose.' Ned climbed up and, in a few moments, the bar came free in his hands. He stepped back down onto the saturated floor and handed the iron bar to Robert.

'It ain't mooch of a weapon,' he said, 'boot y' might do some damage wit' it if y' hafta.' Robert hefted the bar and hoped that he wouldn't have to use it against a musket-toting trooper. He put it down and interlaced his fingers to hoist Ned up to the opening in the wall. Ned tried to put his head through, but stepped back down.

'Ah Jayzus! Me ears is in d' way.'

Robert thought for a moment. 'Take off your leine and let the rain wet you. It'll make you more slippery.' Ned took off the blouse and, when he climbed back up onto the sill, he pushed it outside, then put one arm and shoulder ahead of him and pushed his head through. This time he made it and, when his feet disappeared, Robert heard a thud as the young man hit the ground outside.

'Feck! Oy almos' broke me neck.'

Robert shushed him and that was the last he heard from him until the sky in the east had become tinted orange with the rising sun.

The old sheriff had dozed off a couple of times during the long, rainy night but mostly he sat listening to the raspy breath of his cellmate, measuring time by the old man's breathing. He'd sent the boy on a fool's errand and the longer he was gone, the guiltier he felt about it. He had just begun to fade off into a slumber when he heard a sound.

'Psst! Take dis sack, Oy got some food fer ye.' He looked up and saw Ned at the window. He helped him down before opening the bag. In it were four boiled potatoes, a hunk of gammon, a little jug of poteen and one of the small pistols.

Before he ate anything himself, Robert bent down to Fergus and put a pinch of spud between the old man's lips. The food hovered there, then fell to the ground. Robert feared it was too late for the old tinker but, when Ned put a drop of the whiskey on his finger and touched it to Fergus' lips, the old man roused.

'Sure, Oy t'ought Oy doid an' gone t' heaven an' d' angels give me a swalley,' he said weakly. Ned handed him the jug and he took a long swig of the fiery brew. He looked at Ned with watery eyes. 'T'ankya, lad, have ya got a bit o'dat spud fer a stairvin' man.' Ned gave him one of the potatoes and Fergus took a huge bite from the tuber, stopped in mid chew and reached into his mouth. He pulled out a tooth and looked at it. 'Oy ain' got many o' deese t' spare,' he said, dropping the tooth on the ground and tucking into the first food he'd had in days.

Robert was devouring his spud hungrily and he engaged in a tug of war with Fergus to get the jug from him. It wasn't hard to overpower the old codger and he took a swig from the jar. He felt the cold burn in his throat as it went down, then he handed the jug back to Fergus. The tinker embraced the clay bottle as if it was a lover. The sheriff addressed Ned for the first time.

'Is Joe in on the plan?'

'He is, 'boot 'e wannid all d' mooney in yer purse t' do it. Given d' circumstances, Oy let 'im keep it.' Robert nodded. Their hunger satiated, and their insides warmed by the whiskey, the three men fell asleep.

It was sometime in the middle of the afternoon when they were roused by the sound of a key opening the lock on the cell. Robert reached under his leine for the pistol, which he'd tucked in his waistband, and Ned clutched the iron bar behind his back. The guard was accompanied by a young lieutenant and, ignoring the other two, they concentrated their attention on Fergus. The lieutenant nodded to the guard, who grabbed the sleepy old man and unceremoniously dragged him from the room, pulling the heavy door and snapping the lock shut behind them.

'We shoulda jumped 'em,' hissed Ned.

Robert had considered it but knew that a daylight escape would have been suicidal.

'No, Ned, we stick to the plan. We just have to hope they don't beat anything out of the tinker. If they come back for us, we'll have no choice. Better to go down fast in a fight than rot away here.'

It hadn't occurred to either of them that old Fergus had his own plan to end the suffering.

*

The tinker's wagon pulled into Lackabaun late in the afternoon, but the fellow driving the donkey wasn't the man who'd visited the village every few weeks for the last thirty years. His accent wasn't a West Cork one and the explanation he gave about being the nephew of the late tinker didn't carry much weight. Instead of the usual throng of people who would gather round for the latest gossip, or to make a much-needed purchase, the villagers avoided him as if he had the plague.

He'd had the same reaction on all his stops, but he had his orders and, even if this did seem to him a waste of time, he knew better than to contradict his captain. He decided to spend the night here and he climbed into the back of the wagon to get some sleep. Old Fergus would have enjoyed the hospitality of the various townships but the new man had found the reception chilly, to say the least. Tomorrow, he would travel the few miles to Ballyshee, then onto Inchee Bridge. He dreaded the thought of returning to Glengarrif with no new information because Percival Grey would blame him, not any shortcomings in his own plan.

CHAPTER 24

The guard half-dragged and half-carried Fergus to the office of Captain Grey. The English adjutant was horrified at the manner in which the frail old fellow was being treated, but it wasn't his place to protest so he just followed behind. His captain's cruelty knew no bounds and did nothing to make life easier for either the Irish or the English who were stationed here. Percival Grey believed that any show of mercy would be seen as a sign of weakness, but all his tactics had done was to stiffen the backs of the populace. This was nothing like the lieutenant had imagined when he'd been at Sandhurst. It would have been easier for him to anticipate a volley of enemy gunfire than to watch what he imagined he was going to witness now. They knocked at the office door and it was promptly opened by Jacob, Grey's long-suffering man servant.

Percy Grey's desk was covered with what looked like enough food for a banquet. At first, the lieutenant thought the captain was going to torture the starving old man by eating a meal in front of him but, instead, the commanding officer motioned for the old man to sit down and help himself. Grey held a scented handkerchief in front of his nose, both to mask the smell of the putrid man and to cover his smiling face. He was delighted with his own guile. Fergus knew a man didn't get something for nothing and he declined the offer, even though the tempting aroma of the food was killing him. The man servant poured a glass of claret for his master and Fergus narrowed his eyes.

'A man moight have 'is tongue loosened fer a dram,' he croaked. Percy motioned for Jacob to place another glass in front of the man.

'Not dat shtoof, sar. A Carkman drinks whiskey, not dat pig piss.'

The man's impertinence in criticising his own good taste goaded Percival's temper, but he managed to keep himself composed, sourly indicating to his man that the old fellow's wishes should be complied with. Fergus downed the glass in a single gulp and held it up for more. The captain nodded to his servant, who refilled the glass and, again, the old man swallowed the contents in a single mouthful. The tinker held the glass up for a third refill but, this time, Percy's face flushed with temper.

'No! You're having nothing else until you've given me something in return. Quid pro quo, I give you something and you give me something in return.' His face grew redder as he saw Fergus begin to smile.

'Tis roight y'are, sar, I ain't give ya nothin' in r'turn.' The skinny old man's face was split in a rictus grin now as he motioned for Percy to come closer to him, then closer still, as if he was going to share a secret with him. When the captain's head was just inches away from his own, Fergus spat something in his face. Percival Grey reeled back in horror, grabbed a heavy glass inkwell from his desk and, in act of unmitigated fury, struck the old man on the head. Ferguson the tinker died instantly.

'Get that abomination out of here!' Grey screamed at the guard, who was able to pick up the limp bag of bones with one hand. After the corpse had been removed, and the door closed, Percy Grey looked for whatever had been spat at him. It was a tooth.

*

The commandant fingered the letter of introduction which had been written by Sheriff Wentworth from Kenmare, then held it over a candle flame until it was reduced to ash.

'There you are, Sheriff D'Arcy, you no longer exist.' He called his adjutant into the room and instructed him to take the two remaining prisoners to Seal Point in the morning with a detachment. There, they were to have them strangled and thrown into the bay.

'Who are they, sir?' enquired the lieutenant.

'Just a couple more rebels, best forgotten.'

Back in the cell, the two men were waiting pensively. The redcoats taking Fergus had put a new light on the situation, and they'd had to work out a plan for if they came back for them too. They decided that they'd lure them into the cell, that Robert would shoot whoever was carrying the musket and that Ned would have to dispatch the other with the iron bar. If they came back with three or more, of course, there would be a fight and there were no guarantees as to who would win. It wasn't much of a plan, but it was the only one they had.

Hours passed and no dreaded sound of a key rattling

the lock came. It was time to get the escape plan started. They repeated the same procedure as the previous night and Ned slithered out into the night air. The rain had let up considerably but the weather was still soft with a slow drizzle. Robert handed him the iron bar and the pistol but warned him, for the hundredth time, to use the gun only as a last resort. They waited for Joe's gunshot from the west side of the town.

The gunshot came, followed by two more shots in rapid succession … the nervous sentries had fired wildly into the night. Ned went around to make his move on the guard outside the cellar, but he wasn't there. He must have responded to the fusillade of shots and left his position unattended.

'Shite!' said Ned, under his breath. 'He took d' feckin' keys with him!' He went back around to the window of the cell and whispered to Robert what had happened.

'Use the bar, Ned, and pry the feckin lock loose!' Ned did as instructed and the door was open in no time, both men surprised at how easily the lock had sprung. Must be a French lock, thought Robert. The guard was still nowhere to be seen, so the two men hurried off into the night to find the horses.

Percival Grey had been roused from his sleep by the sound of the gunshots. He was still in a foul temper because that bloody old Irish sod had drunk his spirits, then died before he could get any information about the other prisoners out of him. He told the adjutant to send two of the jaegers after whichever rebel had fired the shot. He guessed that the shooter would head down to the Caha Mountains on the Beara and, if so, he would send a detachment of mounted foot to guard the Healy Pass. Those bastards on the Beara would probably give refuge to the scoundrel, so if he got south of the pass, he'd probably never be caught.

Robert and Ned found their mounts and galloped the horses hard, until they got a couple of miles out of town.

'We have to rest the animals for a while, Ned. When morning comes they'll find out we're missing, then all hell will break loose.' They watered the animals, then carried on towards Knockboy at a trot.

'We'll be past d' town befar daybreak,' said Ned, 'an' If we're lucky an' don' get lost, we should get t' Gougane by noon.' Robert took out his compass and took a bearing, they were going roughly northeast. Ned frowned at the gadget. 'Dat t'ing won' do ya mooch good here,' he said. 'We gotta follow d' lay o' d' land, even if it ain't direck.'

Robert put the device back in its pouch. Ned was right, this terrain was more like Wicklow than what he had become used to in Tipperary. The deputy tossed a potato to the sheriff and it occurred to Robert that, for all his own meticulous planning, Ned had been better prepared than he was.

'It's a lot diff'rint bein' d' hares instead o' d' hounds,' said Ned rhetorically. They continued onwards until the sun rose and, only then did they rest their mounts again, just past Knockboy.

*

Captain Grey was roused abruptly from his sleep by someone frantically pounding on his bedroom door.

'WHAT DO YOU WANT?' He screamed so loud that his voice cracked. His second-in-command entered his room in a state of agitation.

'The prisoners, sir,' he said breathlessly, 'they're gone.'

'That's what I ordered, you blithering idiot,' said Percy

through gritted teeth. 'I wanted them gone.' The lieutenant was sweating and out of breath from the run he'd made from the gaol.

'No, sir, they're gone. They escaped.' Percy's mind was a whirlwind of consequences. If that bastard D'Arcy made it back to Tipperary, his own military career would be over. He'd be lucky if he was mustered out. He would probably face a court's martial. He could live with disgrace but if he was put in front of a firing squad… He shook his head. Think, man, he told himself, think. The lawmen would probably head straight back to whatever fecking town they came from.

'Turn out the garrison!' he barked. 'Guard every bridge and crossroads between here and Millstreet.' The lieutenant was confused, all this seemed like a lot of trouble to catch a couple of rebels. Cork and Kerry were full of them.

'We haven't got enough men, sir. You sent a detachment down to Beara last night, along with two of the jaegers.' His scheme had backfired on him and now he was up to his neck in hot water.

'Get two of the Germans to push them and get two out ahead of them to cut them off.' Maybe if he pushed hard enough they would make a mistake and then … no harm done to him. He was also trying to work out a way of somehow shifting the blame onto the lieutenant. He had never met D'Arcy or his deputy but he hated them both with a vengeance for this. Percival called for his man servant and ordered him to pour him a drink. Jacob was surprised. This was the first time his master had begun the day with a shot of whiskey. It wouldn't be the last.

*

The tinker's wagon pulled into Ballyshee about mid-morning and Michael was there to meet it. He was surprised to find that it wasn't the usual old tinker, but rather some new fellow with what sounded like a Scottish accent. Michael wasn't comfortable with the fellow's story about being the old man's nephew, but he needed his copper pan. The new fellow took an inordinate interest in Michael's accent too and asked questions which made the blacksmith feel as if he was being examined. He asked the price for the pot and the man looked perplexed. This was the first sale he'd made in several days and he hadn't got a clue how to price the utensil.

'Two shillin's,' he said.

Michael frowned. He knew well that a pot of this size shouldn't cost more than a penny or two and he said as much. The spy wanted to get out of there as fast as he could, so he could make his report, so he sold the pan for a penny and immediately turned the donkey around, leaving the valley behind him and heading back toward Ballingeary. His captain would have his report by evening.

*

The Prussian hunters, in hot pursuit, each took an extra mount. They would ride the first horse to exhaustion and then exchange it for a fresh one. They estimated that they could get to Knockboy in two hours. They were only guessing about the destination of the escapees but they had the tracks and their plan was to get in front and wait for their prey to come to them.

Robert and his young companion had begun the climb up the steep slopes of the Sheehy Mountains, which guarded the Lough of St. Finbarr. As they crested a ridge, the younger man turned to check his backtrack.

'Oy t'ink we got company,' he told Robert. The sheriff's eyes weren't as sharp as Ned's, so he pulled the small brass telescope from his bag and pointed it in the direction the deputy had indicated.

He snapped it shut. 'Those are jaegers and if they catch up with us, we're going to be in the shit.'

'Who d' feck aire dese Yay-gers anyway?'

Robert didn't stop to reply, but he spoke as they spurred the Hobbies on. 'They're Prussian professional hunters and we have to find a way of slowing them down, otherwise we're going to get caught in an hour or so.'

The trail narrowed to a path as they got nearer to Gougane Barra and now it was only one horse wide, so they rode in single file.

'You go on ahead, Ned. I'll catch you up in a minute or two.' Robert dismounted, took the sack containing the caltrops, and spread them over the path for three or four yards. The little pieces of sharpened iron would lame a horse if stepped on. This ought to slow you bastards down, he thought, see if you can keep up on foot. He remounted and caught up to Ned.

'I'm hoping we just gained some extra time,' he said. 'When we get to the lake, we'll rest the animals for ten minutes and you can look for your treasure. But ten minutes and no more, do you understand?'

The Prussians had spotted their quarry ahead of them and had spurred their horses into a reckless gallop, hoping to overtake the rebels before they crossed the mountains. Twenty minutes later, they blundered headlong into Robert's trap. Both horses were lamed and would be useless.

Robert was concerned that he'd seen only two of the hunters and he was concerned as to where the other four were. He was unaware that two had been sent to chase a wild goose down on the Beara.

CHAPTER 25

Michael hurried back to the forge, where Morna had preparations underway for their flight to Gortalocca.

'We have to leave at first light tomorrow,' he told her, with a tone of urgency.

The girl looked perplexed. 'So soon?'

'Yes, now go and say your goodbyes to your parents. I'll finish up here and meet you at their house. I don't think that tinker was all he appeared and, the more I think about it, the more I think we should be worried about him. Morna sensed her husband's concern and she left without questioning him any further. Michael gathered up the gammon which had been drying over the forge and checked the baskets for their contents. He slipped a carving knife, along with extra flints and kindling, into a piece of leather, wrapped it tightly and packed it. No matter how many times went gone over the preparations in his mind, there was always something else he would think of.

*

Robert and Ned arrived at the island of St. Finbarr just before noon. Robert held the horses and allowed them to drink.

'Go and find your treasure, boyo, you have ten minutes.' The deputy waded the few yards to the island through the shallow, icy water and disappeared into the cloisters. After only a few minutes, Robert heard him whoop with joy and he came bounding back across the water, holding up a small cloth sack.

'Oy'm a rich man!' he shouted delightedly. 'Oy'm goin' t' Mary Land!'

Robert suppressed a smile. 'We have to complete our mission first, boyo. We should have at least five hours on the Prussians now. How long do you think before we get to Ballyshee?'

Ned looked at the sun and scratched his head. 'Oy'd say we're aboot foive moiles away. We c'n do it on d' Hobbies 'n less den two hours.'

The sheriff had to control his own excitement now. 'The horses need more rest,' he told Ned. 'We'll let them graze awhile and we'll leave in half an hour. That should get us there about mid-afternoon.' Ned sat on the ground and counted his money as Robert hobbled the horses.

*

The trooper from Derry, still in his tinker's disguise, cursed the donkey for being so slow. At this rate it would be almost dark by the time he reached Ballingeary, and at least another hour and a half before he could give his report to the captain. If he'd wanted to, he could easily have pulled the big pistol he carried for protection and arrested, or even shot, the blacksmith. But those hadn't been his orders. He'd been instructed to gather intelligence and report to his superior if he discovered anything out of the ordinary which might lead to the priest's capture. He knew that, if he deviated from his orders, he would be punished. Pussy Grey didn't suffer creativity amongst his subordinates.

*

In a Glengarriff office, a uniformed man paced back and forth. Occasionally, he stopped to look out of the window but he was lost in thought and his eyes saw nothing. He was surrounded by incompetents ... or perhaps they weren't incompetent, but just conspiring against him. He wished he had kept the note from Wentworth. Maybe there was something in it that could have given him a clue as to D'Arcy's intentions. Maybe he'd been sent by the crown to spy on him. Maybe some bastard in London had evil intentions against him … maybe even his own brother. Percival Grey needed something to keep his mind occupied. He shouted for his adjutant.

'Get me the sergeant of the guard and bring me the guard on duty. We'll convene a court-martial as soon as the guilty parties are here.'

The hapless guard could muster no defense against Percy's onslaught. The charges were desertion of his post and dereliction of duty, both of which were capital offenses. Since the passage of the 'Bloody Laws' by Parliament, any offense, whether civilian or military, could be punishable by death. The only options were available to the magistrate, and those were how the punishment could be carried out … by noose, firing squad or the axe. In a matter of moments, the trial was over, and the unfortunate man was sentenced. Percival Grey believed that shooting was too honorable a death so he ordered that the man be hanged before sundown, a traitor's death. The three men left the office, the condemned man sobbing as he was led away. Percival Grey sat at his desk and mopped his brow with a handkerchief. He felt better now that the blame had been placed on someone who would never get the chance to protest. He poured himself a glass of claret and thought about what he would do to that contemptible sheriff once he'd caught him.

*

Ned and Robert pushed their mounts hard as they rode out of Gougane, taking a path which led near to the turnoff towards Lackabaun and Ballyshee. The horses would be able to rest and graze overnight once they had reached their destination. The ground flew by beneath them and, within an hour, they had reached the road to Ballyshee Valley. Only now did they slow their animals to a trot. Ballyshee was a township, rather than a village, in that it had no central area. One-roomed cottages were dotted, seemingly haphazardly, here and there on the valley floor and up the slopes of the mountains which surrounded it. The nearest shop and bar were in Lackabaun.

The two riders followed the stream which ran along the bottom of the valley, and soon they came to the forge which stood alongside it. They dismounted and went in. The furnace was cold and there was nobody about. A moment of panic washed over Robert and he wondered if they were already too late. Two baskets sat, packed, as if waiting for their owners to go on a voyage.

While Robert pondered, Ned went into action. He walked to the nearest cottage, where a portly, middle-aged woman was hanging her washing out to dry.

'Beggin' yer pairdon, missus,' he said, drawing out his Cork accent, 'me harse t'rew a shoe wh'n we w's roonin' away fr'm d' law, an' Oy need a blacksmit' fast.'

The woman was happy to oblige, anyone on the run from the lawmen was a friend to the common folk, and she directed him to the O'Malley cottage. Ned sprinted back to the blacksmith shop.

'Ya bedder go yerself, sar, Oy don' know who yer man is, an' I dawn't wanna scare' im off.' Robert mounted his horse and rode the short distance to the O'Malley cottage. The upper half of the door was open and the inside was dim.

'Michael,' he called out. 'Michael Flynn. Are you in there?'

Jimmy O'Malley came to the door. 'Ain' no Michael Flynn in dis house, stranger.' Robert saw daylight flash into the cottage's interior as a back door was opened, and he heard the scuffle of feet running. Feck, he thought, now I have to run the eejit down. He wheeled his Hobby expertly around to the back of the house, where two figures were running away from the cottage, a man and a slightly built woman. The man held her by the hand and was half dragging and half leading her, as she stumbled alongside him. Within seconds, the rider had pulled in front of them and dismounted but, before he could say a word, the young fellow shouted.

'She doesn't know anything, leave her be!' Michael blurted out breathlessly, standing in front of Morna, and throwing his hands up in submission. Robert held his own hands out, palms up, in a gesture of non-violence.

'What have I always told you, Mikey Flynn? You never, ever, under any circumstances surrender.' The words were familiar to Michael, but the unshaven, grizzled old man who said them was not.

Robert wasn't one to mince words. 'Your mother sent me,' he said, tersely. 'Your father's dead.' The blood drained from Michael's face as he recognised the man who stood before him and took in what he had said. His mind fogged and his stomach turned inside out.

'Mam said you were a bastard and now I know what she meant.' It hadn't made the young man feel any better to lash out and he immediately felt guilty. Robert regarded Mikey pityingly. There had been times when he, too, had reacted the same way to a grievous hurt.

'I don't have time to explain everything now, Michael. The hunters are closing in. They'll be here in a day or so. We have to be long gone by then but my horses need rest and pasture. We'll leave before it gets light tomorrow morning.' With that, the sheriff turned and walked his horse back towards the forge. He looked over his shoulder and saw the girl trying to console the youth.

When Robert arrived back, Ned was happily conversing with a tall blond-haired girl. He thought about Roisin, as she had looked many years before, when she was just a young woman.

'Dis is Mary Galvin,' Ned called to him, grinning. 'She t'inks we're highwaymen, an' she wants t' go t' Mary Land wit' me.' Robert shook his head, Ned hadn't wasted much time. Now, all they needed to do was get themselves out of the valley before the Prussians could make a report.

'I'll take care of the horses, Ned, you go and enjoy your youth.'

Robert led the horses behind the forge to the stream,

where he let the animals drink their fill before hobbling the creatures and turning them out to graze. He watched them and didn't allow a thought to come into his head, enjoying the valley for this brief moment of peace and tranquility.

'I'm sorry, Uncle Robert.' Michael had walked up behind him. 'I don't know why I said that.'

'Agh, no bother, boyo, I understand. You and your da were close, I know. I shouldn't have just blurted it out like that, but you know the way I am. I grieve for your da too but my way is the same as his was, I lose myself in work and try to put the feelings away.'

'You're right,' said Mikey. 'I remember when my sister died, my da worked from morning to night, for weeks on end. Mam was afraid he'd die too, she thought he'd work himself to death.'

Robert nodded. 'When your mother asked me to find you and bring you home, that's all I thought about. It's kept me from thinking about Liam. But when I get you home, then I'll have time and then, no doubt, I'll be as angry and as sorrowful as you are now but, until then, I made a promise to your mam and I shall keep it.'

'How is she?'

'She's destroyed, Mikey. That's why I have to get you back to her. Seeing you is the only thing she has to look forward to.'

Michael managed a smile. He motioned over to where Morna was talking with Ned and Mary. 'I wonder what she'll think of my bride,' he said.

'Your bride?' said Robert, aghast, 'I thought you were a …'

Mikey shook his head, 'No,' he said. 'I'm a backsmith. I put the priest's life behind me. I just want to hammer metal like my grandfather did.'

'My father,' said Robert. 'That was all I wanted until I went off to war, but that's all behind me too.'

Michael voiced a thought. 'Perhaps when we get back to Gortalocca …'

'Too late for me, boyo.' Robert was dismissive. 'Now go and talk to the other young uns and leave me to watch the horses.'

*

Long after nightfall, a rider galloped into Glengarriff on a lathered and gasping horse. He dropped the reins and bounded into the office of the commanding officer. Percival Grey was still at his desk, drinking whiskey. He stood up, outraged at the intrusion but, before he could speak, the young trooper announced,

'I found him! I think I found him!'

Percy hoped he meant that he'd found D'Arcy. 'Where?'

'I found the priest in Ballyshee!'

Percy threw his glass of whiskey at the trooper. 'I don't give a shit about the feckin' priest.'

'He's the blacksmith … and he has the Tipperary accent,' said the man, ignoring the captain's outburst.

'What did you say?'

'He's the blacksmith!'

'No, the other part, you idiot.'

'He has the Tipperary accent!'

Percival Grey sat back down and rubbed his hands together. So that was it. The notorious man-hunting sheriff from Nenagh had seemingly got some reliable information from somewhere about a priest, and the bastard had come all the way down to Cork to arrest him, on Grey's territory. He should be treated like any other bloody poacher.

'Call in my adjutant,' he ordered. 'I'm going to put together a plan that'll catch all the fish in one net.'

CHAPTER 26

Percy was sitting at his desk with maps strewn all around him when the adjutant entered his office. An aide had roused the young lieutenant from a sound sleep with news that he had to report immediately to the captain's office, so he was still buttoning up his uniform as he entered. He stood to attention with his hand to his forehead as Percy went on shuffling from map to map.

'You're out of uniform, you slovenly pig,' growled the captain, who was wearing a dressing gown. 'Ah! I have the bastards,' he said, stabbing a letter opener into a map on his desk.

'Am I correct in assuming you mean the two escaped prisoners, sir?'

'No, you idiot, you are not correct! We are hunting for three rebels, including that bloody priest.' This was the first the young officer had heard about any third quarry and he had no idea who Percival was talking about. Experience, however, told him it was best to keep that to himself.

'Muster the troops,' ordered the captain. 'The bastards will either head north to Tipperary or west to Kenmare and I want every river crossing, bridge and crossroads covered.'

The adjutant looked over the captain's shoulder at the map. 'We haven't got the manpower, sir. You sent a third of the company down to the Beara, along with two of your trackers.'

Percy regarded his subordinate with loathing. 'I don't know why you sent them down there in the first place,' he snarled, through closed teeth. 'Now you have to rectify your mistake. Send a rider down there and bring them back.' Percy was already making a mental note to amend his log, making the lieutenant responsible.

'We'll cast a net from Macroom to Poulgorm Bridge and have the Prussians drive them into it,' he announced proudly.

The young lieutenant shook his head. 'But sir, that would leave gaps wide enough for them to herd a flock of sheep through without our knowledge.'

Percy was loathe to admit that his subordinate was right. 'Alright,' he said, with more than a hint of sarcasm 'if you're such a military genius, what's your plan?'

The lieutenant studied the map for a moment. 'We can deploy the men closer together, in an arc, from Inchee Bridge to cut off the west, to Turnapidogy, cutting off the east. We have enough troops to guard the crossroads at Coolea and Derryfineen, closing the gap north. We can use the jaegers to drive them in and we can set up headquarters at Ballingeary, so we'll be closer to the action.'

The plan did seem to be an excellent one and, if it was successful, Percy would make sure he got the credit for it. If it failed, he would lay the blame firmly at the feet of the Sandhurst graduate.

'How many men have we got available?' asked the commander.

'We can provision the men and have thirty light horse,

along with the two jaegers, in a few hours, sir. At dawn, we can deploy thirty more foot, but they'll take the best part of a day and a half to reach the rendezvous point.'

Percy was ready to throw another one of his tantrums. 'Have them leave, now, damn you! Bugger the provisions, they can get what they need from the Irish!'

*

When darkness came, Robert walked back to the forge and seated himself away from the two young couples, who were engaged in animated conversation. He was amused to see how completely captivated his young cohort seemed to be by Mary Galvin and he thought back to how his brother's heart had been stolen by another golden-haired Irish lass, all those years before. Liam had often told him that, for him, it had been love at first sight but that it had taken a while before he'd managed to get Roisin to fall for him. Robert shook the thoughts from his head, this was no time for sentimentality. He motioned for Ned to come over to him, so they could talk in private. Ned had some information for the sheriff.

'R'member auld Fergus tol' us dat he ditn't know whoy 'e got 'imself arrested?' Robert nodded. 'Well, dere was a tinker here dis marnin', an' 'e spoke wit' a foreign accent. D'ya t'ink it was one o' d' troopers?'

Robert inhaled deeply. This meant that Percival Grey knew where they were now, and that meant he would cover all the escape routes as soon as he could deploy his troops. The Prussians would drive them into a trap.

'Do you think Mikey would leave the girl behind?'

'Not a chance, sar, she's a'ready talkin' aboot d' curtains she'll hang an' d' babies dey'll have.'

'What about you, Ned?'

'If y' mean Mary,' Ned said with a grin, 'sure, she's waited sixteen years fer me t' show up, she c'n wait a coople o' more weeks.'

Robert wasn't as concerned about the troopers as he was about the Prussians. He and Ned had managed to outdistance the two who'd been following them, but there were still four he couldn't account for.

'It would have been harder for us to break out of gaol than to avoid the English pickets, but now that we've got the girl with us, and those feckin' jaegers on our tails …'

Ned interrupted him, he had a plan. 'Ya c'n take Michael an' Morna, an' d' harses, an' light outta here t'rough d' mountains, jus' like y' planned.'

It occurred to Robert that it was the first time he'd heard Mikey's bride's name. 'And what about you Ned? I don't like the idea of us splitting ourselves up, just in case there's another fight. Michael wouldn't be worth a shit in a scrap.'

'Ya ain' use t' bein' d' hunted, sar,' Ned told him. 'Yer t'inkin' loike one o' dem Proosians. Ye go before dawn, jus' loike y' planned, an' Oy'll stay b'hoind. Oy'll let dem sausage-eaters getta good look at me, an den Oy'll take'm back intuh me awn country. D' only arse dey'll see den is deir own arses when Oy run 'em aroun' in sarcles. Oy'll give ye a few days headstairt, an' den Oy'll lead 'em down into d' Beara an' lose 'em.'

'And what makes you think you can get them to follow you?'

Ned smiled a devilish grin. 'Oy'll be wearin' Moichael's priest clothes. Dey'll t'ink dat wharever d' priest is, dat's whar dey c'n foind us all. If y' c'n gimme d' little gun, Oy'll make a racket dey can't ignore.'

'Where will you go on the Beara to lay low? It surely

won't be safe unless the jaegers or Grey give up, and that's not going to happen.'

'Oy gotta place 'n moind. Joe's prob'ly already dere now, drinkin' yer purse droy. Dere's a liddle fishing village called Bunaw, where d' fishermen is only fishermen in d' daytoime, cuz at noight dey smoogle goods in t' avoid d' taxman. Dere's no place bedder fer a pirate den in a nest o' pirates.'

Ned's plan seemed so half-baked that Robert couldn't help feeling doubtful about it, but their situation had changed quickly and he couldn't think of an alternative.

'I think your plan stinks. Why don't I take the robes and lead the hunters away?'

'Beggin yer pairdon, sar,' Ned scoffed, 'but yer so feckin auld dat dey'd run ya down in a day an' den Oy'd be stuck tryin' t' get yer nephew back t' Tipp. You asked me t' trust ya when we stairted dis adventure, an' now you have t' trust me.'

Robert conceded that there was truth in that but he made a vow that, as soon as he got the young couple safely on a stagecoach to Nenagh, he would go back for Ned. Money, he thought, I have no money left. Joe had appropriated the purse he'd brought on the trip, as payment for his part in the gaol-break.

'Ned, I need to borrow some of your money from you so I can pay for the stage fare.'

'Ah shite, sar, y' c'n take d' whole t'ing. Oy'll keep a few shillin's fer meself an' y' c'n keep hold o' d' rest fer me … fer when me and me woife go t' Mary Land.'

'You're going to marry the girl?'

Ned laughed out loud. 'Ya bet yer arse Oy am, sar. Oy'm in love sure.' Robert had to laugh too. It was the first time he'd had anything to laugh about since they were trapped in Percival Grey's murder hole.

'You work fast, Ned, I'll grant you that.'

'A man on a mission can't be wastin' no toime, sar!'

What Ned didn't know was that his poor cousin, Joe, hadn't taken any provisions with him for his escape into the Caha mountains, except for a jug of poteen. When he'd thought he was safe from the troops, he'd had a little drink in celebration, which had led to another. He was caught on the second day by the Prussian hunters. He'd made the mistake of drawing the tiny pistol on a man who was ten yards away and had missed. The jaeger hadn't and Joe was shot through the throat, just above the collar of his leine. Joe's last thought had been that he hadn't even finished the jug.

*

Percival's carriage was ready and waiting for him before the sun rose. It would be more comfortable for the journey to Ballingeary. He had his horse tied to the back so that he could stop the coach just outside of town and make a heroic entrance. Jacob sat up front with the driver and Grey had decided that his executive officer could ride on horseback with the troops. Before he got underway, the two Prussians who'd been sent to chase the rebel on the Beara rode up on winded horses. Without a word, one of them handed a small sack to the captain. He looked inside and a satisfied smile spread across his face.

'Ah, you've brought me a trophy. Good. Was he alive when you castrated him?' The German shook his head. 'Pity,' said Percival, and climbed inside.

CHAPTER 27

Robert slept fitfully. Ned's plan had so many holes in it that he feared for his young companion's survival. It was still the early hours of the morning when he knocked on the door to the room where Michael and Morna slept.

'C'mon, boyo, put your britches on and get your wife out of there.' Morna and Mikey appeared moments later, Mikey blushing as he buttoned up his trews. 'Get your gear together, the sun will be up in two hours and I want us to be over that ridge, north of here, when it does. Michael, give your Franciscan clothes to Ned.' The blacksmith looked perplexed. 'Just do it, don't ask questions.' Michael handed the grey cloak to Ned, who was wide awake by now.

He held it up in front of himself. 'How do Oy look,' he asked, grinning. 'Do Oy look loike a holy priest?

'The divil's own priest, ya sod,' replied Robert.

A few minutes later, Robert had helped the girl up onto a horse and Mikey had pulled himself up behind her with one of the baskets on his back.

'And don't, for the love of God, let her fall off,' snapped the older man. 'We don't have time for accidents.' He put the straps of the remaining basket over his own shoulders and they walked the horses up the slopes, which became steeper as they neared the crest. The deputy had taken up the rear position and he checked their backtrack every few minutes. A light misty rain began to fall. That would delay sunrise for a few extra crucial minutes.

'Dat's grand,' said Ned. 'Dey'll have a haird toime peckin' up yer trail. When youse get t' d top o' d' ridge, keep goin' til ye get t' d' Derrynasaggart Mountains, an' stay in 'em 'til ye get to d' Buggeroffs.' Robert already knew the plan but he sensed that Ned was getting a case of the nerves, like a man before battle, so he let the young man speak. 'Ye should be able t' get a stagecoach in Millstreet an' get t' Limerick. Oy'll meet ye in Nenagh in a few weeks time, God willin'. The last statement made Robert nervous, it wasn't like Ned to put his hope in the Almighty. He too hoped that God was willing because, even if he managed to get Michael home safely, it would be a tragedy to lose Ned in the process.

As they crested the rise, Robert handed Ned the pistol with the pouch containing the lead balls, powder and patches, along with the little brass spyglass, and the long knife which Jamie had made from the end of the sabre.

'I wish you'd reconsider and come along with us, boyo.'

'Ah, Oy'd be a disgrace t' me fam'ly name sure, if Oy w's found consortin' wit' a lawman,' Ned joked. As the horses carried on, Robert turned and looked back. Ned had turned the spyglass towards the path they'd taken from Gougane and was waiting for the trackers to appear.

*

Percival Grey slept some of the way to Ballingeary but his sleep wasn't a peaceful one. In a tormented dream, he found himself back in the boarding school which he'd attended as a child, sent there by his parents at an early age. It was night, the time of day he'd always dreaded, and some older boys had clamped a hand over his mouth and dragged him into the same coat closet they always used. In his dream, he tried to scream, but couldn't. They pinioned him to the ground, face first, and did their worst. Percival Grey could even have endured the excrutiating physical pain, but not the other boys laughing at him, calling him 'Pussy'. There had been no one to tell, no one to help him. He remembered the faces and the taunts, the finger pointing, and he had vowed back then that there would be retribution. He woke in a sweat, took a drink from the silver flask in his pocket and forced himself to stay awake, afraid to go back to sleep.

The troops were gathered in Ballingeary at eight in the morning and at half eight, Percival Grey rode into town on a magnificent, dappled charger. He walked the horse up to his lieutenant.

'What are you waiting for, an invitation? Take the men into Ballyshee and maybe, with luck, we'll surprise the bastards.'

With that, Percy drew his sword and took the lead, followed by a dozen mounted troops. The lieutenant was still assigning men to the trap but, after a few minutes, he followed his commander as the cavalry galloped away to their various assignments with the minimum of instructions. It was a three mile gallop to Ballyshee and Captain Grey held his sword aloft for the whole journey, as if assaulting the entire French army.

Ballyshee's only street was deserted. The sound of galloping horses had alerted the populace and they had all taken cover in their cabins or the fields. Percy was waiting in the forge when the lieutenant arrived. The young man put his hand on the barely warm furnace. It was obvious that it hadn't been lit for a couple of days. Pervical stood with his sabre still in his hand but now, it hung limply at his side. The adjutant waited for orders as the troopers milled about on their mounts. All eyes were on Grey.

He was furious not to have surprised the fugitives.

'Turn everyone out of their shacks,' he ordered the young officer. 'Bring them all here and burn their hovels, every bloody one of them.' A light rain began to fall.

'Sir, if we burn their cottages, most of them will die during the winter.

Percy smiled a sinister smile. 'No, you fool, you're wrong again. They'll all die! Burn the crops and kill the sheep too! These bastards harboured a traitor and, for that, they will pay. Their complicity makes them as guilty as he is and I'll show them no mercy.'

The lieutenant had no choice but to relay the order to a sergeant, who gave the men instructions. The thatch was wet on the outside from the rain, so each cottage must be set ablaze from within.

It took longer than Percival had anticipated but, in time, the worst was done and thirty broken, dejected people stood before him, the women clutching their shawls under their chins. Some of the men were out in the fields, hiding and watching.

Captain Percival Grey thrust his chinless jaw forward. 'I will ask this question of you once, and only once,' he announced to the throng of ragged Irish. 'Where is the priest headed for?' There was a murmur from the villagers as they looked at one another and shuffled their feet, but there was no response.

'Kill the men,' said Grey, to no one in particular, as casually as if he was ordering a glass of claret. The troops looked at each other, shocked for a moment, and Percy began to fume. Were they mocking him?

'Are you all deaf?' he yelled. 'I gave you an order.'

A burly sergeant wrestled a musket from one of the troopers and he shot a man through the chest. The Irishman dropped as if he'd been struck by lightning. There followed a ragged fusillade as the other troopers obeyed the order. Twelve men lay dead, their women folk keening over their bodies, others trying to give comfort to the bereaved.

Ned was watching from high on the ridge, overlooking the Ballyshee Valley. He kept glancing over to the west, where he expected the unhorsed Prussians who'd followed him and Robert to enter the gorge from the direction of Gougane. He was right. Although the rain had washed away most of the tracks left on the stony ground, the smoke rising from the burning thatched had alerted them that something was out of the ordinary. The jaegers trudged wearily down the slope to the village. They had been walking all night, trying to pick up the trail. Ned watched them. When the Germans arrived at the scene, he could see the captain in animated conversation with them. He took out the spyglass and saw Percy flailing his arms around as he screamed at the exhausted men. Ned decided it was time to spring his own surprise. He stood up, presenting a silhouette against the skyline. He stood for almost fifteen minutes, the grey Franciscan robe blowing in the wind, but none of the redcoats noticed him. He considered firing the pistol to alert the English, but decided against it. He might need the powder later.

Finally, one of the troopers who was scanning the hills around the village spotted Ned and excitedly alerted the captain, who promptly pulled a brass spyglass from his saddlebag. Ned and Percival locked gazes, each studying the other through their little telescopes. Percy was the first to snap shut his instrument. One of the Prussians ventured a shot with his rifle and Ned saw the puff of smoke almost a third of a mile away. A couple of seconds later, he heard the report of the weapon. Ned lifted the Franciscan robe and, even though he had his britches on underneath, he knew that the significance of the gesture wasn't lost on those watching him. What he didn't know was quite how infuriated Percival Grey was by the action. The incensed captain ordered the weary Prussians to take up immediate pursuit and Ned watched through the scope for a few seconds more.

'Ah, you boys t'ink yer toired now, wait'll Oy get t'rough wit' ye.' He snapped his telescope closed and took off, west by south.

*

By mid-morning, Robert had led the couple to a road which, in turn, led to Inchee Bridge. There was the off-chance that, if the bridge wasn't guarded, he might be able to get the young couple back to Kenmare by early the next day, then he could go back and retrieve Ned and then his mission would be almost complete. He told Michael to hold the two horses while he reconnoitered the crossing. He took the basket off his back and stayed well away from the road surface. It took fifteen minutes to cover the quarter mile and, when he got to the point where the bridge came into sight, he saw that it was guarded by two mounted redcoats and another two foot soldiers. There were too many of them for him to risk a fight and, in any case, he was virtually unarmed except for the shortened saber. He disappeared back into the undergrowth and returned to the horses.

When he got back, he saw Morna caressing the back of Mikey's neck as the young couple embraced, lost in their own world. They seemed oblivious to the danger they were in and Robert became angry. These young people had to realise what a perilous situation they were all in.

'That's enough,' he snapped. 'There'll be plenty of time for all that shite when we get out of this mess. Michael, I expected better of you, what would your father have thought?' Michael was mortified and he looked down at his feet, the same way that Robert had seen his brother do on many occasion.

The girl leapt to her husband's defense. 'Agh! Ya miserable auld sourpuss, what's d' harm sure?' Robert had to surpress a smile now. It was as if his sister-in-law, Roisin, was talking to him. You didn't mess with the husband of a strong Irishwoman.

The stream had become impassible due to the previous night's rain, so the only hope for the trio was to find a ford. Crossing rivers could be the most dangerous undertaking of a voyage. Robert called a halt. He would explore up-steam while Mikey held the animals. They had been backtracking, going back towards Ballyshee again, and the old man knew they would have to make a break to the north soon, if they were to successfully avoid any potential trap. He moved stealthily through the heavily-brushed banks of the stream. Rain was falling and it helped to mask any sound he made. He heard muffled conversation, it was coming from the other shore of the river. He also heard the sound of running water which meant there was a shallow spot ahead. It was the crossing he had hoped for, but there was still the question of who waited on the other side. He crept closer.

He was suddenly startled by the noise of someone creeping up behind him and he grasped the handle of the short saber tightly. He wouldn't go down without a fight. He was about to strike out when he realised that it was Michael, he had followed him. Robert glared at him, silenced him with a finger to his mouth and motioned for the young man to stay put. He crept closer to the sound of the voices and listened for a moment, then moved back to Mikey, who looked at him questioningly. Robert indicated silence again and crept past Michael, gesturing with his hand for him to follow. They returned to where Morna stood, holding the horses, shifting her weight impatiently from one foot to other. Robert spoke to them in a hushed tone.

'There are two sentries on the opposite bank. We can't cross there and we can't keep going backwards.'

'But there's only two of them,' protested Michael.

'They're speaking French,' Robert told him. 'We're talking about two Huguenots.'

'So what?' replied the young man, with a hint of indignation.

Robert was becoming irked. 'Those men, boyo, have been fighting viciously with the Papists for generations. They know what they're doing. Tell me, how many times have you had to fight for your life, you stupid eejit?' Robert immediately regretted his outburst, but the young fellow seemed completely ignorant of what a life and death situation was.

'Why can't we just gallop the horses past them, and be gone before they can react?' said Michael.

Robert had to admit he had given that very thing a passing thought, the sentries' flintlocks would be useless in the pouring rain.

'And what happens when they bayonet one of the horses? No, we have to think of a way to get them on this side of the river, one at a time, so I can deal with them.'

Michael was beginning to realise that the older man completely disregarded his value in a battle and, although it stung, he said, 'I'll do whatever you say, Uncle Robert.'

Robert looked at the girl. 'And what about her?' he asked.

CHAPTER 28

'Sir, the two trackers you sent after the priest, they're completely exhausted. They haven't slept in two nights and they've been on foot most of that time.' The lieutenant was addressing his captain.

'Aww, what a shame,' replied Percival Grey, sarcastically.

'We have the other four awaiting orders in Ballingeary, sir.'

'Well bring them here. They should be able to ride a Tipperary priest down in a few hours. I don't want him killed, do you hear? I want him arrested and brought back alive.'

'Sir, they're marksman, that's what they do.'

'I will NOT have my orders questioned, lieutenant.' Percy drew the last word out, so as to leave no doubt as to who was in charge.' The subordinate knuckled his forehead in salute and passed the orders on to a sergeant, who selected the lightest and fastest rider for the job.

'What about these women, sir?' asked the junior officer.

Percy looked down at the throng of weeping and wailing women. 'Spoils of war, lietenant. Let the troops have some recreation.'

The young officer felt the bile rise up into his throat and he walked away as if he had some other business to attend to. Percy Grey would have to give that order himself.

The four mounted jaegers were ready to leave in two hours. That had given Ned a three hour lead and he was almost back to Gougane before they started off on their hunt. The Germans were elated that they were finally getting to do what they'd been trained for. They had become bored with the same old routine, but now they were going to track a criminal. They chatted in their low, guttural German, as if they were preparing for a deer hunt, back in Bavaria.

Ned had made a track that would be easy for them to follow. The tops of the stones were wet from the rain but the bottoms were dry so, every now and then, he would stop and overturn some of the pebbles, thereby marking his trail. He left footprints wherever he could in the soil in the forests between ridges, and he broke off twigs of gorse as he hiked. The Prussians soon rode past their weary companions with no time for anything but a wave. They were enjoying the chase.

Just before he crossed the last of the high ground, before descending into the Valley of St. Finbarr, Ned looked back and saw four horseman, in full flight, cresting the previous summit. He felt the hair prickle on the back of his neck. He had to slow them down by making his trail less obvious or they would be on him before nightfall. He changed direction and, instead of going down into the valley, he climbed the ridges to the north. The Prussians might be used to chasing deer, but they'd never come up against a Corkman. They had made the assumption that he would run downhill and that would give him precious hours as they wasted their time down in the valley, searching for signs. Ned travelled on the side of the ridge, opposite the trackers. They wouldn't catch a glimpse of him until he wanted them to.

*

Robert had been trying to come up with a workable plan to ford the river. The rain had begun to ease and that meant the muskets would become usable for the 'Frenchies.'

'I have an idea,' he said finally. Neither of you will like it, but we need to get over that river before nightfall, and before the rain stops. You both said you'd accept my orders and this is an order. I swear I will leave you both in the feckin' woods here if you don't go along with it.'

Morna crept along the bank of the stream behind Robert, who was using the short sword to push aside branches, and Michael followed at the rear. Robert hadn't wanted Mikey to come along but that was the only way he'd been able to get him to consent to the plan. The thorns from the blackberry thicket pulled at their clothes as they crept slowly along an almost indistinguishable path which led towards the river crossing. On the sheriff's command, Morna stood up and strolled towards the river as Robert concealed himself in the bushes, shoving Michael unceremoniously behind him. As the girl approached the bank, the Huguenot soldiers on the other side of the river both stood, one of them levelling a musket at her. Morna feigned surprise, threw up her hands and ran back towards the thicket on the riverbank. The man dropped his weapon and, without taking his boots off, went in pursuit, delighted that the afternoon promised to bring some respite from the boredom. He was across the water in no time, and was almost within an arm's reach of catching her, when Robert stepped out of concealment, crashing the handguard of his sword into the man's jaw. He lay on his back, motionless, his mandible skewed into a hideous position. The girl looked at the prostrate figure and her jaw slackened.

'Scream,' said Robert, almost inaudibly. The girl only managed a feeble squeak and Robert raised the saber over his head as if he was going to deal her a death blow. Morna let out a bloodcurdling scream and Mikey immediately darted forward in her defense. Robert turned on the young man and the look on his face made Michael's knees feel like jelly. He froze as if made of stone.

'Now. Shake the bushes, boyo, as if he's having some fun with the girl. Go on!' Mikey complied and, in a matter of seconds, the second trooper came crashing down the path, wanting to get his share too. He met the same fate as his companion.

'Get the horses and take yourself and the girl across the river. I'll meet you on the other side.' As soon as the young couple were out of sight, Robert slit the troopers' throats as casually as he would dispatch a pig. He wiped the blade off on the second man's coat.

'Pardonnez-moi, mes amis,' he said 'C'est la guerre.'

*

It was long after dark, and just before midnight, when Ned reached the pass which lead into Finbarr's valley from the west. When they'd lost the trail, the Prussians had held a conference and one of them returned to the point where they'd last seen sign of their quarry. He'd picked up Ned's trail now and was following him, while the others still scouted the valley below. Just as the sun had begun to cast a glow on the tops of the mountains, Ned decided he would reveal himself. He collected some dry grass and a few twigs and then, with a spare flint from the pistol and a little black powder, he started a campfire. He pulled down his trews and emptied his bowels beside the fire.

'Here ye go, ye shitehawks, go sniffin' aroun' dis,' he said aloud. Then he began to jog along the same route he and the sheriff had taken a couple of days earlier. If you make the bait enticing enough, he thought to himself, you can use the same trap to catch more than one rat.

The jaegers had indeed noticed the smoke from the campfire and they re-mounted their steeds, to climb the slope up the side of the valley. The three of them thought they would already have ended their sport the previous day but their prey had proved more challenging than they had imagined. The fourth Prussian was now busy navigating the steep terrain on the ridge and, finally, he had to dismount and lead his animal on foot. He was falling behind.

The jaegers had reached the campfire site and were trying to guage how long it had been abandoned. They walked around it, looking for signs.

'Was ist das!?' one of them cried out.

He stripped his boot off and stared at the considerable amount of deposit he'd picked up on the sole of it. When his two companions realised what it was, they roared with laughter, mocking him. The unfortunate German gritted his teeth and vowed to get this schwein of an Irish priest if it was the last thing he'd ever do. He would never catch the priest but it would be the last thing he'd ever do.

Ned left a discernable trail down to the place where the path narrowed. Although rain water now covered the caltrops Robert had dropped there previously, they were still in place. Ned was careful not to step on any of the vicious devices himself. If he was to cripple himself now, the chase would be over before he'd barely even got started. He broke off a branch and stirred the standing water, making it look as if someone had run through it. Then he placed the branch conspicuously at the far end of the trap and hurried to build another fire to attract the jaegers' attention. It did the job and, from the vantage point of another hill, he sat with the spyglass and waited for the show to start.

The Prussians were moving methodically, albeit not swiftly. However, when the tendrils of smoke became visible, they spurred their horses into a headlong gallop, in the hope of catching the resting clergyman. Ned lost sight of them as they disappeared into the narrow gap, but he heard the mayhem which his trap created. The horses screamed and so did the men and, within minutes, three limping animals were lead out by two men. The poor fellow who'd stepped in the excrement which Ned had deposited on the ridge had been pinned under his fallen horse and his thigh was fractured. Ned wondered where the fourth horseman was but he had no time to tarry. The Prussians would be even more determined now.

The fourth horseman, who had followed Ned up and around Gougane, was, in fact, an hour behind the other hunters and, when he came to where the havoc had taken place, the injured man told him what had happened. He took the long way round and caught up with the other two jaegers in less than half an hour. Ned showed himself on the top of a hill, almost half a mile away. When he was certain that he'd been seen, he set about laying another trap.

The fourth Prussian had learned a lesson from what had happened to his comrades and he was in no hurry to take any risks in an effort to end the chase quickly. He would give chase but at a moderate pace and, when the priest stopped to rest, then he would move in for the kill. He would disregard Percival's orders to take the priest alive. This man wasn't like any convict he'd ever hunted before and he wasn't about to take any chances.

Ned was watching his back, and he knew that the mounted Prussian was closing on him at a steady rate.

'Dat's roight, boyo, come closer. Aul' Ned has a liddle surprise fer ya,' he said aloud.

The sun was beginning to set now and, as the light faded, the tracker had a hard time staying on the trail. As darkness closed in, Ned stopped and slipped the Franciscan robe off over his head. He found a clearing in the middle of a thicket of gorse and he filled the robe with grass. He made another fire and propped up the stuffed robe beside it.

'Youse feckers like fire, don'cha. Well, Oy'm gonna give youse a liddle taste o' hell.'

The jaeger spotted the fire immediately and was there in moments. He walked his horse around the thicket, not wanting to get the animal any closer. He tied the horse and walked stealthily, on foot, through the dense mat of thorny vegetation. When he could see the flames from the fire, he squatted in the undergrowth, drew his pistol and waited. Ned began to sing. The soldier caught glimpses of the man by the fire but he didn't want to waste the only shot he had. The priest seemed to be sitting with his back against the large trunk of a fallen tree. From behind the tree trunk, Ned poked the dummy he'd made and it fell over, as if laying down to sleep. After a few minutes, the Irishman made snoring sounds to complete the illusion. The hunter was stealthier than Ned had anticipated and so he was surprised when, without a sound, the man suddenly appeared in front of the fire. The soldier's attention was still riveted by the reclining effigy in front of him and he moved in, holding his pistol out in front of him. When the muzzle was just inches from where the priest's head should be, he was punched a mighty blow on his back. It knocked the wind out of him and, try as he might, he couldn't catch his breath. He dropped the horse pistol to the ground and fought for air. Putting his hand to his chest, he felt the three inches of steel protruding from it. Ned put his mouth next to the man's ear.

'T'anks fer d' harse.'

CHAPTER 29

The sheriff and the young couple went through the two Frenchmen's belongings and Robert took the one pistol and the ammunition. He thought about taking one of the muskets but decided it would be an unnecessary weight for the tired horse to carry. They rifled through the sack of food and found a couple of loaves of heavy meal bread and some salted meat. They packed it all into their baskets, it could be sorted later, and, after crossing the river, they struck out northwards. Michael had been shocked at the ruthless efficiency and brutality with which Robert had handled the two French soldiers and, in a way, he was both in awe of, and appalled, by his uncle's actions. Morna didn't speak. When Robert had held the sabre over her head, she had thought he was going to kill her.

'Do you think those French soldiers will be alright?' asked Michael.

Robert's face lost all expression. 'Say one of your prayers for their souls,' he replied, flatly.

The last Michael had seen of the Huguenots, they had lain unconscious and helpless on the ground and, now, he began to realise why his uncle has sent them on ahead.

'You killed them,' he said.

Robert shrugged. 'All men die. It's just a matter of when and how. If they had done their duty, instead of chasing young Fanny over there, they'd still be alive and we'd be dead.'

'You really can be a bastard, can't you.'

Robert gave a snort of derision and they rode in silence for the rest of the day.

The trio made camp just northwest of Coomagearahy Mountain. They found a place hidden in a ravine, where they could build a small fire to cook some food. Robert unsaddled the mounts and hobbled them, so they could graze the sparse grass without running off. Michael kept Morna company as she prepared a simple meal, using some of the Frenchmen's salt meat for seasoning and adding some of the dried gammon to the copper pot, along with three potatoes. Robert unloaded the pistol and put in fresh powder and priming. He tucked it into his woven belt, under the felted brat that he wore to keep off the night chill. He took a walk to explore the area and to reassess his escape plan. He couldn't shake off an uneasiness about Ned.

By the time he returned, Morna and Michael had finished eating and they sat huddled close together by the fire. Robert took the pot off the fire and began to tuck in.

Mikey was the first to speak. 'How did me da die?'

Robert looked up from the kettle. 'He didn't suffer, if that's what you're worried about. It was quick.'

'But how?'

Robert picked a strand of meat from between his teeth and looked at it. 'Him and Robbie were doing a job and your da felt sick.' He put the piece of meat back into his mouth and chewed it. 'He died on the spot … probably a heart seizure.'

Michael felt a wave of anger rise inside him at Robert's matter-of-fact response. 'You really don't give a shit about anyone, do you,' he said.

The old man threw the food on the ground and stood up. His blood boiled and he wanted to grab Mikey by the throat. 'Don't presume to know me, boy,' he roared, 'You know nothing about me and even less about what I feel and what I don't feel!' He stormed off into the darkness.

Michael pulled Morna close to him, he needed to feel her warmth.

'Yer ooncle's roight, Mikey,' she said, softly. 'Ya don' know how 'e feels.'

Mikey tried to pull away but she held him close. 'He has no more feelings than that sabre he used today,' he said, sulkily.

'No, love, yer wrong. Oy've seen men loike yer Ooncle Robert. Me Da wuz one o' dem. When ya beat on a piece a hot iron wit' a hammer long enoof, it gets hairder. Loife beats men. It makes 'em haird, boot brittle. Me da had me mam to help soften 'im. Yer Ooncle Robert's got nobody.' Michael kissed his wife softly on her forehead, she was right. Morna had seen something in Robert that he hadn't. He went out to look for his uncle.

He found the old man sitting on a stone, looking out into the blackness of the night. As he approached him in the dark, he saw that Robert had his hand on the butt of the pistol which he had tucked under his belt.

'Careful, boyo! You don't want to be sneaking up on a dangerous old man like that!' Robert let go of the pistol and showed his upturned palms.

'I'm sorry, Uncle. It's just that, sometimes, when I think about me da, I get so damn angry.'

'So do I, boyo, that's how us Irish are. When we feel powerless and desperate, we turn it into something we know how to deal with … anger. Let me tell you something about me and your father. There really wasn't that much difference between us, we both needed someone. He had your mam and I had him.'

Mikey was taken aback. His uncle was the High Sheriff of Ormond and, in a way, he wielded more power than even the wealthiest of the gentry. Surely he didn't need anyone.

Robert continued. 'You know, it was no accident that I used to visit Gortalocca a couple of times a month, or that Liam and I would take walks alone in the forest, sometimes for hours. He understood me and he knew that there was a time to give advice and a time to just listen. Everyone needs that.'

Robert's voice cracked a little and, even in the darkness, Mikey could see the old fellow's eyes glisten. If it had been anyone else, he would have put his arm on their shoulder, but this old man was still a formidable presence and Mikey was sure he'd resent it. So he did as his father would have done and he just listened.

'Those two Frog soldiers I killed this afternoon. You think I don't care and you're entitled to think whatever you want. Your father always said that perception is more powerful than reality, and he was right. I feel guilt for it. I feel guilt for all the men I've slaughtered over the years and God knows there's been plenty of them. But I'm not an animal. People say it gets easier each time, but as I get closer to the end of my life, it gets harder. If there had been any way to get past those two without killing them, then I wish I knew what it was.' He shrugged his shoulders and looked out into the darkness again.

Michael knew it was his turn to speak. 'If you'd arrived a day later, Uncle Robert, me and Morna would have blundered straight into those two soldiers. I'd be dead and God only knows what would have happened to her.' Robert nodded, but said nothing, and Mikey changed the subject. 'You never told us the plan to get back home.'

Home, thought the old man, what a comforting sound that word had. His own home, for so many years, had been the spartan room connected to his office in Nenagh and he envied Liam, who had known what the word really meant.

'The plan's flexible, Mikey,' he replied. 'It all depends on the circumstances. This morning I intended for us to stay in the mountains through the Boggeragh, then head north to Mallow, where the three of us would board a stagecoach bound for Nenagh. But I've re-thought the plan now and I think it's best if I get you both to Killarney, put you on a stage, then go back and help Ned. I've been thinking about him all afternoon. We all owe our lives to that man, and I can't leave owing a debt like that. Tomorrow, we head westwards. Now leave me alone with my demons. You go back and make love to your wife.'

*

Ned got the saddlebags from the dead Prussian's horse and went through their contents, stuffing a lump of cheese he found into his mouth. The German had all the implements a hunter could want, including a small telescope. Ned smashed it with a rock.

'Ya won' be needin' dis t'ing anymore, bucko,' he said

to the corpse. He found a horse pistol and he threw it on the ground. 'An' dat ain't mooch use t' me. Oy cootn't hit a wall in a small room wit' one a dem t'ings.' He pulled the jaeger rifle out of its scabbard on the side of the saddle and admired it. It was a piece of art, with images of heroic hunting scenes carved into the walnut stock and inlaid engraving on the metal. 'Betcha dis cost ya more'n a few shillin's, ya sausage-eater.' He threw that on the ground too, then he had an' idea. 'Oy t'ink Oy'll leave a present fer yer mates,' he said, still addressing the dead man. 'Ya don' talk mooch do ya? Dat's good, cuz den ya can't tell'em what d' priest from hell is gonna leave.' Ned took the rifle and removed the lead ball with the worm on the end of the ramrod. Then he packed a triple load of powder, followed by two balls on top. He put the rifle back in the scabbard and put them on the ground next to the dead fellow. 'Hold yer whisht, now, don't be tellin' dem blokes aboot me surprise.' Ned picked up the large pistol he had discarded and put it back into the saddlebag, then mounted the big horse and galloped westwards. He had one more day to keep the Prussians occupied, then he could go down to the Beara and make his escape.

*

A little after noon, there was a loud knock on the door of the inn which Captain Grey had commandeered as his headquarters in Ballingeary. His man servant, Jacob, ushered the lieutenant inside.

'Well?' Percy asked expectantly. 'Have you got good news for me?'

The adjutant cleared his throat. 'I have news, sir,' he said.

Percy leaned back in the cushioned chair which he'd brought by coach from Glengarrif. He clasped his hands together behind his scraggy neck and waited.

'Well?' he screamed finally. 'Are you deaf or just dumb? Give me the bloody report, man.'

The adjutant cleared his throat again. 'Uhh…well, sir… two of the French pickets we put on the crossing near Inchee Bridge were found dead last night. Their throats were cut and it looks like they took a beating.'

'As I suspected. The priest and the rebels headed north.' Percival Grey lunged forwards and slammed both his hands on his desk. 'And that's why we put the blockade there, you imbecile, to stop them! Well we'll set up another one, further north this time.'

'Well…uh… no, sir…' stuttered the young man. 'The … ehhh….'

'Well? Spit it out, man. You're one of his majesty's officers'

'Well, sir … it seems the priest has headed south now.'

Percival was baffled for a moment, then he leant forward. 'The jaegers should have run him down by now.'

The young lieutenant could feel the sweat run down his back. 'The priest has unhorsed three of the jaegers. He led them into a trap … sir.'

Percival's blood had begun to boil. What manner of priest was this? 'So the Prussians have lost five horses in two days? Well then, let the bastards walk! Now, have you got any more *good* news for me?' he said sarcastically.

'Uhm, sir… one of the jaegers suffered a fractured thigh during the ambush and the surgeon is amputating his leg.'

'Well that one can hop! What about the fourth

horseman? He should've been able to catch the priest.'

'It seems he did, sir … the priest killed him.'

That was the last straw and Percival blew his top. 'What kind of priests do they have in Tipperary?' he screamed. 'What about his sacred bloody commandments? The fourth one for a start … Thou shalt not kill!'

'That's the fifth commandment, sir.'

'THAT is insubordination, lieutenant! Get out of my sight!'

The adjutant turned smartly on his heels and left the office, letting the door slam behind him. When he got outside into the fresh air, he inhaled deeply. He could hear Percy ranting from behind the closed door. He had exploded like a volcano and had heaped all his wrath upon poor Jacob. The lieutenant was tempted to intervene but he suppressed the urge. Jacob belonged to the captain and he could do anything he wanted to the old man, short of killing him. Percival beat poor Jacob with a riding crop until there wasn't an inch of his head or shoulders which wasn't reddened or lacerated. Then he threw the old man out and cursed him for bleeding on the floor. Percy sat down and had more than one drink.

CHAPTER 30

A wind had whipped up and Robert felt the chill, even through the brat he wore. He decided he'd given the young couple ample private time and now he sought to sit by the fire for a while, to warm his aching bones. Mikey and Morna lay sleeping a few feet from the glowing embers. They had a blanket over them and they looked warm and comfortable. Robert felt the cold seeping through his body, the chill due partly to the falling temperatures but intensified by a sense of the unknown.

He held his palms out to face the coals, then rubbed them together. He glanced over to where the young couple lay and saw that the girl had her eyes open and was watching him. Her red hair was no longer tied tightly back and it fell loosely around her neck. She looked even younger than her years and the old man suddenly felt very protective of these two young people. Morna lifted Mikey's arm, which had been draped over her, and she gently pulled back the blanket which covered them. Robert averted his eyes because he didn't know if she was clothed. The girl straightened out her simple dress of homespun wool and tucked the blanket around her sleeping husband. She padded over to Robert on bare feet and asked did he mind if she sat next to the fire with him. Robert motioned his head to a place near the fire and Morna sat with her knees pulled up, her forearms resting on them.

'Oy'm frightened,' she said.

Robert closed his eyes. 'So am I.'

Morna looked up at the old man with her soft green eyes. 'Oy can't believe dat. Oy saw how ya dealt wit' dem soldiers t'day.'

'I promise you I was frightened. I was afraid what would happen to you and the boy if the plan failed.'

'Den yer not afraid o' dyin'?'

'I'm afraid of that too. If there is a God, then he'll surely send me straight to hell.'

'Mikey says if ya do somet'in' t'somebody wit' d' intent t' do hairm, den it's a sin.'

'That sounds like something his father would say. If that's true, girl, then I have a lot to repent for. I fully intended to kill those two poor fellows today.'

'But ya believed dat you were doin' it t' save us.'

'Yes, my dear. I was too stupid to think of a better way. I'm afraid stupidity may be a sin.'

Morna changed the direction of the conversation because she knew the old man was suffering and it made her uncomfortable.

'Oy'm scared dat Moichael's mam won' loike me.'

Robert managed a smile. 'Ah, Roisin is a formidable woman alright, but you're no shrinking violet either. You went and showed yourself to those Frog soldiers today and you did it without hesitation.'

'But Oy w's scared shiteless, Ooncle Robbie.'

The old man chuckled to himself. Only Liam

would've had the audacity to call him Robbie.

'Then that makes two of us who were scared shitless, Morna.'

Morna was glad to hear the fierce old man call her by her name. 'Ya need t' get some rest, now, Ooncle,' she said, kindly.

'Don't you worry about me, m'dear, you go back and get some sleep. Us old men don't need as much sleep as you young people.'

Robert stayed awake and worried about Ned and he had good reason for concern. Ned had become so sure of himself that he was about to get careless.

*

Ned had promised the sheriff he would run the Prussians in circles and so, after he'd jogged the horse westwards for an hour, he turned and continued northwards for another hour. He wanted to find the two hunters who Robert had put on foot, days before. When he turned back towards the east, he saw that the remaining jaegers had built a fire and all four of them appeared to be sitting around it. He felt a little uneasy because that was the bait he had used, so he gave them a wide berth and started south again. Ned was happy enough when he was the one playing games, but he was uncomfortable when the tables were turned on him.

The sun was just rising over Ned's left shoulder when he heard the telltale boom of a musket shot. A second later he heard a buzz, like an angry wasp, go past his head.

'Ooo! Ya sneaky bastards. Dat w's close.' He spurred the tired horse into a gallop and, a few seconds later, there was another shot followed by a thumping noise as the projectile hit something with a sound like a drum. The horse stumbled and sank to its knees. Ned picked himself up and tried to look into the sun, where the shots had come from, but he couldn't see a thing through the glare.

'Now ya killed yer own feckin' harse, ya eejits!'

He grabbed the sack of food and weapons from the saddle and tried to find cover. Before he did, he heard a mighty explosion, then silence. He crouched low, running into the bottom of a ravine and heading south. His heart pounded. The sheriff had warned him about the prowess of the Prussians and he had become so carried away with the success of his tricks that he had lost his focus.

With only the thought of escape now running through his mind, he made a quick estimate of how far away the enemy was, probably two hundred yards, and that was well within the range of a rifle shot. He kept on going forwards, pushing his tired legs to their limit. He needed to gain distance if he was to get himself out of the mess his own immaturity had landed him in. He jogged for almost two hours. Before crossing each ridge, he furtively poked his head up and used the spyglass to check behind him. He thought about throwing the heavy horse pistol away. He could make better time if he only carried the knife, the small gun and the food. As it turned out, Ned needn't have worried. Whilst the best of the Prussian marksmen was getting the range, another man was passing the rifles to him and, when he fired what he intended to be a mortal shot at his prey, he used the rifle which Ned had spiked with the extra powder and ball. When the breech of the gun exploded, it took most of his jaw, destroyed what had been his face, and blinded the man who had passed the weapons with shards of steel.

Ned sat beside a stream which fed into the Glengarrif River. He quenched his thirst, ate some of his food and decided he would dispose of the heavy weapons and that way, by tomorrow, he could be down on the Beara. He knew that the refuge there, in the Caha mountains, would be his means of escape. He was just about to throw the pistols into the river when a thought occurred to him.

He tore a strip of yarn from the hem of the priest's clothes. He would make a booby trap to obscure an actual one. He put almost all the powder in the barrel of the horse pistol along with a couple of lead balls, and he tied a bit of string to a stone and buried it in the stream bank, so that only a little of it protruded above ground. He tied the string to the trigger of the cocked gun and placed a little flat stone over the trigger guard, to mask the cord. He tied the small gun to a bush on the path which led to the water's edge, then he tied a heavier, more visible cord to the trigger of that one, stretching it so it would be clearly visible to someone coming for a drink at the brook. Next, he placed the bag of powder and lead balls over the lock of the big gun so that the cocked hammer couldn't be seen. He headed to the Beara peninsula, by way of Rossnagrena, to lose himself.

*

It was morning when the courier galloped into Ballingeary and sought out the second-in-command. The lieutenant read the note, crumpled it up in his hand and let it fall to the ground. He hadn't seen his commanding officer since yesterday, but now he was going to have to deliver the news to the captain and he wasn't looking forward to it. He knocked and the door was opened by poor Jacob. The man had been beaten severely and was in a pitiful state. The captain sat behind his desk and was also a sorry sight. He hadn't taken his uniform off for two days and there were stains on his blouse from everything he'd eaten or drank. His eyes were ringed with dark circles and the young officer thought he looked even more like a ferret than usual.

'Tell me you have some good news today,' he slurred. Percival Grey had begun the day the same way as he ended the previous one and the decanters on his desk were nearing empty.

'The jaegers have sighted the priest, sir. They even got a shot at him.'

Percy looked as if he might either fall asleep or pass out. 'Did they get him?'

'Not exactly, sir.'

Percival stared at his adjutant vacantly for a moment, while his brain tried to process the information. 'Well what the bloody hell does that mean, you moron? Every time you come in here, things get worse.'

'I'm just the messenger, sir.'

'Well give me the bloody message then!' The captain shook his head, as much to clear his brain of cobwebs, as in disbelief at the incompetency he had to tolerate.

'They shot the horse out from under him, sir.'

Percival smiled the smile of a simpleton. Some spit hung on his bottom lip and the lieutenant couldn't take his eyes off the drool, which was destined to join the other stains down the front of his shirt. 'Well, that's good news then, lieutenant.'

'Yes, sir.' The young officer tore his attention back to his superior, who was unravelling before his eyes. 'It is good news, sir. But in the process, they lost two more jaegers.'

The captain stood up, staggered back, then fell into

his chair. 'Wait. How can we lose two men who are shooting at another man?'

'Sir, one of the rifles exploded, sir.'

'Jaeger rifles don't explode, you idiot!'

'This one did, sir. It was one they picked up from the dead hunter yesterday. It seems the priest had spiked the rifle with a double charge of powder and more than one ball.'

'I don't believe it!' screamed the senior officer. 'I'm surrounded by idiots and incompetents!'

'Yes, sir. The thing is, the two hunters who are left are becoming jumpy, sir. The priest could have easily escaped on horseback, but it seems he circled back around to get behind them. They think he might be hunting them.'

'The gutless, cowardly bastards!' Percy managed to stand up by holding on to his desk. 'Which way is he headed?'

'It looks like he's heading back to Glengarrif, sir.'

'Glengarrif? Why the hell would he go to Glengarrif?'

'I haven't the foggiest notion, sir.'

'Well … lieutenant,' said the captain, acerbically. 'When the fog lifts, be sure to let me know, would you? Now get the hell out of my sight! Someone around here has to do some thinking.'

The adjutant left the office and, for the first time, he entertained the thought of relieving his captain of his duties. In his present state, he doubted whether Percival was capable of being in command but, of course, that could be seen as mutiny by those sitting behind desks in London. The young officer considered having a drink to calm his own nerves.

Percival had his own demons to contend with. This priest surely wasn't mortal, he must be something conjured up by the Papists to persecute him. What if the devil was going to Glengarrif to hunt him down? He felt a warm moisture collect around the crotch of his breeches and flow down his leg onto the floor. If he could hunt jeagers, and dispatch them with impunity, what in God's name could he do to an English officer? He would leave right away. He would take a contingent of troops as a guard and lock himself in his quarters at Glengarrif. He would bring back all the troops with him and turn the town into a fortress. Would even that be enough, he wondered. The priest could be anywhere. He seemed to be always one step ahead. Perhaps he was getting inside information, perhaps from the lieutenant. It was a well-known fact that junior officers were notoriously jealous of their seniors. He thought back to how he had felt, back in the days when he was second-in-command.

Percy issued his order. The hunt for the rebels was over and everyone was to return to headquarters immediately.

CHAPTER 31

When Robert and his charges began their ride northwest, the highest peaks of Magillicuddy's Reeks were only just beginning to catch the first rays from the rising sun, and the dark forests were still shrouded in shadow. He hoped that, before tomorrow was ended, they would be in Killarney. On a map, the distance appeared short, but the terrain was undulating with precipitous valleys and steep ridges. The land was carpeted in dense primeval oak forest which had seen neither axe nor settlement. It would be a long trek before they could pick up the little road which skirted Lough Guitane, twelve miles away. From there, the ride into Killarney would be an easy one, along the road which led to Muckross.

After about two hours, and three miles of arduous travel, they came to the road which led from Clonkeen to Kenmare. Robert scouted ahead and, after several mounted redcoats rode urgently by him, heading south, he went back and brought the young couple to the crossing point. Here, they stopped and listened for the sound of horses and, hearing nothing but the birds and the forest noises, they hurriedly crossed the dirt track.

The sheriff broke a branch from a shrub and obliterated the tracks made by the horses. If they stayed south of the peaks of Carrigawaddra and Crohane, they would run into the stream which flowed into the lough. If they found the stream and followed the flow, every brook and rivulet from there on in would eventually enter Lough Leane and Killarney. That meant the threat of getting lost was diminished, or so he thought.

The old man surrendered his seat on the horse to Morna and he walked ahead, occasionally using the short sword to clear any overhanging branches which impeded his progress. His bones ached and the straps of the basket cut into his shoulders. The girl told him to pass the heavy load to her and his ego momentarily tempted him to decline, but he saw the practicality of the offer and passed the burden up to her. Mikey asked why they couldn't take a more direct route, instead of the meandering game paths they were following.

'Animals are smarter than people,' scowled Robert, his sore, aching muscles clouding his temperament. 'They instinctively know the easiest way and they've used these trails for hundreds of years.' Eventually the trail petered out and there was nothing but forest ahead. The old man called a halt at around noon, to rest the horses, he said. In reality, it was he who needed the respite.

'Are we lost?' asked Mikey.

Robert gave him a sour glare in response. 'I know where we are, boyo.'

'Where are we?' asked Michael innocently.

'We're in a feckin' big forest, looking for a stream, that's where.'

Michael looked down and grinned. 'Do you remember when me and Robbie lost Mam and Da in Nenagh market that day?'

Robert narrowed his eyes and the merest hint of a smile crossed his face as he recalled the day. 'I do, and I caught the divil from your mam for it.'

'You held us by the hand and, when we walked down the street, the crowd parted like the Red Sea. All the vendors gave us sweets and food because they thought we were the sons of the High Sheriff.'

'I remember I put you up on my shoulders because you were said you were too small and your mam and da wouldn't be able to see you in the crowd. What were you then? Four, five years old?'

'I was just over four and Robbie wasn't six yet. You know, Uncle Robert, that's one of my happiest memories.'

'Mine too, Mike. For a while there, I got to know just how your father felt every day of his life.' The old man looked wistful for a fleeting moment, then cleared his throat. 'Well, that's enough of that, let's see if we can find this stream or we'll be here all day.'

Morna had been listening to the two men reminisce. 'Oy haird water roonin' a coople hunded yairds back,' she offered, 'on a path dat led off o' dis one, on d' right.'

Robert looked up at her. 'Maybe I should have told you what I was looking for,' he said abruptly, 'and we could have saved all the violins and flowers for later.'

Mikey took the sword and told Robert to ride and he would break trail for the horses. The old man didn't argue. It was time for the younger one to take the lead and, for the first time in thirty years, he was glad to follow.

In no time at all, they reached a brook which came from a spring in the mountains to the west, then curved northwards toward Lough Guitane. The stream was shallow and ran cold and crystalline from its source. The bottom was strewn with pebbles of every shade of brown and cream and, as the horses splashed through, jewel-like trout spooked, skittering in every direction across the shallows.

'If we had time, we could go fishing,' said Mikey.

'And if I had wings, I could fly back to Nenagh and my arse wouldn't be so sore,' replied Robert. He thought about what his young companion had said. 'When we get back to Gortalocca, Mikey, the two of us will go fishing.'

Morna chirped in, 'C'n Oy go too!?'

Robert turned and looked at her. 'Why not,' he said. 'I never heard of a girl going fishing before, but you can be the first.'

That pleased her. 'We c'n all t'ree go fishin', an' Oy'll clean d' fish an' make d' dinner.'

Robert smiled broadly. 'You'd better keep your eye on this one, Michael. She's worth keeping.'

*

Percival Grey returned to Glengarriff and ensconced himself, along with Jacob, in his office. In the outer office, his lieutenant's desk was piled high with paperwork which had been left unattended since the whole business with the priest had begun. The administrative duties of governing the region had been neglected because of his superior's personal obsession with finding the cleric. The junior officer stayed up late. He occasionally heard indecipherable rants coming from the other side of the door which separated the two rooms. It was the last time he would ever hear Percival Grey's voice.

The next morning, after a few hours sleep, the adjutant bathed, shaved and was just putting on a clean uniform when he heard the muffled but unmistakable sound of a gunshot inside the building. With his shirt still unbuttoned, he ran into the hall which was already becoming crowded with soldiers, some dressed, others in just their breeches, all crowded around the door of the captain's office. The lieutenant had a cocked pistol in his hand and, for a brief moment, he wondered if Percival's paranoia was real and that the priest had somehow infiltrated the building and was indeed hunting the officer. The burly sergeant-of-the-guard kicked the door and, when it flew open, the lieutenant went in first. Black powder smoke still hung heavy in the air.

The junior officer scanned the office and first he saw Jacob standing in a corner with his hands clasped over his mouth, his eyes staring wide. The lieutenant followed his gaze and saw Percival Grey slumped over his desk, blood pooling around his face. He made a vain gesture of checking him for signs of life but, judging from the wound in his temple, he knew it was fruitless. He turned the gun on the only survivor left and asked what had happened. The old black servant began in his baritone voice.

'Da massuh wuz drinkin' las' night an' e'd fall asleep an' den wake up fer one maw drink an' den fall asleep again. Early dis mawnin' 'e said out loud … I don' think 'e was talkin' t' me but I ansud anyway. He axed what was goin' t' happen to him an' I tol' a story about Juju. I tol' 'im dat sometimes dere's people dat can call up a spirit 'r a ghost 'r somethin' t' get eve'n wit' someb'dy who did 'em wrong an' dat dere ain't no callin' d' dev'l off once he got stoddit. I tol' 'im dat once d' demon got finished wit' dem Prussians, 'e's gonna walk right through dat door ovah dere an take d' massuh t' hell wit' im. I thought he w's gonna shoot me when 'e picked up dat gun but instead he said dat 'e wasn' gonna let d' pries' win, an' den 'e jus' blew 'is brains out.'

Lieutenant Cuthbert couldn't charge poor, long-suffering Jacob with anything. After all, he'd only told a spook story, the captain had taken his own life by his own hand.

'Go and get your wounds taken care of, Jacob. When the surgeon gets finished, come back here and clean up this mess. Then your duties to Captain Grey are finished. You can continue working here for a salary or you can go but, as far as I'm concerned, you're a free man.'

'Well, suh, if it's all d' same t' you. I gots nowhere t' go an' a free man c'n do whatevah he wants to, so I'll stay right heah an' do whut I w's learned t' do.'

When the office had emptied, the lieutenant remained behind for a few moments. He looked down at Percy and addressed him as if he was still alive. 'Well Pussy, I thought you were a cruel bastard when you were alive and, just because you're dead, my opinion of you hasn't changed. We're out of the priest-hunting business as long as I'm in charge. I don't give a rat's arse which church or what god these people have, I'll keep commerce going. The crown will get its blood money and I'll keep the peace in my own way. So instead of saying goodbye, Captain Percival Grey, I will say, 'Good riddance and I hope you get what you deserve. The priest won!'

Lieutenant, and now acting Captain, Cecil Cuthbert had assumed command.

*

The afternoon sun was quickly losing strength as the trio of travellers arrived at the road which skirted the eastern shore of Guitane Lough.

'We'll carry on for another hour before we make camp,' said Robert. 'From there, it's only about nine miles to Killarney and we should arrive by tomorrow afternoon. Then we can get you two some new clothes and get you on a coach the day after.'

Morna looked aghast. 'Ya mean shop-bought clothes?'

'Well we haven't got time to wait for you to make a dress, Morna, so yes, a shop-bought one.'

It seemed a ridiculous extravagance to the girl. 'Oy never h'd clothes dat came fr'm a shop.'

'Is there enough money?' asked Michael, doubtfully.

'Oh yes,' said Robert. 'Our friend Ned is a rich man and he's allowed us to borrow some of his treasure.'

The young couple were now riding double again, with Robert on the lead horse, when Robert's horse snorted and held its nose high in the air, running out its top lip.

'What is it?' asked the young man as the old sheriff reined his horse to a stop.

'He smells another horse,' said Robert and the old man strained his eyes to see upwind. They waited to see what would unfold and Robert took the horse pistol from his waistband and reprimed it. He tucked it back under his brat and waited, his hand still clutching the grip. Finally, a man appeared, slumped in the saddle of a filthy grey horse which had seen better days. He walked very slowly towards the three.

Robert turned to Michael. 'Whatever happens,' he said quietly, 'you dig your heels into that horse's sides and you get yourself and the girl out of harm's way.' He handed Ned's purse to Morna.

As the animal and rider approached, Robert saw first one man, then another two on foot behind him. A flicker of recognition passed across the sheriff's face. It was the one-eyed derelict from the bar in Killarney a couple of weeks ago, the same one who had expressed an unholy interest in the two Hobbies. He seemed to be unarmed, except for his three burly cohorts. Robert recognised them as the brothers of the livery boy who Ned had cuffed that same evening. The old one-eye spoke first.

'Dems me harses! Oy rec'gnoise 'em an' Oy saw dem farst.'

'They're my horses,' said Robert, firmly.

'No dey ain'. Ya shtole dem offa d' men wit' uniforms on.'

'They're mine,' repeated the sheriff.

'Well, now dey ain't,' said the old fellow. 'Dey belong t' me.' He squinted his one good eye and grinned at the girl lecherously. 'D' garl's moine too.'

Robert turned his horse slightly so the animal's head was out of the line of fire, and he fired through his cloak, hitting the one-eyed desperado in the stomach. The man disappeared into the gun smoke and, when it cleared, he was on the ground clutching his belly.

'Ya killed me, y' harse t'ief,' he rasped. 'Ya killed ol' one-eyed Jack Beatty, an' Oy curse ya.'

The flash from the priming pan had set light to the sheriff's leine, and he was too busy tamping out the fire to hear the man's words. Morna's eyes were as big as saucers, she had never seen a man shot before. What she didn't know was that her own father had met the same fate only days before.

'Aren't we going to help him?' asked Michael. His uncle ignored him and placed the last ball into the big gun, priming the flash pan as he rode slowly onwards, holding the weapon in his lap.

'What happens to the others?' Mikey protested.

Robert rode steadily onwards. 'You kill the head, the body dies.'

CHAPTER 32

Ned spent the night in a tiny grotto at the confluence of a stream and the Glengarriff River. The ceiling was no more than two feet high and the cave, which was under a huge flat stone, was about five feet deep. He hadn't slept much in the last few days and the exertion had taken a toll on his body. His food bag was empty and he poured the last few crumbs into his mouth before slipping off into a deep sleep.

When he woke, the sun was already high. He poked his head furtively out of the cave mouth and looked around, half expecting the Prussians to be waiting. The only sound he heard was the rush of a waterfall. He had calculated that Glengarriff was only a few miles away and he decided that, since no one there would remember who he was, he would venture to the edge of town and get some food, perhaps even some information. As he buried the grey Franciscan frock, he thought to himself; Oy dawn't t'ink Oy was cut out fer dis pries' business. It's fair too dangerous fer a man o' me gentle demeanor. It was late afternoon when he walked into the village.

The pretty little town beside the bay was a beehive of

activity. Red-coated soldiers walked around in groups of two or three and the locals were out in numbers, as if it was a holiday of some sort. A moment of panic swept over Ned as it occurred to him that perhaps there was going to be a hanging. If that was so, then the reason he'd not seen hide nor hair of the Prussians for the last couple of days might be that they'd caught up with the sheriff and the young couple. He found a pub called The Sheep's Tail on the outskirts of the village and he walked inside and placed a penny on the bar. Without asking, the proprietor put a pewter flagon of ale before him. Ned took a long draw on the cup before addressing the bartender.

'Is dere soome kind o' fair 'r celebration in town t'day?'

The taciturn barman's face broke out into a huge smile. 'There is, we're havin' a wake,' he said.

Ned felt the flesh on his arms raise into bumps. 'Who's d' guest o' honour?'

The barman answered with more than a hint of glee. 'It's dat mis'rable fecker, Pussy Grey!'

Ned kept up his casually disinterested expression and pondered for a moment before taking another slug of the brew.

'Did 'e get sick 'r sumpthing?'

The barman leaned in close. 'Da ward is, he blew 'is feckin' brains out.'

Ned drew back. 'Whoy would 'e do a t'ing loike dat?'

The bartender had an explanation, because bartenders always have. 'He w's huntin' fer a priest in d' mountains an' d' priest conjured oop 'n ellymental.'

Ned looked doubtful. 'We don' have dose in Ireland. Dey coome froom Afreeka.'

'Dose is ellyfants, ya eejit. Ellymentals aire soomt'n

like ghosts, boot dey ain't dead people. Ghosts c'n only scare d' shite out o' ya. Ellymentals were never people, dey're loike demons 'r sumpthin an' dey c'n killya if dey want ta.'

'What makes ya t'ink it w's one o' dose ellymentals? Maybe d' auld sod jus' come unglued.'

'Nah, ya don' know d' ha'f uv it, boyo. Da capt'n had a half doozin o' dese Proosian hoonters an' 'e sent d' hounds out t' catch d' priest. Two o' dem r' dead, one is crippled, anudder is blind an' d' las' two are disappeared. Da ellymental prob'ly took'em back t' hell wit' 'im.'

Ned was astonished to discover that his little games had produced such deadly consequences and he felt a slight twinge of guilt. 'Maybe somebuddy wuz jus' playin' wit' dem an' t'ings got outta hand.'

'No!' snapped the bartender. 'Dis ain' by d' hand of any mortal man.'

Ned's stomach grumbled, reminding him that it hadn't been serviced adequately for a few days and he asked the proprietor if there was anything to eat. The owner dished out a plate of boiled potatoes and Ned ate them, almost without chewing, and ordered another plateful with a pint of cool ale to wash it down. Before he left, he enquired if anyone had heard news about his cousin, Joe.

'Dat sheep-stealin' sod got 'imself killed by dem Proosians las' week, down on d' Beara,' said the barman summarily. Suddenly, any guilt about what had happened to the jaegers evaporated from Ned's conscience. He decided he would spend the night in Joe's hovel, then strike out for Kenmare tomorrow. There, he would retrieve the big horses and don his uniform for the last time.

*

Robert took the horse which the unfortunate bandit had abandoned so abruptly after the lead ball struck him.

'This will be of more use to us than to him,' he said. 'I'll turn him loose before we get to Muckross. I wouldn't want to get hung as a horse thief if someone recognises the beast.'

Mikey and Morna were speaking in voices so low that the old man couldn't decipher what was being said, but he knew that he was being judged nonetheless. Morna was still in shock at the brutality of the violence.

'Yer ooncle seems like such a quiet fella, an' den somet'in loike dis happ'ns, an' he doesn't ev'n change 'is expression.'

'That's how he's survived so long, Morna. He shows no emotion at all when he does something that would make someone else hesitate. Uncle Robert has always been a riddle to everyone but himself. He doesn't build up to anger, he just explodes and God help whoever is in his way.'

A little later, the three of them sat around a campfire and the silence was palpable. Robert spoke first.

'There's no joy in victory,' he said. 'Only perhaps the satisfaction that you get to live to see another day.' Mikey and the girl just listened, waiting to hear what would come next.

'If I had to shoot a mad dog, I would do it without a second's hesitation. I would feel remorse afterwards because the dog couldn't help being how he was. Sometimes people can't help what they are either but, when they pose a threat to others, there's no room for reason. I hope those three brothers have learned something. Their leader is lying in the road bleeding his guts out and for what? He probably couldn't get a job because of only having one good eye. Some simpletons think an infirmity is a curse from God. I think, if there is a God, that He has better things to do than to poke out a man's eye.'

'But ya saved us again,' protested the girl.

Robert was weary and he felt older than he'd ever felt before. 'Men like me were once a shilling a dozen. I did what I had to do and now it's the time for reasonable men, those who think before they act. They are Ireland's future.'

'Do you think Ireland will ever be free?' interjected Mikey.

'Free?' scoffed the old man. 'Free from the English? Yes, eventually, I have no doubt. As soon as it costs more to police the island than they can extract, they'll go back home and persecute their own. But free? I doubt it. There will always be the money lenders and the power brokers. I don't think people will ever see a government that gives more than lip service to the common man. There will always be those who can never have enough and those who have next to nothing.'

'That's grim,' said Mikey.

Robert shrugged. 'Just my opinion.'

After a long silence, Mikey asked, 'How's my brother Robbie?'

'He's married now,' replied Robert, 'but he hasn't changed much. You know Robbie. If the roof leaks, he'll buy a bucket to put under it and, when it stops raining, he'll toss the bucket out and forget about the leak. The next time it rains, he'll buy a bigger bucket and that's how he'll go until the roof falls in on him. Then he'll go and whine to your mother.'

'I never understood him,' said Michael.

'Neither did your father, boyo. You and Liam were so alike and Robbie was always jealous of that.'

'I never had any hard feelings towards him.'

'You have some difficult times ahead of you when you get back, Michael. Unless I miss my guess, Robbie has already proclaimed himself the heir apparent and you turning up is going to throw a turd into his soup.'

'But I don't want anything I didn't earn,' protested the lad.

'Well that's good because Robbie won't give you any quarter and I'll bet that, right now, he's making a case to your mother.'

Mikey thought for a moment. 'He always told me that, since he was the oldest, he would inherit the land and the shop. But I thought he was just teasing, trying to get under my skin, so I just ignored him.'

'Ah who knows, son, maybe it won't be as bad as I think once you and Morna get back to Gortalocca. But tread lightly because your mam will be so happy to see you that Robbie's nose will be put right out of joint. Make a bit of a fuss of him. Your brother's always liked being the center of attention.'

'How's Jamie? He was more of a brother to me than Robbie ever was.'

Robert allowed himself a smile at the thought of Jamie Clancy. 'Jamie's still working at Matt's forge. He's very much like your da. If you give him an idea, he runs with it. He has a new wife and a baby. You and him should build yourselves a blacksmith shop in Gortalocca.'

'I used to love watching Jamie and my father working. I swear those two could have a conversation without saying a word. Each seemed to know exactly what the other one was thinking. I thought Jamie would die when he lost his wife and children. I'm glad he's happy. What about Mick Sheridan?'

'Ah Mick Sheridan is immortal,' Robert smiled. 'That man hasn't changed in all the years I've known him. He's still as strong as an ox. He and I have talked about going into the horse trading business when I get back. I'm getting too old for this sheriff malarkey. It would suit me to just buy a decent farm, then buy and trade horses with Mick.'

Michael grinned. 'You'd get bored sure.'

'Well if I do, Mick and I can go out and have adventures, just little ones from now on, mind.' The two men laughed.

'I can't wait to see Mam. I wonder what she'll think of me giving up the priesthood.'

'You can take it from me, boyo, that it will make her happier than you could imagine, to have you safely back in Gortalocca, and married too. She can play the mother hen when you and Morna get a family started. She's a good mam but she'll make an even better grannny. Now you two get some sleep. I'll stand watch, just in case those three thugs get any ideas. If I get tired, I'll wake you and you can take over.'

Morna's curiosity had been aroused by the subject of rivalry between Mikey and his brother and she asked her husband about him.

'Robbie is… well, he's just Robbie. One minute you want to wring his neck like a chicken and the next minute you want to hug him. He can be a pain in the arse … too heavy for light work and too light for heavy work. He's best at telling stories, oh and drinkin' me mam's beer.'

'Oy could help yer mam run d' store,' declared the girl.

'Oh I don't know, Morna, we'll see. I think Robbie might have something to say about that. I'd like to have a pleasant homecoming and not to ruffle the sod's feathers … at least not for a while.'

Morna rolled over on her side and cuddled up next to Mikey. He lay looking up at the stars and thought about how best he should handle Robbie. He had to admit that it put a damper on the joy of going home.

CHAPTER 33

Ned was exhausted from the previous week's journey. The emotional toll, as well as the physical exertion, had left him nearly spent. The surges of adrenalin and the excitement of the chase was all but over and now he had only two tasks to perform. He would go back to Kenmare to retrieve the big horses, then return to Ballyshee for Mary Galvin and bring her back to Nenagh with him. He counted the coins he had in his purse and found there were almost four shillings, that would be plenty. His father had always told him that he could live on the smell of a greasy rag. He left the door gaping open on cousin Joe's cabin and began the walk to Kenmare.

He left the main road just outside Glengarriff and headed due north, towards the ridge of Barraboy Mountain. Once on the other side, he could reach Bunane before dark and get lodgings and a decent meal.

Tomorrow he should reach his goal, Kenmare, and after that he could rest his legs and let the horses do the walking for him. It was one of those days which came late in August, when the sun shone brightly and hot then, with no warning, a cloud would come and dump a rain shower from over the ocean.

*

Robert and his two charges reached Muckross long before midday and he turned the old horse loose as he'd planned. The nag was content to stop and graze and the trio headed towards the town.

'The first thing we have to do is find lodgings and a bath,' he told them. 'I have half of County Cork on my clothes. Then we'll get ourselves a proper meal and find you both some decent apparel for the coach ride to Limerick. You should be home in a few days.'

'What about you, Uncle Robert?' said Michael. 'I thought you'd be coming with us.'

'I have something I need to do and it might take a little while. I have to see what has become of my deputy.'

They were lucky in finding lodgings straight away and, in no time at all, they were fed and ready to do some shopping. Robert looked down and took stock of himself, he needed some clean and simple clothing. A new leine and a pair of breeches would do him but he had decided Mikey needed something more sophisticated, so he bought him a new blouse and a waistcoat, as well as a pair of trousers befitting a gentleman. Morna stood waiting for them, gazing excitedly at the dresses which hung around the shop and, by the time the men were fitted out, she had already selected a dress she liked and she pointed to it.

'No,' said Robert. The girl looked crestfallen. 'We have to go to a proper woman's clothier, my dear. There's nothing suitable in here.'

A few doors away there was a dress shop and, when Robert opened the door, a little bell on it announced their entrance. He ushered Morna and Michael inside the shop and closed the door behind them. The girl looked around her in wonderment. Dresses more magnificent than anything she had ever seen hung in various stages of readiness. She didn't even notice when a girl of about her own age, followed by a woman in her forties, entered the shop from a back room. Both women were dressed stylishly and were beautifully coiffured. The older woman politely inclined her head towards the two gentlemen and, when she turned her attention to the barefooted, waif-like creature who was with them, her expression soured. She instantly assumed that Morna was a strumpet and Morna didn't help matters when her attention was captivated by a red dress.

'No, not that one, m'dear,' said Robert, kindly, and he took a forest green dress off its hanger and held it up against her. The older woman addressed Robert, haughtily.

'That dress will cost you a pound, sir, and I doubt you'll be wanting to spend that much.'

Robert turned to the young couple and he rolled his eyes. 'I'll handle this,' he whispered.

'My nephew and his bride will be travelling to Tipperary tomorrow, to the family estate,' he said, his tone even more condescending than hers. 'We have just returned from an arduous journey and, if you don't want our business, then we'll be glad to take it elsewhere.'

The woman's face flushed red and the young seamstress put her hand over her mouth to stifle a giggle.

'Mother,' she said, 'that dress has been hanging there for over a year. Even if someone could afford it, they wouldn't be able to fit in it.'

The shop owner attempted to hide her humiliation by snapping at her daughter. 'Well then, you handle the transaction, and don't accept less than ten shillings.' With that, she wheeled around and flounced out the same way she'd come in.

'Don't moind me mam,' the seamstress said to Robert, her accent reverting back to Cork in the absence of her mother. 'Sometoimes she fergets where she came from.

'Sometimes we all do,' he said and smiled at her.

'Youse boys go an' git yerselves lost fer a coople o' hours. When ye get back, yer princess'll be all ready.'

Robert bowed at the waist to the young woman. 'Then we leave her in your capable hands, miss,' he said, and hustled Michael out the door and into the street. 'Let's go and get ourselves a beer, boyo, sometimes it's best to leave the girls to themselves.'

*

The sun was stretching out its last few fingers of peach-coloured light from beyond the mountains when Ned arrived in Bunane. He was tired and hungry, but first he needed a pitcher of ale to wet his parched throat. He trudged into a bar and it was uncomfortably crowded with men. He bought a jug of beer and found a place to sit outside. He didn't even bother to use the flagon but just upended the jug and didn't give a damn when a good deal of it escaped the corners of his mouth and dribbled down the front of his shirt.

'What day is it?' he asked a passerby.

'It's d' bes' day o' me life,' replied the man jovially. It wasn't quite the answer that Ned had expected, but he tipped the jug to the merry fellow and took another huge gulp, this time letting it linger in his mouth for a few seconds before swallowing.

A heated discussion was underway inside the bar as to what manner of creature could kill dozens of redcoats and dozens of Prussian mercenaries. Some suggested it was a kelpie who had shape-shifted into a Franciscan. Others insisted that a demon from hell had come to seek vengeance on Pussy Grey, who had sent so many souls there that it was becoming overcrowded with Corkmen. Finally, the proprietor decided there was too much arguing and not enough drinking, and he kicked both sides out. The debate didn't end there, it merely changed venues and, when they got outside the bar, they sought to get Ned involved.

'Whatta ya say, stranger?' said one. 'Do ya t'ink it was a demon 'r a kelpie?'

Ned thought for a moment. 'Maybe it w's a Carkman,' he said, 'pissed off at bein' sent t' hell.' His answer was met with derision.

'Ah sure, all Carkmen are divils alright, but not ev'n a Kerryman could do all dat. How do ya explain dat Poosy's black sarvent saw a ghost 'r sumpthin' come t'rough a locked door, an' put a gun up to d' auld bastard's head an' blow 'is brains out? C'n a Carkman do dat?' Ned had to agree that he didn't think that eve a Corkman could walk through locked doors.

He began to lose interest in the discussion as the beer went to his head and he went back inside the bar. He purchased a few boiled potatoes, which he placed in his food sack, and he found a stable to spend the night. He had hoped to glean some information in the bar, but all he'd got was a bit tipsy and a few spuds. He fell asleep before he'd finished eating the first one.

*

Robert and Michael had a few flagons of good ale in The Brown Cow. The proprietor was an excellent fiddle-player and they lost themselves in the music. Already, the memory of their adventure had begun to alter and the hardships they'd endured didn't seem so bad, now that the end of the journey was in sight.

'I wonder what happened in Ballyshee after we left,' said Michael, rhetorically. The statement brought the old man back to the present and, even though the fiddler played on, neither of them heard the music now.

'I don't think Percival would suffer the indignation of being made a fool of lightly,' said Robert. 'I wouldn't put it past him to have done something ugly.' Both men grew sombre, each silently speculating as to what kind of nefarious retribution the unstable captain might have wreaked upon the village.

'Don't say anything about this to Morna,' said the old man. 'We'll find out in due course what, if anything, happened and there's no need to worry her about her parents now.'

The proprietor stopped playing when a man rushed into the bar and tugged excitedly at his sleeve. The fiddler put his instrument down and listened in rapt attention as the man spoke quietly but in an animated fashion. Now and then, the owner stopped him and asked questions and the man answered, continuing his monologue for several minutes.

'Something's going on,' said Robert. 'As soon as yer man's gone, I'll ask the proprietor. I never knew a musician who could keep a secret.'

The old sheriff waited a while before discreetly approaching the men at the bar, who were already discussing the latest gossip. He listened for a while, then returned to the table with a smile on his face.

'Well, it sounds like Ned is still alive.' he said, his smile broadening.

'How do you know?' asked Mikey.

'Those blokes are saying that a giant ghost, dressed like a Franciscan priest, has slain hundreds of English soldiers in West Cork. You can't kill an apparition, so that means he's still alive, or at least he was when the rumours began.'

'And how is he supposed to have managed that?'

'They say he sticks his finger into the muzzle of the muskets when someone fires at him, and the guns explode.'

'That's daft!'

'It gets even better. Percival Grey is dead. They're saying the priest entered a locked room and blew his brains out.'

'Good riddance! Wait, how do you think Ned did that?'

Robert chuckled. 'I don't know how he walked through the locked door but once he was in, knowing Ned, he probably talked the old bastard to death. A few times, when he wouldn't shut up, I've thought about putting a pistol to my head … or his.'

The old man's mood was buoyed by the rumours from West Cork and he decided that another change of plans was in order. 'C'mon, boyo. We'll go to the stage depot in town,' he said, 'and we'll get you and Morna on a coach to Limerick as soon as we can. I'll get myself a ride down to Kenmare and start looking for my erstwhile partner. He has a lot of explaining to do.'

There was a coach leaving for Limerick at nine o'clock the following morning, Robert counted out the money for the clerk. The tickets were expensive at three shillings apiece but the stage would arrive late afternoon the next day.

'That's fast!' exclaimed Mikey.

Robert shrugged. 'They change horses a few times so they can gallop all the way,' he replied. 'You should be home in a couple of days.' His mind was on getting to Kenmare as fast as he could, so he arranged a coach for himself.

'Yu'll hafta ride up front wit' d' driver,' the clerk informed him officiously. 'D' coach is full o' gentry goin' t' Moll's Gap. After dat, ya c'n ride below.'

'Not a problem,' answered the old man. 'I'll be tying my horses to the back.'

'Dat'll be 'n extra penny, so,' said the man tartly.

Robert didn't feel like arguing, even though he wanted to slap the impertinent sod. He handed the extra penny to the man and cursed his arrogance under his breath. The clerk slipped the coin into his own pocket.

They arrived back at the dress shop just as the middle-aged woman and her daughter were putting the final touches to the dress and they both stopped dead in their tracks. Morna was a grand sight to behold. The long green dress accented her eyes and the lace collar framed her delicate face. The women had talked her into wearing her red hair loose around her shoulders and now they were trying to talk her into wearing shoes.

'Dey pinch me toes,' she had said, 'an' dey make me feet sweat.' The older woman tried to convince her, so she could make another sale, but Morna pinched her lips shut, wrinkled her nose and wouldn't budge on the subject. The men were amused by the scene.

'I'd like to be there the first time your mam and Morna butt heads,' laughed Robert.

Michael raised his eyebrows. 'Ah, it'll be a heavyweight contest alright,' he replied.

CHAPTER 34

Ned woke up with a terrible fierce hangover from drinking too much beer the night before on an empty stomach. His belly growled like a pack of hungry dogs and he had to use his thumb and forefinger to pry open his eyelids. Shite, he thought, Oy'm losin' me touch. The muscles in his legs felt like knots. He tried to eat one of the boiled potatoes but even the smell of it made him feel sick. He forced himself to get up and his head spun. His lips felt like they were glued shut and, when he put his fingers against them, they felt like parchment. Jayzus Croist, he thought, Oy need t' get s'me water inside me. He heard the sound of a stream gurgling at the side of the road and, opening his eyes just a crack, he walked towards the sound of the water and stared at his reflection. Jayzus, Oy look aulder den d' sheriff, he thought and stepped into the icy cold brook. Agh! I have to piss now! He waded further out and settled slowly down into the water.

'Got ten more miles t' walk t'day', he told himself out loud, 'an' den Oy c'n set me arse on a harse an' let him do d' wark.' He closed his eyes now and thought about the girl who was waiting for him in Ballyshee, letting his mind drift away. He hadn't heard a wagon pull up on the road behind him.

'Is dis a proivit conversation?' Ned almost jumped out of his skin and he whipped his head around to see a grizzled old man with brown teeth and a felt cap, sitting on the cart. 'Or do y' mind if Oy jine in?' The old fellow cackled at his own joke.

'Oy w's just discoosin' t'ings wit'meself,' croaked Ned.

'Den yer a madman, so?'

'Oy mus' be,' replied Ned, gathering his senses. 'Oy wannid t' go on 'n adventure an' Oy got more den Oy bargained fer.'

'Oy'm headin' t' Kenmare,' replied the old codger. 'Oy'll trade ya a ride fer yer story.'

Ned stood up, using his hands against his knees to take the strain from his aching muscles, and he waded back out of the water. He hobbled over to the wagon.

'Oy t'ank ya, sar, an' if ya gimme a hand t' get up on dat wagon, me legs'll t'ank ya too.' The old fellow extended a calloused hand and hauled Ned up onto the seat beside him. Ned groaned as he sat.

'Ya looks loike d' cat ate cha an' shat ya out on a dungpile, boyo,' grumbled the old fellow. Ned regarded him with slight indignance and the driver clicked his tongue to gee up the horse. They started out to Kenmare.

*

Robert's stage coach was due to leave earlier than the one Michael and Morna were taking and, before he boarded it, he handed his nephew the purse and a note.

'This is for your mam.' Michael looked at the note questioningly, then back at the old sheriff. 'It's an I.O.U. We've been spending Ned's money and I want to make certain he gets it all back, and a bit more besides.' Mikey nodded and the two men shook hands. When Robert extended his hand to Morna, she pushed it aside and embraced him in a hug, planting a kiss on his cheek.

'T'ankya, Ooncle Robbie. We'll be seein' ya in a coople o' weeks.' Robert blushed and, without looking back, he climbed up onto the seat next to the driver.

The coach driver was a taciturn-looking, middle-aged man who had made the trip so many times that, whenever they rode past something of interest, he would spout a few facts about it in monotone, as if he'd spoken the lines a thousand times before. He stopped the coach for a few moments above Killarney's lakes for his passengers to admire the view below. The old sheriff didn't pay much attention to the scenery, taking the opportunity to check on the two Hobbies tied to the back of the stage. The durable little horses had handled the climb well and, as Robert checked their hooves, the driver came back to admire the beasts.

'Dey ain't many like dat left,' he remarked, then went back to the gentry and helped a woman back into the coach. It wasn't long before they arrived at Moll's Gap, where the tourists reclaimed their luggage and headed for the inn. Robert watered his horses as the driver changed teams on the coach. They galloped swiftly towards Kenmare while Robert slept inside the empty compartment, which was still scented with the perfume worn by the gentlewoman.

*

Ned related his story in dribs and drabs to the driver, who'd offered him a ride in exchange for the tale. A couple of times, he fell asleep in the middle of a sentence and the old man elbowed him in the ribs to wake him up.

'If ya stick me 'n d' ribs wit' yer boney elbow ag'in, Oy swear Oy'll get off an' walk t' Kenmare.'

This story was too good to miss so the codger apologised and asked him to carry on. Most Irish stories needed embellishment to make them dramatic but the young deputy's needed neither exaggeration nor decoration. He had just finished his tale when they rode into Kenmare.

'Dat wuz d' bes' story Oy ever heared, boyo! Ya mus' be d' bes' bullshitter 'n all Oireland,' said the old fellow. Ned shook his hand, thanked him for the ride, and made his way straight to the office of Sheriff Wentworth.

*

Robert was awakened by a sharp rap on the outside of the coach and the driver's voice, yelling in monotone.

'Five minutes to Kenmare!'

The old man opened his eyes and was disorientated at first, until he shook the cobwebs from his head. I'll rest here for the night, he told himself, then I'll head down to the Beara to find Ned. When the coach jerked to a halt, he opened the door and untied his horses. He would check in with Sheriff Wentworth as soon as he had seen to the animals.

*

Ned was ushered into Sheriff Wentworth's office where the sheriff sat, stern-faced and not at all the cordial fellow he'd been on the previous visit.

'Sit!' he ordered, motioning to a chair in front of his desk. 'What has been going on in Cork? I've got conflicting reports and none of them make any sense.' Ned eyed up the bars on the office window. He hadn't forgotten being a 'guest' in the gaol at Glengarriff and he was already making plans in his head. The young sheriff noticed and he smiled.

'You'll bend the bars on my window if you use that thick Cork skull of yours to escape,' he said, his tone more benign now. 'You're not in trouble. I just want to know what mischief you and Sheriff D'Arcy have been up to.'

'We got separated a week ago. Oy don' know what d' sheriff did, boot Oy jus' wannid t' get outta dere.'

Nigel Wentworth narrowed his eyes. 'What have you heard about this murderous Franciscan?'

Ned looked a little sheepish and the sheriff knew that whatever he said next was going to be a lie. 'Oy don' know a t'ink about any priest.' The young man tried to wet his lips with his tongue but he seemed to have run out of spit.

The sheriff was amused by the deputy's distress and he poured a tumbler of water from a glass pitcher on his desk. He extended it to Ned and, when the young man reached for it, he didn't relinquish his grip.

'Not so fast,' he said. 'You give me something and I'll return the favour. Let's start at the beginning, shall we? Is your given name Ned Flood?'

'No, sar, Oy w's baptised, Edmund Flood.'

'You see?' said the sheriff, releasing his grip on the glass. 'That wasn't difficult, was it, Edmund?' Ned took a sip of the water, hoping it would help to detach his tongue from the roof of his mouth. It didn't.

'I'm sure you must be hungry, Edmund.' The sheriff rang a little bell on his desk and an orderly came in immediately. He snapped a salute and the sheriff returned it casually. 'As you were,' he said. 'Bring this man some supper and make sure it's from my own kitchen.'

His subordinate looked pained. 'But, sar,' he objected, 'den dere won't be enough fer yerself.' The sheriff waved him away.

Ned was nobody's fool and he was well aware that kindness could be just as effective in procuring the truth as a lash. He decided to devour everything he was given and then, at least, he'd have a full stomach to face whatever was to come. The young sheriff picked a book up from his desk and pretended to read it, allowing Ned to stew in his own juice while he waited.

There was an impatient knock at the door of the office and, without looking up, Sheriff Wentworth bid the caller to enter. A police sergeant came in and shot a dirty look at Ned before whispering something in the sheriff's ear.

'Well, don't keep the man waiting,' said Wentworth cordially, as if he'd been expecting someone. 'Bring him in.' Robert D'Arcy strode into the office and he had the look of a wild boar gathering itself for a charge. Sheriff Wentworth took one look at the old man and he felt the hair on the back of his neck rise. He was looking at death and death was staring right back at him. He glanced at the pistol on his desk.

'Don't even think about it,' snarled Robert, through clenched teeth. The young officer turned his palms outwards in a sign of surrender.

'That will be all, sergeant,' he said to the trooper. 'Tell the orderly to bring more food. This might take some time.'

Robert turned his attention from Sheriff Wentworth and addressed Ned.

'You alright, boyo?'

Ned nodded. 'Oy woulda been, sar,' he said, 'if you hadn't barged in an' scared d' shit outta d' sheriff. 'E w's just goin' t' feed me.'

Robert turned back to the young man sitting behind the desk. Ned was clearly not in any danger and so his anger began to abate a little.

'Interrogating another man's deputy, before the man can give a report to his own superior, is, at best, bad manners.'

Nigel gave it a moment's thought before he spoke. He knew he was dealing with a hair trigger and a short fuse.

'I apologise, sir. I had been getting contradictory and, frankly, nonsensical reports from Cork and I needed to know what I was dealing with.'

'For what purpose?' snarled Robert.

Wentworth's face flushed. 'I'm afraid to say that it was to satisfy my own inherent curiosity, sir.'

'No matter what you hear, it must be kept in confidence, do you understand?'

'You have my word as an officer and a gentleman, sir.'

Just then, plates of food were brought in and, when the orderly had left the room, the old man turned to his deputy.

'Very well, Ned, proceed. Start from when we parted company on the ridge above Ballyshee. Don't embellish anything and don't leave anything out.'

'Whut about d' gaol-break, sar?' enquired Ned, innocently.

'Hold your whisht!' snapped D'arcy.

Wentworth squirmed in his seat like a boy waiting to hear a story about pirates or ghosts. 'Oh please,' he implored, 'I want to hear it all.'

Robert relented and he had begun to tell the part of the story where they'd got themselves locked up in

Percy's murder hole, when Wentworth stopped him.

'Can I write this down?' he asked eagerly. 'Perhaps I'll write a famous novel about it one day!'

Robert scowled at the interruption. 'The Irish can't read, ya piss drip. You'd have to change the hero into an Englishman … and have him pursued by throngs of mad Irishmen.'

'…or hoards of red Indian savages in the New World!' cried Nigel.

Ned spoke around a mouthful of food, 'Dey got red Injun whores dere?'

'You just shut up and eat your food,' growled the old man. 'You'll get your turn.'

Nigel scribbled notes as the two men took turns in telling their story. It went on well into the night and, by the end of the story, Wentworth was sure he had the makings of a best seller.

'Are you men going back to Tipp now?' he asked.

'Oy've gotta make a trip back t' Ballyshee, farst,' said Ned.

'There is no Ballyshee,' responded Wentworth. 'The annihilation of that village was Grey's last atrocity.'

'Oy saw 'im burn d' town from on d' hill,' said Ned plaintively. 'What else happ'ned?'

The young sheriff told them what he'd heard and Ned thought he was going to be sick. He turned to Robert who gave him a pitying look.

'Oy gotta go, anyways,' Ned told him.

'From now on, we go as a team,' said Robert. 'Go and get yourself some sleep. The sheriff and I have business to discuss. We'll leave tomorrow.'

CHAPTER 35

Things were not going at all well in Tipperary. Acting Sheriff Higgins was experiencing serious discipline problems with his deputies. The men had taken to drinking whilst on duty and the respect which the old sheriff had worked hard to earn was quickly being squandered. The men had begun to extort money as bribes from shopkeepers and vendors, and Nenagh town was becoming a dangerous place to be. Higgins spent more time filling out paperwork to cover the actions of his own men than he did carrying out his own duties. It had started to unravel almost as soon as D'Arcy left and now, it was rapidly descending into anarchy.

Higgins decided that his own failure to mete out discipline was to blame and he resolved to get things back under control. He called the sergeant, who was acting as his adjutant, into his office. The sergeant didn't salute but Higgins ignored the insubordination and told him that he wanted punishment details assigned to the miscreants.

The man drew in his breath. 'The men aren't going to like this,' he said doubtfully.

'This isn't a bloody democracy, sergeant,' said Higgins. 'I want patrols placed on the roads leading in and out of Nenagh, every night.'

The man sneered at his superior. 'Well at least the men will be able to drink in peace,' he scoffed and, without being dismissed, he turned and left the room, slamming the door behind him. Higgins sighed and returned to his paperwork.

*

Things weren't going too well up in Gortalocca either. At first there had been good news when Robbie announced that his wife, May, was with child. Then he had begun to put forward his case to his mother. Since she lived in a bigger cottage all by herself, he'd said, it would make sense for her to move over to Paddy's old place and for he and May to move into the Flynn cottage. He had begun by tentatively making the suggestion then gradually, but inexorably, he arrived at the point where he asked Roisin outright when she was going to move. Robbie was very careful to avoid a full-on confrontation with his mother because that would result in her digging her heels in, and he would never get his way. He switched on his charm and utilised her coming grandchild as leverage. Finally, he convinced Roisin of the logic of his argument and they moved her possessions to the little cottage across the street. There was one altercation, however, and it concerned the big mirror over the fireplace. When Jamie Clancy had come to move it, at Roisin's request, he and Robbie almost came to blows, with Robbie claiming it belonged to the house, not to his mother, and Jamie threatening to smash it over Robbie's head. The mirror was moved to the smaller cottage but it was never hung, a hollow victory.

Roisin noticed that the stock on the shelves of Hogan's was becoming sparse, as items that were being sold weren't replaced. When she brought the subject up with Robbie, he became defensive, blaming the vendors for unreliable deliveries. Roisin prayed that she could hold her world together long enough for Robert D'Arcy to arrive back. He would stand for no nonsense and would put things straight in short order.

Things came to a head when a beer vendor knocked on her door and announced there would be no further deliveries until the overdue accounts had been honoured. Roisin was mortified. In all the years that she had run the shop, the bills had always been paid on delivery of the merchandise. When she brought the situation to Robbie's attention, he told her that he was the man of the house now and that he would run affairs his own way. She had no doubt that, in a very short time, everything that she and her husband had worked for would be lost. For now, Roisin decided that the best way to handle the situation was for her to stay away from Robbie … would that he would let her.

*

Robert slipped quietly into the barracks where the unmarried deputies were housed. Ned was snoring peacefully and Robert made himself comfortable on the cot next to him. The old man lay on his back and looked into the blackness of the dark room. I wonder if being dead is like this, he pondered. He found it hard to sleep, tossing and turning until, just as the sky had begun to get light outside and he had started to drift off into a deep sleep, Ned woke from his slumber.

'Aire we ready t' leave,' he whispered quietly, so as not to wake the other men.

'We've just got a few things to do, Ned, and then we'll be gone before any of these beauties are up and about.'

They made their way out to the stables and there, waiting for them, was Sheriff Wentworth. He was holding a sack.

'I only wish I could go with you boys,' he said, grinning. 'I have no doubt that if I did, I'd have some stories to tell my grandchildren.' He shook Ned's hand enthusiastically. 'I'll send an autographed copy of my book to you in Mary Land,' he told him. Then he turned to Robert and shook his hand. 'I hope I shall see you again, sir. It has been an honour to meet you.' He handed the old man a horse pistol and the sack of provisions. The men saddled up and rode away, leaving Nigel's words echoing in the darkness.

'Safe home, gentlemen.'

'Whadda we got t' do?' asked the deputy.

'Ride to Ballyshee, of course!' said the sheriff, 'Our host has provisioned us.'

Robert felt invigorated but his high spirits were somewhat tempered by the grim look on his companion's face. He had accomplished his mission so far and now he was determined to help Ned find the girl.

'If we take d' road t'ward Clonkeen, we c'n turn off after Morley's Bridge an' be in Ballyshee by late afternoon,' said Ned, rhetorically, and he spurred the Hobby into a gallop. They slowed their horses to a jog as they passed through Kilgarvan an hour later. The lower rim of the sun had just cleared the mountains to the east and the golden disk contrasted against the purple and indigo of the slopes. A few miles more and they would cross the bridge which marked the turn towards the looming peaks. When they arrived at the bridge, there were no redcoats guarding the crossing. The horses' hoofbeats drummed across the old stone arch, disturbing the morning silence.

'We'll rest the horses here for ten minutes, Ned. They need water and I need to stretch my legs.' They both dismounted and walked their animals down to the stream's edge, in the shadow of a stone archway.

They were soon on the road again, riding helter skelter towards Inchee Bridge. Robert recalled that the crossing had been well-manned when he, Mikey and Morna had been there some days before and he told Ned it was better for them to dismount before they reached the bridge and for one of them to approach it on foot first. The younger man was the most likely candidate as his accent would not arouse suspicion if there were indeed troops guarding it. Ned set off and, after what seemed like an eternity to Robert, he returned.

'Ain' no troops dere,' he said abruptly. Robert knew that the nearer they got to Ballyshee, the more anxious the young man was becoming and he had no doubt considered the scouting exercise to be a waste of their time. It was up to Robert to ensure that they didn't become careless now that their final mission had almost reached its culmination.

A little over two miles more and the road made an abrupt turn towards the south. This is where they had forded the river and encountered the two French mercenaries. Robert sniffed the air, hoping that the bodies had been found. The last thing he wanted to see now was the decaying corpses of the two men he had assassinated. The bodies had gone and Robert glanced at the place where the skirmish had occurred. He knew that he had been lucky once again but he also knew that, if he kept up this man-of-action malarkey, one day soon it would be his own name on the parchment scroll that welcomed him to hell.

The sun was almost directly overhead as they climbed up the first slope from the river basin. The forest gave way to scattered, stunted trees, then to yellow gorse and purple heather amidst wiry mountain grass. When they reached the peak of the first ridge, Ned strained his eyes to try and see past the next one, Ballyshee was just beyond it. The old man was conscious of Ned's sense of urgency but he was also dreading what they would find. Years of fighting other people's wars in Europe meant he was all too familiar with the cruelties inflicted by occupying troops on civilian populations and it had always repulsed him. It was one thing to face armed troops in battle, but to commit one-sided atrocities on farm communities was spiteful and barbaric.

Finally, they crossed the last forested valley and the two men steeled themselves for what lay ahead. They walked the Hobbies up the steep slope to the crest and there, below them, lay the ruins of what was once a hard-working little township. Ballyshee had been obliterated. The mud cottages lay collapsed upon themselves, the clay from which they'd been made becoming part of the earth once more. The few stone structures were burnt-out shells and the thatch, which was now in ashes, covered the charred interiors with a fine dust which, from this distance, looked like snow. The walls had already begun to crumble and in a few years time, what were once homes, full of life, would be unrecognisable piles of stones as the Cork landscape devoured the bones of the village.

The wind had picked up now and it blew into the men's faces, bringing with it the sickly stench of decaying flesh. The slopes were speckled with the carcasses of dead livestock, mostly the sheep which the town had relied upon for its existence. As the two descended slowly into the valley, the scope and magnitude of the destruction became ever more apparent. Rooks, ravens and buzzards circled overhead, anticipating the macabre feast which lay scattered on the slopes. They rode past a dead donkey, its eyes milky and its belly swollen. Robert saw that it had received a mortal wound and had managed to drag itself up the slopes in the hope of reaching safety. The droning buzz of bluebottle flies and the raucous cry of carrion birds broke the silence. It occurred to Robert that death was not as quiet as one would think.

Any crops which could be burned had been incinerated, the potatoes and other root crops trampled on by horses. There was evidence that what little remained had been gathered by the survivors. A long rectangular pit of newly-turned earth, which had already been dug through by foxes and dogs, was near the forge. A dug-out hollow exposed the skeletal remains of its newest occupant, as it seemed to reach for the heavens in a grotesque post-mortem plea. Robert knew it to be a hastily-dug mass grave. He had seen this before. Ned had not.

Robert roused the young man from his shock. 'We need a plan,' he said abruptly.

Ned looked at the old man with dead eyes, 'Oy t'ink dis may be our fault.'

Irritation flushed the old man's face. 'It would have happened anyway, even if that bastard Grey had found Michael here.' His anger was not so much channeled at Ned but at the prospect that it might indeed be his fault.

'Is one man's loife warth all dis?' said Ned, flatly.

'Well you can sit here and mourn all you want. You can even dig a grave for yourself if you choose, but I'm going to find out what happened to the Galvin girl.' The old man climbed laboriously up onto his horse. 'When you've finished here, you can meet me in Lackabaun. The people there might know something.'

Robert spurred the Hobbie hard, taking out his frustration on the horse and, after only a few minutes had passed, he heard the sound of hoofbeats coming up fast behind him. He slowed and let the deputy catch up and together they took one last look down on the townland from the heights above, the wind whipping the ashes up into a swirling blizzard, partially obscuring the once thriving and vibrant settlement of Ballyshee.

CHAPTER 36

Roisin soon settled into the little cottage which Paddy Shevlin had built for his family years before. The old pig farmer must have left a little of his spirit there because, despite the situation with Robbie, she couldn't help but smile when she thought about Paddy. He may have smelled like a pig, but never was there a better-hearted man in the village of Gortalocca. She was pleased to be right next door to Jamie Clancy and his wife. Jamie made sure to call in on her every day and his wife brought their baby to visit almost as often. Roisin was happy to practice her grandmother skills with the Clancy child.

Mick Sheridan dropped in to see her every Sunday, with his pony trap, and he took her to the service at the Church of Ireland in nearby Johnstown. They both knew she needed to keep up appearances if she was to maintain the ruse which Liam had used to acquire the property. By all outward appearances, she was still a Protestant, but that was just to keep the English from confiscating the land. Mick was a gentleman and, when they neared the church, he would let Roisin dismount and walk into the chapel as a properly-mourning new widow. It would keep the tongues from wagging.

Robbie had got what he wanted for now and so he gave his mother a wide berth. She saw him occasionally as he walked over to open the shop but when she had any business to take care of, or if she needed any groceries, she would let Jamie's wife do it for her.

She was sweeping out the house one morning when Robbie, seemingly on his way to open the shop, saw her and waved. It was the first acknowledgement she'd had from him since he'd decided he was the boss, and she took one hand off her broom, returning the gesture half-heartedly. She went about her business and Robbie walked over towards her. It was too late for her to go back inside the house and so she stood waiting. He was amiable and gracious towards her and Roisin knew him well enough to know that meant he wanted something.

'I haven't seen ya in a couple o' days, Mam,' he chirped.

'It's been over a week since you kicked me out of my own house,' she said acidly.

'Aw, Mam. I t'ought we'd been t'rough all dat.'

'Oh no,' she replied, 'not by a long chalk.'

'Aw well, dat's not what I come over t' talk t' ya about.' He reached over to put his hand on her arm and she put it behind her back involuntarily. He pulled his hand back as if he'd been scalded.

'What do you want, Robbie?'

'Aw Jayzus, Mammy! Is dat any way t' talk t' yer only son?'

Roisin bristled, both at his insincere tone and at the words he spoke, but she held her composure. Robbie thought he was doing well so far because she hadn't taken a swing at him with the broom, so he persevered.

'Dat auld sod, Gleeson, says if I don't reckon wit' d' bill for d' poteen an' d' beer, him an' his sons are goin' t' come over an' cut me toes off.'

'Isn't that grand,' she replied. 'You won't have to cut your toenails, so.'

'Mam, I'm serious. If you'd seen 'is face when he said it, you'd know.'

'How much do you owe?'

'Almos' eight shillin's.'

'Eight shillings? However did you manage to run up that kind of a bill, Robert?'

Robbie knew he was in hot water now. His mother only called him by his full name when she was about to lower the boom or, in this case, the broom.

'Cuz d' t'ief charges more when 'e sells 'is gutrottin' swill on account.'

'Tell Gleeson that I think it's only fair he charges you a shilling a toe. Tell him, that way, he owes you two more barrels.'

'Mam, please,' he pleaded. 'Yer makin' jokes an' dis is serious.'

'You told me you're the man of the house. Now you want to be a little boy again?'

'Ah ferget what I said, I was in me cups. I'll always be yer boy, won't I Mammy?' Robbie had managed to dig himself out of some of his worst holes with this tactic and it seemed to be working again.

'Your father and I have some savings,' she relented. 'I'll bail you out … but just this once, mind.'

Robbie hugged his mother and kissed her on the cheek. He knew those savings had always been sacred to his family and now he had finally broken the piggy bank.

Roisin went back inside and, when she came back out, she handed him the money. Robbie whistled as he walked away and Roisin went about her work, eight shillings the poorer.

*

Michael and Morna boarded the coach in Limerick to embark on their journey to Nenagh. They would arrive in just a few hours.

Robert and his young companion rode into the village of Lackabaun in the late afternoon. They could feel eyes upon them as the villagers cast furtive glances at the two strangers riding fine Irish horses. If eye contact was made, the villagers would look away and pretend to be otherwise occupied.

'You'd better do the talking, Ned. I'll just pretend to be your idiot companion … again.'

Ned ignored Robert's attempt at levity. 'It's bedder dat way, sar,' he said. 'Oy don't t'ink anybody'll be talkin' t' strangers here, t'day.'

They stopped outside the village shop. It was the local bar, grocery and hardware store and, as such, was the centre of commerce in the little township. For the two men, it was also to be the source of the information they needed. While Robert tied the horses, Ned went inside and ordered two beers.

When Robert walked in, Ned brought one of the tankards over and set it on a little table, leaving the other on the bar.

'You set here, sar,' he told his companion, 'an' if anybuddy tries t' talk t' ya, tell'em yer deef.'

Ned strolled back to the bar and, soon, he had become engaged in conversation with the proprietess.

The plain, dowdy woman was captivated by the young man who seemed to have money to spend and it wasn't long before Ned was back at the table with a huge smile spread across his face.

'We got 'er!' he hissed, triumphantly. 'She has a cousin lives here in d' village an' she's stayin' at 'er house.' Robert went to stand up. 'Set down, sar. She waited sixteen years fer me t' show up. She c'n wait 'til Oy finished me beer.'

Robert dropped back. 'You're so feckin' Irish,' he repied, his face deadpan.

They made their way to the neat little whitewashed cottage which the woman in the bar had indicated and Robert stayed mounted, holding Ned's horse, while the young man knocked on the door. A blonde girl who looked to be in her late teens answered, she was holding an infant. She looked curiously from Ned to Robert and back to Ned, who spoke first.

'Oy'm here t' see Mary Galvin,' he announced.

The woman's jaw fell slack. 'Den ye are d' hoywaymen she's been rattlin' about. Oy t'ought she w's daft, what wit' all dat's happ'ned her.' Ned assured her that he was not the invention of a distressed girl. 'Oy'll go an' ask if she'll see ya.'

Ned could see into the little cabin and, as his eyes adjusted to the dim light inside, he saw Mary cowering in a corner. 'You tell'er dat Oy walked across half 'o Ireland t' git back here an' if she t'inks she c'n get rid o' me dat easy, den she really is daft.'

Mary got up with an effort and shuffled to the door. Her long blonde hair hung in disarray.

'Oy don' t'ink you'll want me anymore, Ned,' she said, almost in tears. 'Oy don' tink any r'spectable man'll want me anymore.'

'Oy heard what happ'ned in Ballyshee an' Oy still came back fer ya. So git yer shtuff an' we'll get outta here an' go far away.'

Mary looked at her cousin. 'Well, Breda,' she said, 'it's goodboy so. Oy prob'ly won' ever be back again.' The two cousins embraced, both trying to hold back the tears. After a moment, Mary pulled herself away and locked the young woman's eyes for a moment, as if trying to etch the memory of her face in her mind, then she kissed the baby's head and turned to Ned. 'Oy'm ready.'

The young couple walked out of the cottage into the daylight and saw Robert with the big horse pistol trained on the forehead of a rough-looking fellow in his forties. They appeared to be locked in a stalemate.

'Tell dis' eejit t' put d' gun down,' the grubby man said to no one in particular. The sheriff's face was expressionless and he motioned to Ned to mount his horse. Ned helped Mary up into the saddle first and she winced with pain as she sat.

'Ah sure good riddance t' d' whore,' shouted the lout. 'She ain' done nuttin' but eat me food an' croy in d' carner fer d' las' week. She's nuttin' boot an' Anglish whore.'

'Shoot 'im,' said Ned, 'ar let me do it.'

Robert shook his head. 'If every arsehole was shot, we'd all be dead.'

The scruffy man scurried towards the door of the cottage, pushing his wife and baby out of the way. When he got inside, he closed the bottom half of the door behind him, more confident on his own territory.

'Ya whore! Mary Galvin,' he screamed. 'If ya w's a real woman, yudda died befar dey could do dat t' ya.'

That was too much for Ned and Robert knew it. His eyes blazed and, before the man could lock the door,

Ned kicked it in and knocked him sprawling inside.

'Don't kill him, Ned!' Robert yelled. A moment later, a sound like a pumpkin being dropped came from inside. Ned walked back to the horses and, without a word, he hauled himself up in the saddle in front of Mary.

'Did you…?' asked the sheriff. Ned shook his head and a sinister smile crossed his face, as he rubbed the knuckles on his right fist.

'I didn't,' he said, 'but he'll be eatin' 'is spuds mashed fr'm now on.' Ned walked his horse to the still gaping door.

'Oy'll be watchin' ya froom now on, ya bastard,' he shouted into the gloomy interior,' an' if Oy ever hear you've said anyt'ing like dat again, Oy'll be back.'

The men walked their Hobbies back to the grocery.

'Stay here, Ned. I need to get some more supplies for our journey.' Robert bought some soap, a brush and a new blue dress of homespun for the girl. The proprietress flirted openly with the old man but it was wasted on him. He just wanted to get out of Cork and back to Tipp. This adventure had already been about as grand as it was going to get. They headed towards Macroom by way of Ballingeary.

There was an inn at Ballingeary, or perhaps hostel would have been a more appropriate term. It was the same place Percival Grey had begun to lose contact with reality. Robert left the young people outside and went in. The most important thing was to provide a bath for Mary. Robert didn't pretend to understand women but he understood people and he knew that sometimes, when a person had experienced something horrific, they felt dirty. He had even experienced it himself, after battle. It was more than the filth of combat. It was a feeling that you had to rid yourself of some real or imagined sin. He couldn't begin to comprehend what the poor girl must be going through. All he knew was that he felt guilty … that somehow he was at least partly responsible for what had happened in Ballyshee.

He handed the package containing the dress to the young girl, along with the soap and brush. She looked at the package curiously, then at Ned.

Robert spoke up. 'He'll be here, girl, when you've finished and then we'll all sit down for supper. There's no rush, we have all the time in the world.' Robert and Ned tended the horses while Mary went to clean herself up. She scrubbed her body until her skin was sore.

It was an hour before the girl returned and she had on the blue dress. Her blonde hair was pulled back, exposing the sweep of her long graceful neck and Robert noticed, for the first time, that her eyes were sky blue. He struggled to tear his gaze from her, even as they sat down to eat, and she grew uncomfortable under his unremitting stare.

'Is dere sumpthin wrong wit me?' she asked.

'No, my dear,' he responded gently. 'You just remind me of someone I once knew.'

'W's she a sweetheart?'

'Ah no, nothing like that,' he said with a hint of nostalgia. His mind drifted back to the first time he had ever laid eyes on Roisin. He always knew that her heart belonged to his brother, Liam, but, although he used visiting his brother as a pretense, he would ride the five miles from Nenagh to Gortalocca as much to see her as his brother. When she wasn't there, he had always felt slightly disappointed.

'Whut ar' ya t'inkin' about'?' It was the kind of question a woman asks, that a man never would.

'Nothing at all, Mary,' he replied.

'Well,' she said, 'Oy w's jus' t'inkin' dat ya know my name, but Oy don' know yours.'

The old man thought for moment. 'It's Uncle Robbie,' he replied.

Ned choked on a piece of gammon and he dropped his spoon. 'Ooncle Robbie?!!'

Robert shot him a look that could curdle a bucket of water. 'It's Sir to you, you horse turd.'

CHAPTER 37

It was mid-afternoon when the stage arrived in Nenagh and a light rain shower was just blowing in from the west, over Lough Derg. The streets were teeming with vendors and shoppers, all oblivious to the worsening weather. A faint stench of rancid meat and over-ripe vegetables permeated the air. It was a typical weekday in the market town, much the same as it had been for the last four hundred years. The coach horses had slowed to a crawl and were winding their way through the crowd. Occasionally, the driver would yell an obscenity for someone to get out of the way and, more often than not, they would shout something equally offensive back at him. Street urchins … ragged orphans who had no means of support … roamed the streets singly and in small groups, trying to steal whatever they could in order to sustain themselves. Morna was overwhelmed with all the hustle and bustle.

'Is it alw'ys like dis, Mikey?'

Michael smiled, it was a scene entirely familiar to him.

'No,' he replied, 'if we'd been here this morning it would have been more crowded.' Morna thought that half of Ireland must be marketing in Nenagh today.

Michael opened the door of the carriage and helped the girl to step down onto the wet, cobbled street. The driver shouted something to him and threw the sack, containing their belongings, down to him from where it had been secured on the roof of the coach. Mikey asked him if he knew whether there was any transport available to take them to Gortalocca. The driver was about to give him a vulgar retort, but he glanced at Morna, then back at Michael.

'Get yerselves back here in fifteen minutes,' he said, 'an' I'll have somet'in' fer ye.'

'We have a quarter hour to kill, love,' Mikey told the girl. 'Let's see if we can get Mam something nice.' He knew his mother's taste well. 'She likes cake made with butter and treacle, and some cream and berries.' They found the fruit quickly enough. In late summer, there were still wild strawberries, blackberries and blueberries aplenty and for a ha'penny, they bought a big sack of the succulent produce. For another farthing, they acquired a large cake, which the baker wrapped up securely for the short trip to Gortalocca. As they arrived back at the coach stop, a jarvey with a pony and trap was just pulling up.

'Good day t' ya, sir,' he said cheerfully to the young man, and tipped his hat to Morna.

'We need a ride to Gortalocca,' Mikey told him.

'Well if ye have tuppence, yer luck's in,' smiled the driver.

'I have sir', said Michael, rattling his purse. On the way out of town, he asked the jarvey to make a quick stop at a bar and he went in. When he came out, he brought with him a stone jar, full of cider, and handed it to Morna.

'If you want to make a good impression on me mam,' he said, 'just hand her this.'

When they reached the edge of town and fields of grain stretched out around them, turning now from green to golden, Michael tapped the driver on the shoulder.

'I'd like to go by way of Ballyartella,' he said, 'if it's not too much trouble.'

The jarvey turned and stared at Michael. 'Ah, yer familiar wit' dese parts so.'

'I grew up here,' replied Mikey.

'I t'ought ya looked familiar. What's yer name?'

'It's Michael. Michael Flynn.' Morna looked at her husband because she had thought the Flynn versus Hogan debate was over, but before she could say anything the driver said,

'Yer one o' Liam's boys so. Let me tell ya a story about yer dear farder, God rest his soul. About twenty years ago … yu'd a bin just a baby back den … I came t' Nenagh from Roscrea wit' a pony an' some tack, but I ditn't have a cart. I met ol' Mick Sheridan. Ya know Mick o'course, he's a mountain of a man but he's got a good heart, Lord luv 'im. Anyhow, he had a pony trap dat b'longed to Squire Johnson. D' auld man had t'rowed it away. Da body was all rott'n sure but d' undercarriage was still sound. So, he get's yer da t' take a look, an' yer da scratches 'is head and he puts 'is hand on 'is chin. It ain't ruined, sez he, it's just almos' ruined. I t'ink fer ten shillin's I c'n geddit lookin' like new, sez he. Well, I nearly busted out in tears cuz he might 's well a said a t'ousand pounds. So yer da asks me if I could afford five shillin's an' I showed 'im me purse an' I only had a farthin' in it. Yer da sez, ya c'n pay me a penny a month 'til you've paid me my five shillin's 'n ya c'n have d' trap so's ya c'n make d' money. Den 'e looks at Mick, ya r'member Mick don'cha, an' 'e says t' Mick, Let's take dis feller down t' Hogan's an' get 'im some food an' a swaller t' seal d' deal. So we all gets t' Hogan's an' dere's yer mam, an' I t'ink she had ya in 'er arms, an' she looks at me an' den at yer da an' she says, I see ya brought me anudder raggedy man t' feed. Now I don' know what she meant by dat but whatever it w's, dey both had a big auld laugh, an' den she kissed 'im. Ah, yer mam loved yer da. Ev'rybuddy loved yer da sure.' The driver's voice cracked as he spoke and Michael couldn't respond because of the lump in his throat. 'Ya look just like yer da did dat first day I met 'im,' said the driver and Michael saw him raise his hand to his face and wipe his eyes. Michael did the same.

The trap was just approaching the mill at Ballyartella when the jarvey halted the pony.

'Listen!' he said. Michael could hear the rhythmic sound of a hammer on an anvil. 'Dat's Jamie!' he exclaimed. 'I recognise d' sound when 'e hammers d' iron. D' ye want ta stop fer a minute t' see 'im?' Michael was torn between going straight to Gortalocca to see his mam and stopping to see this friend of his father, who was like an uncle to him. He was eager to find out what had happened and Jamie Clancy could, no doubt, provide him with the information he needed.

'We'll go and see Jamie,' he said. The driver pulled the trap up to the front door of the forge and, after a few more strikes with the hammer, the blacksmith looked up. He recognised the figure in the coach and he dropped his hammer on the ground and tore off his leather apron.

His voice cracked. 'Liam?' He squinted at Michael. 'Mikey!' he shouted and ran and dragged the young man out of the trap. He wrapped his arms around him so tightly that Mikey could barely inhale. It was uncharacteristic of Jamie to display such emotion and Michael was completely taken aback. Jamie would no more hug a man than his own father would have.

'Go easy, James, you'll break me ribs.'

Jamie let go of him. 'Oh Jayzus, Mike! Fer a second dere, I t'ought ya were yer farder's ghost,' he said. 'C'mere t' me and let me tell ya, dere's a real shite storm goin' on in d' village, an' yer feckin' useless brudder is 'n d' middle of it.'

Jamie turned to the jarvey. 'Billy, is it alright wit you if I stand on d' back o' d' trap while ya drive Mikey home. I got a lot t' tell 'im.' The driver told Jamie to climb on board and, as the pony trudged towards Gortalocca, the story of the goings-on there unfolded.

Mikey felt the blood rushing to his head as Jamie related the story, and the blacksmith felt his own anger rise too.

'Yer mam tol' me t' keep me temper in check, Mike, an' so fer her sake I'm tellin' ya t' do d' same. We don' want her t' get caught in d' middle o' dis. I owe 'er too much t' cause 'er any more grief.'

Michael agreed. He had watched his father keep a cool head when most would have flown off the handle. After all, hadn't he managed to live with his mother for all those years? Michael had never seen him lose control of himself. He closed his eyes and swallowed deeply. Try and be like your da, he told himself.

The trap came to a halt outside the little cottage which had once belonged to Paddy Shevlin and Jamie jumped off the back.

'Let me get yer mam! I don' want 'er t' faint when she sees ya.' Jamie ran into the house without knocking and, as he was getting down from the trap, Michael heard his mother reading the riot act to the blacksmith. There was silence, then Roisin burst out of the door with Jamie hot on her heels.

Mikey's feet had barely touched the ground when he was overwhelmed by his mother. She squeezed the breath out of him and kissed him a hundred times. He could taste the salt of her tears as they wet his face.

'I knew you were alive,' she wept. 'I told everyone that you were alive. They said you weren't but sure I knew you were.'

Michael took her by the shoulders and pushed her away a little so he could see her face. 'I thought you said you never cried, Mam?'

'Agh, these last few months, Michael, I've cried enough to fill the Shannon.'

He wasn't used to seeing his mother as vulnerable as she seemed now. She had always been the rock upon which their entire family was built. Roisin began to regain control of herself and she pushed Mikey a little further away now as she addressed the jarvey.

'And where have you been, Billy Reardon? I thought you'd at least have paid your respects when Liam....' Roisin hated the word 'died' and, even now, she had a hard time saying it.

'I'm sorry, missus. I jus' couldn't come. Ev'ry time I t'ink o' Liam, I still get a lump in me t'roat an' I'm full o' tears.'

'It's full o' shite y'are, Billy Reardon. Ya always were an' ya always will be,' she said in mock anger, wiping her face with her apron. She turned her attention to the pretty young lady in the beautiful green dress who was still seated in the trap and who, up until now, had been neglected. Roisin looked her up and down, from head to toe, before saying, 'You'll have to excuse these louts, miss, they have the manners of a billy goat. I'm Roisin Flynn, I'm Michael's mam.'

The country girl was flustered by all the excitement and, when she responded, her reply was almost inaudible.

'Oy'm Morna. Oy'm Michael's woife.'

Roisin felt her knees buckle, the same way they had when Jamie had announced that her son was outside, and she looked at Michael, then back at the beautiful red-haired girl.

'I beg your pardon, dear, I don't think I heard you correctly with all this commotion going on.'

'Oy'm Michael's woife,' said Morna, a little slower and slightly louder.

Roisin's head spun as she found herself suddenly caught between confusion, elation and jealousy. She turned to her son.

'What about the priesthood, Michael?'

'I didn't get ordained, Mam. I had second thoughts about it a few months ago. When I fell in love, it changed everything.'

Roisin closed her eyes. 'Oh, my boy, your father would be so happy to know that.'

'What about you, Mam? Are you happy?'

Roisin looked back at the girl. 'Your beautiful wife is like a princess and, if she doesn't climb down from that carriage, I'm going to have to climb up.' Morna leapt down onto the ground and Roisin enveloped her in her arms. 'You saved my son's life, my dear,' she whispered, 'and I will love you like my own daughter.' The girl embraced Roisin in return.

'An' Oy promise t' be a good daughter,' she replied, 'an' a good woife.'

While all the fuss was going on, Roisin had noticed

Robbie out of the corner of her eye, standing at the door of his cottage. He had watched his brother's homecoming and had been waiting to see if Uncle Robert had returned with him. Finally, when he was sure that the coast was clear, he meandered over to the gathering. He stood mute, looking at each face to guage his position. When Mikey became aware of his presence, he walked over to him. Robbie regarded him through narrowed eyes.

'So you're alive, are ya?' he said, softly enough that his mother wouldn't hear him. 'Well, dere's been some changes aroun' here an' I'm in charge now.'

Michael hadn't expected a warm welcome from his brother but he hadn't expect outright hostility either. He felt somewhat hurt but he didn't say a word in response.

'You jus' showin' up doesn't change a t'ing. Who's the girl?' Here was something Mikey could provide an answer for.

'She's my wife.'

'Dat makes no diff'rence. I gotta wife too, an' mine is pregnant.'

'Well congratulations, Robbie. I'm very happy for you.' Mikey extended his hand to his brother but it was left hanging in the air as the older sibling turned and began to walk away.

'An' anudder t'ing,' he snarled, 'don' go tryin' any o' dat sneaky underhand shite Da pulled.' With that, he turned and disappeared into the house their father had built. Mikey looked down and realised that his hand was still extended.

Morna, Jamie and Roisin walked up to Mikey as he stood staring at the door which had just been closed in his face.

'What was that all about?' asked Roisin.

'Nothing, Mam, don't worry about it. Listen, let's all go in the house and then we can have some cake and a cup of cider.'

Jamie rushed off and, within a few minutes, he had returned with his wife and baby. They had the most enjoyable evening any of them could remember having for a very long time, and they listened to Michael's tales about life outside County Tipperary. Across the road, Robbie wasn't enjoying his evening at all.

CHAPTER 38

There were only two rooms available at the inn and Robert told Ned they would share one and let Mary have the other. The young man was loath to let her out of his sight but Robert explained that it was best for her to have her privacy. He told him she didn't need someone pawing at her while she was in such a fragile state. Ned agreed, but only because the sheriff was his superior. In actuality, he would have given anything to be on top of the girl tonight.

Robert couldn't sleep. Ned thrashed about and mumbled, even shouting incoherently from time to time. Nightmares, thought Robert, he knew them well. In a way, conflict and battle were easy. The enemy was standing in front of you and you did whatever you had to in order to survive. The demons that came afterwards were a different matter. They haunted the recesses of your mind and, as soon as it got dark and your defenses were down, they would crawl out and attack. They say you never die in your dreams, that you always wake up just before the coup d' grace is delivered. Perhaps that's the torture of it, pondered Robert, for you to have to live through it, time and time again.

After a couple of hours tossing and turning, Robert gave up on the idea of sleep and he went downstairs to the darkened bar. He wasn't alone. Sleep had eluded Mary too and she sat at a table, her face in her hands, crying. Robert sat down facing her.

'Can't sleep either?' he asked quietly.

'Oy don' t'ink Oy'll ever be able t' sleep again,' she sobbed.

Robert put his hand gently on hers. 'I've felt that way too, Mary, in the past.'

'Will it ever go 'way?'

'It will o'course.' the old man said, but he wasn't convinced.

'When?' she implored.

'When all the good things fill up your mind and push out the bad ones,' he said softly.

'What aboot what me coosin's husband said? Dat a real woman woulda died farst.'

'Agh, he's just an eejit! He has no idea what terror is. Some things are worse than dying. You know that better than I do and I'm an old man.'

'Oy wish Oy'd died, like me da did, when dey shot 'im.'

Robert squeezed her hand. 'Woman, the reason you didn't die is because you still have something important to do. That man upstairs, trying to sleep, loves you enough to go through his own hell to get back to you. You saved his life.'

'Do ya really t'ink dat's d' reason?'

'I really and truly do, Mary.' The old man still wasn't convinced.

The golden-haired girl looked at him quizzically and her face was like a child's. The old fellow felt as protective of her, as a father would his daughter.

'Ya know,' she said, 'fer a hoywayman, ya know a lot o' t'ings. Maybe ya shoulda bin a priest.'

Robert laughed out loud. For your penance, he thought, hold out the hand that did it and I'll cut it off.

'I wouldn't have made a very good priest,' he said. 'Now, let's see what they have behind the bar. Maybe we can find a little something to help us sleep.'

He rummaged around on the shelves and found a bottle of French brandy which Percival had overlooked. He poured them both a half cupful and they sipped it slowly. The girl yawned.

'Give it another try,' he said. 'Perhaps you'll be able to drop off now.' She began to pad away on bare feet, then stopped, turned back and gave the old man a hug.

'T'anks, Ooncle Robbie.'

Robert poured himself another cup of brandy and sat alone in the darkness.

The sky had just begun to get that early morning glow in the east, about an hour before the sun makes its appearance, and the silhouette of the mountains was deep indigo against the deep blue of the sky. Robert picked himself up painfully from out of the chair. One of the gifts of age, he thought. At least you knew you'd lived to see another day when the aches and pains reminded you. He went outside into the cool morning air and breathed deeply … and coughed. It was time to check on the horses. The journey had been almost as hard on them as it had been on the old man. Both animals were about a hundred pounds lighter than they had been at the beginning of the adventure. Robert stroked the side of the animal nearest to him.

'We've spent all this time together,' he said, out loud, 'and I've never even given you boys a name. Well, you're brothers and you're Irish, so how about Bran and

Sceolan? They were two heroic Irish beasts too. They were the war hounds of Cu Chulain and…'

Ned appeared from out of the darkness and startled the old man. 'Oy been oop fer a coople o' hours,' he said. 'You was sittin' in in d' bar sleepin' so Oy let y' be.' Robert hadn't even realised that he'd slept. 'Oy had a converstion wit' d' harses meself a bit earlier,' Ned continued. 'Dose two are good listeners.'

Robert inspected the animals. He said that when they got to Macroom, later that afternoon, it might be best to give the creatures a few days rest and let them put a bit of weight on before pushing them any further. Ned took a look at them and agreed that it was indeed a good idea to give them a chance to recover.

'Maybe we all need a few days,' he said.

Robert thought for a moment before he spoke. 'There's no rest for the wicked, Ned. As soon as I can arrange passage, I shall go directly to Gortalocca and then I can take it easy. You and Mary can stay with the horses and, after a few days, you can come and join me.'

'Ah now Oy don' know about Gartalocca. Oy wanta see Mary Land.'

'So you still have that notion in your head?'

'Oy do, sar, but Oy may have to wark fer a few more years t' save enough money.'

Robert smiled. 'Oh I don't think you'll have to wait that long, boyo. Do you remember I said I had business with Wentworth, back in Kenmare? Well I sold him the big horses. I thought I might get about ten or twelve pounds each for them but he was feeling generous with the town's money and he was so excited at the prospect of writing that book of his that he gave me fifteen pounds each for the beasts. You have thirty pounds now, boyo, and, when you get to Gortalocca, you'll get another five from me once you deliver the horses to Mick Sheridan. That'll be enough to get you and Mary to Mary Land and enough to buy a real piece of land.'

Ned was completely overwhelmed. He had thought himself a wealthy man when he'd had the five pounds which Fergus bequeathed him. Now he had thirty and, soon, he was to have thirty-five pounds.

'Sar…Oy…'

'Don't say anything, boyo. I've accumulated money over my years as sheriff. The salary was generous and there were, let's say gratuities, given to me. I lived a simple life in my quarters in the castle and it turns out that money never meant much to me. It was all I had and now it really doesn't seem important at all.'

'What 'r ya gonna do when ya get back t' Tipp?'

'I'm going to be a horse trader, Ned. No more adventures for me. I shall leave that to you, but you can bet your arse that if I was twenty years younger, I would be going to Mary Land with you. Now let's get the horses saddled. We might as well hit the road early.'

Robert went back into the boarding house and left a few pennies on the bar for the brandy. He tapped on Mary's door. It opened immediately and she stood, ready to leave.

'Still no sleep?' he asked. She shook her head and walked past him. It'll be a long time before she rids herself of her demons, he thought.

*

In Gortalocca, Michael's homecoming festivities were continuing well into the night. There were stories to tell and gossip to share. The young man had been proud to introduce his wife to the gathering and things were going swimmingly, then the cider ran out.

'Michael,' said Roisin, 'go over to your brother's house and get him to open up the bar so we can carry on our party there.'

'I don't think that's a good idea, Mam.'

'Nonsense. Robbie's your brother. He won't mind and, besides, he should be hearing about life outside in the big wide world too.'

Reluctantly, Mikey acceded to his mother's wishes and he crossed the road to the Flynn cottage. A light came from the window. Michael had secretly hoped that the occupants would be asleep so he would have an excuse not to knock. He tapped tentatively on the door.

'Who is it?' came a slurred reply from the interior.

'It's Mikey.'

'What d' feck do you want?'

'Mam wants you to open the bar.'

'Tell 'er t' go t' sleep,' came the reply.

Michael waited for a moment before he decided what he should tell his mother. He came to a decision. I'm not covering for you anymore, Robbie, he thought. I'm going to go across the street and tell Mam that you said no, and that's exactly what he did.

'What did you say to him,' she snapped, in a feeble attempt to mitigate the conduct of her eldest son.

'I told him exactly what you told me to, Mam.'

'Well how did you say it? Maybe he was upset at the tone of your voice.'

Mikey tucked his bottom lip behind his teeth and rolled his eyes. Although Roisin was overjoyed to have her youngest back in the fold, she bristled at his impertinent expression and she stood up, putting her hands on her hips. Jamie Clancy intervened.

'I have a key,' he said. All eyes turned on him and he smiled an enigmatic grin and raised his bushy eyebrows.

'I didn't know that,' said Roisin, indignantly. 'Where did you get it?'

'I gottit from Liam. Ye go over t' d' store an' I'll meet ye dere.'

The group filed out of the cottage and Jamie went next door to his house. As they gathered around Hogan's padlocked door, Jamie reappeared.

'Gimme some room,' he said. 'I hafta use me key.' The gathering separated and Jamie pulled out a short iron bar and broke the hasp off the door. He laughed at the shocked expression on Roisin's face.

'Da bar is op'n fer business, missus,' he said, and bowed as he held the door for her.

The contents of the beer kegs were already low and Jamie tipped one of them on its side as Mikey filled some flagons with the cloudy liquid.

'They're just dregs,' he said, 'but they'll have to do us until there's another delivery.'

Roisin's face flushed, she was mortified. There had been a delivery less than a week before. Robbie must have had a celebration or two with his mates. Michael picked up a clay jug which at one time had contained poteen and he shook it. It was empty.

'Business must be good, Mam,' he said. Roisin averted her eyes, which were threatening tears.

The festivities had just begun to take off again when Robbie appeared at the door brandishing a hefty walking stick.

'Get outta here, ya thieves! I'll brain youse wit' me stick.'

Michael stepped forward, hoping to defuse the situation. 'I'll fix the lock and I'll pay for the beer.'

'Feckin' right ya will!' he screamed, 'an' dere ain't none o' yuz welcome in dis place ever again.'

Jamie Clancy had heard enough and he pulled himself up to his full six feet and three inches. 'If ya want ta start sumpthin' here, ya'd better start wit' me,' he snarled. Jamie was a quiet, gentle man but his tall stature, muscular as it was from his years in the smithery, could be imposing, especially when he used this tone of voice. Robbie took a step backwards as if he was going to swing the stick, but Jamie stood his ground and the two men locked stares. The drunken man was the first to blink.

'I'll know how much beer ya drink, an' I'll be expectin' ya t' leave yer money on d' bar.' He turned and staggered back out into the night, leaving silence among those assembled.

'Ah, he'll be sorry for what he said tomorrow,' blustered Roisin, trying to hide her humiliation at her son's latest outburst. 'He probably won't even r'member, sure. C'mon, let's have a drink.'

CHAPTER 39

They set out for Macroom long before the sun rose over the mountains. A strong wind had whipped up from the southeast and grey clouds were threatening to obscure the last stars. Late summer had begun to surrender to autumn and the fair weather that had been their companion for most of the adventure was giving way to storms, which grew in intensity as the seasons changed. The bushes alongside the road rattled like old bones in the howling gale.

'Looks loike d' wedder is goin' t' close on us t'day, sar.' Ned had to shout to be heard as the gusting wind tried to whip his words away. Soon the rain began to pelt down, not soft Irish rain but huge drops that had probably originated in some tropical sea to the south.

'I was hoping we could make Macroom today, Ned,' yelled Robert, 'but if this gets any worse, we'll have to find some shelter until it passes.'

By the time they came to Inchigeelagh, both riders and horses were drenched through to the bone. The wind had all but abated, the squall had passed, and now the sun was playing tag behind the clouds. They passed through the village and had to move aside as several mounted redcoats rode by. Robert's heart was in his mouth but the soldiers paid no heed to them and galloped past in the direction of Macroom.

'Jayzus, sar,' gasped the deputy, when they had gone by, 'Oy w's scared t' death fer a second.'

'You and me both, boyo,' exclaimed the old man. He noticed that Mary had hidden her face and, when she looked up, he could see she was terrified.

'We'll rest the horses, Ned,' he said abruptly. 'You go and water them. I'm so sore I don't think I can walk.' Without a moment's hesitation the young man followed his orders, leaving Mary and Robert alone together.

'Did you recognise any of those men, girl?'

'No, Ooncle Robbie. I couldn't ev'n see deir faces. I only saw d' red coats.' Robert breathed a sigh of relief.

'Yer no hoywaym'n, are ye. Oy mean yer not t'ieves.'

'No, you're right. The last time I stole something, it was a dead man's uniform and his name. That was forty years ago and I haven't taken the name or the uniform off ever since. I've hidden behind them.' The girl's eyebrows knitted with a question that she didn't ask. 'I became Robert D'Arcy, a captain in the Irish foot, and in the end, even I forgot who I really was. If I'd been brave, I would have gone back to the blacksmith shop my father owned and I would have swallowed my pride and admitted that I was wrong. My vanity and conceit led me down a different path.'

'But yer a brave man…'

'I'm a coward. My brother was a brave man and so is his son Michael, and so is Ned, but not me. I hid behind my duty and I gave up the things that are really important. I thought there would always be time, but here I am, already an old man, just fighting to stay alive.

If I live long enough, perhaps I'll find a way to repent for my sin of self-importance.'

They reached Macroom early in the afternoon. The squalls had persisted and now the rain fell constantly in a downpour. They put the horses in a pasture on the outskirts of town and, after an initial burst of exuberance, the two animals settled down and began to graze. Robert gave the farmer a shilling and said there'd be another when Ned came to claim the beasts in a few days. They walked to the town centre in the bucketing rain and found an inn right in front of the old castle ruins. They sat down to a meal and some beer and Robert enquired of the proprietress, who informed him her name was Shelagh, if accommodations could be provided. Shelagh showed them a pair of rooms, side by side on the third floor, and Robert handed her a shilling for both. She gave him a penny in change.

Mary turned in early and Ned went up not long after her. Robert stayed downstairs in the bar and listened to the local gossip. The two hot topics of conversation were the death of Percival Grey and the demon priest who haunted the mountains to the south. A few claimed to have seen the eight foot, sometimes twelve foot, apparition dressed in the grey garb of a Franciscan, with fierce red eyes that glowed like coals. They considered the latter to be a saviour or, at the very least, an ally against the English.

'It might be a divil from hell,' one man offered, 'boot it's our own divil.'

Robert wondered what they would think if they knew that the 'divil' himself was sleeping right over their heads. He called it a night as the bar emptied out and he carried a cup of poteen up to his room with him. Guilt is the Achilles heel of the Irish and Robert still couldn't help feeling that, if he'd done something different, then perhaps there would still be a village called Ballyshee. Ned wasn't in the room when the old man arrived. Robert drank his whiskey and fell into a fitful slumber.

*

Michael and Morna slept late; the journey to Gortalocca had been taxing. Roisin began her household duties early. Now there were three people crammed into the tiny twelve by fifteen cottage but she didn't mind because at least she had company. Jamie stopped by and he had his tools with him. He was on his way to repair the lock on Hogan's door. He knew that, if it wasn't done promptly, Robbie would nag and harp on about the damage like an old woman. Half an hour later, Robbie appeared at the door. He looked at the young couple sleeping on the floor.

'Is 'e goin' t' sleep all day? He's got Clancy doin' all 'is work.'

'What do you want, Robbie?' asked Roisin, ignoring the remark.

'Him an' Clancy drank all d' beer las' night. I need money t' get anudder delivery.'

'What about the empty shelves? You must have made a profit on the groceries.'

He gave it some thought before he answered her. 'Wit' May havin' yer grandchild, she's eatin' a fierce lot o' grub.'

Michael had been listening to the conversation and now he sat up.

'Robbie, you are full of shite,' he said, stretching.

Roisin cast him a withering look. 'I'll thank you to mind your tongue in my house, boy. If he's full of shite,

I'll be the one to say so.' Robbie was delighted with his mother's defense and he smiled smugly at his brother. Mikey was irked that his mother was defending Robbie, even though he'd lied to cover his own arse.

'I'm going to go and help Jamie,' he said.

'He don't need yer help!' yelled Robbie

'Ah he does sure,' replied Michael, casually. 'Who else is going to hold your head steady while he pounds a nail into it?'

'See, Mam. He's no sooner back an' 'e's startin' trouble. Tell 'im!'

'Jesus, Joseph and Holy Mary! You're like a couple of spoilt kids. Michael, go way out of it. Take Morna with you and go and help Clancy.' Roisin knew she would have to separate the two brothers before it came to blows. Without another word, Mikey took Morna by the hand and stalked off out the door, the girl stumbling behind him.

They found Jamie working and fuming at the same time. It was clear that he had something to say and Michael doubted that it would be good news. Morna picked up a broom and began to sweep the floor of the bar; it was a pig sty.

'Dat feckin' brudder o' yours,' he said, as if spitting nails. 'He jus' tol' me dat if anyt'ing happ'ned yer mudder, he would evict me from me own house. I tol' 'im dat 'e oughta say it in front o' 'is mam, an' he jus' smiled like d' fox dat ate d' chicken. I wannid t' brain'im wit' dis here hammer.'

Before Mikey could respond, Robbie sauntered in, smiling. He held a purse up and jingled the few coins in it. The smile disappeared from his face when he noticed the girl sweeping the floor.

'Get 'er outta here! I tol' yuz las' night dat ye ain'

welcome inside.' So he had remembered the outburst from the evening before. He hadn't been as drunk as his mother had thought. Morna propped the broom against the wall and, with Robbie's eyes still on her, she walked outside into the feeble sunshine.

Jamie addressed Robbie. 'Dis door is rotten on d' bottom. It's gonna need a new one soon.'

'You stick t' yer smithin', Clancy,' sneered Robbie. 'I'm d' carpenter aroun' here.'

'I was jus' sayin' dat…'

'I heard what ya said, I ain't deaf, and I'll t'ank ya t' mind yer own business.

Clancy put his tools into his canvas bag and left, followed by the young couple. Robert watched them go.

'I don' t'ink much o' yer wife's looks eider,' he shouted after them.

Morna turned on him in a flash. 'Da pigs in Cark got better manners den you have!' she spat.

Robbie felt the sting of not having the last word and he threw the broom down onto the road in front of the shop.

When they returned to the cottage, they found Roisin busy making preparations for the evening's meal. It was a labourious endeavor and she had begun it almost as soon as the hearth was cleaned after breakfast. From the frenzied way she worked, it was clear that something was troubling her.

'What's the matter, Mam?' asked Michael. She abandoned her work and slumped heavily onto a chair at the table. Morna took up cutting the spuds and turnips where the older woman had left off and Jamie stood at the door in silence.

'Jamie, m' cuishla, could you leave. This is a family matter.' Jamie felt the sting of her words. Since he'd been orphaned at eleven, the Flynns had been the only family he'd known. Roisin saw the look on his face and she changed her mind. 'I'm sorry, Jamie, you stay. You're as much a part of this family as anyone.' Mikey sat opposite his mother at the table and motioned to Jamie to join them.

'If it's me and Robbie who are upsetting you, Mam, I promise I'll try harder to get along with him.'

'I know you will, son. You're like your father, and so are you Jamie Clancy.' She grabbed Jamie's hand and looked at Mikey. 'Your father always said that Jamie was like his first born.'

Jamie looked down at the table. 'He was more of a da t' me den me own farder.'

Roisin dabbed her eye with a corner of her apron and straightened herself in her chair 'Well Liam wasn't perfect,' she said sternly. 'but I wish he was here now because he always had a plan. If anything complicated it, he just made a new one.

'Like Ooncle Robbie,' offered Morna.

Roisin bristled at the comparison. 'He was nothing like his brother Robert,' she snapped. Morna felt her face flush with embarrassment at the rebuke, and she turned back to the vegetables.

'Well he knew how to control Robbie anyway, but now that he's gone …'

'Liam alw'ys had t' stay on the sod's arse dough,' ventured Clancy. 'As soon 's 'e took 'is eyes off 'im, he'd go wanderin' off wit' 'is friends. If Liam had anyt'ing impart'nt t' do he'd come an' ask me t' help.'

'Don't you think I know that, Jamie? But that was then and this is now. I only put Robbie in charge a little over a month ago and already things are starting to fall apart. I've spent nearly half our savings and soon I'm going to have to dip into the money we've always held in reserve for the lean years. Next month, the rents will be due and, if I let Robbie take over that job, we'll be ruined altogether.'

'Mam, let me and Jamie collect the rents,' said Mikey.

'That would only cause trouble, Michael.'

'What the divil has happened to you, Mam? I never knew you to be afraid of trouble. You know it makes sense.'

Roisin dabbed her eyes again. 'I don't know. I know what I should do but I just can't do it to Robbie.'

'An' dat's d' problem, missus,' sighed Jamie. 'He c'n play ya like a fiddle, an' 'e knows it, an' he t'inks you don't. Lookit, I gotta leave an' go do me own wark 'r Matt'll be raisin' hell down at d' forge.' Jamie stood up, kissed Roisin on the cheek and left, telling them that he'd see them later in the evening.

'I don't know what I would have done after your father died if it hadn't been for Jamie.'

'Did you know that Robbie threatened him this morning? He told him if anything happened to you, he would evict the Clancys?'

'Ah no, now I can't believe he would say something like that,' declared Roisin.

Mikey shrugged his shoulders.

CHAPTER 40

Robert was already downstairs, and Shelagh had just begun to ladle out some porridge into his bowl when Ned came down. He was smiling and his smile grew wider as he sat down opposite the old man. Robert glowered at him.

'Oy never touched 'er,' protested Ned, holding his hands up, as if that would somehow prove it. 'Well, Oy touched 'er, boot Oy never … well, ya know.'

Robert exhaled a sigh of relief. 'Good man, Ned.'

The young fellow basked in the compliment. 'She just wannid to coodle, so Oy just coodled her.'

Robert started shovelling the gruel into his mouth and Ned caught the attention of the landlady. She brought over a big bowl for him and, before he had the spoon halfway to his mouth, the sheriff said,

'You know, boyo, you're not half as daft as you look.'

Ned took his spoon the rest of the way to its intended destination. 'T'anks … Oy t'ink.'

The golden-haired girl came floating down the stairs, barefoot, just as Robert pushed his bowl away from him. Mary had that same self-assured elegance the old man had seen before on another golden-haired girl. Her simple blue dress did nothing to detract from her slender, willowy form. Robert looked at the deputy and smiled. You have her right where she wants you, boyo, he thought. The three travelling companions sat and relaxed in each other's company. This time, there was no one chasing them and no need for haste. It was a relief to all of them that events had finally stopped happening at breakneck speed.

'You two sit here awhile, I'm going to see if I can get a coach to Mallow.'

Robert strolled across the street to the stage depot and let the misty rain envelop him. The summer's prolonged sunny spell was over and things were back to normal. It was a little over twenty-five miles to Mallow and, if he could get passage out of Macroom before noon, he should arrive just after dark. Although the fare of thuppence seemed a stiff price, he paid it gladly to save his arse from riding all the way on horseback. When he returned to the bar, Ned and Mary were locked in each other's eyes.

'I hate to break this up but I have something to give you. Let's call it Mary's dowry.' He put the bag of coins on the table, imagining that it was a tax he had to pay for interrupting the lovers. 'It's only money, Ned, not worth losing your life over, and neither are the horses. I'll leave you the pistol too, but only use it if you have to protect yourself and the girl. If I was you, I'd spend the next couple of nights right here. I'll be leaving in an hour for Tipp and I can meet you in Gortalocca sometime next week.'

Robert went up to his room, wrapped the pistol in his brat and brought it back down, putting it on the table in front of Ned. He shook the young man's hand.

'Thank you, Ned, he said, then he kissed Mary on the cheek. 'You take care of him, girl, he belongs to you, now.'

The old sheriff walked out the door without looking back and the young couple watched him go. None of them could know that it would be the last time they ever saw each other.

*

Inside Nenagh Castle, loud shouting could be heard coming from the sheriff's office and the fat sergeant who sat at the front desk smiled. Bernard Higgins was being hauled over the coals by the chief magistrate and, although the adjutant had no idea what it was about, it made him happy to know the officious prig was finally getting his comeuppance. The door opened.

'I'll see to it, your honour,' the acting sheriff assured the judge, penitently. 'The man will be punished severely, sir.' The judge brushed him aside, grunted and stormed out.

It seemed that one of the deputies, a fellow by the name of Willie Egan, had solicited a bribe by force from the bureaucrat's favourite butcher, Charlie Quinn. When Charlie refused to pay, the deputy had beat him so severely that he hadn't been able to work for several days. When those in high office discovered they had to procure their meat from a different vendor, they were furious and they demanded retribution.

Back in his office, Higgins yelled for his desk sergeant, who strolled in with a slovenly gait.

'I want William Egan arrested and brought before me, Sergeant.'

The adjutant stood, slouching, which made his big belly protrude even further. 'Willie is well liked by d' udder men,' he said, doubtfully. 'No one is goin' t' be happy about dis.'

The colour rose in Bernard's face. 'My job is not to make the other officers happy, you cretin!' he screamed. 'My job is to keep the peace.'

'An' a fine job yer doin'… sar,' snorted the sergeant. He turned and sauntered out, leaving the office door ajar behind him.

Higgins asked himself what D'Arcy would do. The Bloody Laws, which had been introduced years before, stated that any man who stole more than five shillings could be hanged, but D'Arcy had always maintained that, if hanging was to be used as a deterrent, it should only be done so for the most serious of offenses. If he was to hang a popular deputy, there was always the chance that the other men would mutiny and then redcoats would have to be called in to quell the revolt. Higgins paced his office, his hands clasped behind his back. The punishment must be severe but not so severe as to cause a rebellion.

Finally, Bernard decided that the man would be stripped of his uniform, tied over the barrel of a cannon and flogged with a cat-o'-nine-tails. He would use the small contingent of redcoats in the castle to mete out the punishment. There was no love lost between the police and the Army. Although fifty lashes could kill a man, thirty would be sufficient to serve as an example to the other deputies and the man would then be brought out into the market and put in the stocks for three hours. This would be a public spectacle, even if it was not the hanging which the town was anticipating.

The punishment was delivered the next morning. The contingent of police stood at attention throughout the flogging process and every time the man screamed, and scream he did as each lash bit into the skin on his back, the deputies would shift their weight uncomfortably from one foot to another. Egan passed out several times and the flogging had to be called to a halt until he was doused with a bucket of water and thus revived. After all, a whipping was only useful if the recipient was aware of each stroke. When it was done, before he was put in the stocks, a red hot iron rod, an inch in diameter, was burned through his ear. From now on, he would forever be recognised as a criminal, lucky to have escaped the gallows.

Higgins made his way back to his office and he felt sick to his stomach. Although he had witnessed dozens of beatings during his years in service, this was the first one that he himself had ordered. Whenever D'Arcy presided over the affair, the blood hadn't bothered him much. Now, however, he found it impossible to get the metallic smell out of his nostrils. The man's screams had seemed more terrible too and he had found the sight of the iron burning through his ear disturbing. It was still early in the day but he wanted a drink. The brass clock on his desk read half nine as he poured himself a glass of whiskey.

*

There were no other passengers on the Mallow to Limerick coach when Robert boarded it and so his thoughts were uninterrupted. He had initially hoped that he and Ned would simply find Michael, then spirit him away. Now he wondered, had he taken the young deputy's advice and gone into the mountains by way of Macroom, whether it would have made any difference to the outcome. The image of self-assurance and fierce resolve which Robert presented to the world was no different to that of his younger brother. He wondered if they were both frauds. Ah Liam, he thought, if only you were alive, we would take a walk and share our doubts, just us two brothers Flynn. Suddenly he had an urge to reclaim his birth name. When he got back to Gortalocca and started up the horse business with Mick, they would call it 'Sheridan and Flynn.' He liked the sound of it and mouthed it to himself.

'Did ya say somet'in'? the driver called down. Robert realised he'd been talking out loud to himself and wondered was he going daft or just getting old.

*

'You know, Mam, that door Jamie fixed is going rotten. It's going to fall off its hinges one day.'

Roisin turned to her son and smiled. 'I'm not surprised, Michael, it's the original one from when my da bought the place almost fifty years ago.'

'I was thinking that Jamie and I could build a new one.'

'That's a good idea, son, get Robbie to help you.'

'Why don't you just break all my fingers and be done with it, Mam?'

'Ah stop. Robbie worked with your da all the time.'

'No, Mam, Robbie stood around and picked his nose while Da worked.'

'Go on out of that. Sure it might even bring you two boys closer together.'

Mikey pursed his lips and shook his head. 'The only way I'm prepared to get closer to that gobshite is if I stick me foot up 'is arse.'

'Michael Flynn! And you nearly a priest! You spent too much time down in County Cork and now you're beginning to sound like one of those gasbags.'

Morna overheard Roisin's remark and stiffened. 'Ain't nuttin' wrong wit' Carkmen,' she sniffed.

Roisin was momentarily without words. This girl was half her size and she dared to bristle like a badger in defense of her home county and her husband.

'Go build your door, Michael.'

Morna took off her apron, threw it aside and was about to walk out the door with her husband when Roisin softened. The storm clouds in her mind had parted.

'I'm sorry, Morna, I didn't mean to upset you.' Michael's eyes widened. Never in all his life had he heard his mother apologise to anyone. She would perhaps do some little endearing thing if she found out she was wrong about something but 'I'm sorry' was just not in her vocabulary. Morna winked and squeezed his hand.

When the young couple arrived at the old church which Liam had used as a carpenter's shop, Mikey had to use his shoulder to push the door open. The rusty old hinges squealed in protest and, as the door finally swung open, a startled mouse scurried out.

'I see Robbie's been busy,' he said, sarcastically. The tools were hung in tidy rows, just as his father had left them, but they had begun to rust. Boards were stacked neatly in piles and the little stool which Liam had used to rest on during his last few seconds was toppled over on the floor. Michael was filled with emotions, a jumble of grief, love and respect.

'Da,' he said. 'I'm going to make you proud of me. I'm going to do what you taught me.'

Hanging from the rafters were a few ancient pine boards which had been there for as long as Mikey could remember. They were almost three inches thick and over a foot wide and he thought they must have come from a once-mighty tree. Between the two of them, Michael and Morna wrestled a couple of the planks down to the floor and Mikey set his wife to work, cleaning the rust off the tools with a bucket of lard, using some fine sand as an abrasive. The girl's hands quickly turned red from the corrosion but she was working with her husband and that was motivation enough for her. By the day's end, the door was nearly complete. It just needed hinges now and Jamie could supply those from the forge.

They didn't have to search out Jamie because he found them just as they were closing the door.

'Howaya,' said Jamie, using the usual Irish rhetorical greeting. 'Whatcha buildin', Mikey?'

'Building a door. I need hinges for it though.'

'I got some in a bucket back at the house. Don't know what style ya want. Pick one.'

Morna looked from one to the other, taking it all in. They all made their way to Jamie's cottage and the girl watched while the men rummaged through the bucket. She had enjoyed working with her husband and was eager to learn more.

'Dis one's called a buck hinge,' Jamie said. 'Me and yer Da invented it here in Gortalocca. Ya see?' he said, demonstrating it to Mikey. 'Ya don' have to cut a mortise fer it. It has teeth dat look like a deer's horns, so ya c'n just bang it in, an' den ya put a coupla screws in it t' hold it fast.'

It made sense to Morna now. Her knowledge of her

native language was sketchy but she knew that 'buck' was 'pocan' in Irish. 'Pick one' must be how Tipperary people pronounce 'Pocan'.

One day, the village was to have a new name.

CHAPTER 41

If their coach kept to its timetable, thought Robert, he would be in Limerick by that evening. His head had begun to pound, even though he hadn't drunk anything stronger than a single beer the night before. When his coach changed horses in Charleville, he would find an apothecary and buy a little laudanum or opium for his throbbing head … penance, he thought, for Ballyshee and the hundred other places and deeds. He pulled shut the curtain which covered the little window, but even the light which escaped around its edges hurt his eyes. The jostling of the coach and the pounding of the horses' hooves exacerbated the beating drums inside his skull.

They finally arrived at the depot in Charleville and Robert alighted from the coach, squinting his eyes against the glare. The driver gave him directions to the apothecary and he made his way there as gingerly as he could, each footfall more punishing than the last. As he entered, even the tinkling of the doorbell drew a curse from him. The chemist gave him a small vial containing the remedy and Robert uncorked the glass container immediately, taking a sip before walking back out into the street. It was unbelievably bitter in his mouth but he knew, from experience, that relief was on its way. When he returned to the coach, a new team of horses had been hitched and the driver was ready to leave. A fat, well-dressed gentleman, along with his considerably younger wife, had taken a seat opposite him. The woman's perfume was sickly sweet and almost made him gag, but his mind was already becoming dimmed as the narcotic took effect and he was soon fast asleep and dreaming.

He awoke, startled and disoriented. The fat man had kicked him in the shins.

'Ya were talkin' in yer sleep,' he growled. Robert mumbled an apology and thought about the strange dream he'd had. He had been in a huge dark room with a flaxen-haired woman. He knew it was either Mary Galvin or Roisin, but he couldn't remember which. They were running away from a ghostly apparition who flew above them, like a witch from an old folk tale. Robert held the fair-haired woman by the hand and dragged her behind him until she could run no more. He pushed her behind him, into a corner, and swung a stick over their heads, taunting the phantom, daring it to come and get them. He had been determined to make a stand and face the spectre, no matter what it was. He tried to shout at the witch but, instead of words, all he could manage were guttural sounds and grunts … then the fat old fellow had kicked him and the dream had ended. Robert would have liked to go back to sleep to see how it all ended but, like all dreams, it had gone. He dozed for the next hour until they reached Limerick's city walls.

Although he had eaten nothing since breakfast, the very thought of food revolted him. The laudanum had not only fogged his brain but had also turned his stomach. The pain in his head was gradually returning as the drug wore off and he went straight to his room, snuffed out the candle and lay in his cot. He resisted as long as he could before uncorking the little bottle which contained the narcotic. He took a small sip and let the darkness embrace him.

Almost immediately, another dream began. This time, he was in Gortalocca and a storm was building on the Clare side of Lough Derg, whilst another brewed to the south, over the Silvermine Mountains. It wasn't a typical late summer storm, but rather a maelstrom. Dark purple and grey clouds wrapped themselves around each other and lightning flashed and thunder boomed like distant artillery. Robert had experienced tempests before, when he'd fought in the South of France and Spain, but he had never seen anything like this. The storm was all around them, threatening to engulf them in its chaos. He gathered the villagers together and ushered them into a root cellar. He recognised them all but their faces were devoid of expression and, try as he might, he couldn't prevent them from wandering off aimlessly, like errant sheep. No sooner would he bring one back to the safety of the cellar, when one or two others would escape. Finally, there was no alternative other than to give up and they all drifted away, leaving him alone in the shelter. When he awoke, he was covered in sweat, not the perspiration of exertion, but the thick, cold, clammy excretion of fever or fear. He lit the candle and lost himself in the flame. He fell asleep again and this time, there were no dreams.

*

There was a storm brewing in Gortalocca. It may not have been an epic one like the old man had envisioned in his dreams, but it was one which could be equally destructive to the village. Michael had finished painting the door. He had decided on ochre yellow because he remembered that his mother loved the colour and had always wanted a door that shade. At almost two hundred pounds in weight, the door was extremely heavy and even if he could manage to wrestle it over to Hogan's himself, it would be impossible for him to hang it on his own. He had no wish to risk another argument so he decided not to ask his brother for help. He went back to the cottage and, as he approached the door, he could hear the telltale clack clack of a spinning wheel coming from inside. He found Morna sitting at the wheel, while Roisin knitted in the corner, where the sunlight illuminated her work. She was knitting a blanket for Robbie's expectant wife.

'Mam, the door is ready to hang but it's too heavy for me to do it alone.'

'Get your brother to help so,' said Roisin absently, dropping a stitch.

'No!'

Roisin lowered her knitting into her lap. 'What did you say?'

'I said no, Mam.'

Roisin wasn't used to hearing the word, especially from Michael, and she was already irritated about the knitting. She glared at her son. 'Go and tell Robbie that you need help and tell him that I said so.'

Reluctantly, Michael went across the narrow street to his brother's house. His mother's temper was legendary and he already had taken the dangerous step of treading on it. He knocked at the door and Robbie's wife answered.

'I need help to hang a new door on the store,' he said, before she could speak.

His brother's voice boomed out from inside the darkened house. 'Feck off!'

It was the response Mikey had expected so he added, 'Mam said you have to help me.'

There was a moment of silence. Mikey expected his brother to accede to their mother's demand because, when she said to do something, it was never a mere suggestion.

'You can tell her to feck off, too!'

Michael was taken aback. He hadn't expected that response and he certainly wasn't about to convey the message to his mother. He turned and walked back to the old church, at least he could claim sanctuary there. The door groaned in protest as he entered and he heard the scurry of mice inside.

'If I tell Mam what Robbie said,' he told them aloud, 'I'll be sharing this place with you.' He was deadly serious. Roisin wasn't above killing the messenger. He lifted up one corner of the newly manufactured door and kicked a stool under it with his foot. There was a wheelbarrow leaning against the wall and he moved it to just outside the door. Standing the door up on its end, he walked it out into the sun, moving it from corner to corner. When he got it outside, he dropped it onto the barrow and it landed with a heavy thud. He wheeled the barrow down towards the shop and, as he passed his mother's cottage, she appeared at the open door.

'I thought I told you to ask Robbie to help.'

'I did ask him. He told me to feck off.'

'Did you tell him that I said he had to help?'

A sinister smile flickered across the young man's face. 'I did, Mam. He said you could feck off too.'

As he hurried along towards the shop, he looked behind him and smiled again as he saw that his mother's backbone seemed to have been replaced by a broomstick. He wished he could hear what was about to unfold but he would have to make do with watching from a safe distance. Roisin marched across the road to the Flynn house and flung open the door without knocking or bothering to close it behind her. A moment later, the silence was broken by a loud crash, followed by his brother's plaintive voice.

'Jayzus, Mam! Ya almos' cracked me feckin' skull.'

'If you'd only stand still for a minute and give me another chance, I'll break it!'

There was the scuffling of feet, then another crash.

'I gotcha now, ya gobshite.'

'I t'ink yer after killin' me.'

Robbie came stumbling out of the cottage as if the house had spit him out like a cherry stone. He had one hand to his forehead and he was using the other to keep himself from falling face-first into the road. Mikey couldn't help but smile as he watched from the safety of his vantage point. The next thing, Roisin appeared at the door with a clay bowl in her hand.

When Robbie thought he was out of her range, he turned to his mother. 'Have ya gone mad, woman? Only a witch would try an' kill 'er loving son.'

'A witch, is it? You wanna see a witch? I'll show ya a witch.'

Roisin heaved the bowl at him and it whizzed past his head, narrowly missing him.

Mick Sheridan rode up just in time to catch the last round of the fight. When Roisin saw him, she straightened out her apron and smoothed her hair back.

'Well. Mick,' she said, smiling sweetly at him. 'You're just in time, I'm after baking some scones.'

'It looks like dat scone's only half baked,' he responded,

looking at Robbie.

'Ah, we were just having a discussion sure,' she said calmly.

'It looks more loike a CONcussion t' me,' he grinned.

'They're your favourite scones … the ones with the currants in them. C'mon over.'

'T'anks, I'll be dere in a few minutes, missus. I jus' wanna say hello t' Mikey.' In reality, Mick wanted to stay and witness round two. Roisin walked back to her cottage in a demure, ladylike fashion and got ready to welcome her guest.

Just as Mick caught up with Mikey at the shop, Robbie arrived too and the second round began.

'What did ya tell'er, ya rat bastard?' Robbie hissed. His mother was out of earshot but he wasn't taking any chances.

'You said to tell her to feck off,' said Mikey, feigning innocence. 'I just did what you told me.'

His answer infuriated Robbie and he took a swing at his brother. The blow glanced off Mikey's cheek but nevertheless, it hurt, so he returned the favour and popped his brother on the forehead, in the same place Roisin had left her mark.

'Ouch! Ya little shit bird. See, ya can't take me even after Mam's softened me up.' The two brothers began to grapple and wrestle and the fight rolled out into the dirt road.

'Dat's what I like about Gortalocca,' said Mick Sheridan. 'Nuthin' ever changes. Now you lads enjoy yerselves, I gotta scone waiting fer me wit' me name on it. An' by d' way, Mikey, it's good t' see ya again. Nice door.'

CHAPTER 42

Ned and Mary packed their sparse belongings and readied themselves for the four day ride to Nenagh. Shelagh was loathe the see them go, not that she would particularly miss their company, but rather the extra shilling she'd been charging them for their tiny, windowless room. For her part, Mary was glad to be leaving. Every time she saw a red-coated soldier, she stiffened with fear and searched his face for any sign of recognition. Even if she had identified one of her violators, she would never have mentioned it to Ned, afraid that his own peculiar code of honour would compel him to exact revenge, regardless of the consequences. Shelagh waved them off.

'Safe home,' she said.

They made their way to the edge of town, paid the farmer for watching the Hobbies and began the trip northwards to Kanturk, hoping to reach there before nightfall. As they passed through Millsteet, a beggar tried to grab the reins from the girl, but he was rewarded for his trouble with a swift kick in the face from Ned.

'Don't let any o' dese sods slow ya down, Mary,' he'd told her. 'We got miles t' go before dark.'

They left the mountains behind and the foothills surrounding them became gentler. They had crossed the bridge at Blackwater River by late afternoon and that meant they only had five miles to go before they reached their first day's destination. The three-day rest had done wonders for the horses. They had put weight back on and had regained their strength. Tomorrow, they would make it to Charleville and, from there, would retrace the trip taken just days before by the sheriff.

Things had settled down in Nenagh. The flogging and branding of the deputy had convinced most of the men that Higgins would no longer tolerate their shenanigans. Even the desk sergeant had become a good deal less insubordinate. He had, in the past, felt the lash at the hand of D'Arcy and he had no desire to repeat the experience. Higgins was able to command more respect now that the men knew indifference and leniency were no longer something he would turn a blind eye to.

A couple of the deputies were still drinking whilst on duty, Connolly and Gallagher. They were unlikely friends, united only by their love for the hard stuff. Connolly had been a deputy for many years. He was a rail thin man with a stern face, or at least it was stern when he was sober. Gallagher, on the other hand, was a big man with an easy smile, well-liked among his fellow troopers. Nevertheless, regardless of everyone's affection for the fellow, some measure of discipline had to be administered and so Higgins ordered the sergeant to assign them both to overnight picket duty, outside the town. The hope was that if they had to stay away from the bars, it might serve to diminish their thirst.

The two men left the castle on foot just before dark to assume their post. They passed a dishevelled man approaching the castle as they left and he gave them a salute which they didn't return.

'Did ya ever see dat eejit givin' us a salute,' scoffed Gallagher. 'Silly fecker mus' t'ink he's sumpthin'.'

'He is sumpthin',' said Connolly, his face deadpan. 'He's a piss trickle.' Gallagher laughed heartily. The dour old deputy had a way with words.

Robert arrived at the castle gates but was unable to talk his way past the guards. They didn't recognise his face and, without his uniform on, they were not about to let him through. He had begun to lose his temper with the two guards on duty but relented, telling himself that they were just doing their jobs and that he probably did look a sight. He would walk to Gortalocca instead. As he passed the livery stables, he spotted a light flickering inside. Perhaps he could borrow a horse and save himself the five mile walk. He went inside and saw Billy Reardon sitting on a stool, the tack from his pony trap scattered around him. He was busy polishing the brass paraphernalia and, when Robert walked in, he was startled.

'Jayzus,' he cried, 'ya scared d' shite outta me! What can I do fer ya?'

'I need a horse, Billy. I don't fancy walking all the way to Gortalocca.' As soon as the sheriff spoke, Reardon recognised him immediately

'Sir! I didn' recognise ya. Ya look like sumpthin' d' dog t'rew up! Jus' let me put d' harness back t'gedder, sir. Eider dat 'r ya c'n take d' cob over dere. Ya know I took young Mikey Flynn back home a week 'r so ago.'

That was music to the old man's ears. He had accomplished what he'd set out to do and now he was even more anxious to be on his way. Billy, however, had other ideas. First, he was determined to relate the tale of how he'd met Liam and he went into the same long story he'd told Michael, this time with added embellishments. It had started to get late.

The two guards had just reached their post when Gallagher produced a canteen.

'If ya start drinkin' water now,' the skinny fellow warned him, 'yu'll be pissin' all night long.'

'It ain't water,' grinned Gallagher, just as the aroma of poteen reached Connolly.

'C'mere, gimme a nip o' dat.' The big man handed the tin canteen to his companion and he took a long draught of it.

'Oi, take it easy, ya pig! Dat has t' last all night.' He snatched the container back and shook it. 'Jayzus, if dats a nip, I wouldn't wan'cha t' bite me,' he said sourly.

Connolly decided to have some fun with the big fellow. He knew he was more than a little superstitious.

'Hey Gallagher, didja' hear about d' terrible monster down in Cork?'

Gallagher felt the hair on his skin rise. He wanted to hear the tale but it was dark and he had a fear of monsters, terrible or not. 'No,' he replied.

'Well I'll tell ya. Down in d' mountains, a priest conjoured up a divil, an' it murdered a couple a hundr'd redcoats.'

'Ah go way outta that. Priests can't conjour up divils.'

'Back in d' aulden days dey could. Dat's how dose man-eatin' sheep came about over in Connemara.'

'Dat was in d' aulden days, dey can't do it now.'

'Dey can o'course. Dey teach it to 'em at priest school sure. Dey jus' don't do it much anymore, cuz once dey conjure one up, it's alive f'rever an' it roams d' land, doin' what it w's conjoured up fer.'

Gallagher looked about him, nervously. 'Dem feckers down in Cork 're all liars. Sure, dey'd see a badger an' d' next t'ing, it's a bear.'

'I heared it from a fella fr'm Limerick,' Connolly assured him, 'an' dey're too thick t' make up lies.'

'Let's hope it's still down in Cork so.' They passed the canteen back and forth as Connolly expounded on the story.

'Dey say it rides a black horse dat spits fire outta its nose instead o' snot. Dey say it burned down a village called Ballyshite.'

'Who'd name a village Ballyshite?'

'Corkmen would, dat's who.'

Gallagher conceded that they might and he gave it some more thought. 'How long d'ya t'ink it takes fer a demon t ride all d' way from Cork t' Tipp?'

Connolly was beginning to enjoy the uneasiness of his companion. 'I wouldn't be surpris'd if it w's already here. Ya know how dem t'ings are.' The big man's mind had become a little blurry and he decided he needed another drink. The tin container was getting close to empty and the night stretched out ahead of them.

The old man listened patiently to Billy's stories about Liam. Like every Irish jarvey, Billy liked the sound of his own voice, and his yarns led him seamlessly from one anecdote to another. Although Robert was eager to get back to Gortalocca, he was also enjoying hearing about his dead brother. When the stories looked like threatening to continue into the night, he pointed out to Billy that the brass wasn't going to polish itself and that it was getting close to midnight and he had to be going.

'Do you have a saddle for that plug?' he asked. Billy rummaged around and found a dried-out old saddle. He wiped the dust off it with a rag and put it on the cob. The girth was old and cracked and Robert hoped it wouldn't break and dump him into the road. That would be far too untimely an end for an otherwise perfectly good adventure. The light draught horse was as wide as the big charger he was used to riding, but several hands shorter, so it was easy to mount the animal. Billy handed the sheriff a riding crop.

'Yu'll be needin dis,' he said. 'Dat dead-sided mule won' pay ya no heed widdout spurs on yer feet.'

Robert slipped the lanyard of the crop over his wrist. 'I'll bring her back first thing in the morning, Billy.'

'Ya bedder had, sir. She ain't mine an' I don' wan'cha t' have t' hang me fer a horse t'ief.'

'I did the stealing. I'd have to hang meself.' said Robert, grinning.

'Safe home, Sheriff D'Arcy. I'll see ya in d' marnin'.'

The old man gave him a nod and began to walk the horse out of town. He tried squeezing the animal with his thighs but it offered no response. He kicked it with his heels and still nothing. He tapped it on the rump with the crop and, finally, the reluctant beast managed to trot for a few steps before falling back into a walk.

'You're a old lazy bastard,' said Robert aloud.

Connolly had polished off the last few drops from the canteen and he held it over his mouth, shaking it to make sure nothing remained.

'You c'n stand d' farst watch, boyo,' he said. 'I'm goin' t' shut me eyes fer a bit.'

Gallagher was every bit as inebriated as his companion but he was still jittery from the spook stories

Connolly had filled his head with. Every shadow and every rustle startled him from his stupor. The wind whipped around, ratting the trees like bones and adding to his trepidation.

Robert reached the first turnoff, just outside Nenagh. If he hadn't stopped at the livery, he thought, he could be halfway to Gortalocca by now. He whacked the horse on its rump hard enough to sting the animal out of its lethargy and they began to gallop towards home.

The wind carried the sounds away and the sentry didn't hear Robert's horse until it was thirty or so yards away. He felt the hair prickle on the back of his neck. He kicked his sleeping companion but Connolly just rolled over. He levelled his gun in the direction of the approaching sound and fired into the darkness.

Robert heard the shot, followed immediately by the angry buzz of a musket ball as it whizzed over his head. The horse heard it too and reared up on her hind legs. The saddle girth snapped, just as the rider was about to shout a warning to the sentries, and Robert began to tumble off the horse. Before he hit the surface of the road, a second shot rang out and an ounce of lead hit the old man just below the ribs.

Life is full of if's and maybe's and, no matter how well-laid a plan is, there is always a measure of chance involved. If Robert had chosen to walk instead of ride … if he hadn't become impatient with the horse's slow gait … if the cinch strap hadn't broken and thrown him, the second bullet would have missed its mark as widely as the first. Robert had danced with danger most of his life and he'd always enjoyed the devil's own luck, but fortune was a fickle mistress. She may flirt with a man for a while but, in the end, she took no lovers and now she had jilted the old man.

Robert lay in the road. He felt no pain and he knew that painless wounds were the most mortal. He put his hand to his belly then held it up in front of his face, the blood was black. He had been shot through the liver. He might live for an hour or he might live for a week. He closed his eyes and prayed that it would be the former.

Just as the two guards carefully approached the supine body lying in the dusty road, a misty rain began to fall …. another if. If the rain had started a moment earlier, the powder would not have ignited in the flash pan and the musket would not have fired.

'Maybe he's a horse t'ief, 'r a bandit,' said Gallagher, hoping he was right.

Connolly used his bayonet to push the man's hair aside and took a look at his face. 'Oh Jayzus Christ!' he cried. 'We killed D'Arcy! We'll hang sure!'

Robert tried to speak but he hadn't enough air in his lungs. That's good, he thought, with clarity, the ball went through the lungs. That means I'll be dead soon.

'See if he's got any money on 'im, Gallagher. We gotta get ourselves out o' here.'

'We can't jus' leave 'im 'ere.'

'If 'e's got money, we c'n get away before anyone finds out what we done.'

The shock had rendered both men stone cold sober and now Gallagher began to cry.

'Jayzus, sir, I'm sorry.' He sobbed as he relieved the sheriff of his purse and handed it to his companion. 'Now we're t'ieves 's well 's murderers.'

'Dey c'n only hang ya once,' said Connolly.

The old man formed his mouth around a word.

'He's tryin' t' say sumpthin,' said the young deputy, and he bent closer to Robert to hear what he hoped was forgiveness.

'Whattid 'e say?'

Gallagher looked at Connolly in astonishment. 'He said feckin' eejits….'

CHAPTER 43

The lathered horse arrived at the livery stable just as Billy Reardon had finished putting the harness back together, and it went straight into its own stall. The jarvey knew something was wrong. He saw its saddle was missing and he went over to inspect the winded horse, finding flecks of blood on the animal's flanks. After examining it for wounds and finding none, Billy realised something must have happened to D'Arcy. He headed immediately to the castle.

The two guards at the castle gate watched as the obviously distressed man ran towards them, yelling.

'Shutcher gob, Billy Reardon. Yu'll wake d' whole garrison,' said one of the men. The jarvey paused to catch his breath and the guards looked on in amusement.

'Looks like Billy fell off d' wagon again,' laughed one to the other.

'I ain't fell off any wagon, but I t'ink d' sheriff fell off 'is horse.'

'Be quiet, man,' ordered the first sentry, sternly. 'Sheriff Higgins is here, ya daft eejit, asleep in his quarters. If you wake him up, he'll put ya in d' stocks.

Now go way wit ya.'

'I mean Sherriff D'Arcy …' The pudgy old fellow bent over and put his hands on his knees. He inhaled deeply and screamed, 'HELP!!'

'Jayzus, Billy!' yelled the first guard. 'Now ya've done it! Yu'll have woke everyone in d' whole place. There'll be hell t' play!'

Billy Reardon looked from one sentry to the other and realised he wasn't going to get any help from them so he inhaled deeply, cupped his hands around his mouth and screamed.

'HEEELLP! MURDER!!!'

If the guards had had a shovel, they would've dug a hole and crawled into it. They just looked helplessly at each other and waited for the inevitable. They didn't have to wait long.

Sheriff Higgins came running out of his quarters, tucking his shirt tails into his still unbuttoned trousers. He was furious.

'What in God's name is going on out here!' he yelled across the courtyard to the two guards.

'It's Billy Reardon, sir,' shouted one of them. 'I think he's gone mad.'

'I ain't mad, Mr. Higgins, an' I ain' drunk eider,' screamed Billy, in a state of near hysteria. 'It's Sheriff D'Arcy… I t'ink sumpt'in terrible's happ'ned t' 'im!'

'Sheriff D'Arcy is down in Cork, man.' stated Higgins, abruptly.

By now, Bernard Higgins had closed the distance between them and arrived at the gates but that didn't stop Billy from shouting.

'He ain't, sir. I was jus' talkin' wit' 'im an hour ago. He couldn't get past d' guards so 'e was goin' on t' Gortalocca. I gave 'im a harse.'

Billy's story had a ring of truth about it and Higgins knew there was more to this than the ravings of a demented Irishman. He cast an acidic look at the two guards and asked Billy why he thought something had happened to D'Arcy.

'Cause d' harse showed up wit' blood on 'im.'

'Have my horse saddled up and bring him to the livery,' the sheriff barked to one of the guards. 'Turn out a few deputies and have them meet me there.' He turned to Billy and said, 'Get a grip on yourself, man. We'll go to the stable and get this sorted out.'

Robert lay alone on the Lough Derg road and looked up at the starlit sky. He coughed and a bit of bright foamy blood oozed out from the side of his mouth. He had always wondered how he'd die. He wondered now whether, if he could get his feet under him, he might be able to elude the inevitable just one more time. He tried to push himself up but it just made him cough up more blood, so he settled back and gazed at the night sky again. He had the same feeling the headache medicine gave him. His mind became foggy, his thoughts vague and he began to drift away. He was in a forge and he was young again.

Higgins arrived as Robert D'Arcy's last spark of life spluttered and died. He dismounted and felt the neck for a pulse, then he took a handkerchief from his pocket and wiped some of the blood from the old man's face, almost tenderly. He addressed the lifeless corpse of his superior.

'By God, sir, you were a stern old bastard. But I don't think anyone ever really knew you. You've died as you chose to live … alone. God rest your soul.'

Higgins was right and he was wrong. It was true that Robert Flynn D'Arcy's steely exterior had always given a harsh impression to most. But he was wrong about him being alone. Robert had a best friend, his younger brother, Liam. Now the two best friends and brothers were reunited once more and Robert Flynn was not as alone as Higgins imagined.

Sheriff Bernard Higgins assumed the role of commander. The other deputies arrived and surveyed the scene of the incident. Higgins picked up the empty canteen and sniffed it.

'Find Connolly and Gallagher,' he ordered, his tone one of disgust. 'They have a lot to answer for.'

Connolly and Gallagher had been making their way eastwards, toward Ardcrony. As the sun rose, they excited the deep forest and spotted a few cottages.

'We need t' get outta dese uniforms,' hissed the skinny man.

Gallagher's world was crashing in around him. 'I ain't gonna run,' he stated bluntly. He dropped his musket and walked towards the road that led to Nenagh.

'Yer feckin' mad,' spat Connolly, as the young man walked away.

One of the cottages had laundry drying on a hedgerow and the older deputy began a stealthy approach in the half light of dawn. Just as he was taking some clothing, a woman screamed from the doorway. A second later, her four young sons bolted through the open door and confronted Connolly. He tried to fire his musket but he'd forgotten to reload it after shooting the sheriff. The young men surrounded him like wild dogs worrying a sheep. He feinted with his bayonet and tried to face them, but he was surrounded. Rather than close on the armed man, one of the fellows picked up a stone and threw it at him. Taking the cue, the others began to pelt him with rocks. Finally, one struck home and knocked the deputy senseless. He dropped his musket and they fell in on Connolly to teach him a lesson.

The two deputies were brought before the sheriff that afternoon. The magistrate was sent for and a jury hastily convened. In a matter of a few minutes, and in accordance with the law, both men were found guilty of murder. Before their sentence was read out, the men were allowed to speak in their own defense. Gallagher showed remorse and Connolly tried to place all the blame on his cohort. The judge was having none of it. It had been decided that both men were complicit in the killing of the sheriff and they would be hanged in two days. It was left to Higgins to decide what means of execution would be utilised. He sentenced Gallagher to be hanged from a gallows. Connolly didn't fare as well. His vain protestations of innocence had infuriated Higgins, who was a gentleman and a man of honour. The older deputy would be put on the back of a donkey cart, and a noose placed around his neck. Death would not come swiftly for the coward. In two days' time, the sentences would be carried out in front of the castle gates. Higgins intended it to be a spectacle and an example of how justice would be administered from now on, even with lawmen.

The town was teeming with crowds of people when Ned and Mary arrived.

'Is it alw'ys like dis?' asked the girl.

'No,' replied Ned. 'Dere mus' be sum'thin' happ'nin' t'day.' He craned his neck to try and see what was going on as they rode their horses forward, through the throng of humanity. People cursed and swore as Ned muscled the horses through the tide of peasants. He stopped and asked a trader what was the reason for the festivities. It was as he suspected, a hanging was due to take place. Sheriff D'Arcy had wasted no time in reasserting his authority, he thought. He asked a second man what the crime was and the man told him two men had killed the sheriff. Ned's skin prickled and he felt a sensation of numbness sweep through his body, starting at his head and working its way down to his feet.

'Do you mean Higgins?' he asked, hopefully.

The man shook his head. 'No,' he replied, grinning. 'It was that bastard, D'Arcy.'

Ned felt his face flush and he nudged the Hobby over until it stepped on the man's foot.

'Ouch! Ya stupid fecker.'

Ned kept ploughing forward until he could see the faces of the murderers. He recognised them immediately as two of his former colleagues. A new wave of numbness engulfed him, sweeping away his anger towards the lout he'd just trampled on.

Gallagher was marched up to the gallows, his hands tied behind his back. He was asked if he had any last words. He opened his mouth as if he was about to say something, then closed it when words failed him. A hood was pulled over his head and the noose tightened around his neck. He didn't wait to be pushed from the gibbet and, as he stepped off, the only sounds to be heard were the thrum of the rope as it came taught and his neck as it snapped.

Connolly was fighting as he was dragged out next, loudly protesting his innocence and screaming about injustice. He was put on the back of a donkey cart and a sack was pulled over his head. Seconds before the cart was wheeled away, Higgins cut the bonds that held his hands. Connolly struggled and kicked, pitifully trying to haul himself up in an effort to grab a last few breaths. Higgins pulled a pistol and shot the man, dead. He remembered the words of Sheriff D'Arcy.

'There is no room for malice in the administration of justice and no one should ever take joy in a man's death, no matter what evil deed he's done.'

Ned and Mary left the crowd behind and continued on towards Gortalocca. Ned didn't want to find out about his mentor's death from any stranger, he wanted to hear it from Michael's mouth.

In his mind, men like D'Arcy were immortal. They aren't, of course, and soon the world forgets they even existed. Robert had known that. Ned was yet to learn it.

CHAPTER 44

It was just before noon when Ned and Mary walked the horses into Gortalocca. First they had to find out where Mrs. Flynn lived so they could deliver the news. Ned tied both animals up outside the crowded village store and opened what looked to be a newly-painted yellow door. The place was abuzz with people talking about a shooting and what had happened on the lake road a couple of nights before, and the snippets of conversation Ned caught made his guts tighten. There was a young man behind the bar, doling out refreshments, and he directed Ned next door.

They left the Hobbies tied and he and Mary trudged to the cottage. The shock had begun to wear off a little and Ned hoped he could trust himself to speak. Death was always an acquaintance but some deaths were unfathomable. He knocked and Michael answered the door, solemn-faced. He recognised Mary, of course, from his time in Ballyshee but he didn't immediately remember Ned. Nevertheless, he ushered them both into the house and closed the door behind them.

Morna and Mary locked in an emotional embrace for

a moment and Ned was left standing awkwardly. Tears came to Mary's eyes when Morna asked her what had become of Ballyshee. Mary held the delicate young girl's shoulders and pushed her to arms-length. 'Dere is no Ballyshee, mo chuisle,' she said and her own eyes filled.

'What aboot me family?'

Mary hugged her close again. 'Dey're gone, love. Yer da got shot along wit' mine an' yer mam and a few udder women wen' off intuh d' hills an' we nev'r seen dem again.'

Morna rested her head on Mary's shoulder and began to sob.

'Oy'll go back an' see if Oy c'n foind'em, Morna,' volunteered Ned.

'You'll do no such t'ing,' Mary snapped at her future husband. 'It's too late now. Da moun'ains 's a'ready ate dem up.'

Morna reached out and took Ned's hand in hers. 'She's right. Ya already done enoof an' Oy won't have ya takin' yer life in yer hands again.'

'Oy swear Oy'll go if ye want me to. Oy gimme ward on it.'

Roisin spoke up for the first time. 'You will not,' she said. 'I just lost one old man who gave me his word he'd find someone for me. I won't be party to sending a young one out on a fool's errand.'

She picked up two letters from the table. 'I have two letters here,' she announced. 'They're from Sheriff Robert Flynn.' She saw no need to address the dead man by his usurped name. 'One is addressed to me and the other is for all of you. I'll read yours.'

'I, Robert D'Arcy, being of sane mind, do bequeath the following:

Six pounds sterling to my nephews, Michael Flynn

and Jamie Clancy, in the hope that they will build a permanent blacksmith shop in Gortalocca.

Three pounds to my nephew, Robert Flynn, in the hope that he will find his way.

Three pounds to Ned Flood, who was like a son to me, in the hope that he and his wife will build a new life for themselves in the colonies. I only wish that I could accompany them on their adventure.

The remainder of my estate, which amounts to eleven pounds, four shillings and thruppence, I leave to my late brother's wife Roisin.

'There's an addendum here,' she said, 'a note that says an additional four pounds, two shillings and sixpence is owed to Ned, for miscellaneous expenditures.'

Ned shook his head and, after he'd coughed to clear his throat, he managed to speak. 'Ferget dat pairt,' he said. 'Ooncle Robbie has a'ready taken care o' dat.'

'As you wish, Ned. In that case, I have just one final request to make of you. Would you bring Robert's body back here to Gortalocca? He was as much a part of this town as his brother was and I want the two of them to lie side by side.'

Mikey stayed with his mother and the two girls, while Jamie accompanied Ned to Mick Sheridan's cottage, to get a wagon. After their brief explanation, Mick quietly went about hitching a horse up to a wagon for the job of retrieving the dead man's corpse and the three of them set out for Nenagh to perform the grim duty.

While the young people talked amongst themselves, Roisin re-read her letter from Robert.

My dearest Roisin,

If you are reading this note, then I am dead, and I expect no tears to be shed over me. I know that you hold me in disdain, and for that I am heartily sorry, but one thing that binds us together is our love for Liam. As well as being my brother, he has always been the only true friend I ever had and only now, as I pen this letter, alone in my office, am I beginning to come to grips with my own grief.

I have done my best to watch over Gortalocca for as long as I was able, fulfilling a promise I made to myself and to my late brother all those years ago. I consider my vow upheld, and now it is up to you to take over. If my mission has been successful, then your son has been reunited with you. If not, then I tender my apologies and trust that you know I did my best. Perhaps, one day, you will think fondly of me.

Yours, sincerely and affectionately,

Robert Flynn

Robert's body had lain in state in the big hall at Nenagh castle and various dignitaries had come to pay their respects. Higgins had presided over the funeral, which had been carried out in the English tradition.

Ned provided entry to the castle for the two Irishmen and, and after a brief but animated discussion with the new sheriff, they removed the body and returned to the village.

Roisin had already made arrangements for Robert to lay in the Flynn cottage, in the same place Liam had occupied just two months before. Robbie had kicked up a fuss, saying that he wouldn't share the house with a stinking corpse, but big Mick Sheridan and Ned Flood had convinced him to take his wife and spend the night at Hogan's.

When it came time to honour the dead man with stories, Michael asked Ned what had become of him after he separated himself from the party. Ned was a natural born storyteller and he captivated his audience with tales of the chase involving the jaegers, down in County Cork. Even Robbie showed an interest.

'What happ'ned t' d las' two Prussians?' he asked, when Ned came to the end of his story.

Ned shrugged his shoulders. 'Dunno. Oy w's a bit too busy t' foind out,' he replied innocently.

'You're a legend, Ned Flood!' declared Mikey, clapping Ned on the back.

Ned looked down on the pale corpse of his former mentor. 'Oy don' wanna be no legen',' he said, sorrowfully. 'Dere's a legen' layin' dere. Dem folks us'ally die young, an' us'ally dey die vi'lently.' He took Mary's hand. 'Oy wanna doy peacef'lly, layin' nex' t me woife, when Oy'm ninety years auld.' He gave her hand a squeeze.

The next day, Higgins and his sergeant arrived in Gortalocca early for the interment. The day was coloured slate-grey, the perfect backdrop for a funeral, and rain drizzled steadily. Higgins was surprised to find that his predecessor was no longer dressed in his uniform, but wore a simple leine and pair of trews.

Both Mary and Morna kissed the old man's forehead, then stood back, making way for Roisin to approach the coffin. She leaned over it.

'I never really knew you, Robert Flynn,' she whispered, 'and I blame myself for that.' She kissed his cheek. 'Thank you, thank you for everything.' She stood back as the lid was nailed shut and the coffin lowered into the earth, alongside Liam.

Afterwards, Higgins approached Ned and offered him the sergeant's position, in the hope that it would tempt him back into the service.

'No t'anks, Oy'm done wit' all dat,' he said. 'Me an' me wife are goin' t' Mary Land.'

Mikey asked him when he and Mary intended to leave.

'After Oy had a drink t' d' auld man's mem'ry,' he replied.

The funeral party moved off to the Flynn cottage and Mick stayed behind with Jamie. They began to fill in the grave and the noise which the earth and gravel made, as it hit the top of the casket, was a sound all too familiar to them.